A Wedding in Provence

Also available by Katie Fforde

Living Dangerously
The Rose Revived
Wild Designs
Stately Pursuits
Life Skills
Thyme Out
Artistic Licence
Highland Fling
Paradise Fields
Restoring Grace
Flora's Lot
Practically Perfect
Going Dutch
Wedding Season
Love Letters
A Perfect Proposal
Summer of Love
Recipe for Love
A French Affair
The Perfect Match
A Vintage Wedding
A Summer at Sea
A Secret Garden
A Country Escape
A Rose Petal Summer
A Springtime Affair
A Wedding in the Country

Katie Fforde

A Wedding in Provence

C
_____
CENTURY

5 7 9 10 8 6 4

Century
20 Vauxhall Bridge Road
London SW1V 2SA

Century is part of the Penguin Random House group
of companies whose addresses can be found at
global.penguinrandomhouse.com.

Copyright © Katie Fforde Ltd 2022

Katie Fforde has asserted her right to be identified
as the author of this Work in accordance with the
Copyright, Designs and Patents Act 1988

First published in Great Britain by Century in 2022

www.penguin.co.uk

A CIP catalogue record for this book is available from
the British Library

Hardback ISBN 9781780897608
Trade Paperback ISBN 9781780897615

Typeset in 12/16 pt Palatino LT Std
by Integra Software Services Pvt. Ltd, Pondicherry

Printed and bound in Great Britain by Clays Ltd, Elcograf S.p.A.

The authorised representative in the EEA is Penguin Random House
Ireland, Morrison Chambers, 32 Nassau Street, Dublin D02 YH68

www.greenpenguin.co.uk

For my dear friend Jane Wenham-Jones 1962–2021
with very much love

Acknowledgements

The same names crop up frequently in my acknowledgements, which indicates how incredibly loyal and kind people are. This is my opportunity to thank them.

As always, Bill Hamilton and everyone at A. M. Heath.

Richenda Todd, who saves me, year after year, from making ghastly mistakes in public.

Again, my sister-in-law Susan Makin for telling me about rural France in the 1960s.

Selina Walker, best editor and dear friend. Her assistant Sophie Whitehead. The team behind me who are so crucial in the whole business including: Sarah Harwood, Charlotte Bush, Evie Kettlewell, Mat Watterson, Claire Simmonds, Sarah Ridley, Ceara Elliot, Jacqueline Bissett, Linda Hodgson, Helen Wynn-Smith, Laurie Ip Fung Chun, Hope Butler, to name but a few. As my team, you are all vital to me. I am so grateful!

To previously unsung friends and fellow writers: Jo Thomas, A. J. Pearce, Jill Mansell, Milly Johnson, Janie Millman, Judy Astley, Catherine Jones, Bernadine Kennedy, and all the greater writing community. We keep each other going when times are tough. Not sure where I'd be without you all but I know it wouldn't be much fun! Sadly missing from this list is our darling Jane Wenham-Jones. No longer with us, but never to be forgotten.

Chapter One

Paris, Autumn 1963

Alexandra still couldn't quite control her excitement. She was in Paris! True, it was only for twenty-four hours, but the October day was bright and full of possibility. She loved Paris, although she'd only visited it once, years ago, when her nanny had taken her, so that she, the nanny, could visit her boyfriend. Paris had made a deep impression on her and she was enjoying every moment of being there.

Tomorrow, she would get on a train to Switzerland and go to a finishing school, or whatever her well-meaning, unimaginative guardians thought was a good idea. But today was hers and she'd already done quite a bit of exploring.

She pulled the belt of her mac a little tighter as a gust of wind caught her where she stood at the foot of Montmartre, looking up at the Sacré-Cœur, thinking how beautiful it was. She was about to set off up the very many steps towards it when she heard a little scream behind her. She turned to see a pretty young woman with blonde hair, her hands held against her face in a gesture of horror. There were potatoes and onions rolling away from her feet and a broken string bag in her hand. She was on the verge of tears.

'I can't believe this!' the woman wailed. 'You think a day has started badly and it just gets worse and worse!'

Alexandra couldn't ignore her. The woman didn't seem much older than she was at just twenty, and was obviously very upset. She was also speaking English, albeit with an American accent.

'Come on! It's all right. I'll help you.' Alexandra crouched down and started gathering up vegetables into the skirt of her mac.

'It's so kind of you to help,' said the woman, sounding slightly less as if she were about to cry. 'But unless you've got a bag, we might as well just leave all this here!'

Alexandra looked at her lap: the woman had a point; she couldn't walk with all this clutched to her stomach. 'We could fill our pockets, I suppose. Oh, look at that garlic!' Accustomed as she was to tight little garlic bulbs, the large purplish item, the size of a tennis ball, reminded her of the cookery course she had recently finished in London. The first thing Mme Wilson had said was how pathetic the garlic was in England. This garlic was very obviously French.

'Take it if you like,' said the woman. 'I have no pockets. I'm never going to get to use it now.'

'I'm sure things aren't that bad,' said Alexandra soothingly. 'Put what you can in your handbag—'

The woman waggled a tiny box purse in Alexandra's direction.

'OK, my pockets, then. And I can put some in my handbag, although maybe not the cabbage.'

Alexandra's bag was an antique postal bag and was fairly capacious but not big enough for something the size of a human head.

'It's so kind of you, but I haven't got anything I could put vegetables in. I don't even know why I bought them. I'm supposed to be having a dinner party tonight and I don't have a menu! I can't cook and I can't even shop for one! My husband is going to be so disappointed in me.'

'Is he quite a new husband?' Alexandra felt he must be, given how young this woman was.

'*Very* new. And at this rate I wonder if we'll make it to a year. Tonight is the first big dinner party he's asked me to arrange and I've already failed!' The woman was still distressed but not weeping. 'Look, can we go somewhere and get a drink? Even just a coffee? I haven't spoken English to anyone except my husband – and of course he's American, like me – since we got to Paris. And that wouldn't be so bad except I don't speak French!'

Alexandra was naturally kind-hearted and couldn't ignore the appeal from this young woman who must have been terribly lonely. 'Why not? Here's a nice café – have you had lunch? I haven't. And I do speak French. Not perfectly, of course, but well enough.' Alexandra was hungry. Keen to enjoy every minute she had in Paris, she had got up too early to be given breakfast at her *pension,* and had done a lot of walking.

'Oh! I would so love to go somewhere and not have to fight with the waiters to make myself understood!' said the woman. 'My name is Donna, by the way.' She put out her hand.

3

'Alexandra,' said Alexandra, shaking Donna's hand briefly. 'Now, let's eat.'

When they both had plates of *steak frites* and a bottle of wine in front of them, and had eaten several mouthfuls in silence, Donna put down her knife and fork. 'I'll just tell you my story quickly,' she said, 'then I want to hear about you.'

Alexandra smiled. 'Go on then.'

'Well, I grew up in Connecticut. Married young to a very nice man, Bob, who my parents approved of, and then his job sent him to Paris. Which sounds so romantic, and it is really, but not when you don't speak the language, your husband is out all day and you have no friends. I have no one to talk to except the maid and she doesn't speak English – and hates me! My parents aren't happy about me being so far away and keep writing letters asking if Bob can't be transferred back to the States. Well, it's my mother, really.' She paused for breath. 'That's pretty much me summed up. Paris is a beautiful city and I'd love to get to know it better,' she sighed. 'Now it's your turn.'

'You haven't told me about the dinner party yet,' said Alexandra, 'but I will give you the salient facts about me. I grew up in London and don't have any parents, although I do have relations who look out for me. I was living a lovely life with friends in a big house owned by my family, and now I have to go to Switzerland.' She paused. 'The relations found out I wasn't behaving in a way they considered suitable, so they've told me I must buckle down and do what they say.'

Put like that, it didn't seem very dramatic, but at the time it had been awful. She'd been away at the wedding of her close friend Lizzie, and had come back with David, fifteen years older and her best friend, to see the house blazing with light. After she had stopped worrying that the house had been burgled, which took about two minutes, she realised her relatives from Switzerland had let themselves into the family property. Her and David's easy life was over. David didn't even go back into the house; he went to stay with a friend until the coast was clear. Fortunately the relatives hated London and didn't stay long, but their orders to Alexandra were clear; she must go to Switzerland the following month.

'That's awful that you don't have parents! But you do have relations? Why didn't they take you in when your parents died?' asked Donna.

'I don't know, but I'm really glad they didn't. I had lots of nannies and people to look after me, and I didn't mind. My relations want what's best for me, absolutely, but I would never have been happy living with them.' Alexandra had to have a sip of wine to help her recover from the thought. 'They're very straight-laced and buttoned-up. I'm a bit of a free spirit.'

'Gee!' said Donna. 'That sounds so – dashing!'

Alexandra laughed. 'It was fun, particularly when I met my special friends at cookery school.'

'You're a trained chef?'

'No! Certainly not, but I can cook fairly well now. I did a few professional cooking jobs with my friend Meg, who's a brilliant cook.'

5

'If only she were here now!' said Donna, obviously remembering the dinner party she'd been trying to forget.

'Do you mind if I ask you something a bit personal?'

'Go ahead,' said Donna. 'It's so good to have someone to talk to; I don't care about being discreet.'

'I know the feeling. I had a lovely friend who was – is – a man, but girlfriends are a bit different, aren't they?'

Donna nodded. 'What did you want to ask me?'

'Is Bob's job well paid? I mean, if money is no object, you could find someone who'd cook for your dinner party and you wouldn't have to worry. I've done jobs like that myself.'

'I had someone! I had booked a chef and then they sent a message to say they couldn't come. Bob said, "Oh, you can do it then, honey, it'll be fine." Then he closed up his newspaper and went to work. His mother always did the cooking when his father had business people over to dinner. He thinks women can do these things automatically, just because they're women.' Donna suddenly looked as if she might start to cry again.

'And you didn't say, "No, I can't do it"?'

Donna looked down at her plate in shame. 'No. I want to be the sort of wife who can cook for a dinner party. I didn't want to disappoint him.'

Alexandra didn't reply. She tried not to look reproachful but suspected she had failed.

'Could you do it for me, Alexandra?' said Donna, sounding very young and helpless. She was leaning forward, her long blonde hair trailing into her wine glass.

Alexandra thought about the short time she had to enjoy Paris. 'But you need a proper French chef! There must be hundreds of them. We're in Paris, after all.'

'But do you know of any I could contact? The one who cancelled today couldn't think of anyone.'

'It doesn't mean there aren't any.'

'Well, I realise that. But how would we find one in time for tonight?'

Donna had a point. 'I agree it is very short notice – but there must be agencies we can try.' Alexandra, who considered herself resourceful, realised that it would be nearly impossible to find a chef to cook in a private kitchen at such short notice if you had no contacts.

'Would you do it for me?' Donna pleaded, putting on all the charm, using skills that no doubt worked well on her father and Bob. Alexandra found she wasn't immune, either. 'If you're not a trained chef, you have at least cooked meals before,' Donna finished.

'The thing is, I only have today to see Paris . . .' Alexandra paused, thought for a moment – and decided that Switzerland and all it represented could wait. She had some money stashed away in the inner pocket of her handbag, traveller's cheques she'd bought with the money she'd earned in London. Her relations knew nothing about it. She'd use that to spend a little more time in Paris. She was already booked into a very reasonable *pension*. She could send a telegram, tell her relations she had met a friend in Paris and was staying for a bit. After all, they'd done without seeing her much for years. A few more days wouldn't make a difference. And where better to improve her French than in Paris?

She smiled at Donna. 'OK, I'll do it. But with you, not for you, and I don't want to be paid. The thing to do here is to buy your way out of trouble! The French are brilliant at ready-made food. We'll buy pâté, lots of cheeses and a gorgeous dessert, and then all we have to worry about is the bit in the middle.'

'You make it all seem so easy,' said Donna. 'I am so glad I met you. You look so glamorous, but you're so kind. I'd have thought you were French if I didn't know otherwise. Is your scarf Hermès?'

Alexandra nodded. 'It was a present from my uncle. When he came over to London last month, he realised I wasn't a child any more and gave me something I really wanted to wear.'

'With your mac, the belt, you look sort of—'

Alexandra sighed. 'I know. I've always looked different from other people my age. I've always gone my own way a bit, fashion-wise.'

'I was going to say you're like Audrey Hepburn. You're so – cool. And very stylish.'

'Honestly? So! Let's finish our lunch and then sort out your dinner party. We may need to buy a shopping bag or two!'

But she couldn't throw herself into shopping and cooking until she'd dealt with sending the telegram to the people who were expecting to meet her off the train in Switzerland the following day. First, she had to compose the perfect message so her plan to stay in Paris for a few days would seem to them like a good idea. Then she had to send it, which probably meant finding a large *bureau de poste*.

They stayed at the restaurant table, and Alexandra took out a dog-eared notebook which she had previously used to write down details of the antique bits and pieces she used to buy and sell as a money-making hobby when she lived in London.

'Can I help with the wording?' asked Donna after she'd watched Alexandra cross out a few attempts.

Usually Alexandra was good at telling her relations what they wanted to hear. When she'd lived in the family house in London, she had managed to keep hidden from them for a long time the fact that she had had no paid female companion. But this telegram had to imply that what she was doing was exactly in alignment with what they wanted for her. As their primary concern was that her French wasn't good enough (they considered it too colloquial and rustic), this was what she now focused on, while emphasising she was only delaying her arrival in Switzerland by a short time. She had considered saying 'a few days', but then decided not to be too specific.

'No, thank you, I think I'm there. What do you think?' She read her efforts out loud.

'Great! And while you've been doing that, I've had a wonderful idea. We'll phone it through to Bob's secretary and ask her to send the telegram. Then we don't have to wait any longer before getting going on the dinner party.'

It didn't take much persuasion for Alexandra to agree to this.

'After all,' said Donna, 'it's a tiny thing compared to bailing me out of my predicament. You only met me on the sidewalk, we're not even friends!' She frowned. 'Well, I hope we are now, but you know what I mean.'

Donna had also located the telephone in the *bistrot* so once Bob's secretary, whom Donna described as 'scarily efficient and not at all attractive', had had the telegram dictated to her, Alexandra and Donna were free to shop. It was going to be an enjoyable afternoon.

Chapter Two

⁂

'It's so great that you can talk to the cab driver,' said Donna a few hours later when they loaded bulging bags into the boot of a taxi.

'You can too, if you practise,' said Alexandra. 'What's the address?'

Donna lived in a very good *arrondissement* near the Eiffel Tower. Alexandra resolved to send a postcard, borrowing Donna's address, to her relations. They'd be very reassured. The address of the small *pension* where Alexandra was staying wouldn't be nearly as impressive.

And Donna's apartment was glorious. It had high ceilings, huge rooms with herringbone parquet floors and marble fireplaces, and tall windows that opened on to balconies and Paris and beyond.

'This is lovely!' said Alexandra, looking around the salon, thinking that Bob must be doing very well to be able to afford such a beautiful apartment.

'It is. But you wait until you see where I have to cook.'

Alexandra followed Donna into the kitchen. 'I see what you mean!' she said, horrified. 'It's like a corridor with a sink in it!

'How am I supposed to produce a dinner party in here?' asked Donna. 'It's hard enough to make coffee and toast.'

It was more like a scullery, fairly long, but very narrow. It had a shallow sink and a plate rack above, the only thing which reminded Alexandra of the beloved kitchen she had left behind in London.

'I don't suppose you are expected to produce dinner parties, really,' Alexandra said. 'I expect your cook would have done what we have, and brought in things from outside.'

'Or maybe people entertain in restaurants. That's what Bob should have suggested really, but we're American!'

'That's all right,' said Alexandra, as Donna did seem a bit shamefaced. 'We've bought pâté, fresh bread and butter for the starter, and the most wonderful Gâteau Saint-Honoré for the pudding, so we've only got the chicken dish to do.'

'That is the most beautiful dessert,' said Donna, looking at the confection which had sat on her knee during the taxi ride, encased in a white cardboard box. Golden spheres of choux pastry sat on a circle of puff pastry topped with whipped cream. A circlet of spun sugar was the final touch. 'But no one will think I made it.'

'They don't have to think you made it,' said Alexandra. 'My nanny told me when I was in Paris before that no Frenchwoman would dream of *making* a cake or a tart for a formal dinner.' She paused. 'Now, what shall we do with the chicken?'

Donna gave a gasp of horror. 'Don't you know? You bought all those vegetables and herbs – I thought you had a recipe in mind!'

'I soon will have a recipe,' said Alexandra confidently. 'Look, here's a *Larousse Gastronomique*.' She pulled out the large and very battered book from the shelf. 'Thank goodness there was a copy of it in the apartment.'

'We rented it furnished,' said Donna. 'I expect they consider it essential, unlike effective plumbing and drains that don't smell.'

'I hope my French is up to obscure technical terms.' Alexandra realised that Donna was looking at her uncertainly. 'Why don't you set the table? That can take ages!'

'Oh yes. I could find the plates too. There are hundreds of plates and glasses, all shapes and sizes.'

'See if there's something attractive to serve the pâté on,' suggested Alexandra. 'And also for the cheese. I think we should unwrap it.'

She was glad when Donna went back into the dining room because she wasn't quite as confident as she made out, and didn't want to be watched or talked to while she went through the book. However, she had done a cookery course, and had helped her friend Meg, who'd done the same course, cook directors' lunches, so she had a bit of experience.

It wasn't long before she decided to put down what was thought by many to be the Bible of French cuisine and just get going. She didn't have enough time to translate obscure culinary terms – the course she'd done in London had been for young women, not chefs.

She began by chopping a few onions and lots of the purple garlic bulb that had so appealed to her when she saw it rolling into the gutter.

She was glad she'd had the foresight to ask the butcher to divide the two chickens into pieces. They needed tidying up but she didn't have to bash her way through anything too large. She threw all the leftover bits into a pot with the onion skins, some whole onions, carrots and a bunch of thyme. She had no plans for a stock but thought it might come in handy.

Several hours passed and, at last, the tiny kitchen was filled with the delicious smells of chicken, wine and mushrooms. There was a sauce to pour over the portions and chopped parsley to go on top of that. Alexandra was tired. She wanted to go back to her *pension* and lie on her bed and do nothing. Cooking a simple chicken dish wasn't nearly as easy as everyone pretended it was, or at least, not for her. But she had really enjoyed helping Donna, and was very sad to think that they probably wouldn't see each other again. They'd become friends as they worked out which glasses went where and speculated about what the dinner guests might be like.

'And you're sure there'll be someone to serve for you?' she said, reluctant to leave even though she was tired.

'Yes, yes. Bob's secretary organised that when she set up the dinner party. She booked the chef too. I must tell her they didn't turn up.'

'You should!' said Alexandra, who had started to resent the non-appearance of a trained professional quite early on.

'But at least now I can give you this.' Donna put an envelope full of French francs into Alexandra's hand. 'Don't argue. Just get in a cab and go back to your lodgings. But promise you'll come back in the morning to hear how it went?'

'I promise,' said Alexandra, suspecting she might be called upon to help clear up as well, in spite of the hired waitress.

'I don't know what I'd have done without you, Alexandra!' Donna said. 'You've been so brilliant.'

'I've really enjoyed myself! I just wish . . .'

'What?'

'That I could spend more than just a few days in Paris.'

'Oh, I'd love that!' said Donna. 'We could explore it together and I'd learn not to be terrified of the waiters.'

Alexandra laughed and then sighed. 'What I need is a proper reason to stay, like a job. If I was working for grand people my relations would probably approve. I'd be improving my French with people with the right accent.'

'What qualifications do you have? Shorthand, typing?' asked Donna.

Alexandra shrugged and sighed again. 'I have no qualifications. I'm fit for nothing.'

'That's certainly not true! Look what you've done for me!'

'I loved doing it.' Then she and Donna shared a long hug before Alexandra got into the tiny, creaking lift.

*

15

When Alexandra presented herself at the elegant apartment at eleven o'clock the following morning, she found Donna in a state of excitement.

'It was amazing!' she said to Alexandra, without waiting for an exchange of how-are-yous. 'I am so grateful to you I cannot tell you!' Donna took Alexandra by the arm and led her into the salon. The long windows were open and there was a little table set on the balcony. 'Sit down. I'm going to bring you coffee and dessert and then I'll tell you some wonderful news.'

Alexandra was very happy to sit and watch Paris go by below her in the sunshine. Donna appeared with coffee and a plate of profiteroles and cream: Gâteau Saint-Honoré in its component parts.

'I met the most gorgeous man!' said Donna. 'Don't worry, not like that. I'm married to Bob and nothing will ever change that. But this man has a job for you! What about that? He also had a gorgeous woman with him, but that's not the point. Can you imagine? When I told him about you, he was so interested, especially when I mentioned your family house in Belgravia.'

Alexandra's heart leaped. She really didn't want to go to finishing school in Switzerland, especially not when there was a chance she could stay in Paris and have fun with Donna.

'What's the job? Do you know?' Alexandra now really wanted to stay in Paris so badly, she'd try anything. Although the gorgeous man probably wanted a bilingual secretary who could not only speak French but do shorthand too – in both languages.

Donna made a face. 'I don't really know, but the good part is, it's only for a month. Your relatives might not mind you staying for a month. Families like dates, I've discovered. Mine really didn't want us to come to Paris but when I said it was only for a year, they felt a lot better about it.'

Alexandra nodded. 'I think mine would be the same, but I need to know what sort of job it is. I may not be able to do it. I told you I couldn't do shorthand, for example.'

'He didn't say anything like that. He said you must be able to cook, which you can, speak English and French, which obviously you can, and drive. Can you drive?'

'Yes,' said Alexandra, 'but I'm not sure I can drive in French.' She tried to imagine herself driving through Paris and felt a little daunted.

'Oh, you mean in Paris? I see your point. Parisians make up their own rules about how to do it.'

Then Alexandra got over her defeatist attitude. 'I did learn to drive in London, and if I can do Hyde Park Corner, I'm sure I'd get used to Paris. For a month, you say?'

Donna nodded. 'Your family would like that, wouldn't they? You'd have a month of really brushing up your French, although I think it's perfectly fine as it is, and then you can go to the finishing school.' Donna paused, not something she did often. 'What do they teach you to do there, do you think?'

'Oh, I don't know. How to write cheques, how to address the nobility and how to get in and out of sports cars without showing your pants.'

Donna laughed delightedly. 'In America pants are things men wear. But never mind that: here's his card.

You're to go to that address at two o'clock today for an interview. All the information is on there. If you need a reference, Bob will give you one.'

Alexandra inspected the card and her spirits lifted. 'He's a count! My relations will love that. If I get the job, I'll have to send them details.'

'Of course! Now, what are you going to wear for the interview?'

This did give Alexandra pause. She had very few clothes with her. 'I don't have a lot of choice. Most of my things are probably already in Switzerland. They were sent ahead so I wouldn't have heavy luggage to deal with on the train. I have some pyjamas, a change of underwear, this dress, a pair of slacks and a cardigan. That's it, more or less.'

'And your Hermès scarf.'

'Yes, but while it may be useful, it's not a whole outfit.' Alexandra looked down at her dress, which was fitted, sleeveless and knee-length. It was a 'meet your relations dress' and it would have to do for an interview. 'I think this is fine. It may smell slightly of cooking but perhaps, being a Frenchman, he won't mind that. He's not judging me for my clothes, after all; he wants to know if I'm suitable for the job.' She paused. 'Are you sure he didn't mention what sort of job it was?'

'No, but don't worry. He didn't mention any secretarial skills or accountancy, and surely he would have done if he'd wanted those?'

'I'd be much keener on going to Switzerland if I thought they were going to teach me things like that. Although I'm sure they're awfully boring, secretarial skills and grown-up arithmetic would be useful.'

Donna patted Alexandra's knee. 'I'm sure you'll be fine. And it'll be so cool having you in Paris. I'll have a friend!'

'Oh, I know! I would love that.'

'Are you absolutely sure about that dress? We could look in my closet – I could lend you something? You are a bit taller so my clothes would be short on you, but that may not be a bad thing.'

Alexandra smiled. 'I think this dress will be fine. I wore an apron when I cooked in it yesterday. Though if you have some lovely scent I could spray on myself, I'd be delighted. To disguise the faint *eau d'oignon*.

'Perfume!' Donna cried out. 'I have so much I could take a bath in it. Now, I thought we'd have an early lunch, no wine, and then after your interview we can celebrate.'

'I may not get the job,' said Alexandra. 'I've never actually been to an interview before. Have you got any tips?'

Donna shook her head. 'I've never had a job.'

'I've done lots of catering jobs, and I used to deal in antiques. But I've never had a nine-to-five sort of job.'

'Antiques? How exciting!'

'A friend of mine has a stall on the Portobello Road market. He let me put my things with his. He taught me all I know.'

Alexandra allowed herself a moment's reflection. Her life had been very good in London, sharing a large house with friends, earning money cooking or waitressing with one of the friends and doing the antiques stall with another one at weekends. She was a person who made the best of things, but life in Switzerland was going to feel lonely and confined. At home she'd be stuck with her boring, formal relations and at finishing school she'd be surrounded by girls she'd probably have nothing in common with.

'At least let me do your make-up,' said Donna. 'All my spare time was spent practising how to put on eyeliner without smudging it. You have such lovely eyes; it will be such fun emphasising their beauty. He'll have to give you the job!'

Chapter Three

As Alexandra walked through the doors of the tall, elegant building for her interview that afternoon, she was more nervous than she'd expected to be. Usually she had a lot of confidence, and it didn't matter if she didn't get the job. She hadn't planned to have one, after all. She could have a few days in Paris and then hop on the train to Switzerland having had an enjoyable holiday.

But she found her lips were dry as she asked for directions at Reception and hesitated before knocking on the door of the office. She took a couple of deep breaths and told herself she was ready.

Having been asked to enter she found herself in a room with two grand desks in it. At one, by the window, a man was writing, and at the one directly in front of her was the sort of woman who might well be described as a dragon.

She was wearing a very smart black suit which could easily have been Chanel, had perfectly groomed hair, two rows of pearls, a too-white face and thin lips. Alexandra got the impression she avoided smiling to hold back the formation of wrinkles. It was only partially successful.

Alexandra now wished she'd borrowed something to wear from Donna's extensive wardrobe. Her own outfit had travelled from London to Paris and witnessed a lot of rather desperate cooking involving onions, garlic and cream – the apron may not have been adequate.

As there was no point in regretting her clothes, Alexandra put on her best French accent, greeted the woman as politely and formally as she could manage and gave her name.

She received a nod of the head and a return of the greeting and an invitation to sit down at the chair in front of the desk.

'I am Mme Dubois; I will be conducting this interview.' Then she handed Alexandra a form. 'Please complete this, mademoiselle. Here is a pen.'

On impulse, Alexandra added five years to her age and then completed the form in her best handwriting. She described her last position as 'company chef', although she wasn't quite sure if *chef d'entreprise* quite described cooking lunch for board members of City banks. But it was the best she could come up with.

As she handed back the completed form, she consoled herself that as a first job interview it was already pretty tough. This meant that future interviews, where the result was more important, would probably seem easier. Being interviewed by a terrifying Parisienne looking at her disdainfully was surely a baptism of fire which would strengthen her for the future.

Mme Dubois read the form, which caused her to raise her eyebrows a couple of times. 'So, you are English?'

Alexandra nodded.

'But you speak French?'

Alexandra felt she'd demonstrated that fairly well already, but she nodded.

'You are a reasonably competent cook?'

Alexandra nodded. 'I said – on my form.'

'Mam'selle, you wrote that you were the head of a company, and I suspect this is not the case.' She narrowed her eyes, the nearest thing to a smile that she could manage. 'Possibly your French isn't as good as you think.'

Alexandra murmured apologetically.

Her interlocutor continued, 'And you can drive?'

Alexandra produced her English driving licence as proof of this, praying Mme Dubois wouldn't look beyond the first page and discover her real age.

Far from it. Mme Dubois barely glanced at the licence before handing it back between the tips of her fingers. 'That seems satisfactory,' she said. 'The position is only for a month. You knew this?'

'I did, madame.'

'Very well, mademoiselle. This position is for a nanny – the children's permanent nanny is away visiting her mother who is sick. Do you have the relevant experience?'

Alexandra took an inward breath. The thought of her looking after children was a bit of a shock; she'd hardly ever met a child, let alone cared for one. On the other hand, she'd had plenty of nannies herself and knew a good one from a bad one. 'Certainly, madame,' she said.

She was ready to explain that she hadn't written this on her form because she didn't know the job required nannying skills, but Mme Dubois didn't seem to care.

'There are three children in the family. They are older. Will you be able to cope with this?'

Alexandra nodded, relief that her charge wasn't a newborn baby making her positively enthusiastic. 'Oh yes.'

'And three children? You will manage?'

'Definitely.' This probably was a bit over-confident but it was only for a month, surely that couldn't be too difficult? She could take them on outings to the tourist destinations of Paris. Donna would come to help – it would be fun.

Mme Dubois studied her for several unnerving seconds. 'You understand that we require the position to be filled urgently, or we would not consider anyone like you. However, the Count has been informed of your background, and as it is only a very temporary arrangement, you may be suitable.'

'Thank you,' said Alexandra, duly humbled.

'We will check your references, and if they are not satisfactory, you will be dismissed forthwith.'

Alexandra had given Donna's husband Bob as one reference, and the female cousin with the grandest name that included a title as her other. She really hoped the cousin wouldn't denounce her. 'Of course,' said Alexandra meekly.

'You look very young for your age, mademoiselle.'

Mme Dubois's gimlet stare drilled into Alexandra in such a haughty way, it made Alexandra find her backbone. When she had written down the wrong date of birth on her form she had anticipated this question. Although in general she knew she looked fairly mature for a twenty-year-old, it was possible she'd be challenged. She gave the woman a sweet, wrinkle-inducing smile. 'I know. I have always considered myself to be extremely fortunate.'

This induced a rise in one perfectly plucked eyebrow. 'Good.' Mme Dubois opened a drawer and produced a fat envelope. 'This is half the money you will be paid; you will get the remainder when you leave. And your train ticket.'

Alexandra's hand had been outstretched to take the offered envelope. 'Train ticket?'

'Yes. The position is in Provence: you travel to Marseille. You seem surprised?'

'Yes! I didn't know – no one mentioned – I thought the job was in Paris.'

Mme Dubois looked at her as if this suggestion was odd. 'But no, I thought this had been made clear when it was suggested you come for an interview.'

Alexandra's mind was in turmoil. It had never occurred to her that the job wasn't in Paris. Now she had no idea if she wanted the job or not.

At that moment, the man who'd been working in the corner got up and crossed the room to speak to her.

'Mademoiselle, you would be looking after my children and, naturally, they are very dear to me. Can I trust you to look after them for me?'

Several things occurred to Alexandra all at the same time. The first was that this man was extremely attractive, the second was that he must be the man Donna had met at the dinner party, and finally that she felt she couldn't let him down.

'Of course, monsieur.' Too late she remembered his business card said he was a count and corrected herself. 'M. le Comte.'

He was tall, with hair that was almost black and dark eyes fringed with long eyelashes. He had a long, slightly hooked nose and a mouth that curled at the corners.

He was, Alexandra realised with a sinking feeling, almost impossible not to fall in love with. At that moment she felt she would go to the ends of the earth for him, let alone to Provence.

M. le Comte bowed slightly. 'Thank you, mademoiselle, I am very grateful.' Then he left the room.

'Good!' said Mme Dubois, a bit more unbending now Alexandra had obviously been passed as suitable by her employer. 'I will write you a quick itinerary. You depart from the Gare de Lyon. I suggest you take some light summer dresses as it can be very hot in Provence even in autumn. You will be collected at the station when you arrive. There is a housekeeper at the chateau, so really your job will be very easy.' She went on to relay a few more details of what was expected.

Alexandra smiled stiffly. As Mme Dubois relaxed she became more tense. 'I will do my best to be satisfactory.'

Mme Dubois bowed and very nearly smiled properly. 'But of course!'

Donna had arranged to meet Alexandra in a café near where Alexandra had her interview. Donna was bouncing with eagerness to hear how Alexandra had got on, while Alexandra just wanted to sit and sip a glass of cold water. She planned to follow this with a glass of cognac to calm her nerves.

'Well?' said Donna. 'Did you get the job? Will they tell you later? Shall I order champagne?'

Alexandra nodded. 'That would be lovely. Although I'm not sure we're celebrating.'

Donna gave the order while looking at her sharply. 'Why not? Didn't you get it? Antoine – the man you met – seemed desperate when we spoke last night.'

'I did get the job.' Alexandra watched as the waiter filled her glass. 'But it's not quite what I thought it was.'

'What do you have to do?'

'Be a nanny, but it's not that I'm worried about. The job isn't in Paris; it's in Provence!'

Donna's face fell. 'Oh. I had hoped—'

'I know! So had I! I thought we could have had a lovely time in Gay Paree.'

Donna still looked full of disappointment. 'I was so looking forward to having a friend in Paris. Now I'll never see you again!'

'You'll see me when I come back. In a month. I have to come back to get the train to Switzerland.' Alexandra was partly telling herself this. Although she had willingly accepted her task, she had misgivings. Provence seemed remote and far away from civilisation and she had no idea what her relations would say.

They drank their champagne and then, partly to cheer up Donna, who was looking so bleak, Alexandra said, 'Let's go shopping. I need underwear.'

'Monoprix. That's where you want to go. I can take you.' Donna smiled a little sadly. 'It's not quite the Champs-Élysées but it's what we need.'

Chapter Four

Alexandra was excited all over again the next morning when the train left Paris, but she knew she was in for a long journey and had come prepared.

Donna had insisted on coming to the station with her, and bought two filled baguettes, fruit and a bottle of Perrier water. The previous day, Alexandra had taken Donna to the Left Bank and sought out the famous English bookshop, Shakespeare and Company. She bought a French/English dictionary and two novels for the journey. Donna had wanted to donate the *Larousse Gastronomique* to her but Alexandra had said it was too heavy to carry and was part of the fixtures and fittings of Donna's apartment. Their farewells were surprisingly emotional, considering they had only known each other for a very short time.

A few hours later, Alexandra had eaten her picnic, peeling the apples with her Swiss Army knife, which she never travelled without. Across the aisle was a man and his wife and he also had a knife. It was an Opinel clasp knife that he used to attack ham on the bone. It made her little knife seem too dainty for words.

She'd read most of one book (rationing herself so she'd have something for the month ahead) and studied the dictionary carefully, several times. She spent a long time looking out of the window before at last the train trundled into the station.

The scenery, especially latterly, had been wonderful. The countryside had been painted gold by sun and the changing season. She'd passed fields of sunflowers, yellow and brown, and lavender fields, harvested now, so the grey bushes crawled over the hills like fat cater-pillars. Grape-pickers in large straw hats, baskets on their backs, gathered fruit from vines that were scarlet in the sunshine. Villages of golden stone clung to the hilltops. And even though it was October, the light – the reason artists went to Provence, Alexandra knew – was still special. While she looked out of the window, she tried very hard not to think about the man in the office, the Comte de Belleville, the children's father. She did not believe in love at first sight. She may have only been just twenty but she had quite a lot of second-hand experience of love. The various nannies and compan-ions who had looked after her over the years had mostly been young and hadn't held back from telling Alexandra when their hearts were broken. She had resolved from an early age (she had been about ten) not to succumb to love if she could possibly help it.

Since then she had discovered that being in love wasn't all bad, but to fall in love with someone you really didn't know was the height of folly. It was not going to happen to her, however good-looking the man might be.

*

She'd grown stiff during the long journey and staggered a little as she climbed down off the train. A man in blue overalls, who had somehow identified the English nanny, greeted her in heavily accented French she could only just understand.

'Mademoiselle! You are late! You must hurry. I am late too now! My name is Bruno.'

'*Bonjour*, Bruno. My name is Alexandra,' she said but he didn't listen. Instead he took her new little case with her new clothes in it while she clutched on to the airline bag and her handbag. In these two bags were her tools for life and she'd be lost without them.

Bruno seemed friendly, but in a great hurry.

'Well,' he said, 'there has been a small calamity.'

How could a calamity be small? Alexandra wondered.

'The housekeeper, Mme Carrier, has been called away. Her mother is ill.'

'Oh? The same as the mother of the nanny?'

Bruno didn't know or care about the nanny. 'You will have to cook for the children. But don't despair' – Alexandra wasn't given to despair and she didn't intend to start now – 'the gardener will bring you vegetables and fowls. Food from the estate. As normal.'

Although she was struggling to understand Bruno's dialect and his speed of delivery she heard 'fowls' and hoped he meant fairly young chickens, not tired old boilers who were only good for stock. She gave a mental shrug (being in France was beginning to affect her) and thought that maybe the chateau would also have a *Larousse Gastronomique*. In a month she'd have time to get to grips with it all.

He led her to an old blue truck and put her case into the back which, going by the odour, had last contained animals. She hauled herself up on to the seat beside him. While he went round to get in himself she wondered how Mme Dubois in Paris would have described this agricultural vehicle.

Her chauffeur talked and gestured and exclaimed as they rattled through the smaller roads and lanes until at last the chateau came into view at the end of an avenue of trees.

It wasn't enormous by chateau standards, but it was still a substantial property. It was square with large, fat towers at either end and seemed to grow out of the soil. It was constructed of huge stone blocks and looked as if it had been designed to withstand anything. Now, creeper that was beginning to turn the colour of fire in the afternoon light covered a good part of the walls. Castellations on the towers could have been decorative or could have indicated the chateau was of a great age, and the hills behind made it seem protected. Alexandra had a sudden strange feeling that it looked like home.

But as Bruno charged up the avenue Alexandra reminded herself that it wasn't home, the job was only for a month. However, she found her heart was beating faster – she wanted to do a good job. She'd promised the children's father he could trust her, and she couldn't let him, or the children, down.

Bruno hammered at the front door of the chateau using the knocker, which was the ring in the nose of a bronze model of a bull's head. Immediately a deep barking started, obviously from a large dog. Alexandra jumped but Bruno was unimpressed. He huffed impatiently when no one opened it instantly, although it wasn't long before the big door was dragged back.

'*Ah, bonjour!*' said Bruno as the door opened wider. 'I have brought you your new nanny!'

The dog, who was indeed large, was black and white with floppy ears and a thin tail, trotted out. He sniffed Alexandra and gave her hand a cursory lick.

Once she knew she wasn't about to be eaten, Alexandra looked at the three young people who were guarding the door more effectively than the dog. The eldest was a girl of about fifteen wearing slacks and a roll-neck sweater – she could hardly be described as a child. There was a boy, almost as tall but obviously younger, and another smaller girl in a faded dress with smocking and puff sleeves who seemed the only one who was the right age for a nanny. Her heart went out to them. She'd had nannies inflicted on her when she was past the age for it to be appropriate and it wasn't fun. She understood why the older girl and her brother were looking at her with a mixture of hostility, resentment and defiance. The little girl was anxious, and clung to her brother.

The eldest two looked very like their father, with his hair that was nearly black and his dark, heavily fringed eyes and mouth made for smiling, although they certainly weren't smiling now. The youngest one looked quite different, with fair curly hair. Her big brother had his arm protectively around her. She must take after her mother, Alexandra thought.

'We don't need a nanny,' said the eldest girl, her chin up, speaking French.

'I'm sure you don't,' said Bruno. 'But your papa says you have to have one. And here she is. I must go now.' He ran back to the truck, collected Alexandra's case from the back and almost pushed her through the door. Then he roared off, making Alexandra feel her only friend had just left her, and was shooting off down the avenue.

Her three charges looked at her and Alexandra looked back. She recognised her young self in their expressions and cast her mind back to nannies she'd got on with – there'd been a couple. She'd liked them because they respected her and didn't talk down to her.

'Hello,' she said in English. 'Do you speak English?' She had been told that they did as their mother was English, which was why they'd wanted a native English speaker to be their nanny.

The eldest girl lifted her chin.

Alexandra repeated herself in slow, schoolgirl French.

'*Non!*' said the girl.

Alexandra asked them their names in the same way, slowly with a very English accent to her French.

The eldest girl didn't speak but her brother said, 'Félicité,' using the French form of the name and gesturing to his older sister. 'I am Henri. And this is little Stéphanie. The dog's name is Milou.'

Alexandra nodded. That was what Tintin's dog was called in the French version of the books. If these children knew those books it would be something she could talk about, although she was determined to speak to them in English. They may well not want

34

her to know they spoke English and she decided that she would keep the fact she spoke French more or less fluently a secret too. People were allowed secrets, she felt.

'I am Alexandra,' she said in French, and then went back to English. 'I'm very hungry. Can you tell me where the kitchen is, please?'

'*Non!*' said Félicité, still defiant.

'Very well,' said Alexandra, 'I will find it for myself. Maybe Milou will help me?'

Milou obliged and together they went through the long passage to the back of the house; possibly Milou was hungry too.

The kitchen was large with a huge black range against one wall and a big, scrubbed table in the middle. Next to the range was a small armchair, with a lot of squashed cushions on it. In the corner was a grandfather clock, which ticked loudly. There was a sink, several large cupboards around the walls that almost reached the ceiling and, in front of the range, a rug on which Milou lay down.

Above the range was a long wooden rack, possibly designed for drying clothes but hanging from it instead was everything that might go in a kitchen apart from furniture. There were copper saucepans, frying pans of every size, ladles, strainers, sieves and what looked like medieval weapons of war, bunches of herbs, tea towels, and a teddy bear who had obviously been washed and hung out to dry.

To Alexandra's relief, in one corner she saw a fairly modern gas stove next to a large bottle of gas. There was also a large armoire, its door ajar, revealing bowls and casseroles, dishes, plates – everything you might need to eat from or to serve food. But the room was freezing, even though it was only October.

But first things first, Alexandra told herself. It was a long time since she had eaten her picnic on the train.

'I'm very hungry,' she said in English and then repeated herself in slow, painstaking French.

Félicité shrugged but Stéphanie, who obviously hadn't quite taken in the instructions about language said, 'I'm hungry too!' in perfect English.

'Stéphie!' said Henri, more in sorrow than in anger, 'we're only supposed to speak French!'

'That's all right,' said Alexandra. 'It's fun to play a prank on someone but it isn't funny if it goes on too long. What do you want to eat?'

She addressed Stéphie, who shook her head, obviously still embarrassed by her recent faux pas.

'OK,' said Alexandra, mostly to herself. 'Is there a fridge?'

She'd stopped expecting help and so started opening cupboards and doors and eventually found a large larder a short way down a passage. In here she found a pat of butter on a plate, a selection of cheeses and one of the fowls Bruno had referred to. She would think about cooking that another time; now she wanted bread.

Carrying the butter and some cheese she thought was Comté, the nearest thing to Cheddar available in France, she went back to the kitchen. She was pleased to see the children were still there.

'Where is the bread?' she said in her loud, slow French. She was trusting that the eldest girl would play the game. Everyone knew the children spoke English, but Alexandra addressing her in French should mean she would have to reply.

Félicité indicated with her head where Alexandra should look. 'In the pantry,' she said in English. 'But it's probably stale.'

'When did you all last eat?' Alexandra was worried. It was six o'clock. Had they eaten at all that day?

'We had croissants for breakfast,' said Stéphie. 'And apples for lunch.'

'OK,' said Alexandra. 'Let's find some food.'

The pantry was beyond the larder and in it she found a wooden bread bin, in which were a couple of hard baguettes and a *pain de campagne*.

Hoping she'd find a knife saw-like enough to cut it, she picked up the round brown loaf and took it back to the kitchen. If the housekeeper was going to be away for long, she'd make a few changes; things needed to be a lot handier.

There was a knife on a magnetic rack against the wall. Alexandra sawed through the loaf until she had four decent-sized slices. Then she proceeded to make cheese on toast.

The smell of toasted cheese, and the sight of it bubbling on the bread that Alexandra had put on a round bread board, brought Alexandra's charges to the table like moths to a flame. When she saw how eagerly they tucked in she cut up the rest of the loaf and used all the cheese to put on top. She hoped them having full stomachs would make them unbend to her a little.

Sitting in a kitchen, albeit a cold French one, reminded Alexandra of her London life, when she and her friends would sit around the kitchen table, eating, laughing, chatting about life. They'd shared the large London house in recent months, making it a very happy place. Could she make this house happy? On her own with three unhappy children? It would be hard. Although Félicité was not really a child any more.

She got up from the table and went to inspect the range. She opened the fire door. 'Does this work, usually?'

Henri nodded. 'It needs lots of wood, but yes, usually it works. There's a wood shed.'

Alexandra smiled at him. If she could get at least one of her charges on her side it would make everything so much easier. 'Could you find me some wood and some kindling? You know, small sticks to get the fire going. And some newspaper.'

Henri picked up another piece of cheese on toast and set off. Alexandra decided this was not the moment to teach table manners; after all, she had asked him to get the wood. She hadn't said 'when you've finished eating'.

It took Alexandra a little while to get the range going and once she had, she realised it would be another matter to keep it in. But it was cheering to hear the crackle of the wood and realise that eventually there would be a little heat. It had been a golden October day but now it was getting chilly.

'Henri, you must show me where the wood is. I can't rely on you to fetch it for me.'

'Mme Carrier used to swear at the range a lot. She struggled to keep it in overnight,' Henri confided.

'OK, in which case, I'll content myself with lighting it in the morning and keeping it going in the day.' She put on another couple of logs. 'Anyone fancy hot chocolate?' she asked. She really felt like a glass of wine but until she had properly settled in and found where it was kept, she'd have to make do. Hot chocolate, served in bowls the French way, would help a lot.

There wasn't much milk in the large jug in the larder but a thorough rummage through the various packets in the cupboards came up with a mix that only required hot water to make a milky cocoa. Alexandra put some milk into a pan, the contents of the packet, a lump of chocolate and some water and heated it on the stove. Eventually, she poured the foaming drink into bowls she knew were usually used for drinking coffee.

Soon they were all sitting round the table, sipping their drinks. The room was beginning to warm up as was the cheerfulness level. Neither was as high as Alexandra would have liked, but an upward curve was positive.

Alexandra had very little to go on, but thought that Stéphie must be about eight or nine. She saw the little girl yawning a few times. Perhaps Stéphie needed more sleep than the older two and hadn't been getting it.

She gathered the empty bowls and put them in the sink, resolving to wash them tomorrow. Although it was probably not the official nanny way to behave, she always preferred washing up in the morning when there was sunshine, rather than standing in a dark kitchen when she was tired.

She reached for the teddy. 'This little chap must be quite tired. I wonder where he sleeps?'

'He sleeps with me!' said Stéphie immediately and then looked at her siblings in case she'd revealed too much to their unwanted nanny.

'OK. Does anyone know where I sleep?' asked Alexandra. 'I'd ask Teddy but I'm not sure he speaks English.'

'He's called Clive,' said Stéphie.

'Oh? That's a good name. Why is he called that?'

Stéphie gave a little shrug. 'It's his name.'

Félicité pushed back her chair, making a horrible scraping noise on the stone floor. 'The nanny's room is ready. Mme Carrière did it before she went. We'll show you.' She paused. 'It has a sofa and chairs. You can stay in it.' Her meaning was clear: Stay in your quarters, Nanny, and don't come out!

Alexandra flinched inwardly. Had she ever been so completely hostile to any of her nannies or governesses? She felt a flash of shame when she realised she probably had.

'I'll just make up the stove and see if we get a bit of hot water out of it. At least we know that Clive doesn't need a bath,' she said. When she'd put on logs, fiddled with draughts and levers she didn't understand, she straightened up.

'Let's go!' Although she sounded positive and cheerful, inside she felt incredibly tired and a little disheartened.

At least the chateau is beautiful, she thought as she followed her charges up the elegant staircase to the upper floors.

Her room, as indicated by Félicité, was one of a suite of rooms designed for children and their personal servants. It wasn't luxurious but the nanny wasn't expected to sleep in a garret, obviously. It had a full-height window and a small balcony giving a nice view over the grounds at the front of the chateau, and was large enough to have a sofa and a couple of armchairs arranged around a small table in the window. There was a chest of drawers and a desk against the wall, and the bed was a double with pretty hangings. If she did have to live in it, it wouldn't be bad. It was fairly simple but it looked clean. The bed was ancient, she realised, but that certainly wouldn't bother her tonight.

'Will there be hot water if anyone wants a bath?' she said to her little group.

'No,' said Félicité. 'The nanny is expected to wash in her room with a bowl and a jug of water.'

Alexandra was keen to get Félicité on her side but this was a step too far. 'Oh come on! What sort of novels have you been reading? But talking of reading, I wonder if Clive likes being read to?'

Stéphie nodded assertively. 'Yes, he does.'

'Let's find something he'd like and I'll read.' She did remember how much she liked being tucked up in bed while someone read her a story.

Everyone went to Stéphie's room, which was pretty and had twin beds in it. It had a little bookcase full of books. Alexandra went over to it and read out the titles. 'Oh! *Milly-Molly-Mandy!*' she said and then realised her childhood favourite might be a little young for Stéphie.

'OK, we can read that if you like.' Stéphie sounded resigned and condescending but Alexandra wondered if she was secretly happy to go back to a book written for smaller children.

She picked it up. 'Get your night things on and do your teeth and then I'll read.' She discovered that, although she never would have thought of herself as the sort of person who told people to clean their teeth, she was settling into the role.

Stéphie took her pyjamas into the little bathroom and Félicité and Henri got on to the second bed.

'Are you keen on *Milly-Molly-Mandy*?' Alexandra asked.

'Of course not!' said Henri.

'We have to stay with her until she goes to sleep,' said Félicité, 'and of course, make sure you're not cruel to her.'

'Fair enough,' said Alexandra, wondering if she should actually supervise the teeth-cleaning and then deciding not tonight.

She wandered round the room looking at things and came across a china model of a horse that was in several pieces. She was examining the head when Stéphie came back. 'It was an accident!' she said, suddenly upset.

'We know,' said Félicité gently. 'It's OK.'

Alexandra put down the horse's head. 'I may be able to mend that for you later.'

'Our last nanny didn't read to us much,' said Stéphie. 'She said we were old enough to read to ourselves.'

'And of course you are,' said Alexandra. 'I understand that. But I still love being read to.'

Henri and Félicité settled on to the second bed while Alexandra lay down next to Stéphie and opened the book.

She'd read one of the stories and then saw that Stéphie was fast asleep. The other two seemed to be enjoying being read to but she asked them quietly, 'Shall I go on? Stéphie's asleep.'

'No,' said Félicité quickly. '*Milly-Molly-Mandy* is a bit young for us.'

Alexandra got off the bed carefully, so as not to disturb the little girl, pulled up the covers and tucked her in. Then she went to the broken horse. 'Would you like me to mend this? Would Stéphie like me to?'

Félicité shrugged in a very Gallic way. 'Stéphie would like it. I don't care. But it was mine.'

'I need to get my things up from downstairs,' Alexandra said. She tried not to look at Henri in a meaningful way but he took the hint anyway.

'I'll get them.'

'You mustn't take advantage of Henri. It wouldn't be fair. He's very kind and helpful,' Félicité said as he left the room.

'OK,' said Alexandra, following him out and making her way to her own bedroom, Félicité trailing behind.

She had brought her handbag up with her. She knew she had glue suitable for china mending in it because she'd found it when looking for make-up, before her interview. She remembered buying it just before her friend's wedding and it had been kicking around in the bottom of her bag ever since. She took her bag over to the table.

'If you go and get the horse, I'll see what I can do.'

As Félicité went, Alexandra realised that in spite of her nonchalant attitude towards it, the ornament obviously meant a lot to her.

Twenty minutes later, Henri and Félicité were sitting on Alexandra's bed while she sat at the table, scraping glue off the edges of the broken china with her penknife.

'It is odd for a girl to have a penknife in her handbag,' said Henri, unable to keep silent about the oddness any longer.

'It's a Swiss Army knife,' said Alexandra. 'A friend from London gave it to me. He said everyone ought to have one.'

'Was he a boyfriend?' asked Félicité.

Alexandra looked up and smiled. 'No. He is my best friend, probably, but there's nothing romantic about us.' She thought about David, who had kept an eye on her and later her friends, in London. He was more like an older brother, and homosexual, something they never really spoke about, so their relationship was never going to be anything different.

'Why are you scraping all the glue off?' said Henri. 'Why put it on if you're going to take it all off again.'

'It's to make sure there isn't any excess to ooze out when I put the pieces together.' She paused. 'I don't suppose you've got any sort of tape? Sticking plaster would do.'

Henri, who was obviously fascinated by the mending process, obligingly fetched a roll of sticking plaster. It was rather old and took Alexandra a while to get into but eventually the little horse was sitting on the table, together once more, his pieces held together by strips of sticking plaster.

'That's amazing!' said Henri. 'It looks as if he's been patched up in hospital.'

'He'll look better tomorrow when we take the tape off,' said Alexandra, hoping her china-mending skills hadn't deserted her. 'I'll show you how to do it if ever there's anything else that needs mending,' she said to Henri.

When Alexandra had cleared up her things and put the tops back on the two substances involved in the mending, she said, 'What time do you two go to bed? Normally?'

'When we like,' said Félicité defiantly.

'Oh good,' said Alexandra. 'So if I went to bed now, you'd lock up the house and let Milou out? Things like that?'

'No,' said Félicité, horrified. 'You must do that. You're the grown-up.'

'All right,' said Alexandra. 'But you'll have to show me what to do.'

Milou had a bed in the kitchen but although he went out obediently enough, barked twice before doing what was required and came back in, the bed in the kitchen didn't seem to appeal.

'Does he usually sleep with one of you two?' Alexandra asked.

'He's not supposed to,' said Henri, 'but he gets lonely downstairs and howls. It's a terrifying sound.'

'Well, if he wants to sleep with one of you, that's fine. I don't want howling. I'm really tired.'

45

'Does sleeping in such a big house make you nervous?' asked Félicité, obviously hoping she would say yes.

Alexandra shook her head. 'In London I used to sleep alone sometimes in a much spookier house than this one.' She shrugged, although when she was younger, a gap between nannies or companions was something she'd dreaded. She looked at Félicité directly. 'I had a lot of nannies when I was growing up, sometimes when I was too old to have one, like you.'

Félicité looked away, obviously not wanting to acknowledge any similarity between her and this Englishwoman who'd been inflicted on them.

'Was your father away a lot too?' asked Henri.

Alexandra shook her head. 'No, I'm an orphan. But it's OK, I never knew my parents.'

'We've got a father,' said Henri, 'but our mother lives in Argentina. We never see her.'

'Oh, that's sad,' said Alexandra, probing for information as if it were a sore tooth; she was ready to draw back at any moment.

'It's fine!' declared Félicité. 'What sort of a mother leaves her children? We don't want to see her.'

'It's handy she lives in Argentina then, isn't it?'

Henri frowned. He would like to see her, Alexandra thought. But what about Stéphie? When had their mother left? Would she even remember her?

A yawn erupted from nowhere. 'I must go to bed,' said Alexandra. 'I'll trust you two to brush your teeth and settle Milou for the night. We've locked the doors. Time to sleep!'

'We didn't shut the hens in,' said Félicité. 'The fox will get them if we don't.'

Alexandra took a breath and refrained from asking Félicité why she hadn't mentioned this before. 'Right, we'd better do that then. You'll have to show me.'

As she followed Félicité and Henri out of the back of the house and into the yard, across the yard to the henhouse, Alexandra resolved to make sure this was done much earlier in the evening. She'd have to make a list of chores for herself.

In the desk in her room was some faded writing paper with a drawing of the chateau on it as well as the address and telephone number. Alexandra dithered for a couple of minutes and then decided it would be a good idea to write to her relations using this paper. She was determined to be more adult about her situation and would start by telling them that things hadn't worked out quite as she expected, although she admitted to herself that she wouldn't have been so keen to share this information had she been working anywhere less salubrious and suitable for a young woman of her background. But as she was now in a large chateau, looking after the children of the Comte de Belleville, she didn't have to worry about this.

Chapter Five

❧

Alexandra was woken in the morning by Stéphie, who appeared in the doorway of her bedroom holding Clive, her teddy. 'Is it time to get up yet?'

Alexandra, who'd had a restless night and had just fallen into a deep sleep, reached out for her little travel clock and peered at it. It was hard to see in the dim light and it took a while before she made out that it was only half past five.

'Not really,' she said. 'But if you go and get your pillow you can get into bed with me for a bit while I sleep a little more.'

Stéphie trotted off and was back before Alexandra had snatched more than forty winks. Stéphie had *Milly-Molly-Mandy* with her.

'Will you read to me?'

Alexandra considered, her eyes still closed. 'I think you could read it to yourself for just a bit. It's very early.'

'I can't read,' said Stéphie.

This made Alexandra wake up. 'Can't you? Not at all? How old are you?'

'Nine. And I can read a little bit.'

Had Stéphie said she couldn't read to get her attention, or could she really not read? 'Why don't you read to me? I like being read to,' Alexandra said.

Stéphie stumbled along but was obviously struggling. Alexandra frowned. 'Do you go to school?'

Stéphie shook her head. 'It's too far away. Our last nanny couldn't drive.'

'I can drive,' said Alexandra. It had been one of the conditions of her employment. 'Was your last nanny with you for long?'

'Years and years. She used to do sums with me.'

'What about Félicité and Henri?'

Stéphie was wriggling about and seemed not to be interested. 'We did have a governess for a while and, after she left, they went to our neighbours, who had a tutor. But then they moved away.'

'How did they get to the neighbours?' Surely if the older children could be transported to a neighbour, they could go to school.

'Bruno used to take them across the fields.'

'How long ago?' asked Alexandra. How long *was* it since these children had received a proper education?

'I don't know,' said Stéphie, who obviously didn't care.

Alexandra decided that because she was only there for a month, she couldn't enrol the children in school in a foreign language and undertake to get them there unless they were very keen to go. However, she could help Stéphie with her reading. At nine she should be reading better than she was, surely. Alexandra had been a very early reader herself; it had been part of her defence system.

'Would you like me to help you with your reading, Stéphie?' Alexandra asked, struggling to a sitting position.

'We haven't got the proper books,' said Stéphie.

'Books that have words in them are the proper books,' said Alexandra. 'Let's have a look.'

They were doing quite well and Stéphie was gaining confidence when Alexandra's door was opened and a furious Félicité stood there. 'You're not supposed to teach Stéphie! That's not a nanny's job!'

Alexandra looked up and said calmly, 'Well, thank you, Félicité. If you'd care to write out a list of my responsibilities and another of things I'm not supposed to do, I'd be very grateful. I've never been a nanny before.'

'I like reading with Alexandra,' said Stéphie. 'She makes it fun.'

Félicité tossed her head. 'OK, well, if you like it, you can. Now it's time to let the hens out.'

'Ooh,' said Stéphie, abandoning *Milly-Molly-Mandy* and getting out of bed. 'I like doing that. I like collecting the eggs too, unless any of the hens have gone broody.'

'Off you go then,' said Alexandra. 'Let's hope there are eggs. Then we can have them for breakfast.'

'I only like them boiled with soldiers,' said Stéphie. 'And soldiers are difficult with French bread.'

'Get the eggs; I'll sort out the soldiers.' Alexandra frowned. 'Have we got any bread?'

Félicité, who obviously didn't share Stéphie's enthusiasm for collecting eggs, nodded. 'I expect someone who works on the farm will leave some. There's a little village nearby that has a *boulangerie*.' She smiled coldly. 'They know we haven't got a housekeeper now, and only a new nanny.'

'That's good,' said Alexandra, ignoring Félicité's snooty attitude to her current profession. 'When's the market in the local town, do you know? I need to get some clothes. All mine are probably in Switzerland by now.'

'Why are they in Switzerland?' asked Félicité, her imagination caught.

'I was on the way to Switzerland when I stopped off in Paris and decided to get a job and this is it!' Alexandra wondered if she should add that she'd thought the job was in Paris, but didn't. 'As you know, it's only for a month, while your nanny is looking after her mother.'

'What were you going to do in Switzerland?' asked Félicité.

'Stay with my relations, go to a finishing school, something like that.'

'But why would you go to a finishing school?' asked Félicité, who appeared to know what one was.

'That's what I thought,' Alexandra said. 'Why? Which is why I chose to have a job instead.'

'Although you've never been a nanny before.'

'To be honest, I didn't know the job was for a nanny. I just knew I had to cook, drive, speak French—' Too late she remembered she'd been keeping the fact that she could speak French to herself. 'A bit, I can speak French a little. And I thought, what better way to improve my French than having a job?'

'Why did you think you could be a nanny when you hadn't ever been one before?'

It was a fair question. 'I reckoned I'd had lots of nannies and I could just do what they did, more or less. Although none of mine could drive or cook or speak French. Except one who taught me' – she caught herself again – 'a bit of French because she was French. She took me to Paris. I loved it.' She hadn't loved the fact that her nanny had spent a lot of time ignoring Alexandra and making love to her boyfriend, but she had got used to it and explored Paris on her own. 'So, is there a market in the town?'

'It's today,' said Félicité.

'I'm going to get up now,' said Alexandra.

'I'll see you downstairs,' said Félicité.

Watching her and Stéphie leave the room, Alexandra felt she'd made a little headway with Félicité. Which was good. Félicité was intelligent and knew the house and the area – she'd be a good person to have on her side.

Down in the kitchen, Alexandra lit the fire in the range before she did anything else. It was a beautiful, golden day outside but there was mist about and a chill in the air. The kitchen was cold too, although there was a basket of eggs on the table, with some long narrow baguettes and a round, brown country loaf. There was also a large pat of butter wrapped in paper, and some cheese. Some helpful person had indeed been to the *boulangerie* for them.

Henri had brought in more logs and sticks and was looking at the food in a hungry way. 'Can I have some bread and butter?' he asked. 'Bruno doesn't usually bring bread. It must be because you're new.'

'How do you get it usually?'

'You can walk over the fields to the village. I go sometimes. Or someone drives.'

'Then of course you can eat it!' said Alexandra.

There was an exchange of looks among the children which told Alexandra they had been expecting her to say no.

'I'll cook some eggs. What about French toast? That's my favourite.'

'What's French toast?' asked Stéphie. 'I want boiled eggs.'

'You can have boiled eggs if you want but French toast is nice. Is there any jam?'

'Greengage jam, from last year,' said Félicité.

'I'll get it,' said Henri.

'I must learn where everything is,' said Alexandra, finally content that the range would stay in at least for a bit.

Breakfast was a cheerful meal although Alexandra did find herself missing tea. She knew she'd have to get over that. She had concealed a packet of tea in with her clothes, now in Switzerland. But for a month she'd have to drink coffee, hot chocolate or the *tisanes* she generally found to be disgusting.

'Now I think we should go to the market and hope they sell something I can wear,' said Alexandra.

'How will we get there?' asked Stéphie.

'We'll go in the car,' said Alexandra. 'I wonder where it is?' She looked at Henri, hoping his helpful nature would lead him to tell her. It did.

'It's in the barn,' he said. 'Shall I get it out for you?'

'How old are you, Henri?' asked Alexandra. 'What is the legal age for driving in France?'

'I've been driving round the property since I was small,' said Henri, grinning.

'In which case, do please get the car out for me.'

While Henri was doing this, Alexandra was in the kitchen checking she had everything she needed, including her handbag and purse, when Stéphie said, 'What about Milou?'

'What about him? Should I give him more food? What have I forgotten?' Alexandra had shared a dog in London but she'd never been in sole charge before.

'We have to take him with us!' Stéphie insisted. 'He'll be lonely on his own.'

'Couldn't Clive look after him?' asked Alexandra, hoping the teddy shared Stéphie's caring nature.

Stéphie looked at Alexandra in disgust. 'He's a teddy bear! What can he do to look after Milou?'

Alexandra suppressed a sigh. 'OK, but you'll have to take care of him. Can you find his lead?' At least the dog had a collar.

But not a proper lead, she discovered. 'He always just follows us when we run around outside,' said Félicité as if a dog on a lead was an incomprehensible concept.

Henri gave a short blast on the horn of the car, adding to the sense of panic that was beginning to rise in Alexandra.

'Well, let's leave him here!' she said. She was going to have to cope with driving a car she didn't know to a place she didn't know, with three young people she didn't really know either. Adding a large dog was asking for trouble, in her opinion.

'We can't,' Stéphie insisted. 'Here, we'll use my scarf as a lead.'

Alexandra sighed. 'OK. Now into the car everyone. Henri? Can you move? Much as I'd like to, I can't let you drive us to town.'

There was a fair amount of discussion – argument even – about who should sit where and in the end Félicité sat next to Alexandra in the front and the others went in the back. Milou took the middle, so he could lunge forward every so often. Apparently he didn't want to go in the bit at the back designed for luggage or dogs; it was obviously too far away from the action.

To Alexandra's relief the car was very similar to the one she had driven in London, owned by David, her antique-dealer friend. She'd learnt to drive on a car like this and so she set off with confidence.

It was a lovely sunny day now: the first autumnal mists had been burned off and it was starting to warm up. Alexandra wished she had something resembling a summer dress to wear rather than the formal, now grubby dress she'd worn so much in Paris. It had been fine for her interview but wasn't right for the country. She had put a cardigan on over the top but realised she looked dressed for the city. More importantly, she felt wrong. However, she was confident that the market would have everything she needed. She began to enjoy herself.

Henri turned out to be very keen on giving Alexandra advice on how to drive. He leant over her shoulder telling her what to do and was obviously feeling the frustration that males often do when watching a woman do what they consider to be their job.

They got to the end of the drive. 'Which way now?'

'Left,' said Henri.

'We've never had a nanny who can drive before. Usually Mme Carrier takes us to the market if we go,' said Stéphie, enjoying the novelty.

'Just tell me if I start driving on the left,' said Alexandra, picking up speed now they were on the road.

The little town of Saint-Jean-du-Roc wasn't far away and soon Alexandra was crawling through the streets deciding where best to park. She found a spot and everyone got out, Stéphie hanging on to Milou. Milou was used to vast acreage to roam in and wasn't really keen on being confined by a scarf, although he was very sweet-natured and clearly adored Stéphie.

Alexandra had brought a couple of baskets with her; she gave one to Félicité and took the other herself.

'When we've got all the food we think we need I'm going to buy some clothes. While I'm doing that, you can have a good look round. Maybe, if you're good, you can buy something for yourselves.' She should probably have kept bribery until she really needed it, but remembered how frustrating and dull it could be shopping when you couldn't buy anything. Although she doubted anyone could be bored here: it was so full of wonderful things and people.

'I haven't got very much money, though,' she added belatedly. 'I need to find out how to get housekeeping money.' She realised that she had been employed in a hurry before things she would need had been put in place. It made life quite tricky. Luckily Alexandra was resourceful. Mme Dubois should have asked her about those skills instead of worrying about her references.

'Can't help, I'm afraid,' said Félicité, who didn't seem quite as sorry as she should have been.

'There's a bank over there,' said Henri. 'That's where you get money from, isn't it?'

'Yes,' said Alexandra, 'but you can't just go in and ask for it. Still, I do have traveller's cheques. I could cash one of those and use that until we find out.' She said 'we' deliberately. She wanted everyone to feel like a team.

The food stalls were eye-opening in their colour and variety. She longed to have David with her, or another friend, Meg, both of whom loved cooking and food. They'd be in heaven. Her current companions were a bit more blasé and wandered off as soon as Alexandra started her shopping.

There were stalls filled with grapes, melons, apples and pears. The colours were so glowing she imagined she could feel warmth coming from them. Peppers, which in England tended to be green and considered exotic, were red and yellow, and as big as a hand. Garlic bulbs the size of cricket balls, courgettes and aubergines like purple balloons. Even the vegetables Alexandra was more familiar with, like carrots, cabbages and potatoes, seemed bigger, better and more beautifully presented.

She had a basket full of onions, potatoes, garlic and carrots and was buying some peppers and aubergines when Stéphie appeared. 'Milou has escaped.'

'Oh, love!' Alexandra knew there was no point in being angry. 'Can you try and catch him? Then we can put him in the car until we've finished. It's probably a bit confusing for him, being in this crowd.'

Stéphie disappeared again and Alexandra headed towards a cheese stall. There was no earthly point in being in France if you didn't buy cheese, she decided. She was also tempted by stalls selling jam and honey, soap and lavender products. There were also cured meats and prepared foods, like cooked chickens, vats of bœuf bourguignon, cassoulet, and bouillabaisse, a rich fish soup.

She had just been offered an olive by an attentive stallholder when Milou appeared at speed, colliding with the man next to Alexandra and causing him to spill his carton of olives all over her.

There was a welter of apologies, both Alexandra and the man (who she had time to notice was young and very handsome) fighting for the privilege of taking the blame.

Stéphie and Henri arrived in Milou's wake. Félicité joined them more slowly.

'Sorry! He just saw you and dashed off!' Stéphie explained. 'He loves you!'

'He hardly knows me,' said Alexandra, continuing to speak French without thinking.

'It was my olives that poured oil all down your dress,' said the young man. 'Oh, I know you!' He addressed Félicité and her siblings and then turned to Alexandra. 'I'm a friend of Antoine. Indeed, I am his lawyer.' His remorse increased. 'So I must apologise even more! I have ruined the clothes of a friend of my good friend le Comte.' He took hold of her hand and kissed it. 'Maxime de Marais at your service. Now, what can I do to make amends?'

'Ah!' said Alexandra. 'I am so pleased to meet you. I have been given your name if I need help with anything. I had a letter with information on it saying I wouldn't be able to get in touch with le Comte but you could do it for me.'

Maxime bowed. 'And now I have covered you in oil. I must immediately make amends.'

Alexandra laughed. 'It's all Milou's fault, but if you want to do me a favour, could you escort this lot to a café? I need a little time alone to buy clothes.'

'Clothes? From here? Mam'selle, it is hardly an appropriate place . . .' Maxime sounded outraged.

'I need something now, not when I can find the right shop,' Alexandra said. 'And don't worry, I needed clothes before Milou's accident.'

'Then I will take the children to a café,' said Maxime. 'With the greatest of pleasure.'

As he didn't immediately move, Alexandra put her hand in her bag, remembering the letter she had written to her relations on the train. 'And if you could find a stamp and a postbox for this, I'll forgive you for everything.'

Maxime took the letter and then kissed her hand again. 'We'll be in the café across the road. I'll order you a glass of champagne.'

'What are we celebrating?' asked Alexandra, smiling.

'We're celebrating our meeting,' said Maxime. 'Come along, children. And keep a hold of Milou. He's done well this morning, but let's not push our luck!'

59

A little burst of joy accompanied Alexandra to the stall she had spotted earlier. It sold cotton dresses in bright prints and pretty, off-the-shoulder styles. It was a peasant look that would have been very out of place in London, where styles were mostly rectangular, skirts were short, and geometry ruled. But here, in the autumn sunshine, gathered dresses with flounces and frills seemed appropriate. She bought two, and was impressed by the price and charmed by the free neck scarf that went in the paper bag along with the dresses. She discovered that flirting was part of the language and found it made her smile. It was respectful but enjoyable too.

A couple of stalls along from the one that sold dresses was a more sober set-up. Here traditional clothes for working men hung from hangers. There was the blue jacket that workmen wore in several shades of blue; there were trousers and jeans, long cotton coats and boiler suits.

It was the boiler suits that attracted Alexandra. There were famous pictures of women wearing these during the war and Alexandra felt there was a lot to recommend them to someone who was going to be living in a French chateau in the autumn. It took her a while to convince the stallholder that she wanted one for herself but amid much laughter she finally had one in her hands and held it up against her. The arms and legs were too long but she could roll them up.

She was just wondering if it was too long in the body when the stallholder said, 'Would you like to try it on? Here? In my van. There is a mirror.'

'*Superbe*,' she said, and in no time she was in the van, taking off her oil-covered dress, climbing into the boiler suit. It was perfect! It needed a tight belt round the waist to give her shape and – a thought occurred to her and she found the neck scarf she'd been given and put that on. She turned up her collar and reapplied her lipstick. Great! She was delighted. She got down from the back of the van and paid for two boiler suits because, she explained to herself, she may never be able to get one again. They were useful and comfortable and, with the addition of a belt, she was certain, sexy.

She couldn't be away from her charges too long so she decided not to look for a stall that sold belts: she'd make do with the wonderful scarlet scarf. She felt like a revolutionary and found her way to the café with an extra spring in her step. Alexandra had discovered that she liked flirting, and having Maxime to do it with, even for a morning, was delightful.

Her group had a good outside table, with an excellent view of the square and the market and Maxime looked up when Alexandra joined them. '*Mon Dieu!* You have changed, and somehow you have made the uniform of the French worker into a stylish outfit!' His expression told her he wasn't just being polite and Alexandra returned the smile.

'*Merci du compliment*! Are we really having champagne?' she said to Maxime as he handed her a glass. 'How delightful! What are you having?' she asked her charges.

'I'm having champagne,' said Félicité defiantly, obviously waiting to be told off.

'Excellent,' said Alexandra, thinking one glass would probably be fine for a fifteen-year-old, especially if they had something to eat.

The other two were drinking soft drinks. Alexandra clinked glasses with Maxime. 'This is so kind of you. Can I invite you to have lunch with us? While we're here, it makes sense to eat.' If he accepted, she'd have to nip across to the bank to cash a traveller's cheque; she hoped they were open.

'I am ahead of you,' said Maxime, bowing slightly. 'I have already asked for menus. And you will be my guests, of course.'

'That's wonderful,' said Alexandra, having taken a few sips of champagne. 'I would have needed to get some cash and wasn't sure if the bank would be open.' She paused. 'Although I suppose on market day, it would be.' Although she'd been given half her wages, her shopping in Paris as well as in the market just now had made inroads into them.

Maxime, having made to give her more champagne before she put her hand over her glass, said, 'You shouldn't have to worry about money to feed these children. Antoine may not be a millionaire but he can afford to feed his family – and their nanny.'

Alexandra shrugged. 'There don't seem to be arrangements for me to have money for housekeeping. Or food, really. Although Félicité did say someone brings bread at the moment.'

'And things from the farm,' Félicité clarified. 'But of course there isn't a lot of variety.'

She sounded a bit jaded, Alexandra thought. It couldn't be a great life for a teenager stuck away in a chateau, miles from young people her own age. 'Stéphie told me you don't go to school,' she said.

'Papa is going to arrange a new, proper governess when he gets home,' said Félicité.

'Don't you fancy going to school?' asked Alexandra. 'I had governesses for most of my education but I did go to boarding school for a couple of years and I really enjoyed being with girls my own age.' This was a slight exaggeration of course but she had felt lonely a lot of the time before she went.

Félicité shrugged, as if such things were not for her to think about.

'I'd quite like to go,' said Henri. 'I love my sisters, of course, but I do miss playing games and things.'

'I hated school,' said Stéphie.

'She was bullied,' said Félicité, 'and I got into a fight and decided to leave. It was then that Papa hired a governess. But she didn't stay all that long.'

Alexandra had also got into a bit of trouble defending the girl everyone was picking on and she too had decided to leave before she was asked to. Her guardians had got her a very strict governess after that. Luckily she didn't stay long either.

'What would we like to eat?' asked Maxime. 'I recommend the *salade niçoise*. It is very good here.'

Alexandra was putting a perfect forkful of anchovies, olives and hardboiled egg into her mouth when she became aware of being looked at. Two elegant Frenchwomen were glaring at her in a way that was surprising.

'Oh, look,' said Stéphie. 'There's Grand-mère.'

To her absolute horror, Alexandra watched, helpless, as two formidable women in their fifties processed across the square towards her. Briefly she calculated her chances of getting through the tables and chairs to the *toilette* before they arrived, but they were determined women – she had no chance.

Félicité, Henri and Stéphie got up and greeted their grandmother politely. They nodded to her companion, who was obviously familiar to them. Maxime also got to his feet, and bowed; he knew them too.

The briefest of harmless conversation passed before Grand-mère turned her attention to Alexandra. 'And who are you?' she said in perfect, accentless English.

'I'm the nanny,' said Alexandra, who didn't think her name was relevant – she was only the nanny for a month, after all.

'Really?' said Grand-mère, obviously surprised. 'What a strange choice, if you don't mind my saying. I must speak to my son-in-law about this!'

Then she and her acolyte turned and moved away.

'That was interesting,' said Alexandra brightly, trying to pretend she wasn't remotely offended.

'Don't worry about her, she's very snooty,' said Stéphie kindly.

'And you're only here for a month,' said Félicité. Although she probably hadn't intended to sound sympathetic, Alexandra felt that her attitude towards her temporary nanny did seem to have softened a bit.

After that, it was a very enjoyable lunch. Maxime promised to address several things Alexandra had been worried about – the most serious being the need for some housekeeping money. Maxime gave the children some francs to spend in the market while he and Alexandra enjoyed a cup of coffee. He offered her cognac to go with it, but Alexandra shook her head. 'It's a lovely idea but I'm responsible for three young people and a dog in a car that's still unfamiliar.'

He bowed. 'Very sensible.'

They fell into a companionable silence, Alexandra enjoying the feeling of the sun on her face. A lot had happened to her in the last few days and she'd hardly had a moment to take it all in. Now, in the sunshine, with a very handsome, companionable young man, seemed a good time to think how well things were turning out.

A little later they set off for home. Once again, Stéphie, Milou and Henri sat in the back, and Félicité in the front next to Alexandra. Driving out of the town was easier than driving in had been as most of the stalls had gone and with them the people and the cars.

'We must take the tape off the little horse when we get back,' said Alexandra, in English. 'And see if he's mended now.'

'He's a girl!' said Félicité crossly.

'Is he? You can't always tell with horses. What's her name?'

'Alice!' said Félicité, obviously going for the first name that came into her head. 'And I noticed at lunch that you suddenly spoke very good French for an English nanny!' She was accusatory now.

'I know! It's amazing how quickly one picks up the language when you're actually living in the country,' said Alexandra.

Félicité suddenly developed an interest in the passing hedge, but Alexandra could tell that she was smiling.

When they got home Félicité and Stéphie rushed up to get Alice the horse. Everyone went to the kitchen and while Henri got the range going, Alexandra peeled off the sticking plaster.

'There we are,' she said. 'That's quite a nice repair, although I say so myself.'

'It's OK,' said Félicité, although Alexandra could see she was pleased.

'It's wonderful!' said Stéphie, and flung her arms round Alexandra's neck and hugged her. 'Thank you!'

Alexandra suddenly felt quite tearful.

Chapter Six

The next few days went well and Alexandra was beginning to feel another three weeks or so would be fine. She hadn't heard back from her relatives to say she had to rush to Switzerland and she found she enjoyed the pace of French provincial life. The only slightly worrying thing was that Maxime had telephoned to say that the nanny who was looking after her mother would not be returning. That, however, Alexandra decided, was a problem for Antoine to deal with; she couldn't help.

She was in the kitchen writing labels for some pear jam she had made to use up the quantities of fruit she and the children had picked the previous day. Her feeling was, as a nanny, she should get her charges to do practical, outdoor things when she wasn't reading with Stéphie or looking in the library for things she thought Félicité and Henri might like. She was just doing this last task, feeling pleasantly domestic, when the loud jangle of the doorbell followed by a volley of deep, terrifying barks from Milou broke the silence.

She looked at Félicité to see if she knew who it might be. She shrugged.

'No one ever calls round,' said Henri. 'We're too far away from other people.'

'Not far enough, obviously,' said Alexandra, putting down her pen. She was wearing one of the off-the-shoulder dresses in a bright print that she'd bought at the market and had tied up her hair in the sash that had come with it. A glance in one of the mirrors she passed showed a peasant in festival clothes – the opposite of the sophisticated young woman she had been in London. She'd also gained a bit of tan from being outside watching Henri and Stéphie climb trees.

So she was put out to be confronted by the two extremely elegant and formal women who had asked her who she was at the market. Although she was wearing her pearls, the real ones as opposed to a long string of fat, fake ones which had gone with her other luggage to Switzerland, she still felt a bit like a farm hand, not a proper nanny.

'Can I help you?' she asked politely in French.

'May we come in?' asked Grand-mère, speaking English.

Alexandra didn't think she could say no so she opened the door wider. She was ushering them into a salon – a room that would have been lovely had it been used more frequently – when Henri appeared. Stéphie wasn't far behind and then came Félicité.

'Children,' said Grand-mère. 'I'm pleased to see you.'

Alexandra wanted to get them all settled so moved ahead and opened the French windows so that light filled one end of the room.

'Do please sit down.' She gestured towards the sofa and chairs. 'Can I get you some refreshment?' She continued in English. 'Would you like coffee? Tea? A cordial of some kind?' What did you offer middle-aged women at this time of day, which she guessed (the charming French timepiece on the mantel had stopped) was late morning.

'A glass of wine would be acceptable,' said Grand-mère.

Alexandra flew along the passage to the kitchen, grateful that she'd found a few wicker-covered demi-johns filled with rosé in a larder. Henri had explained this wine was produced on the estate and just for people who lived there. She found a jug and filled it. There were good glasses in a cupboard in the salon, which she hoped weren't too dusty. She found a tray and added a jug of water; she was fairly sure Félicité would ask for wine and she wanted to be able to dilute it. Possibly Henri, too. She had let them have well-watered wine a couple of times and she was aware Félicité might well try to show her up as a bad nanny.

When she arrived back in the salon, Félicité, Henri and Stéphie were sitting in a row opposite the two women. Alexandra realised she didn't know either of their names and hoped it wouldn't matter. One of the benefits of English was that you could go quite a long time without ever mentioning someone's name. They didn't know her name either, she assumed.

The wine-pouring seemed to take a lifetime and while it was performed no one spoke until Félicité said, 'Can I have some?'

Alexandra put an inch of wine in the bottom of a glass and filled it with water. 'Here you are.'

'Mademoiselle,' said Grand-mère imperiously. 'Do please sit down. We need to consider your position here.'

Alexandra opened her mouth to say she was only there for a few more weeks but closed it again. Grand-mère might say something useful.

'I know you're not here permanently but the education of my grandchildren has been neglected too long already.' She paused. 'I have decided to move in here and take on the task.'

There was a chorus of horrified gasps from the children. Alexandra glanced at them and saw real anxiety.

'But, Grand-mère,' said Stéphie, 'you hate it when we visit! You wouldn't like staying with us!'

The two older women exchanged glances. Grand-mère's friend raised an eyebrow, possibly acknowledging that Stéphie had a point.

'Stéphanie is correct,' said Grand-mère, 'but I have many beautiful, fragile things in my house. Here you live . . .' She hesitated, picking her words. '. . . in a very informal way.'

'We do live informally,' said Alexandra. 'As befits a household of young people. I think you might not be comfortable here.'

'We wouldn't be comfortable,' said Henri.

'Henri,' said his grandmother, 'you're forgetting yourself. For the education of my grandchildren, I am willing to make sacrifices. I will personally make sure my grandchildren do not grow up as savages.' She gave Alexandra a very formal smile, as unlike an expression of pleasure as a growl. 'So, my dear, it will not be necessary for you to continue here. I am taking over the household. You can go home.'

Stéphie gasped in horror. Félicité and Henri looked at each other in panic. 'No!' said Félicité. 'I mean, Grand-mère, it is very kind of you, but really – we're fine! We don't need you to sacrifice yourself.'

'I will be the judge of that, *petite*,' said Grand-mère more kindly.

'But you don't like Milou!' said Henri.

Grand-mère nodded. 'Milou will live in his kennel outside.'

'But he hates it outside!' Henri protested.

'He'll howl!' Stéphie added.

'Then he will be put somewhere so we won't hear him howl,' Grand-mère went on relentlessly.

'But why?' wailed Stéphie, obviously upset.

'Because, *ma petite*, you are growing up with no education!'

For the first time Grand-mère's friend nodded in agreement but still didn't speak.

'But that's not true!' the little girl went on. 'Alexandra is teaching me to read!'

Both women looked at Alexandra with interest. 'Oh?' Then they turned back to Stéphie. 'Can you show us?'

'I don't think Stéphie would like—' Alexandra broke in, unable to bear the thought of the little girl being tested in this public way. But before she could express her objection Stéphie got up eagerly.

'Of course!' she said. 'I'll go and get *Milly-Molly-Mandy*!'

Although the staircase was made of stone, Stéphie's sandals could be heard slapping against the steps as she flew to fetch the book.

71

'It's kind of you to help the little one with her reading,' said Grand-mère with surprising warmth. 'But what can you do for Félicité and Henri? They will be obliged to take exams at some time. They may wish to go to university. Without my help they'll know nothing of the classics.'

Swallowing her surprise that this conventional woman should be thinking about university for her grandchildren, Alexandra said, 'I could possibly arrange for a Shakespearean actor to come and teach them. He's an excellent teacher.' She was confident about this; David had taught her all about antiques as well as teaching her to drive. 'I feel it's better to study with someone who can make the language really come to life.'

'That would be good!' said Félicité quickly, enthusiasm almost disguising her anxiety.

The two women had a quick conversation in French that was too fast and quiet for Alexandra, who was sitting across the large salon, to understand.

After they had stopped, no one spoke. Alexandra couldn't tell if Félicité had heard what had been said or not. But her knee was bouncing up and down and she was pulling at her fingers in a worried way. Henri was staring at the floor.

At last Stéphie appeared with *Milly-Molly-Mandy* and Alice, the mended horse.

'Here's what we're reading!' she announced. 'And here's a horse that was broken. Alexandra mended it. I want her to stay!'

Alexandra was touched.

'So do I!' said Henri.

Félicité, naturally, was less eager to express her enthusiasm for Alexandra. 'Her cooking is OK. And she can drive,' she added.

Grand-mère became thoughtful. 'Show me the horse please. Hmm,' she said thoughtfully, having spent a long time examining it, holding it up to the light and squinting. 'You've done quite a good job. I have a piece – a soup bowl, sentimental value only – I'd like repaired.'

'Alexandra will do that for you, Grand-mère,' said Stéphie. 'But only if you don't send her away.'

'Let me hear you read, *chérie*,' she said.

Stéphie did very well, Alexandra thought, pleased that the early-morning sessions had proved so productive.

'That's very good, Stéphanie,' said Grand-mère, a little surprised.

'Does that mean you won't come to live with us?' asked Stéphanie.

Grand-mère got to her feet and her friend did likewise. Alexandra had the strangest impression that Grand-mère was amused and possibly a little relieved, although her features didn't move very much.

'You say you know someone who can teach Shakespeare and other classic texts?' she asked.

Alexandra nodded. 'As I said, he is an excellent teacher and he could certainly provide references.'

'And this person would be willing to come here and teach my grandchildren?'

Alexandra nodded again. 'It would only be a temporary measure, until the children's education can be more formally arranged.'

Grand-mère shrugged. 'It would be better than nothing, I suppose.'

'Do you think', Alexandra asked hurriedly, 'that the Comte would be happy with the arrangement?'

'If you can vouch for this person, as I said before, it would be better than nothing. I will of course be keeping a very close eye on the arrangement. Hortense? *On y va?*'

'That was nerve-racking,' said Alexandra after she'd closed the door politely behind the two *grandes dames*.

'You don't want to leave early, do you?' asked Henri.

'Certainly not,' said Alexandra. 'I love it here.' She had been very touched by her charges' insistence that they wanted her to stay. She also thought of the life in Switzerland she was anticipating – living with formal relatives who told her what to do or a finishing school teaching her things she either knew already or had no interest in learning. Discovering how to support children without their parents along with living in France was an adventure. And she'd quickly become fond of prickly Félicité, Henri, helpful and stoic, and little Stéphie, young for her age but affectionate and loving. What she really liked, she realised, was the fact that they needed her.

'Really?' asked Félicité, incredulously. She was surprised and possibly disappointed; she'd tried so hard to make Alexandra's life difficult.

Alexandra nodded. 'Now I'm going to telephone my friend to see if he can come and teach you Shakespeare. Maybe we could put on a little bit of a play for your grandmother?' A thought occurred to her. 'Your grandmother seems very French but she speaks perfect English. Has she ever lived in England?'

'She is English,' said Henri, 'but she prefers the French way of life. And maybe the weather.'

This made sense. And of course, she remembered now, the children's mother was English. 'And who's her friend?'

Henri shrugged. 'Mme Sologne. They go everywhere together.'

'OK,' said Alexandra. 'I'll go and telephone my friend David, then let's take some bread and cheese and some fruit into the garden and have lunch.'

Chapter Seven

A routine had quickly developed. Stéphie would come into Alexandra's bed early in the morning and they'd read together. Then they'd get up, see to Milou and let out the hens, light the stove and cook breakfast. Félicité and Henri would appear when they were hungry. As this was at about eight o'clock, Alexandra didn't think it was necessary to wake them. Stéphie's reading was coming along nicely and she seemed to appreciate having Alexandra to herself first thing.

Alexandra had also learnt to love the hens and surprised herself when she found she could pick one up while it was sitting and retrieve the eggs.

'That's very brave,' said Stéphie, impressed. 'I don't like it when they flutter.'

'I don't like birds in the house,' said Alexandra, 'but hens are different. And it's lovely having fresh eggs every morning.' She now had a basket with a dozen of them in it. 'Do you want soldiers again?'

'Yes, please.' Stéphie took hold of Alexandra's free hand. 'Can we make a cake later?'

'Of course. We've got better at making them, haven't we?'

'We're all very good at eating them,' said Stéphie seriously, and then smiled, pleased to have made a joke.

Alexandra laughed and hugged the little girl to her. 'Practice makes perfect!'

A few days later, Maxime drove up to visit them.

'Are you at home for morning calls?' he said, having kissed Alexandra's hand.

'It seems we are,' said Alexandra. 'We weren't doing anything very exciting.'

'It is quite boring living in the middle of the countryside,' added Félicité.

'I do hope your *gouvernante* doesn't share your opinion,' Maxime said to her. 'I have had a telephone conversation with your papa. Among other things we discussed he told me that he needs this young lady' – he looked at Alexandra – 'to stay for another two weeks, so six weeks in all. Will that be possible?'

Alexandra considered. 'It might be, but I'd need to tell my relations in Switzerland. Could you send them a telegram for me? I'm not entirely sure—'

'I will send the telegram. You go now and compose it. Félicité? Can you lead me to some rosé? Writing telegrams is very fatiguing. Alexandra will need sustenance when she has done this task.'

Alexandra laughed and ran upstairs to her bedroom where she could think in peace. She didn't try to make her telegram brief, in order to save money; the estate could presumably afford to pay for as many words

77

as she needed. In the end she was pleased with what she'd written.

So sorry but I have been asked if I would stay on at the chateau for another two weeks as the Comte de Belleville has been further delayed abroad. I feel it is my duty to continue to care for his children who are my responsibility. I will be in touch the moment I know when I can come to you. I am looking forward to seeing you.

It was very long for a telegram and Alexandra wondered if she should have said she was looking forward to seeing them. For one thing, it wasn't really true, but she wanted to appear as if she was doing her best to honour their wishes. She had reminded them she was working for a count, in a chateau, and that she had responsibilities. All good things, she felt.

While she was spending the Count's money she added a telegram to David. *I'm staying an extra fortnight. Do try and come!* She added the telephone number that was on the writing paper. He hadn't said if he was coming yet and she wanted to give him a nudge.

She found Maxime and the children in the salon with a tray with glasses and a jug of wine.

'Here's my telegram to my relations in Switzerland and another to my friend in London who I'm hoping will come over and teach Shakespeare to Félicité and Henri. Their grandmother is worried about their education. I am a bit, too, although Stéphie and I enjoy reading together.'

Maxime nodded. 'Do you not want to go to school?' he said to Félicité and Henri.

They both shook their heads firmly but Alexandra felt they did this from habit and that they hadn't really considered the benefits that being at school could give them.

'I could drive you to school,' said Alexandra. 'If you wanted to go.'

'I'll go if Papa says I have to,' said Félicité with her bottom lip stuck out just a tiny bit.

'We'll let him decide then,' said Alexandra. How long had their father been away from home? Too long, probably.

That night the telephone rang and Henri, who had answered it, said it was for Alexandra.

'David!' she said as soon as she realised who it was. 'How wonderful to hear you! Can you come and stay? I've missed you so much. I actually love it here' – she'd said this for the benefit of the children originally; now she realised it was true – 'but I miss having someone to talk to and gossip with!'

'I'd love to come, actually,' said David. 'I haven't got any theatre work coming up and a trip to a few French flea markets and *brocantes* would spice up the antiques stall. I've managed to get some lovely references from important-sounding people.'

'That's wonderful!' said Alexandra.

They chatted for a bit, Alexandra filling David in on everything that had happened to her since he'd dropped her off at the station in the chilly dawn just a couple of weeks previously.

'Is the chateau big?' said David. 'It's just I was talking about it to an old friend in the pub and he said he'd heard of it and may even have visited. He knew of Saint-Jean-du-Roc.'

'Well, it's a chateau! It seems big. I haven't actually explored everywhere yet. Some of it is fine and some needs a bit of decoration and repair.'

'It's just that I know Jack would really like to come with me. He could teach the children music and maths. He's really a musician but apparently he did maths at university, which makes him actually qualified – unlike me.'

'Oh, I'm sure we could find space for him. I might have to consult the children's grandmother, but she'd probably be delighted that he can teach two important subjects.'

'He's not . . . well . . .' said David. 'We're just friends.'

'David, you know I wouldn't mind . . .'

'But your employers might object to a gay man teaching your children, especially if they think he's brought his boyfriend with him.'

Alexandra sighed. She couldn't help thinking that what David said was true. 'Well, I can't wait to see you both. When can I expect you?'

'I'll telephone you. We have a couple of things to sort out first, as you'd expect.'

'And of course, you may not be needed for long. I can't even promise you'd be paid properly.'

'Oh, that's all right, we can stay with you for a couple of weeks and then tour round, or just go home. We'll see you soon, my darling girl!'

When she'd put the phone down, Alexandra realised that having David at the chateau would make all the difference. Although she hardly felt it, she was just a little bit lonely.

The following afternoon Alexandra was lying on her back enjoying the feeling of the autumn sun on her face. Maxime had come for lunch, bringing an apricot almond cake, a local delicacy, as well as cheese and wine, and chocolate for the children. Now he'd gone home and everyone was relaxing in the garden.

Alexandra was very near sleep. It was strange but she felt more at home in rural France than in the tall London house where she'd grown up. She was determined to enjoy every second of her time here.

A shadow across her face caused her to open her eyes. Standing above her, blocking the light, was a woman, who, from that angle, seemed incredibly tall. Alexandra sat up and then got to her feet, feeling slightly off balance and caught out.

She looked around for the children, who'd been lying in the grass with her, reading, while she'd closed her eyes. Only Milou was with her now and he got up too, not exactly growling, but rumbling.

'I've come to collect my children,' said the woman with quiet determination.

Alexandra blinked and moved sideways so she wasn't blinded by the sun. The woman was dressed in an elegant two-piece outfit in a soft caramel colour that was better suited to a smart restaurant than a garden in the French countryside.

'I'm so sorry,' said Alexandra. 'I think I must have dozed off for a few minutes and I'm totally confused. What did you say?' While it was true about her dozing off, she wasn't at all confused. She just needed time to compose herself.

'I said, perfectly clearly, that I've come to fetch my children. I am Lucinda de Belleville. Can you call them?' She had a lot of confidence and spoke in a way that showed she was used to having her own way.

Alexandra put on a helpful smile as she realised she was talking to the children's mother. 'I could, but I have no idea where they might be. There are several acres of grounds here, or they could be inside. I'm sure you know that the chateau has many rooms. Why don't we go in and I'll get you a cold drink? They might appear of their own accord.'

'I was hoping to just get them into the car and then go to my mother's house. She doesn't know I'm here.' Lucinda made irritated noises as she followed Alexandra through the patch of long grass into the courtyard and, from there, into the kitchen. Alexandra could feel her frustration and crossness burning into her back.

'I'll show you through to the salon,' Alexandra said soothingly. 'Would you like wine or something soft?'

'I can find my way to the salon, thank you,' Lucinda said. 'This used to be my house!'

'And as they used to be your children, maybe you would know best where they're likely to be?'

Lucinda looked murderous. 'They are still my children!'

She left the room briskly, her stockings making a swishing sound as she walked, presumably heading to the salon. Alexandra realised her last remark had been a little rude, and felt guilty as she found glasses and a carafe for the wine.

'Félicité, Henri, Stéphanie! You have a visitor – one you'll be very pleased to see!' she called up the stairs. She wasn't entirely sure the children would be pleased to see their mother, but it was a fair assumption and it would make up for her earlier rudeness.

She was gratified to hear footsteps running down the stairs. The three of them appeared, slightly out of breath.

'It's your mother,' said Alexandra. 'She's in the salon.'

'Our mother!' said Félicité, frowning. 'What the hell is she doing here?'

A tiny bit of Alexandra felt she should reprimand Félicité for this, but the rest of her thought there was probably a reason for the girl's reaction.

'Let's go and find out. Stéphie? Would you be a dear girl and carry in the water? It makes the tray so heavy.' Really, Alexandra felt that Stéphie would like a job. Having something to do could be helpful in a possibly worrying situation.

'Well, I've found the children!' said Alexandra as they all came back into the salon. 'Now, what would you like? Rosé? Water? A mixture?'

Lucinda took no notice. She was staring at her children as if she'd never seen them before.

'You've grown so much,' she said with a crack in her voice. 'I hardly recognise you.'

'Papa has sent you lots of photographs,' said Félicité, an edge of sarcasm in her voice. 'That should have helped.'

There was a lot of resentment there, thought Alexandra, wondering how old Félicité had been when her mother left.

'It doesn't matter now,' said Lucinda. 'I want you to come and live with me, now I'm back.' She smiled and Alexandra saw that she was actually very beautiful as she opened her arms.

But no one moved. Alexandra had gleaned that Félicité had been young when Lucinda left, so Stéphie must have been a tiny baby. This was not going to be easy.

'Come on, my darlings. Do neither of you want to give your mother a hug?'

'Papa won't want us to live with you,' said Henri. 'We've got Alexandra to look after us.'

'I'm sure Alexandra is doing her best, but what you need is a mother's love, not that of a paid employee.'

'Why didn't you think of that before?' said Félicité, her resentment evident.

'Darling, when you're older you'll understand these things. I'll explain it all to you then.'

'I'm fifteen,' said Félicité, 'in case you've forgotten. Explain it to me now!'

'What a very rude person you've become!' said Lucinda crossly. She looked at Alexandra. 'It's typical of my husband to employ someone who is far too young and inexperienced for the task. Are you a Norland nanny?'

A picture of brown-uniformed women taking enormous prams full of children to Kensington Gardens floated into Alexandra's head. 'I think Félicité is too old for that sort of nanny,' she said.

'Now, maybe, but in the beginning, when she could still be moulded, that's when she should have had a properly qualified nanny.' Lucinda sighed. She clearly had strong opinions on the subject. 'Now it's too late. She has terrible manners.'

Alexandra felt that if she cared so much about how her children were brought up, she shouldn't have abandoned them.

'I haven't got terrible manners,' said Stéphie, possibly resenting her feeling of guilt by association.

Lucinda turned her attention to the little girl. 'Who are you?'

Alexandra felt sick. What sort of a woman would ask a question like that?

Stéphanie looked at Félicité, Henri and Alexandra in turn.

'She's our sister!' said Félicité, angry now.

'No, she's not!' said Lucinda indignantly. 'Not unless your father had an *affaire* I didn't find out about!'

Alexandra cleared her throat. 'Excuse me, but I don't think this conversation is suitable for children. Henri? Will you take Stéphie and see if you can find some biscuits? She knows where they are.'

'Madame,' she went on once Henri and Stéphie had left. 'I can't believe you've forgotten how many children you have!'

'Of course I haven't! And that little one isn't mine!'

Alexandra looked at Félicité for an explanation.

'Stéphie's parents died when she was tiny. Her father was Papa's best friend. Papa brought her to live with us,' Félicité explained.

Alexandra got up and poured wine into glasses and handed one to Lucinda. She and Stéphie had this sad beginning in common, but, unlike Stéphie, no one had taken her into their family, like Antoine had. He must be a very kind man, she thought.

She carried the tray of glasses over to Félicité without really thinking. But it was up to Félicité if she took one or not. Alexandra took a glass and had a sip. She had no idea how to handle this situation; she just had to play it by ear and hope it turned out all right.

'I see,' said Lucinda, who'd also drunk some of her wine. 'Well, I don't want her, sweet as she is. I just want my own children.'

'Stéphie is like a sister to us. We are a team,' said Félicité.

The other members of the team came back into the room at this moment, the smallest of them holding a plate of biscuits.

Lucinda took a biscuit, looked at it, and obviously wished she had a plate to put it on. Seeing this, Alexandra wondered if she should get one, but then her protective instincts overruled etiquette. She needed to stay by her charges.

Milou, an opportunist, went over and sat by Lucinda, his big head about six inches above her knee. Lucinda took a tiny bite and then gave the rest to the dog. 'Really, you should teach the dog not to beg,' she said to no one in particular.

No one replied to this statement. Lucinda cleared her throat. 'I do understand, children, that you haven't seen me for a while. But I'm back from Argentina now and would like you to come and live with me. It's my turn to have you.' She smiled, obviously hoping that, as children, they would understand the concept of turns.

'Well we don't want to,' said Félicité. 'We're happy living with Papa.'

'But you're not living with Papa! You're living with – Alexandra. Do you really want to live with someone who's paid to take care of you, instead of your loving mother?'

'Yes,' said Félicité bluntly and, Alexandra felt, flatteringly.

Alexandra cleared her throat to get Lucinda's attention. 'Actually, I couldn't possibly let the children leave this house without specific instructions from M. le Comte telling me that is what he wishes.' Alexandra delivered a smile she hoped would end the discussion, although she knew it wouldn't.

'I am just as much the children's parent as he is,' said Lucinda reasonably. 'My instructions should carry the same weight.'

'I was employed by M. le Comte.' Alexandra was also being reasonable. 'It was to him I gave my promise to look after his children. *All* his children.'

'That doesn't matter. I am here now. They are my children and I want to take them. They need to be properly educated. Possibly in an English boarding school. You can stay here with the little one.' Lucinda's smile was much more convincing than Alexandra's had been.

'No!' said Alexandra and Félicité at the same moment, equally horrified at the thought of them being sent to England. 'I can't let the children be separated,' Alexandra went on vehemently. 'And I can't let them leave the house with you either.'

'This is ridiculous!' said Lucinda, getting up and walking to the window and then turning back into the room. 'I'm going to take them to my mother's house. You've met her! She wrote and told me! You can have no problem with that.'

Alexandra bit her lip. 'The thing is,' she said apologetically. 'I have no proof that you are who you say you are, and I can't guarantee that you will take them to their grandmother's house. And I don't know if they want to go.'

'We don't,' said Félicité quickly.

'You can't speak for your brother,' said Lucinda.

'Yes, I can,' Félicité said. 'Can't I, Henri?'

Henri nodded. 'And we're not going anywhere without Stéphie.'

Lucinda gave an exasperated sigh. 'This is ridiculous! You'd have thought your father would have asked me before he took on another child!'

'Why?' said Stéphie.

'Because – because – well, he should have done!' Lucinda's frustration boiled over. 'I'm leaving. But I'll be back. With my mother!' She made this sound like the ultimate threat.

'That would be delightful,' said Alexandra. 'I think she has a bit of broken china she wants me to mend for her. She could bring it with her.'

'So you're good at mending china, are you?' said Lucinda.

'She's very good,' said Stéphie.

Lucinda stalked across to the mantelpiece and picked up a figurine of a shepherdess. 'Then mend that!' She threw it on the floor where it smashed into hundreds of pieces. The children gasped in shock, and even Milou growled at this act of destruction. Lucinda left the room with a toss of her elegant head.

Alexandra collapsed on to the sofa. 'Oh my goodness! She's hard work!' She didn't want to criticise the children's mother in front of them but couldn't keep completely silent.

'Will you be able to mend the ornament?' asked Félicité.

Alexandra shook her head. 'I'm sorry but it's in far too many pieces. Was it precious?'

Félicité shrugged. 'I don't know. I think Grand-mère gave it to Papa one Christmas.'

Stéphie giggled.

Henri picked up the carafe and poured some wine into Alexandra's glass 'Here you are,' he said, holding it out to his carer and protector. 'It might cheer you up.'

Alexandra laughed. 'Thank you, Henri! I'm sure that as your nanny I should refuse it, but that was a bit stressful, wasn't it?'

Félicité was looking pale and anxious. Henri sat down next to her and Stéphie, most anxious of all, hugged her big sister's arm.

'I think we should ring Maxime,' said Alexandra, having taken a sip of rosé. 'He'll know what to do.'

'Why do we have to do anything?' said Henri. 'We don't want to go with her. What else is there?'

'The thing is . . .' Alexandra began.

'She might be able to *make* us go with her,' said Félicité. 'I don't know. She is our mother.'

'It would be much better if your father could tell us what to do,' said Alexandra.

'I wish he'd come home!' Stéphie wailed. 'We need him to look after us!'

'We've got Alexandra,' said Henri.

'And Milou,' said Alexandra. 'Do you know? When your mother found me in the garden, he was with me and he growled! What about that!'

'He never growls unless there's another dog,' said Stéphie, impressed.

'I know!' Alexandra felt her small lie was justified. He hadn't growled properly, just grumbled a bit.

'I want Alexandra and Papa!' said Stéphie, her voice beginning to break.

'Well, let's ring Maxime and see if he can get your father to come home.' She didn't say that when their father arrived, she would probably have to leave. Stéphie might want them both, Alexandra and her papa, but she didn't really need them.

'Papa is always very difficult to get in touch with; his work takes him all over the place,' said Félicité.

'Maxime will sort it out,' said Alexandra, sounding more confident than she felt.

Chapter Eight

❧

Maxime was in his office when Alexandra called him. She had sent Henri and Stéphie away to see if there were any more eggs, promising them chocolate mousse if there were. Félicité was sitting on the sofa, looking pale and unhappy.

'The children's mother was here!' said Alexandra, less calm now she felt she could be. 'She wants to take them away to live with her. Only not Stéphanie. I didn't realise she wasn't actually related to the other two.'

'Lucinda? Lucinda is here?'

'She's just arrived back. She'll be staying with her mother, apparently. Where is the Count? Could he be asked to come home? And can I legally stop Lucinda taking Félicité and Henri?'

'She can't drag us out of here against our will,' said Félicité.

'Félicité says they don't want to leave, but what's the legal position?' Alexandra asked.

'I don't know, but I can find out and I'll cable Antoine and tell him to get home as soon as possible.'

'Do you know when he might be here?' asked Alexandra, hoping she didn't sound pathetic. She was used to solving her own problems and needing help was disconcerting.

'I can't tell you that, I'm afraid, *chérie*, but don't worry. He'll come as soon as he can. I'll send the cable now.'

Alexandra told Félicité what Maxime had said.

'It'll probably take at least four days for him to come,' said Félicité, sighing. 'He travels all over the world. He could be anywhere. China possibly. Although if it's China it'll take even longer for him to get here.'

'Well, let's hope it's not China,' said Alexandra. 'Come and see if the others found some eggs. And even if they haven't, I think we should make chocolate mousse anyway.'

A few days passed before they heard from Maxime that the Count was on his way home. Alexandra suggested they prepared David and Jack's rooms, who were due to arrive the following evening. Rather to her surprise the children agreed and they set off to the rather distant part of the chateau where their new tutors were to stay.

Félicité found some wonderful antique, lace-edged bed linen in an armoire. Henri fixed a wobbly leg on one of the beds and Stéphie picked vases of flowers for both bedrooms and the bathroom. Henri said men didn't like flowers, but Alexandra said that sometimes they did.

'What will David and Jack expect me to do? Write essays and things?' said Félicité, obviously a bit anxious about the impending arrival of her tutors.

'I've never met Jack, but I expect he'll be nice if he's a friend of David's. I don't know what David is like as a tutor, but he was a very good friend to me in London. He had a flat at the top of the house where I lived, but he used to cook for me, he taught me to drive, he taught me all about antiques—'

'But he wasn't your boyfriend?'

Alexandra laughed. 'No. He was more like an older brother, or an uncle. He was always giving me good advice. He was the one who taught me how to mend china, only I got better at it than he was quite quickly.' She didn't think it was appropriate to explain that there was another reason why David could never have been a boyfriend. 'He's quite a bit older than me, too.'

'How old?'

'About thirty-five, I think. Too old for me.'

'Papa is thirty-five,' said Félicité.

Alexandra thought about Félicité's father. She had only met him that one time in Paris but he had made a big impression on her. And although she was five years younger than she had stated on her application form, she didn't think he was too old for her at all. But of course, he would think that she was too young. Maxime was nearer her in age, so why wasn't she thinking about him, instead of M. le Comte?

'Do you like music? And maths?' she asked.

'Henri is brilliant at music,' said Félicité. 'Have you heard him play the cello?'

'That was Henri? I have heard little phrases of music but I thought it was a record.'

'He's very shy about people hearing him play, but he's very good. He should have proper lessons really.'

93

'I'll speak to your father about it,' said Alexandra, feeling very remiss that she hadn't known about Henri's talent.

'As for maths,' said Félicité, 'do they matter?'

'I didn't take any exams in maths but I know how to budget. Jack might expect a bit more of you than that. But I can almost guarantee that both David and Jack will be good teachers.' Alexandra gave a rueful smile. 'As long as your grandmother is satisfied, and your mother, of course.'

'My mother!' Félicité tossed her head. 'She has no right to come here and demand that we live with her!'

'Your father is coming and will sort that out, so you have no need to worry. Now, is there anything else you can think of that David and Jack might need?'

Alexandra and Félicité looked around the room together. It was sparsely decorated but with what Alexandra thought was a *lit à demi-ciel* which gave the room some grandeur. It had a high top, protruding about a foot from the wall, from which hung (somewhat threadbare) curtains. In England it would be called a half-tester bed, but she remembered one turning up on a stall on the Portobello Road when she was there selling antiques with David, and being given the proper name.

'Grand-mère likes to dry her face on a linen towel,' said Félicité, 'but I couldn't find any.'

Alexandra laughed. 'They're men, they'll be fine with the towels they've got.'

As she and Félicité walked back to the kitchen, Alexandra asked, 'Why isn't there more furniture here? I mean, there's enough, but it's not full. Is there a reason?'

Félicité shrugged. 'I know that Papa inherited the chateau and the title from his uncle. It happened before I was born, but maybe Papa and my mother just bought the minimum of furniture they needed then. I think my mother liked the idea of living in a chateau but didn't really like living in the country.'

'That would explain it, I suppose. Now, I wonder if we've got anything to eat except chicken?'

'Chicken is what the farm produces,' said Félicité. 'That and a few pigs and sheep.'

'David is a brilliant cook,' said Alexandra. 'You'll enjoy his food, I promise. And he's going to love the produce. You laugh at me getting excited by garlic at the market – he'll go into ecstasies.' She paused. 'He can be a bit . . . flamboyant.'

Félicité laughed. 'Grand-mère may hate him.'

Alexandra shook her head. 'No, she'll love him. He'll make sure of it. I just hope his friend does the same.'

The following afternoon, Alexandra and the children were sitting at the table under the trees on the terrace at the side of the chateau, playing rummy, when two men pushed open the wrought-iron gates that opened on to the area. One of them called, 'Anyone at home?'

Alexandra put down her cards and rushed over. 'David! You're early! I wasn't expecting you until tonight!' she said and threw herself into his arms.

After a few moments hugging and exclaiming, David said, 'Lexi! You look different! When I saw you last, you were all elegant, like Audrey Hepburn. Now you're a sultry peasant, in your off-the-shoulder dress and bare feet. More like Brigitte Bardot.'

Alexandra laughed. She had missed his teasing. 'I'm like this during the day, but not when it gets colder in the evening and I put on a cardigan.'

'Meet Jack – Jack, this is Alexandra who you've heard all about. Lexi – this is Jack who can teach maths and music and is very interested in the area.'

Jack came forward to take Alexandra's hand. She noticed that he limped slightly and had a stick. He was older than David – in his fifties – with thick, greying hair and dark eyebrows over kind, twinkling eyes. Any worries that Alexandra had had about him being suitable vanished. He seemed just as nice she had promised the children he would be.

'Hello,' he said. 'Delighted to meet you at last and thank you so much for inviting me.'

'We're delighted to meet you too. Félicité? Henri? Stéphie? Come and meet your tutors.' Alexandra didn't want to make too much of introducing David and Jack to her charges. She felt they'd be more receptive if they could just observe them for a little while. 'Would you like something to drink?' she said. 'Something to eat?'

'That would be delightful,' said David, who had shaken everyone's hand. 'We did have a snack on the way here, but we wouldn't say no to something. Maybe some cheese?'

'We always have cheese,' said Stéphie, who liked to be helpful. 'I'll bring some.'

David smiled at her. 'Thank you so much. That would be very kind.'

'I'll get the wine,' said Henri, obviously a bit shy and glad of an excuse to escape for a bit.

When Stéphie and Henri had gone, David turned to the dog. 'And who is this handsome chap?'

'That's Milou,' said Alexandra. 'He looks after us. He's very good at it.'

'Does he sleep in a kennel to repel intruders?' asked Jack.

As Alexandra knew that Milou slept with Stéphie or Félicité but didn't want to say in case it caused embarrassment, she changed the subject. 'I hope you like goat's cheese,' she said. 'Most of the local cheeses are goat.'

'There's an opportunity for someone to make a joke about old goats,' said Jack, 'but I think I'll refrain.'

'How did you get here?' asked Alexandra a little later when she'd seen the new arrivals had everything they wanted.

'We brought the car,' said David. 'It's parked in front of the chateau. Then we realised no one was in, so came round the side and found you here.'

'It's good that you've got the car,' said Alexandra. 'It'll give you some independence.'

'Yes,' said David. 'I want to buy some antiques.'

'And I just want to explore the area,' said Jack.

'Why?' asked Stéphie.

Jack smiled at her. 'I was here on holiday before the war. When I heard David here talking about coming

I thought: This is my chance. It's handy for me that I teach maths so I've got an excuse to come.'

Stéphie seemed satisfied with this explanation.

'And, of course, if I buy too many antiques, I'll have to rent a van anyway,' said David, 'in which case, Jack can drive the car home.'

'Would you like me to teach you a card trick?' Jack asked Henri, who'd been building card houses while David and Jack had their cheese and some pâté.

'Do you know one?' asked Henri.

Soon Jack was shuffling cards and getting Stéphie to pick one and it wasn't long before Henri knew the trick too. 'Arithmetic is really helpful for card tricks,' Jack said finally. 'As well as a bit of magic.' He took a card from behind Stéphie's ear and caused a lot of giggling.

Alexandra couldn't help noticing that while Henri and Stéphie were quickly relaxed with David and Jack, Félicité held back. Alexandra found herself understanding the older girl completely. She wasn't interested in card tricks and didn't want to be forced to learn anything against her will. And yet Alexandra knew if Félicité wasn't taught at home she'd probably be sent away to school.

'I do hope you two men are going to be good teachers,' said Alexandra. 'So far I've had the children's grandmother wanting to move in to look after them, probably so they learn proper manners, and their mother wanting to take them away and possibly send them to boarding school in England. But if you two can teach them something maybe everyone can stay here.' She smiled at the group. She was partly saying this to gently remind Félicité what her options were. 'I'd better go in and do something about dinner,' she said.

'I'll come and give you a hand,' said Félicité.

Alexandra didn't do more than smile her thanks but inside she was amazed. It was the first time Félicité had volunteered to help, even if it was to distance herself from her new tutors.

'And the market is tomorrow?' said Jack at dinner, a few hours later.

'Yes,' said Alexandra for at least the third time, 'we'll go in my car – the estate's car – as usual. You'll both love it, I'm sure.'

'What, the car? Or the market?' asked Jack.

'I am absurdly excited at the prospect of the market,' said David and then yawned. 'Now, if I can remember how to get there, I think I'll take myself off to my palatial quarters.'

'I'll come too,' said Jack. 'Delightful as this is, enjoying this charming company and eating such delicious food, it's been a long day.'

The moment the men had left, Alexandra said, 'Now, Stéphie, I must get you off to bed too. You must promise not to tell your grandmother I let you stay up so late.'

'It's even past my bedtime!' said Félicité, helping her sister with the heavy chair.

'And don't you dare confess that to Grand-mère!' said Alexandra. 'We'll never hear the end of it!'

By the time the hens were shut in, Milou had had a last prowl around and everyone except Alexandra was in bed, she surveyed the kitchen. It was where they'd enjoyed a very jolly meal but now it looked a mess. David and Jack had bought wine on the ferry so there were empty bottles as well as numerous glasses and far too many dirty plates. Alexandra had been distracted by the company and the chat and the range had gone out. There would be no hot water until it was lit again. She sighed and decided to leave it. The mess would all still be there in the morning. She didn't need to worry about it now. All she could think about was her own bed and sleep. But she was content as she went up the stairs; David and Jack were going to work out brilliantly.

Chapter Nine

Alexandra was in a very deep sleep when she was awoken by Milou barking. It wasn't the full-throated deep bark he used for intruders, but it was still a noise. He must have heard something and gone down to investigate. Alexandra thought she should do the same. It was probably David or Jack wanting something from this end of the chateau.

Knowing Milou was down there already gave her courage but although she wasn't a nervous person and was accustomed to being in a large house on her own, she was trepidatious. She pulled on a light dressing gown but didn't put on slippers which clacked on the stairs. She wanted to be silent.

She was aware that Milou's noises had changed to a strange whimper she hadn't heard before and when she reached the hall she saw he was on his back legs, his front paws on the shoulders of a man. She could hardly see him because the dog was in the way but she knew it was Antoine.

He was talking to Milou in a low voice, in French; she couldn't quite follow what he was saying but it sounded very fond.

At last Milou jumped down and then saw Alexandra and came up and barged into her with his shoulder, in case she was feeling left out. The Comte de Belleville looked up. 'Ah, Alexandra, is it not?' he said in English.

Alexandra thought her name had never sounded so wonderful. She cleared her throat. 'Yes. I heard noises and thought I should investigate.' She spoke in English too. Her French was good but not perfect and she didn't want to make a mistake.

'That's very brave of you.' Antoine looked at her in silence for a few moments.

Alexandra felt very conscious of her long cotton nightie – she'd bought it from the *brocante* stall at the market in Saint-Jean-du-Roc together with the simple cotton wrap she wore over it. Her hair was down over her shoulders, in need of a trim. She wished she'd had warning of his appearance; she'd have at least got dressed.

'I knew Milou would protect me if need be. Can I get you something? Have you been travelling for hours?'

'Yes, and yes. What is there to eat?'

Alexandra remembered that the kitchen was in a state but she also remembered she had made onion soup the day before. 'I have some soup. Why don't you go into the salon? I'll bring it to you.'

'Nonsense,' said Antoine. 'We'll go into the kitchen. Will the stove be in? I'm cold.'

He'd set off down the corridor before she could stop him. He halted at the door of the kitchen having switched on the light. The single bulb hanging from the middle of the ceiling made the kitchen look more than just the site of a drunken party, it looked spooky, like a crime scene in a film. Alexandra was mortified. Antoine was looking at the table crowded with glasses and bottles, the draining board piled with dirty plates, and the floor, which had piled-up saucepans on it.

'What on earth's been going on in here?' he asked. 'In case it isn't what it seems?'

'This', Alexandra said with dignity, 'is the remains of our dinner. I have arranged for two tutors to come and teach the children. Your mother-in-law agreed it was a good idea. They arrived yesterday and I was too tired to do the washing up last night.'

'Why is washing up your job? You are employed as a nanny, are you not? We have Mme Carrier for cooking, don't we?'

She managed a smile, hoping it didn't look as if she was complaining. 'It's just me at the moment. Would you like some soup?'

'Just you?' He looked at her intently, not for the first time. 'What happened to Mme Carrier?'

Alexandra could hardly remember. 'Her mother is ill, I think.'

'You look far too young to be taking on all this.'

Alexandra was bitterly regretting lying about her age on her application form but then realised she probably wouldn't have got the job if they'd known she was only twenty. 'Would you like the soup?' she asked again.

'Yes, please,' he said, and Alexandra went to the larder to fetch it.

When she came back with the pot in her hands, he was lighting the range.

'I haven't found the knack of keeping that in over-night, I'm afraid.' She ladled some soup into a saucepan and took it to the small cooker. It was 'French onion' as taught by Mme Wilson, at her cookery school. But although Mme Wilson was French, Alexandra didn't think her version of it would compare with the real thing, which her boss would be accustomed to.

She cleared a space on the table while Antoine was snapping bits of kindling and by the time he'd re-turned with some logs, she had a space on the table and a lot of the dirty dishes organised into a pile in the corner. She toasted some bread, piled grated cheese on it, and put it back under the grill.

The fire in the range was going well and the table more or less cleared before Antoine turned his atten-tion to his supper. Alexandra put a bowl of steaming soup in front of him and next to that, a plate of cheese on toast.

'Please remember I'm English when you're eating it and don't compare it to what you're used to having.' She wished she'd stayed silent. She was making excuses for herself before he'd even tried it.

'This is good!' he said, slightly surprised.

The soup had simmered on the range for a long, long time and the onions were dark brown. Alexandra had been aiming to impress David with it, although in the end they hadn't had it with supper; David and Jack had filled themselves up with pâté and cheese and so they'd all gone straight on to the inevitable chicken casserole. Now, she thanked the god of English employees who had to cook for Frenchmen for this accolade.

'Do you want anything to drink?' she asked. 'I could get you some wine . . .'

'Cognac please. Do you know where it is?'

As she went to fetch it, Alexandra wondered if she should have pretended she hadn't discovered it, and drank at least some of it. She was still wishing she hadn't lied about her age. She must remember to tell David she was supposed to be twenty-five.

'Bring a glass for yourself,' Antoine said, 'and tell me how my children are. Do you like them?'

'I love them,' Alexandra heard herself saying, when a moment's thought would have made her more circumspect. 'They are delightful. Stéphie and Henri are easier of course.'

'But Félicité is more of a challenge? I am accustomed to governesses telling me she's wilful and uncooperative.'

Alexandra was offended by this. 'She is more of a challenge, but I sympathise with her. She's too old for a nanny, really. She needs a companion.' She remembered when she was promoted from having a nanny to having a companion. It had seemed a big thing at the time, an advantage, but really it hadn't been that different. There were good and bad companions in the same way there were good and bad nannies; good ones were good, and the bad ones were bad.

'She's not "playing you up"? Is that how you say it?'

'Not really. And why should she obey a young woman who's not much older than herself? Not very much older, anyway,' she added hastily. 'It's why I thought we should have tutors. It was after their grandmother came to say she was worried they weren't getting an education. And their mother—'

'Yes?'

'She talked about sending Félicité and Henri away to boarding school in England.'

'You know that little Stéphie isn't . . .'

'Yes. I was a bit shocked when your wife—'

'Ex-wife.'

'Appeared not to know her. I found out then that Stéphie is adopted.' Alexandra paused. 'She and I are very good friends.' She didn't tell him that Stéphie got into her bed in the mornings so they could read together and that someone had not paid enough attention to teaching her to read. She'd been quite happy muddling through her job as nanny, doing what seemed to work best. Now her boss was here she wished she was properly qualified. 'The older children adore her, of course.'

'Yes. They missed their mother very much when she left and so when Stéphie came about two years later, they gave her all their affection. It was charming, but also a bit concerning. They might benefit from having Lucinda back in their lives.'

Alexandra wondered if they would when she seemed keen to send them away but didn't comment. It wasn't her place, and it was accepted wisdom that mothers were a good thing. Not having had one herself, she didn't really know.

'More brandy?' Antoine held the bottle up.

'No, thank you. I should probably make up your bed or something.' Alexandra hadn't been in his bedroom ever – there had been no reason to go, but at least she knew where the sheets and other bedlinen were kept.

Antoine smiled at her suddenly and Alexandra felt herself melt.

'I think you should go back to bed. I can manage my sheets.'

'The mattress might be damp—'

'It won't kill me. Don't worry about me, Alexandra – if I may call you that?'

Alexandra nodded. She would never tire of hearing her name on his lips.

'You are here for my children, not to be the house-keeper.' While he didn't say it out loud, his expression said, 'Run along now.'

'Well, if you don't need me, I'll see you in the morning.' Alexandra smiled politely and left.

Once she was back in her room she gave herself a very strict talking-to. 'You are not in love with him; it's quite impossible that you should be; you don't know him! He's not even that good-looking! He may be dark and have lovely eyes with long lashes but when did you become so shallow as to like someone because of what they look like?'

She rattled on to herself in this vein as she brushed her teeth again, brushed her hair and eventually got back into bed. It took her ages to get back to sleep.

She was woken by Stéphie shaking her. She felt as if she'd only been asleep for about an hour.

'Alexandra! Wake up. Papa is here. Come down and see him!' Stéphie ran out of the room, leaving Alexandra half tempted to allow herself a bit more sleep.

But then she realised she couldn't stay in bed when she'd been invited to meet Papa, although unlike Stéphie, who was wearing her dressing gown and no slippers, she needed to be dressed.

She didn't let her desire to hurry stop her paying proper attention to how she looked, though. She brushed her hair (again) and coaxed it over her shoulder so while it was loose, it looked tidy. She put on a clean dress and added her cardigan and the espadrilles she had bought at the market the last time they had been. She dithered about make-up. She was the nanny, it was first thing in the morning, it would look very odd, and as if she was trying to snare M. le Comte, her boss, if she arrived in the kitchen in full *maquillage*. But she couldn't ignore the fact she was going to see a very attractive man she could (just possibly) be in love with. There was a compromise!

She dabbed a bit of lipstick on her finger and patted it on to her lips so it hardly showed. She put a bit of eyeliner round her eyes and carefully rubbed it off again so only the tiniest trace remained, and she inspected her face for flaws. The tiniest dab of powder applied to the end of her nose, and she decided she'd done all she could and went down to the kitchen.

'Oh, you're dressed!' said Félicité, who wasn't.

'I do try to get dressed every day,' said Alexandra, sounding a hundred times calmer than she felt. 'It's got to be a habit with me. Good morning, M. le Comte,' she said formally.

There were many reasons why she shouldn't appear too familiar with her boss and one of them was that she knew Félicité would be absolutely furious if she thought Alexandra was trying to ingratiate herself with her beloved papa.

'Papa came home in the middle of the night!' said Stéphie, still very excited at the wonder of this event.

Alexandra and Antoine exchanged a glance. 'I heard him,' said Alexandra. 'At least, I heard Milou. I went down to see what was going on.'

'That was brave of you,' said Félicité. 'Weren't you scared it was burglars?'

'I knew Milou would protect me if I needed protecting,' Alexandra said. 'Shall I make breakfast? I see the range is going well.'

'Papa knows how to make it stay in,' said Henri.

'Good morning, Alexandra,' said Antoine. 'She was very brave to investigate my arrival, but perfectly right that Milou would protect her. Do you know, children, in England they have a book where the nanny is a dog?'

'*Peter Pan*,' confirmed Alexandra. 'I did always think that was a little strange when I was growing up. Still do! What did we think about breakfast?'

'I'm starving,' said Henri.

'Me too,' said Antoine.

Alexandra smiled at them both and went to find her apron, glad that she'd bought something prettier to put over herself than the overall the previous chatelaine of the kitchen had worn.

'Come and see the hens, Papa,' said Stéphie. 'Alexandra can pick them up!'

Antoine and his youngest daughter walked through the corridor to the courtyard while Alexandra focused on the kitchen.

She turned on the tap to get the washing up started at the same time as she got going on breakfast. As always there were plenty of eggs but there was also some leftover ratatouille and some local sausages. She put some duck fat in a pan and cut up some sausages. Soon she had a couple of things sizzling away.

'Good Lord!' said a carrying male voice. 'The smells are from heaven!'

'Or from Provence,' said David, 'whichever happens to be nearer. Good morning!'

Both David and Jack were dressed and well groomed and ready to be sociable.

Inevitably, Antoine and Stéphie chose this moment to come back into the kitchen.

Usually, Alexandra liked people and having a full kitchen didn't put her off but just now she stifled a desire to scream. Just at that moment she wanted everyone to go away and leave her to cook and wash up. She was a nanny who cooked, nothing more. But there was no one else who could act as hostess so she had to make the introductions.

'Ah, Jack, David, good morning! I hope you slept well. Let me introduce you to . . .' She hesitated. She knew his name but at that moment she could only think of him as Antoine or Papa, neither of which would do.

Antoine got up. 'I am Antoine, Comte de Belleville – these children's father. Am I right in thinking you are here as tutors?'

'That's the idea,' said Jack. 'I'm Jack Andrews, maths and music. I'm properly qualified to teach maths but I'm also a professional musician.'

'And I'm David Campbell: actor, antiques dealer, gourmand and gourmet, and most importantly friend of Alexandra's. Shakespeare is my speciality, or at least, it's why I'm here. We only arrived yesterday so no one has learnt anything yet.'

'Except I can do a card trick,' said Henri.

'That was just a little ice-breaker,' said Jack. 'I do intend to teach you algebra.'

'What's algebra?' asked Stéphie, intrigued by the word.

'Difficult,' said David. 'Shakespeare is much more fun.'

'Hey! Algebra can be fun too!' said Jack. 'But you may not need to learn it yet, Stéphie.'

'How do you propose to teach Shakespeare?' asked Antoine.

Alexandra withdrew to her stove. They could talk amongst themselves now. She could focus on getting people fed.

'That was a stupendous breakfast,' said David a little later. 'I was expecting a bit of baguette and butter and maybe a croissant.'

'We'd have to drive to get bread in the morning,' said Alexandra, 'and I thought you'd all be hungry.' She meant she thought Antoine would be hungry, and how he felt was somehow very important to her.

'Do you intend to start lessons immediately?' she asked.

'Do we have to?' said Stéphie. 'Papa has only just got back! We need to hear all about his adventures.'

'Maybe we should have a day to get used to each other before we start lessons,' said Jack. 'David and I could go to the local town – Saint-Jean-du-Roc?' Antoine nodded. 'And possibly buy some things, to save Alexandra some work—'

'It's market day,' said Alexandra. 'I could give you a list.'

'No one wants to come with us?' asked David, looking round the kitchen. 'I see that no one does.' He smiled. 'So, when we've done the washing up—' '

'No need!' said Alexandra. 'Really! I'll be fine on my own.'

She and David knew each other very well and as their eyes locked she managed to convey to him how much she wanted everyone out of the way.

'Children, we should assist Alexandra—' said Antoine.

'No! Really, you need to be together, after so many months apart.' She paused. 'And really, I want everyone out of my kitchen!'

'It's not your kitchen,' said Félicité.

'While I'm cooking in it, it's mine!' said Alexandra, more sharply than she meant to. She moderated her tone. 'I mean, while I'm responsible for the meals it is my place of work. You go and get dressed and then you can spend time with your father. He must have missed you dreadfully.'

'Neatly done, Lexi,' said David when everyone had left. 'You're doing very well here.'

'Thank you. I've had to learn an awful lot in a very short time and it is a bit exhausting sometimes.'

'I can't wait to get to the market, buy some wonderful Provençal specialties and cook for you, instead,' he said. 'And I like the children. They're very bright and we can have fun together.'

'I'm very glad to hear it. I've had the grandmother and the mother more or less telling me I'm not fit to care for them. If they could learn a bit about their English heritage, I'd feel less inadequate.'

David frowned. He obviously wanted to argue but Alexandra flapped her hands at him. 'Go to the market. It's best to get there early.' Although it was already too late to be early, she thought.

She just had a bowl of really hot water and a saucepan on the stove boiling some more in case the hot water ran out when Antoine appeared.

'You must let me dry the dishes—' he began, picking up a cloth from the bar in front of the range.

'No, M. le Comte!' said Alexandra firmly. 'Please! I am happy to do this. Go and be with your children. They have missed you badly.'

Alexandra realised she'd put her hands on her hips and must have been looking very confrontational as she spoke to her boss. She smiled, to soften her commanding appearance, and he laughed.

'In which case, I will do that – I have presents for them. But really, we must get some more staff.'

'That would be a good idea.'

He smiled ruefully. 'I'll see to it. And please call me Antoine. I don't like using my title unless I have to.'

She nodded agreement and he left.

Later that day, Stéphie came up to Alexandra while she was in the courtyard picking grapes from the vine that grew under the eaves and said, 'Isn't it lovely that Papa is home?'

'It certainly is,' Alexandra replied. 'You must be so thrilled.'

'Yes, because while Félicité and Henri have their mother – and I don't like her at all – I only have Papa, so it's nice for me when he's home. Although of course the others like him too.'

'And I'm not sure they like their mother very much either,' said Alexandra. 'But when they get used to her being here, they may like her more.'

'Do you think so? I think she's very rude, although she is pretty and smells nice.'

Alexandra couldn't help wondering how Antoine would feel about Lucinda after not seeing her for years. 'Is being pretty and smelling nice enough?' she asked, not expecting Stéphie to understand her question.

'I shouldn't think so. Félicité says being pretty isn't important,' Stéphie said and then paused. 'I think you're very pretty. Maybe it's not important but it is nice.'

Alexandra laughed and put her free arm around her. 'Come on, let's take these grapes back to the house. David, my friend who came yesterday, is cooking supper tonight. We can have grapes for pudding.'

'Oh,' said Stéphie, disappointed. 'I'd rather have pudding like you make. With fruit and the biscuity stuff on the top.'

'Fruit crumble is all I'm fit for after cooking a proper meal,' said Alexandra. 'But we'll ask David about it. I'm sure he can make it too.'

Chapter Ten

❦

David was in the kitchen surrounded by food supplied by the market and every cooking utensil he could find. He was jointing a couple of chickens for dinner, which involved a chopper and a lot of noise.

'Don't tell me off,' he said, when Stéphie and Alexandra arrived. 'I know I was always telling you off for being untidy when you cooked, Lexi, but I'm getting my bearings. Until I know what's here, I can't be tidy. But I'll put it all away in a minute.'

'We've brought grapes for pudding,' said Stéphie. 'Only I like crumble.'

David paused in his dismembering. 'Right. I'll do you a deal. If you can find grape scissors, so people don't pick at the grapes and leave little stubs on the bunch, I'll make a crumble. Or maybe ask your nanny to do it.'

'Her name is Alexandra,' said Stéphie sternly. 'And she's very good at crumbles.'

'It's about the only pudding I make at the moment,' said Alexandra. 'Shall I be your kitchen assistant, David? And Stéphie, do you have any idea where you might find grape scissors? In the dining room perhaps?'

'Grape scissors are an affectation,' said Jack, passing Stéphie as she skipped out of the door. 'Ordinary ones will do.'

'At a pinch, dear boy, but we are in a chateau,' said David. 'We should have higher standards.'

Alexandra and Jack both laughed, and then she turned to put wood into the range.

'Alexandra,' said Jack. 'Can I do that for you? Or maybe bring in some logs? If you show me where they are.'

Alexandra hesitated, wondering if Jack would manage with his stick.

'I'll be fine,' Jack said, obviously reading her thoughts. 'Just lead me to it.'

Alexandra picked up the log basket and led him out through the corridor of storage rooms and sculleries to the courtyard and directed him to the wood store, which, fortunately, was still full of firewood. 'Here we are. It's all wonderfully dry, which is lucky. I don't think we'd have a chance with that range if it wasn't.'

She and Jack started throwing logs into the basket. When the basket was full Alexandra said, 'if you could learn how to keep the range in overnight I'd be grateful. The Count can do it, but I feel I should know too.'

'Then why don't you ask the Count to show you?' said a voice behind her.

Alexandra jumped. 'Oh! I just thought you might be busy.'

'And won't Jack be busy, teaching my children algebra and card tricks?'

Jack laughed. 'I will be busy, and so will they, but we all need time to enjoy our surroundings. David's considering putting on a play.'

'Really?' said Antoine. 'Why?'

'He says the best way to understand Shakespeare is to act it,' said Jack. 'But we might not have time.'

'I think that sounds a splendid idea, if there is time,' said Antoine. 'I like the idea of my children being taught in a less conventional way than they'd experience at school.'

'School has its advantages,' said Alexandra quietly.

'Schools haven't worked well with my children so far,' said Antoine, 'but I'll be happy to discuss it with professionals.'

'Right,' she said. 'I'm going back to the kitchen to make a crumble. It's Stéphie's favourite.'

'May I talk to you about Stéphie sometime?' said Antoine.

'I'll be happy to talk about her any time,' said Alexandra, smiling. 'Just now she's looking for grape scissors. We can have grapes as well as crumble. I thought she might find some in the dining room.'

Antoine shrugged. 'I have no idea where they might be. Maybe you should help her look? She's very fond of you.'

'It's mutual. I'll go and find her.' She paused for a moment. 'You won't forget the logs, will you?'

As she went back into the house, she realised she'd started giving orders to a member of the French nobility; probably not the best way to further her career as a nanny.

She found Stéphie in the dining room, in front of a large, very ornate sideboard. She was sorting through the knives and forks, presumably looking for grape scissors.

'I wish Félicité was here. I need her help!' She picked up a fork. 'Oh, these are pretty. We haven't used these for ages,' said Stéphie.

Alexandra picked up another one, admiring the ornate tracery and pattern. 'They are nice, aren't they? David will admire them. He's an antiques dealer as well as a teacher.' She put down the fork. 'Shall we eat in here tonight? What do you think?'

Stéphie jumped up and down. 'I think it's a lovely idea. We can celebrate Papa coming home. Usually we only eat in here when we have Grand-mère and it's all rather stiff and we're not allowed to talk much, but I like the plates and the forks.'

'And are there special glasses?' Alexandra asked.

'In the cupboard.'

'Will your father mind if we use them? Would you like to find out?' Alexandra had a feeling that if Stéphie asked, her papa would agree and she thought she should keep out of her boss's way until he'd forgotten she'd ordered him to bring in the logs. 'It would be fun and nice to eat somewhere other than the kitchen.'

'I'll go and find Papa.' Stéphie was out of the door before Alexandra could ask about the grape scissors.

Alexandra decided to look for Félicité. She hadn't seen her for a while and Stéphie would even enjoy sorting out cutlery if her big sister was with her.

She found Félicité sitting on her bed staring out of the window. There were tears on her cheeks.

'Oh, honey, what's the matter?' said Alexandra before she remembered that Félicité was touchy and might respond better to a less emotional approach. 'Are you OK?'

Félicité gulped and nodded. 'I expect so.'

Alexandra sat on the bed next to Félicité. 'But you're not sure?'

There was a big sniff. 'I know all about it. It's just now it's happened I feel weird. And it hurts and I want to cry.'

Light dawned on Alexandra and she felt a wave of sympathy. 'You've started your period?'

Félicité nodded.

'I remember starting mine. It was horrible at first. I just couldn't believe it would happen every month. Have you got everything you need?' Alexandra couldn't remember who had told her about this stage in a woman's development and if they'd provided her with pads and a belt.

'No. Grand-mère told me about them but she said she didn't have them until she was sixteen. She seemed to think that if you had them before that it meant you flirted with boys and were bad.'

'Oh well, that's certainly not true. And I can help you out with what you need for now. Have you got a pain? In your lower back?'

'Yes! How did you know?'

Alexandra laughed. 'It's usual. You need a hot-water bottle and possibly an aspirin.'

'In France they put them—'

Alexandra stopped her. 'I have some you can swallow.' She did not want to know the finer details of how the French administered pain relief. 'A hot drink would help. Hot chocolate? My nanny used to put a bit of brandy in mine.' Alexandra paused. 'Would you like me to try and get hold of your mother?'

'Absolutely not!' Félicité seemed to be in no doubt about this.

'I'll get what you need.'

Just as she reached the door Félicité said, 'Why did you still have a nanny when you had periods?'

Alexandra shrugged. 'Well, she was called a governess but she didn't teach me anything – I was at school then – but she wasn't a companion either. I don't think my relations, the people looking after me, quite knew what I needed.' She waited in case Félicité had any other questions and then left the room.

She got downstairs to find Antoine and Maxime in the hall, talking and laughing and banging each other on the shoulders. They were obviously pleased to see each other.

'Can we invite Maxime to dinner?' Antoine asked. 'Will there be enough?'

'If David is cooking there will be more than enough.'

Maxime took hold of Alexandra's hand and kissed it. 'You are even more beautiful than when I last saw you.'

Alexandra laughed, to hide her embarrassment. 'Hello, Maxime.'

'You two seem to know each other better than I realised,' said Antoine, smiling but without amusement.

'Maxime has been a great help to us,' said Alexandra. 'Especially when he got you to come home.' She thought for a minute. 'Why don't you have a glass of wine on the terrace? It's a lovely evening.'

'Will you join us?' asked Maxime.

She shook her head. 'You two need to catch up with each other and I have things to do.'

Stéphie shot out of the dining room. 'Where have you been? And where is Félicité? We're not ready!'

'I don't suppose David is either, so don't worry. Félicité isn't feeling well so she may stay upstairs for a while. I'll go and see how David is getting on. Maxime is here. He and your papa are going to have a glass of wine on the terrace. You could take it out for them – save me a job. And maybe some olives?'

'I'd rather finish doing the table. I've found lots of lovely things! No one's ever let me look in that cupboard before.' Stéphie went back into the dining room to finish her task.

Alexandra went into the kitchen to discover that David, who'd always been a very calm presence in London, wasn't calm now.

'David!' said Alexandra looking at the array of dishes and saucepans on every surface, all with something in them. 'This is very unlike you. You're always so well organised in London!'

'I know!' He threw his hands in the air in a theatrical way. 'I think France has gone to my head rather.' He paused to smile at Antoine who had come in, possibly for the wine. 'Just seeing the wonderful produce at the market made me buy everything and now of course I want to cook everything.'

Alexandra turned to Antoine. 'When we lived in London together he was always sorting out the scrapes—'

'You lived together in London?' Antoine suddenly seemed cold and rather haughty.

Alexandra and David both tried to explain at the same time. Then Alexandra held up a hand to David.

'I'll do this. My family has a large house in London. When I was studying cooking in London I shared the house with David, who had a separate flat at the top of the house, and two friends. And Meg's dog,' she added, as if this would make Antoine stop looking so disapproving. 'David kept an eye on us girls. And I had known him for a couple of years before.'

Antoine smiled, still disdainful. 'And your parents? They were happy with this arrangement?'

Alexandra found it difficult to meet his gaze but she forced herself. 'My parents have been dead since I was very small.'

Antoine frowned. 'But who looked after you?'

'A series of nannies and companions. It's why I feel so well qualified to be a nanny, I have had so many. My relations supervised me from Switzerland.'

'Did they know you were sharing the house with a single man?'

'Not really,' began Alexandra, blushing because they didn't know anything about it.

'I think maybe we need to tell Antoine everything,' said David.

Alexandra swallowed. It was very possible that Antoine would ask David to leave immediately. She really hoped not. Apart from anything else, she'd have to finish cooking dinner.

'I am homosexual,' said David. 'Which means while I loved Alexandra practically like a daughter, I'm not remotely tempted to see her as anything else. It is ironic that the person who could in England be classed as a criminal is actually the very safest person she could have shared a house with.'

Antoine's brows drew together in thought as he considered this.

'My relations wouldn't have understood or been happy with me living with someone like David,' said Alexandra. 'Although they should have been.'

'Well, I will endeavour to be more broad-minded. I think it is illegal in England? Not here in France,' said Antoine. He smiled and his expression relaxed. 'You are welcome in my house. And now I must find some wine.'

Alexandra felt a wave of relief. 'Maxime is joining us for dinner, David,' she said. 'And Stéphie is preparing for a banquet in the dining room.'

'As am I, in the kitchen,' said David with a bow.

Alexandra caught Antoine smiling as he left the room to go to the cellar. It would be all right, she decided.

Alexandra was pleased to see Félicité arrive in the dining room while the table was still being set. She went over to her. 'You could have stayed upstairs. I would have told people you had a headache.'

Félicité gave a quick half smile. 'It's OK. People would have asked questions. I can't bear the thought of people talking about me.' She paused. 'Although that is mostly Grand-mère. She finds me very disappointing.'

'I'm sure that's not true, but well done for coming down, anyway. Stéphie has arranged a *placement*, so you must find where you're sitting.'

At Alexandra's suggestion Stéphie had written place names on some lovely old-looking name cards she had found in the sideboard which, David informed them, when he came in to see how they were getting on in the dining room, was really called a credenza.

Also at Alexandra's suggestion, Stéphie had put her father at the top of the table with Félicité on one side and Stéphie on the other. Henri was next to Stéphie. After that, Stéphie had lost interest rather and just focused on writing names on cards and finding every obscure piece of cutlery the credenza drawers contained. This included snail tongs with matching forks and a very decorative set of cutlery for hors d'oeuvres.

'My goodness,' said Antoine when he came into the dining room holding several bottles of wine. 'We really are having a banquet!'

Alexandra and Stéphie looked up. 'Indeed we are,' said Alexandra, 'although it's just possible we won't need every single knife, fork and spoon that are out.'

'Alexandra said that it's nice to get everything out sometimes,' said Stéphie, just a bit defensive. 'And they are so pretty! We can't see them when they're just in the cre – the cupboard.'

'That's very true. And seeing everything reminds me that we should invite my mother-in-law for a meal.' Antoine didn't look terribly pleased at the prospect. 'Fortunately we have Alexandra to help us.'

Alexandra wasn't absolutely sure if he was being sarcastic but decided probably not.

Félicité came over. 'And what about my mother? Do you have to invite her for a meal too?' She did not sound happy at the thought.

'I think so, *chérie*,' said Antoine. 'But we don't have to think about that now.'

Alexandra could see that Félicité was upset at the prospect. She knew some of this would be because of her period but she also had very valid reasons for not liking her mother much.

'The trick,' said Alexandra, 'when there's someone you don't want to invite, is to invite lots of other people too, then they're diluted and it's better. Look, here's Maxime. We could invite him when we invite Grand-mère?'

'You are experienced in the art of entertaining?' Antoine asked.

'A bit, yes,' said Alexandra firmly. She realised he found her confusing and hoped he realised she would do whatever was necessary for the children in her care.

Antoine nodded.

'I'm going to see how David is getting on in the kitchen, and make a start on the crumble,' she said briskly and left the room. 'Then we must find Jack.'

'I am ready, more or less,' said David, wiping his brow with the back of his hand a little later. 'You take the anchovy tart and I'll take the stuffed tomatoes.' He paused. 'I did them because the tomatoes were amazing, like pumpkins! And not everyone likes anchovies.'

Alexandra laughed to herself as she took the tart. She'd known David would be excited about the produce. She was excited about it herself, but she didn't love cooking in quite the same way David did, or her friend Meg, who was one of the girls she'd lived with in London. Food was Meg's passion, and her other friend, Lizzie, was passionate about dress-making – any kind of sewing really. What was her passion? Alexandra liked lots of things, antiques, living in France, and she had come to love her charges in a very short time. But her passion seemed to be her boss – a state of affairs that couldn't go on.

She put the tart down on a mat, leaving space for the stuffed tomatoes.

'My goodness! A veritable feast!' said Jack, who had appeared from his room.

'Oh my God,' said David. 'I didn't know we were having snails! How terrifying!'

'We're not having snails!' said Stéphie. 'We just wanted to put out the tongs.'

'Oh, that's all right then.' David looked exaggerat-edly relieved to make Stéphie laugh, which she did.

'Maxime, could you help me pour the wine?' said Antoine. 'Do sit down, everyone. I think we should eat this delicious repast without delay,' he said. 'Stéphie, have a tomato.'

Everyone followed his lead and soon everyone had food on their plates.

'*Bon appétit,*' said Antoine.

He had looked at Alexandra before he said it but she didn't think she should take the role of hostess. It was one thing when they were eating in the kitchen, but this was more formal.

'Well, isn't all this delicious!' said Jack after everyone had started eating.

'And I thought Englishmen couldn't cook!' said Maxime teasingly.

'I didn't know men could cook,' said Stéphie.

'Well, they can,' said Alexandra. 'And David does it very well.'

'*Chérie!*' said Antoine to his youngest child. 'Your papa can cook. I just don't get the opportunity.'

'Because you're not here very often,' said Félicité.

'Yes, when will you come home and live with us all the time?' asked Henri.

Antoine didn't reply immediately. 'When I can,' he said, a little bleakly.

'Can I propose a toast?' said Maxime. 'To the return of the conquering hero!'

'What's a conquering hero?' Stéphie whispered to Alexandra.

'It's someone who is very successful and probably rather warlike,' her papa replied. 'And I'm afraid I'm not one.'

'Just as well!' said Jack. 'The young people want peace these days. There's been enough war.'

There was a murmur of agreement.

'Is there a piano in this establishment?' Jack went on.

'Oh yes,' said David, considerably relaxed by the success of his dinner and the very good wine that Antoine had provided. 'We love a sing song round the old Joanna.'

'He means piano,' said Alexandra to Félicité, who also seemed happier now, having been made to laugh several times.

'There is a piano in the music room,' said Antoine. 'But I don't know if it's fit to play. It was my wife's. It was too expensive to ship it to Buenos Aires when she left.'

'She tried to make me learn but I don't have her gift,' said Félicité.

'*Chérie*, you were only five! Not everyone is a musical genius,' said Antoine, patting his daughter's hand.

'Your mother was musical, was she?' asked Jack. 'That's interesting.'

'But I can't play the piano,' said Félicité, a touch defiantly. Alexandra couldn't tell if she really minded about this or not.

'You mean, you couldn't when you were five,' said Jack. 'I'm here to teach maths and music and some kind of instrument would be helpful but we don't all have to learn to play the "Moonlight Sonata".'

'That is a shame,' said Maxime. 'It is the only thing I can play.'

'I like playing the piano,' said Henri. 'But I prefer the cello. A friend of Papa's gave me his, when he no longer wanted it.' Then Henri blushed scarlet and tried to bury his head in his food.

Jack glanced at Henri. 'The cello is a wonderful instrument. Do you read music, Henri?'

'A little,' said Henri, addressing the plate in front of him, still bright red. 'There was a book that came with the cello.'

Félicité broke in, rescuing her embarrassed brother from being the focus of attention which he so obviously hated. 'I can pick out a few tunes on the piano.'

'That's called playing by ear,' said Jack. 'And it's very useful. But I can teach you how to read music, which means you can play things you've never heard before.'

'Although the piano will need tuning. I'm not sure—' began Antoine.

'I may be able to sort it out a bit myself,' said Jack. 'If not, we'll find a tuner, won't we, Alexandra?'

Alexandra smiled and shrugged. 'I'm just the nanny, I'm not sure I'm qualified to find a piano-tuner.'

'Sweetheart, you're not qualified to be a nanny,' said David cheerfully and then stopped. 'Forgive me,' he said to Antoine. 'I've known Lexi for a long time. I've always teased her. I'm quite sure she's a perfectly splendid nanny.'

'She *is* a perfectly splendid nanny,' Stéphie repeated.

'Thank you, darling,' Alexandra whispered to her. Louder, she said, 'Would you like me to help you with the next course?'

'I'd like help as to which it should be,' said David, looking at Antoine. 'Cheese or pudding? Are we being English or French?'

'Cheese, please,' said Antoine. 'I'll open another bottle of wine. However, the children may prefer something sweet now.'

'David makes wonderful desserts,' said Alexandra.

'I'll help,' said Félicité unexpectedly.

'I found the grape scissors,' said Stéphie, pleased with herself. 'We have grapes with cheese. And usually, they're pudding.' She frowned. 'Grand-mère doesn't approve of pudding. She says it makes people fat.'

'My grandmother doesn't think people should be fat,' said Félicité as they carried dirty dishes through to the kitchen.

'Are you feeling OK?' asked Alexandra. 'Do you need another painkiller?'

'No, thank you. I feel better now.' She gave a little smile. 'Stéphie's right. You're quite a good nanny.'

They put the cheese on the table at the same time as the two puddings. There was an apple crumble and chocolate mousse. Stéphie thought she was in heaven. The adults drank cognac and became talkative. Stéphie, unnoticed, ate quite a lot of the mousse until she began to yawn.

'I think it's bedtime,' said Alexandra, looking at Antoine. When the children's father was present, was it still her job to declare an end to the evening?

'Oh yes. Stéphie?' said Antoine, who'd got into a discussion with David and Maxime about truffles.

'Alexandra will put me to bed and stay with me until I'm asleep,' said Stéphie.

'I'll come up too,' said Félicité.

Henri, aware that if he stayed he'd be the only young person, got up as well.

'I'll come and kiss you all goodnight,' said Antoine, smiling proudly at his family.

Alexandra heard him do that shortly after she had retired to her bedroom. It made her smile. Stéphie would sense his presence even though she was probably fast asleep by now.

Chapter Eleven

Some days later, at lunchtime, Alexandra was in the kitchen stirring the soup that David had started making that morning and had set on the wood range to cook. Alexandra had left the library, now a schoolroom, where she had been helping David with his Shakespeare lesson. It had involved an awful lot of laughing – not something Alexandra had previously associated with Shakespeare – and people taking parts and reading aloud. Everyone had thoroughly enjoyed themselves. Jack had joined them briefly and then carried Henri away for a music lesson. The chateau was now a very different place from how it had been when Alexandra had first arrived.

Antoine came in as Alexandra was putting baguettes into a basket and arranging cheese on to a plate.

'Well, that's that done!' said Antoine. 'I've invited my mother-in-law to lunch.' He paused. 'And I had to invite my ex-wife as well – they were together at the time. I also invited Hortense, my mother-in-law's friend.' He paused. 'Will David cook, do you think?'

Alexandra nodded. 'Or I will.' She was a bit offended by the assumption that only David could cook. Although she'd find cooking for those particular people single-handed a bit daunting. Everyone would watch her, possibly wanting her to fail. But she *had* been employed partly for her cooking skills. 'Should you invite Maxime, too?'

'If you'd like me to.' He raised a Gallic eyebrow at her.

She ignored the eyebrow, knowing it meant he thought she was interested in Maxime beyond friendship. Although perhaps she *should* develop feelings for Maxime – he was very good-looking after all. 'He's extremely helpful and charming.'

'You're right. Maxime is a good friend and he may flatter Lucinda out of her pouting.' He was thoughtful for a few seconds while Alexandra continued with the lunch preparations. 'Her ego is bruised and it makes her irritable.'

'When have you invited everyone for? I do hope it's not today.'

'Of course it's not today!' said Antoine, outraged at the suggestion that he might do such a thing. 'It's tomorrow.'

Alexandra made a noise, an exclamation that meant tomorrow was hardly better than today, and that she was a bit put out about it.

'I'm sorry,' said Antoine apologetically. 'When we got into days that were convenient, tomorrow was the only one possible.'

'I'm sure it's not my place to comment on your social calendar,' said Alexandra, her chin lifted.

Antoine seemed to find her indignation amusing. 'I have infinite belief in your ability to cope with any emergency,' he said. 'Besides, you are English: no one will expect anything wonderful.'

Alexandra pursed her lips, trying not to join in his merriment. She was part flattered, part insulted, but mostly she wanted to laugh with him.

'Shall we have this lunch in the garden?' she suggested.

'Oh yes. Why not? We have a lovely spell of weather. It's always better with the children's grandmother if we can make it less formal.' He watched Alexandra as she inspected a bunch of grapes. 'How did lessons go this morning?'

'Well! If you go to the library you can read a part. David likes everyone to join in.'

'Is that a tactful way of asking me to leave you to do your work in peace?' The eyebrow lifted again, and the curl at one corner of his mouth was irresistible.

Alexandra nodded, trying to be serious, but she couldn't help returning his smile.

'Stéphie!' said David the next day, after twenty-four hours of cooking and a certain amount of shopping. 'The table looks absolutely ravishing! Like an Impressionist painting. You've done a terrific job.'

They were on the terrace, under an awning of vines, dappled with autumn sunlight. It did indeed look like a painting, thought Alexandra. She wished it could have been for a party with jolly guests, old friends, people she liked. As it was, the guests were mainly people who were critical and made the children tense, and, as she knew from personal experience, anxious people were never at their best.

Stéphie, who was unaffected by the anxiety troubling the rest of the household, beamed. 'Alexandra helped.'

'You did all the hard work, darling,' said Alexandra.

'Grand-mère won't like the flowery cotton napkins from the market,' said Félicité. 'She only likes linen.'

Alexandra had thought she liked linen too until she'd realised she would have to wash it. She needed to talk to Antoine about buying a washing machine. The chateau had probably managed perfectly well without one when there were more staff, but while it was just her and a girl from the village – whom, blessedly, Antoine had hired to help her – there needed to be more mod cons.

'I just thought a touch of colour would be nice,' said Alexandra. 'And those fabrics are a very Provençal thing, after all.'

Félicité and Stéphie looked at her, bemused, for a few seconds and then went back to inspecting the table. 'Don't forget water,' said Félicité.

'The flowers are so pretty,' said Alexandra.

'Yes and they don't take up too much space,' said David. 'There'll be so many dishes on the table, there's hardly room for flowers. But those little posies are just perfect.'

'Grand-mère will say they're weeds,' said Félicité.

'And we'll say there is no such thing as a weed, only a flower in the wrong place,' said David primly.

Félicité gave a shout of laughter Alexandra hadn't often heard. 'Oh, please say that, David! I can't wait to hear what Grand-mère says in reply!'

'They look like proper flowers to me,' said Alexandra, seeing that Stéphie was a little offended. She tried to think of some flower names. 'That's a fuchsia – and isn't that pink daisy-like thing a cosmos? And those are definitely marigolds. They look lovely!'

'You grandmother is a starchy type, I gather?' said Jack, arriving with two large jugs of water in his hands. 'Still, Henri's practised his piece for hours. He's really gifted on the cello. She'll be impressed by that, if nothing else. He's almost a prodigy.'

'Our mother will want me to play,' said Félicité with a sigh. 'She was disappointed with me when I was five; she'll be even more disappointed now I'm fifteen.'

Alexandra opened her mouth to say something sharp indicating that if you wanted your daughter to learn to play the piano you should stay around to teach her, but then shut it again. She and David had had a couple of conversations on the subject. He had said, 'I know your parents left you, Lexi darling, but they didn't have a choice. Lucinda, of course, did have a choice, but no one ever knows what's going on in another relationship. We shouldn't judge.'

'I'd be delighted to give you piano lessons, Félicité,' said Jack. 'Any time. It's just Henri's so keen with his cello. But if you want to—'

'No, thank you,' said Félicité. 'I don't like playing the piano. I just don't want my mother being disappointed.'

'You do have a delightful singing voice,' went on Jack. 'There are more ways of being musical than playing the piano. David here plays the piano perfectly well, but he doesn't have a musical bone in his body.'

'Do you mind?' said David. 'That's an outrageous thing to say! Now I must go and check on the food. We could put some of it out now if we keep it covered. Do we know if our guests are likely to be punctual?'

Alexandra was about to say she didn't know when Félicité replied, 'I expect my mother will be late. And she'll come with Grand-mère so they'll both be late.'

'That's fine,' said David. 'I wasn't doing a soufflé but good to know I can let the daube just bubble away. It may be too hot to eat it anyway, in which case we'll just have cold meat and salad now, and have the daube another time.'

Alexandra followed David back into the kitchen. 'You've gone to so much trouble, David,' Alexandra began, feeling guilty that David, who was here to teach, was doing so much of the cooking, which she felt she should be doing.

'You know I love doing it, Lexi,' David said. 'I love all the amazing produce, and I've got the kitchen to work for me now, so it's a joy! And I think this is going to be very difficult for everyone, particularly the children.'

'I know.' Alexandra sighed. 'I'm not sure who I'm most worried about, Félicité or Stéphie. Although maybe it will all go over Stéphie's head.'

'I don't suppose it'll be a barrel of laughs for you, either,' he said.

'But I don't really matter!' She laughed. 'I do matter, of course I do, but this lunch – the children having

137

both their parents in the same place for the first time since I don't know when – is going to be tough. And their grandmother, who is – well – you'll see.'

'I'm looking forward to it. In my line of work any extreme sort of person is an opportunity to study character. Now, shall we have a little stiffener? Just us?'

Alexandra laughed. 'Go on then. I'll have a tiny glass of rosé and then not drink later. I just want everything to go well! For – well, for the children.'

'And you don't care about how it goes for the children's father?'

Alexandra couldn't stop herself blushing and so busied herself with tidying up the bunches of grapes that filled a huge platter. Stéphie's grape scissors were proving a godsend. 'I want it to go well for him too, of course, but he can look after himself. The children need me.'

'Although Antoine would do a perfectly good job of—' David stopped suddenly.

'What would I do a perfectly good job of?' asked Antoine, arriving in the kitchen, his arms full of bottles.

'I was just reassuring Lexi here that she needn't worry about this lunch. And that no one will be unkind to the children when you are here.' David was very firm.

Alexandra blushed some more and trimmed a perfectly good bunch of grapes.

'David is right, Alexandra,' said Antoine. 'I am well able to protect my children. But I appreciate that their happiness concerns you so much.'

Bravely she looked up at him. 'You know I take my duties very seriously.' She picked up the platter and fled.

They'd set up a serving table under a fig tree and she put down her burden there, putting a napkin over the grapes to keep off the flies. There was already a bowl of figs and some late peaches, very nearly past their best.

As she tweaked what was on the table, she wished she didn't feel so embarrassed whenever she was in Antoine's presence. It was so unlike her! The fact he was her boss wasn't really relevant. They both knew she was doing a good job, so why did he make her feel so unsettled?

'I do hope Maxime comes early,' she said to Félicité, who'd appeared by her side. 'Everything always seems more relaxed when he's here.'

'Don't I make you feel relaxed?' asked Jack, who had arrived with Henri.

'You do, but Henri's grandmother is terrifying. And so is his mother. I need lots of protection.' She smiled, making out she'd been joking all along. 'When are you going to play your piece, Henri? Can I suggest you do it before lunch? Otherwise people will sink into the wine and the food and then all remember the time and rush off.'

'I'm not sure it's quite like that in France,' said Jack. 'But do let's do your piece first. It'll put the terrifying *grand-mère* in a good mood. You play so well.'

Alexandra gave Jack a warm smile. She deeply appreciated how good he was with the children. 'I'm so glad you decided you wanted to visit France, Jack.'

'Well, I've always had a longing to go back to Saint-Jean-du-Roc so when David told me he was going there, or very nearby, I couldn't resist.'

'Why have you always wanted to see it?' asked Henri. 'It's not a famous Provençal town, like Aix-en-Provence or those other places where famous artists painted.'

Jack shrugged. 'I was here for a brief holiday once. I wanted to see if it had changed because of the war.'

'Oh, look! Maxime's coming,' said Alexandra. 'The terrace is very well placed, isn't it? You can see people arrive from a distance.'

'It's a pity we can't slam down a portcullis, and repel marauders, eh? Félicité?' said Jack.

Félicité giggled.

Because they could be seen coming, everyone was at the front door to admit Grand-mère, her friend Hortense and, of course, Lucinda. Only Jack was absent. He was preparing the music room, which included dusting the piano, something no one had thought to do until Stéphie wrote her name on it with her finger.

Alexandra didn't need to be part of the welcoming committee and she had things she could be doing, but she didn't want to miss the moment and wanted to be able to scoop up Stéphie if she felt left out.

'Ah! Penelope!' said Antoine. He kissed his mother-in-law three times. 'Hortense . . .' She also got three kisses. 'And Lucinda.' His ex-wife got a kiss on each cheek.

'Now,' he said, speaking English, 'Let me introduce Mr David Campbell, who is teaching the children English with an emphasis on Shakespeare.'

David behaved just as any grandmother or mother would wish. He was polite, charming but not too informal. When he and Grand-mère had finished their exchange he said, 'Now where's Jack got to?'

'He's in the music room,' said Henri. 'I've prepared a piece for you to hear.'

Alexandra noticed Henri didn't look at anyone when he said this, unsure whom he needed to impress.

'Maybe you'd like to play your piece now, Henri?' said Alexandra encouragingly. He seemed very nervous and she still thought the sooner the performance was over, the better.

'Yes,' said Antoine. 'Let's go and hear him. Lucinda, I think you will be very impressed by our son.'

David excused himself and headed off to the kitchen. Félicité followed him there but Alexandra went to the music room. She'd overheard Henri playing but this was an opportunity to hear him properly. She decided to stay outside the door to listen, so his audience wasn't too big.

Jack was at the piano. Everyone was sitting down, and Henri picked up his bow. Jack turned round to check he was ready when suddenly there was a gasp from Grand-mère. It became a cough, and she took out her handkerchief while Lucinda asked if she was all right.

From the doorway, Alexandra wondered if she should fetch water, but Grand-mère insisted she was perfectly all right, brushing her daughter's concern away with irritation.

Alexandra happened to look at Jack and noticed that he had gone very pale and then red. Then he turned back and fiddled with his music.

'Are you going to play or not, Henri?' asked Grand-mère sharply.

'We are very impatient to hear you play, Henri,' said Antoine, smiling.

'Yes,' agreed Grand-mère. 'I didn't mean to sound so sharp.'

Félicité seemed surprised. Possibly her grandmother didn't often apologise.

Jack started with an opening phrase at the piano, stumbling over the first couple of notes. He was obviously nervous too, Alexandra realised.

Then Henri began to play. The melancholic notes of Saint-Saëns filled the room. Alexandra stopped breathing. It was so beautiful, so moving, she felt time stand still. The boy was so absorbed in the music, at one with his instrument. His mother was staring at him as if she didn't recognise him. Then she noticed Grand-mère. Tears were pouring down her face. Was she really ill? Alexandra waited until the last note had been played and then fled back to the kitchen, wondering if Grand-mère might need a doctor, or at least somewhere to lie down where it was cool.

Alexandra and David were outside, putting things on the table and fiddling with the table arrangements when Stéphie joined them. 'Henri played really well but Grand-mère has gone all weird,' she announced.

'Oh no! Is she ill?' asked Alexandra. She had arranged a sofa in the salon so Grand-mère could lie on it while they waited for the doctor, if he was summoned.

Maxime, who had followed Stéphanie, said, 'Not really ill, I don't think. She went pale and had to sit down. Lucinda is looking after her.'

'I hope she liked Henri's playing,' said Alexandra. 'It was so . . . moving.'

'She wept. The Saint-Saëns is a very moving piece. It was afterwards, when Antoine introduced his teacher, that Penelope felt faint.' Maxime sent Alexandra a reassuring smile.

'Well, I hope she feels better soon,' Alexandra went on. 'Everyone's gone to a lot of trouble over this lunch. I don't want it spoilt by Grand-mère having the vapours.'

'What does that mean?' asked Stéphie.

Alexandra was very tempted to tell Stéphie she'd enlighten her later, but held firm: good nannies did not avoid questions. 'It means people feeling a bit faint for no apparent reason. Now, have we got everything?'

'We'd better have,' said Félicité. 'We couldn't fit anything else on!'

Eventually the rest of the party came through from the music room and was seated; drinks were poured and toasts exchanged. It seemed to Alexandra to take forever. Everyone was talking about how beautifully Henri had played – everyone except Henri, who hunched down in his seat as if trying to pretend he wasn't there.

Alexandra was at the far end, away from the honoured guests but near to David so she could help him replenish and change dishes frequently.

Things seemed to be going quite well up the other end of the table. Penelope was a bit quiet, as was Jack. Lucinda, on the other hand, seemed full of energy.

'Of course, he'll have to go to Paris to study. That talent will never be appreciated in this backwater of France,' she was saying, her clear voice carrying down the table.

Félicité was thoughtful and Henri, once he'd got over his initial shyness, just seemed really hungry, ignoring his mother's plans for his future. Stéphie was full of beans, delightedly telling everyone how she'd found some beautiful glasses in a cupboard and had helped wash and dry them. She was drinking water out of one now.

'We have to hope they will all be intact when the meal is over,' said Lucinda, removing the glass from Stéphie's hand.

Alexandra was hurt on Stéphie's behalf. The little girl had been so careful with the glasses, putting a cloth in the sink and on the drainer, washing one glass at a time. Had she been nearer she'd have said something. She muttered all this to David who said, 'Just as well you're not nearer, then. The nanny can't snap at the mistress of the house even if she's an ex-mistress – ex-wife – something! Can you be an ex-mistress?'

Alexandra laughed, and caught Maxime's eye. He raised his glass to her and she nodded in reply.

She was just beginning to relax – the guests were now all eating grapes and cheese and generally shedding their best-behaviour manners for something less formal – when David suddenly frowned.

'Hello! Who's this arriving in such a beautiful car?'

Alexandra turned and saw a cream-coloured Rolls-Royce with its top down proceeding down the drive. She felt hot and cold at the same time and ended up feeling sick. 'Oh my God!' she said. 'It's my relations!'

Chapter Twelve

Alexandra had time to inspect her relations as they disembarked from the vintage Rolls-Royce that had transported them for fifteen years or so. Her cousin Hubert was at the wheel. He was in his early thirties, slightly bald, with sloping shoulders and a weak chin. He was, Alexandra knew, the one everyone wanted her to marry. No one wanted her fortune to go out of the family.

His passengers were older, early sixties but full of energy. Cousin Clothilde and Cousin Aimée, elegantly dressed, wearing hats, emerged, looking around them with evident approval.

'Alexandra!' said Aimée, seeing her there on the doorstep. 'How very – rural you look.'

Alexandra stepped forward and kissed her cheek. 'Cousin Aimée. Did you tell me you were coming?'

'No,' said Clothilde crisply, 'we thought it would be fun to surprise you.'

Alexandra's mind flew back to that night in London, only a couple of months ago, when Clothilde and Aimée, accompanied by one of the older, male relations, had 'surprised' her when they descended on the family home in London where Alexandra was living. It had not been fun for anyone.

Antoine arrived at her side, making Alexandra suddenly feel supported and yet anxious. It was his house; all she had to do now was to explain why a Rolls full of her relations had just turned up on his doorstep. She swallowed. It was not going to be easy.

'Antoine, may I introduce you—' Then she remembered you were supposed to introduce the man to the woman first. 'Clothilde, may I introduce you to the Comte de Belleville?'

She saw her cousin's naturally haughty expression soften as she heard the word 'Comte' and the rest of the introductions went well.

Antoine was supremely gracious about this sudden invasion. 'Please do come in. Would you like to refresh yourselves . . .?' He turned to Alexandra.

'Do follow me,' she said, 'I'll show you to the . . . ladies' room.' She didn't quite know how to describe the room to which she was leading them. 'Downstairs loo' didn't really cover it. It had probably been built for some other purpose. It was fairly large, had a small sofa in it, and Stéphie had filled it with flowers and bunches of dried lavender. Alexandra was grateful that they'd been expecting Grand-mère for lunch. Because of her, there were beautifully embroidered antique linen hand towels and eau de cologne on the dressing table.

While her cousins were making themselves comfortable, Alexandra looked in the mirror in the hall, aware that 'rural' probably meant 'peasant-like'. She was wearing her favourite dress from the market and had tied her hair back using the belt of the dress as an Alice band; she had espadrilles on her feet. With no make-up, she looked about twelve. She hadn't been dressing for her starchy relations that morning – she'd been dressing for Lucinda, who, she realised, was the sort of woman who would be jealous of any other woman just because she was female. Thus, Alexandra had tried to look as young and nanny-like as possible. David had said she'd pulled it off perfectly. She could hardly run upstairs and put on her kitten heels now!

'I think Antoine has taken Hubert outside to join the party,' Alexandra said when her cousins emerged. 'We'll join them.'

Don't give them a choice of where to go, she thought; just put them where you want them.

'You call your employer by his Christian name?' asked Aimée. 'Is that usual?'

'I've never thought about it.' Alexandra refused to sound apologetic, although now it was pointed out to her, it probably was a bit odd. 'He asked me to.'

'Very well. Let us meet the family. I must say, Alexandra, it was something of a relief to us to see you were employed by the aristocracy. I do hope your French is improving because of it.'

'Monsieur,' said Clothilde, when her party had consumed some bread, cheese and apple crumble, served to them by David, who was fascinated to see the relations Alexandra had talked to him about so often, but whom he had never met. 'I think we should talk. We need to discuss how long Alexandra will be here.'

'We should,' agreed Antoine. 'Would you like to come with me? Do, please, bring your wine,' he said to Hubert.

'I'll stay here, if you don't mind,' said Hubert.

Although she had not been invited, Alexandra went too. She felt she needed to be there, although she didn't blame Hubert from wanting a short break from his tiring female relatives.

They went to the salon, which suddenly, Alexandra noticed, looked faded and in elegant disrepair. There was a long streak of damp next to the window, partly obscured by curtains which had obviously been there a very long time.

'Monsieur,' said Clothilde again as soon as everyone was seated. 'How long do you need Alexandra?'

Alexandra coughed loudly. She wasn't a piece of furniture being lent out. 'I want to stay until the children are – settled.'

Clothilde gave the sort of patronising, don't-speak-when-your-elders-are-talking smile at which she was so expert. 'I should imagine the Count will want to find a nanny who is properly qualified and maybe not quite so young.'

'Alexandra has been doing an excellent job with them so far,' said Antoine. 'The children are very fond of her, and my eldest daughter, who is fifteen and so at a difficult age, will take a long time to settle with someone new.'

Clothilde seemed surprised that Alexandra, who had always been a bit of a problem to her family, seemed to be so valued. 'How very gratifying. As you will know, we have had to bring Alexandra up from a distance. It has not been easy.'

Alexandra studied the patch of damp, wondering for about the millionth time why the family hadn't just scooped her up and taken her to live with one of them the moment she was orphaned. Donna had asked this question in Paris and Alexandra had brushed it off. But it was something she had thought about often, on and off, over the years, and had come to the conclusion that none of her relations really liked children and therefore wouldn't put themselves out for a baby. She felt she'd had a lucky escape; she might have ended up just like them.

Antoine smiled. 'So, it won't inconvenience you if she stayed with us here until the spring?' He smiled. 'After all, you can have no need of a nanny.' His expression indicated he had made a joke and intended people to laugh, but underneath he was serious.

Alexandra caught her breath. She had no idea that Antoine might need her that long and her heart leaped at the thought.

'Until the spring?' It was Cousin Aimée who answered. 'I suppose we could enrol her into the finishing school near us for the summer semester afterwards. I can see that being with you has improved her French.' She leant forward. 'You will understand that we only want the very best for Alexandra, and that school is the best in Switzerland, and is guaranteed to give her all the . . . sophistication she currently lacks.'

Alexandra noted that her heel was bouncing up and down in frustration and got up. 'Well, I'm so glad that's all settled. Now, Cousin Clothilde, Cousin Aimée, I think we should let the Count get back to his guests. Would you like to see the garden?'

As Antoine also got up the moment she did, the cousins did too. 'Oh no,' said Cousin Aimée, 'it's kind but we must get on. We only called in here to reassure ourselves you were happily settled. We're going to Aix. Maybe you could tell Hubert the route, Alexandra? Could you go and fetch him? Tell him we'd like to leave.'

Alexandra didn't protest but she knew she'd been sent away so they could talk about her and she was determined to make sure she knew what they said.

Alexandra was surprised to find Stéphie waiting outside the door of the salon and then realised that Félicité and Henri had probably been taken over by their mother and she had been left out. She put her finger to her lips. 'I want to listen for a moment or two.'

Together they leant near the door so they could hear better.

'Monsieur,' said Aimée to Antoine; she had a very carrying voice. 'I think it's only fair to tell you that Alexandra doesn't come into her fortune until she is twenty-five.'

Stéphie and Alexandra looked at each other in amazement. Then there was a sharp exclamation and the sound of furniture being scraped across the floor. 'Alexandra's fortune is of no interest to me,' said Antoine at his most aristocratic.

Alexandra's mouth went dry and she gripped Stéphie's hand. 'Quickly, darling, run and tell Hubert the others want to go. I must stay here!'

'All right, but promise you'll tell me everything later!' Stéphie whispered back.

'Of course!' said Alexandra. 'Now run!'

She watched as her ally fled, obviously excited to be part of a conspiracy. Alexandra strained to hear more of what was going on but they'd obviously moved across the room to where the windows gave on to the view of the distant mountains; she couldn't hear a word, only a distant mumbling.

She stepped back as Aimée and Antoine came out of the salon. They were obviously surprised to see her.

'Oh! You're there!' said Aimée.

'I'm going to make sure Hubert knows where he is going,' said Antoine, and passed through into the hall.

Aimée stood at the door of the salon and regarded Alexandra in confusion. 'Erm – I wonder if you could bring us some tea?' she said. 'Clothilde has a little cough and I think a hot drink would be soothing.' She didn't move, obviously waiting for Alexandra to go.

There was to be further private discussion about her situation, Alexandra realised. They'd got Antoine to leave the room and now Aimée was getting rid of her.

She went off down the corridor and then nipped back the moment she heard Aimée close the door. She would ignore the request for tea. Clothilde didn't know she'd wanted it, anyway. Alexandra knelt and put her ear to the keyhole. Luckily she could now hear them fairly clearly.

Aimée was sounding apologetic. 'Did I make a dreadful mistake telling him that about her fortune? He obviously didn't know anything about it. I should have kept quiet.'

A chair scraped. 'We don't know Alexandra's attitude to her fortune. Maybe she tells everyone she meets. You couldn't have known that she hadn't.' Clothilde was reassuring. 'And you didn't say she'd also come into it when she got married.'

Aimée gave a little laugh. 'Not even I am as foolish as that. Wretched Hubert! Why won't he make a play for her? We know how wayward she is but she's a very lovely girl. If he doesn't marry her before she's twenty-five someone else might. I can't abide the thought of all that money going out of the family! It doesn't bear thinking of.'

It occurred to Alexandra that obviously Aimée thought about it quite a lot.

Aimée was still speaking. 'I must say, being a nanny seems to be bringing the best out in her. It's making her a better marriage prospect than she already is!'

'Don't worry too much. I don't think Alexandra has any idea she'll get her inheritance on her marriage, even if it happens before she's twenty-five.'

'Doesn't she? Oh, no harm done then. But I'll talk to Hubert about it. He doesn't seem interested in any other girl at the moment, does he?'

Alexandra was aware that she was shaking. She went down the corridor to give herself a couple of minutes to recover from what she'd overheard. It was outrageous that she hadn't been told she'd get it if she married. As for marrying Hubert, she'd infinitely prefer to stay single!

The car, a very well-maintained Rolls-Royce Silver Wraith dating from the 1940s, caused quite a delay to the departure of the party from Switzerland. Maxime, David and Antoine all wanted to inspect this beautiful machine. Hubert was delighted to talk about his precious car for a while: normally people didn't pay much attention to him. Only Jack and

Penelope were missing. Apparently they had gone back to the music room.

Then Lucinda appeared wanting something and Maxime and David rushed to do her bidding. So it was just Antoine, Alexandra and Stéphie who were still there at the end, to check for the nineteenth time they didn't need anything (this was Alexandra, not wanting them to return precipitately) and close the doors. Hubert started the engine, which purred expensively, and then Clothilde, who was sitting in the front, put her hand on Hubert's, stopping the process.

'Goodbye, Monsieur,' she said loudly, as if the engine made any real noise. 'I should just make sure you know, Alexandra is very precious to us.'

'I am a father myself,' said Antoine, very haughty. 'I understand perfectly.'

Antoine didn't move until the car had reached the gates at the end of the drive. 'Stéphie?' he said. 'Go and find Félicité. Alexandra, we need to talk.'

'Do we really?' said Alexandra quickly, watching Stéphie run off with dismay. 'You know all you need to know, and there are guests. Lucinda is already annoyed at being abandoned. You should really get back to the party. I'll make some coffee—'

'It won't take long,' he said.

Alexandra's mouth went dry as she followed him into the house and back to the salon. Why did she feel that nothing was going to be the same after this? Would her being an heiress make him treat her differently? Surely not! And what about her not being twenty-five yet? He still didn't know how old she was. She could be twenty-three. A couple of years added on wasn't a major deception and everyone knew it was allowable to lie a little on a curriculum vitae. He'd said himself how well she was doing at the job. She decided to take control of the situation. She wouldn't say anything about the fortune and hope that somehow he'd forget it.

But the moment they were in the salon with the door closed, she found her heart was pounding and she could hardly breathe, let alone think of something to say to get her out of trouble.

Antoine didn't speak for what felt like hours. 'I think you've misled me, Alexandra.'

She shook her head.

'You're not what you appeared to be,' he said. 'I might have to let you go.'

She swallowed and coughed and cleared her throat and eventually found her voice. This was desperately unfair. She was going to fight to keep the job she loved. 'What do I appear to be?'

This wasn't quite what he was expecting, she realised.

'I thought you were a very efficient young woman from a good family who knew how to handle troubled adolescents and children.'

'I am!' she said, her equilibrium beginning to restore itself. 'And I don't remember those requirements being part of the form I filled in.'

'True,' he said. 'But there was a space on the form for your age and it seems you did not fill in that part correctly.'

She put her chin up. 'I'm sorry I lied about my age on the form but I thought that woman – the one who interviewed me – wouldn't give me the job if I . . . was a bit younger. And I really wanted the job! I thought it was in Paris,' she added, without intending to.

'Why didn't you walk out when you discovered it wasn't in Paris?' he asked.

She couldn't tell him it was because of him. She shrugged extravagantly. 'You've met my family. I wasn't in a hurry to go to Switzerland to be "finished".'

'You thought rural Provence would be more fun?'

She laughed. 'Yes, I did. And it is!'

'How old are you really, Alexandra?' Antoine asked, frowning. And before she could work out what age she could get away with he added, 'The truth, if you please.'

'I'm twenty.'

There was a brief, colloquial exclamation from under his breath. 'Had I known—'

'To be fair to you,' Alexandra interrupted quickly, 'you thought there was a housekeeper here when you employed me. Twenty is not too young to be a nanny. You only required me to cook, drive and speak English. I can do those things. I have managed everything and without the housekeeper. I had no help when I first came; it was only the children and me.'

Antoine didn't speak for a while and then shrugged. 'I thought I was leaving my children in the care of a responsible adult.'

'You did. I am responsible – I have proved myself to be so; and I am an adult – old enough to get married, anyway.' She really wished she hadn't said this; she wouldn't have done if she could have thought of anything else she was old enough to do.

156

'None of that makes you any older,' Antoine pointed out, still frowning.

'Surely you should judge me on my actions and not my age?' Alexandra wasn't given to feeling sorry for herself but she felt again that she was being treated very unfairly. 'When I came the children hadn't eaten, the chateau was freezing, and there was only a bit of stale bread and old cheese to feed them on. There was no housekeeper, no help in the house and no money to feed the children with. I had to buy food at the market with my own money. But I managed.' She was horrified to hear a break in her voice. I must be tired, she thought. It's been a long difficult day.

He didn't respond immediately, but when he did, his manner had softened. 'I am so sorry, Alexandra. You should have never been put in such a position. You have managed brilliantly. Supposing I had taken on a woman in her thirties, say, who didn't have your resourcefulness and courage? They could not have managed anything like as well.' He paused. 'I just wasn't expecting you to be an heiress.'

Alexandra took some calming breaths. She'd always taken her potential fortune for granted and felt it was so far out of reach it wasn't worth thinking about. Although this afternoon had altered that. Her money could be much nearer to her than she had thought. 'Does it change anything?'

Antoine looked down at something on the floor for a long time. 'No. It changes nothing. Which is just as well. And I have forgiven you for the exaggeration of your age so I won't deprive my children of their beloved and responsible companion.'

157

Alexandra had to sit down. She felt weak with relief.

'Which is just as well as I will have to go away again fairly soon.'

The bubble of joy that had risen in her for a second burst. 'Oh.'

'I came back before my work was finished because Maxime told me how things were here, and how Lucinda was talking about taking the older children away. When I have things sorted out, I'll have to go back to Paris.'

'Do you always have to work away from home?' She wouldn't usually have the courage to ask this although she'd thought about it for a while.

'Yes. Unless or until I find a way of earning enough to keep the chateau and the farm going without regular injections of cash.' He gave her a paternal no-need-for-you-to-worry-about-it smile. 'Now we should go back to the party, and see how our guests are getting on.'

As they walked back to the terrace together, Alexandra gave a silent sigh of relief. Her fortune hadn't lost her her job, and her relations had given her permission to stay here until the spring. The thought made her heart lift.

Chapter Thirteen

⚜

When Alexandra went into the kitchen, she was pleased to see the very large kettle and another pot sitting on the range for boiling water. The amount the range usually provided was never going to be enough for the piles of washing-up the lunch party had created. She glanced out at the terrace to see David clearing the table, and Stéphie helping. No one else was visible.

The washing-up could take days, Alexandra thought, her spirits suddenly descending into cold water, like the puddle on the floor by the sink. She should get on and start doing it.

But rather than scraping plates and stacking them and generally doing useful things, she sat at the kitchen table. Milou came in, and sensing she was unhappy, came and pushed his face into hers. Ignoring his dog-breath, she put her arm round him. He was so big it was almost like hugging a person.

'What's up, chicken?' said David, coming into the kitchen with a basket full of dirty crockery. 'Did seeing your illustrious relations make you homesick for Switzerland?'

Alexandra instantly felt better and she laughed. 'Certainly not! But they were very exhausting and don't you think it was rude appearing with no notice? And then disappearing off to Aix like that? I felt it was outrageous.'

David shrugged. 'It was a bit high-handed, I suppose. Although as aunts they were very amusing, almost as good as the aunts in P. G. Wodehouse.'

This made Alexandra smile. Thinking of them like that put them in perspective. 'They want me to marry Hubert, you know.'

It was David's turn to smile. 'I don't think that will happen.'

'Why not? I may be wayward but I'm a very lovely girl. I have that on the best authority!'

David shook his head, still amused. 'Your cousin Hubert bats for the other team: I'd lay folding money on it.'

'You mean . . .?'

'He doesn't like girls, however lovely or wayward.' There was a wistfulness to his smile now. 'If that was all it took, I'd make a play for you myself.'

Alexandra got up and poured a kettle of water into the battered enamel bowl they did the washing up in. 'You mean a marriage of convenience? I like Hubert, he's nice and very kind, but marry? *Je crois que non.*'

'Well, they've gone now.'

'And they didn't want to stay the night! Think how awful that would have been!'

'Are there enough habitable bedrooms?' asked David. 'Although bed linen wouldn't have been a problem.'

He unloaded his basket, presumably so he could go back to the table outside and fill it again.

'Do you know? I have no idea how many decent bedrooms there are here. I've only seen the ones I need to see.' Something stirred in her brain. 'We must explore,' she said. 'It would be really useful to know something like that. Do you think people would come on holiday here? Can you pass me the plates?'

'Of course they'd come!' David handed over the pile. 'The English love France! There's so much to do here. It's an antiques collector's paradise. Just the little stall in the market is like gold dust!'

'I know,' Alexandra agreed. 'I've bought a couple of little things myself when I've been there. Just to keep my hand in. After all, I won't be a nanny forever.' She felt quite sad about this and rubbed her cloth over the plates thoughtfully. She didn't want to leave this family; they and their happiness had become so important to her.

Alexandra and David had got through quite a bit of the washing up when Félicité and Henri came in holding packages wrapped in elegant paper and curled gold ribbons. Stéphie followed with nothing, her chin high and her bottom lip firmly clamped by her top teeth. She was very obviously trying not to show her disappointment.

'Mummy's gone home,' said Félicité, 'and she's given us presents. Not Stéphie though.' She didn't sound enthusiastic and glanced at Stéphie nervously.

'Open them!' said Stéphie. 'It's all right. She's not my mother. I do know that.'

Félicité's present was a beautiful pale blue writing folder. It was leather, with all sorts of little pockets

161

and places for letters and pens and stamps, everything you might need in order to write to someone. There was also a beautiful pad of paper and envelopes lined with tissue paper to match. Henri had been given one the same except that it was dark red and the envelopes were plain.

'There's a note in mine,' said Henri. He opened it. 'Oh. It's so we can write to Mummy when we go to boarding school.'

Stéphie took in a shaking breath. Alexandra could see she was about to burst into tears at any second.

'Oh!' she said, getting up. 'I've remembered something! No one move. Especially not you, Stéphie!'

She flew upstairs to her bedroom to the cupboard where she'd put the bits and pieces she'd bought from the *brocante* stall. She picked up one of the items, put a bit of tissue paper round it and then ran back down to the kitchen, offering a prayer to whichever saint was in charge of such things that her plan would work.

'I bought you this, Stéphie,' she said. 'But I didn't want to give it to you until I had something for Félicité and Henri. But now they've got their writing sets . . .' Alexandra kept on praying, this time to the saint who cured disappointment. She so wanted to make Stéphie smile.

'Oh! It's a little range!' said Stéphie, having unwrapped it. 'Like we have here. Only tiny!'

'Yes,' said Alexandra. 'And I think if you put methylated spirits in it, you can light it. It's not new, I'm afraid.'

'And not an antique,' said David, observing from across the table. 'But definitely worth collecting. Really,

I should hire a van and fill it with stock and take it all back to the Portobello Road.'

'I love it!' said Stéphie. 'It has little saucepans and everything. It's wonderful! Thank you so much!' She gave Alexandra a huge hug, genuinely delighted with her gift.

Antoine came in. 'What's going on?'

'Mummy bought us presents,' said Félicité, 'but not Stéphie. Alexandra has given her a toy cooker.'

Alexandra couldn't help herself; she looked up to see him looking at her. She suddenly felt terribly awkward.

'That's very kind of Alexandra,' said Antoine, obviously feeling as awkward as Alexandra was.

'It was so thoughtless of Mummy not to think of Stéphie,' said Félicité, saying what everyone was thinking. 'And if she thinks I'm going to go to boarding school in England and write her letters with envelopes like this, she's in for a nasty shock!'

Alexandra opened her mouth but didn't speak. Although she agreed with Félicité completely she was sure there was some rule that meant you weren't allowed to criticise your parent even if they were wrong. No one said a thing.

'You're looking tired, Lexi. Why don't you go up to bed?' said David suddenly. 'You must be exhausted. All the cooking and arranging everything—'

'You did the cooking,' she began.

'But I didn't have very frightening relations from Switzerland arriving without notice,' David went on.

'You don't have to worry about reading me a story,' said Stéphie, kindly. 'Papa will do it.'

Antoine nodded. 'I will. You go, Alexandra.'

She went, not knowing whether she felt cared for, or dismissed. By the time she got upstairs she no longer cared; she discovered she really was tired. But before she let herself fall into bed she wrote a letter to her cousin Hubert in Switzerland asking him for a copy of the will which gave details of her inheritance. He would get the letter when they all got home from their grand tour. Then she did her teeth and was asleep in seconds.

Stéphie ran into Alexandra's bedroom in the morning. She was already dressed. 'I'm not reading this morning, Lexi,' she said. 'I'm going out with Papa!' She ran out again while Alexandra wondered how she felt about Stéphie calling her Lexi. She decided she quite liked it.

She got up and dressed in a clean dress and her one cardigan before going downstairs.

David was there, frying sausages. 'I'm starving,' he explained. 'After you went to bed no one wanted any supper. Jack seems to be sickening for something and Antoine has taken the children out, so I'm making breakfast for whoever's left to eat it. Which I think is just us.'

There were fresh baguettes and a basket of croissants on the table. 'I am jolly hungry.' She picked up a croissant and put it on her plate. 'Did you go out for bread too? You must have been up very early.'

'I do wake early, as you know, but Jack went to the village. He wanted to take my car somewhere later and so bought bread and *viennoiserie* before he left. That translates roughly as croissants, by the way.'

Alexandra reached for the butter. 'Stéphie called me Lexi this morning. I like it. Did the children have any breakfast?'

He nodded. 'Croissants and hot chocolate. With Antoine and the children away it means we've got the day to explore the chateau.'

'Oh, that would be so much fun! After all the dramas of yesterday it'll be lovely just being with you and not having to think what I'm saying all the time.' She paused. 'But I'd feel awkward snooping around the chateau without asking.'

'Me too,' said David triumphantly. 'So I asked Antoine if we could. He said, "Help yourself and don't overlook the cellar and find something nice to have with your lunch. We'll be out all day."'

'Oh, that is nice!' She finished her croissant and reached for the bread.

'Leave room for the sausages, they're local,' said David, getting up to fetch them. When he'd put one on Alexandra's plate he said, 'You know, not long ago you wouldn't have needed to ask permission to explore an empty house. You'd have just done it and trusted you wouldn't be found out. Why the change, I wonder?'

'Oh. Well, I expect it's just because I'm a bit more mature than I used to be,' she said. 'And maybe being a nanny has given me a sense of responsibility.'

'Maybe,' said David, after a pause, obviously not convinced.

The chateau was bigger than Alexandra had realised. There were rooms at the back she had never needed to go into. And outside there were disused buildings: a wash house and what looked like a dairy as well as a house next to the stables where presumably the grooms once lived. There was a *pigeonnier* too, a little way away from most of the buildings and two storeys high. Its past was clear from the bird droppings, obviously accumulated over many years, but, as David said, it would make a perfect house to rent.

'It's like a village, with houses clustered round the big house,' said Alexandra. 'Only instead of the cottages just belonging to the big house, they're there to service it.'

'It's a rather disturbing thought, isn't it?' said David.

A little bit separate from the house, across a lawn, was another building that David said was probably an *orangerie*. 'Imagine, growing your own citrus,' he said. 'Your own lemons for your gin and tonic.' He shook the door. 'It's locked. Do you mind if we have another look at the stables?'

'They were so grand, weren't they? I'd happily live in them myself!'

Later, as they walked back to the house, David said, 'There is a lot of potential here. If Antoine really wanted to, he could have these buildings done up and rent them for the summer. Or even year round. Artists would come to paint, writers to write, and *les Anglais* to be objectionable and loud on their holidays.'

Alexandra laughed. 'You're not very kind about your fellow countrymen.'

'They're not very kind about me,' said David.

Alexandra didn't speak immediately. She was aware that there were things that went on in David's life that he would never tell her about. 'But I'd forgive them if they brought in enough money so Antoine didn't have to go away all the time.'

'I agree, it's not good for the children being without a parent,' said David. 'And now Lucinda's here, determined to take over Félicité and Henri's lives, that leaves little Stéphie even more parentless. Just as well she's got you, Lexi.'

'I do feel quite maternal about her, I must say.'

'She loved the little stove. Did you buy it for her?' David asked.

'Yes. I knew it would appeal to her. I do wish Lucinda would be a bit more thoughtful. Those children all think of themselves as true siblings. It's not fair of her to treat them differently.'

'I think Stéphie will be all right, with you fighting for her, Lexi.' He paused for a second. 'Do you want to tell me how things went between you and Antoine yesterday?'

Alexandra had known David would ask this so wasn't unduly surprised at his change of subject. 'Well, he knows how old I am and that I'm an heiress but that I'm not due to inherit until I'm twenty-five.' She didn't tell David about her getting it sooner if she married; she was still getting used to that idea herself. 'And although he did originally say he should send me away, he realised it wasn't really a good idea.'

'Quite right too! You're the lynchpin of this family,' said David. 'Now come on, let's go to the cellar and find an amusing little bottle of something.'

'And after lunch, I'll make a cake,' said Alexandra. 'I think I'm missing Meggy and Lizzie from when we lived in London. Mme Wilson didn't do cakes really, but Meg did.'

'I'm sure a cake will go down well.' David patted her on the shoulder. He understood her feelings without her having to go into too much detail. 'And why not send Meg and Lizzie a postcard? Let them know how you're getting on.'

Alexandra had just added a dusting of caster sugar to the top of her cake when Lucinda came into the kitchen.

'Hello,' she said. 'I hope you don't mind me letting myself in. I came in via the terrace. I've brought round some prospectuses for Antoine to look at. Schools for Félicité and Henri,' she clarified.

There were a couple of shocked seconds before Alexandra and David sprang into life.

'Would you like some tea?' said Alexandra, hoping Lucinda would say no. David had brought some from England but it wouldn't last forever.

'Oh – no, thank you,' said Lucinda. 'But some hot water with a slice of lemon would be lovely.'

'What about a piece of cake?' asked David, a knife hovering over it.

'I never eat cake,' said Lucinda looking surprised to have been offered it. 'Did you make it, David? Why?'

'I made it,' said Alexandra, trying to sound insouciant. 'I felt like making one and I thought the children might like it.'

'Oh, please don't give it to Félicité! She's all right now but if she got fat, her life would be a misery.' Lucinda smiled quickly. 'Well, not a misery perhaps, stuck here in the country where no one will see her, but girls at boarding school can be very cruel.'

'So why would you send her to one, then?' Alexandra realised too late that she was just the nanny and wasn't paid to have opinions.

'She's got to be educated! And not all the girls she'll meet will be bitches.'

Alexandra went to find a lemon for Lucinda's hot drink. She might not like her, but she felt that Lucinda did have a point. It was important that Félicité had a proper education.

Alexandra's cake was greeted far more enthusiastically by Antoine and the children, who saw it before they saw Lucinda, who was sitting impatiently at the table.

'Cake!' said Henri. 'I love cake!'

'You live in a country where they produce the most beautiful gateaux,' said Antoine. 'Why the excitement about something that looks quite a plain confection to me?'

'In France we have gateaux; this is cake. They're not the same,' said Henri. 'Grand-mère makes us English cake sometimes.'

'Tsk,' said Lucinda. 'I must ask her not to do that. It'll make you fat.'

'Can I have some, Lexi?' asked Stéphie.

'Of course.' Alexandra picked up the knife that was ready. 'What about you others? Antoine? It's an English speciality. A Victoria jam sponge, as seen in the very best English homes.' She had decided to overlook his remark about it being a plain-looking confection.

He laughed. 'In which case, I would be honoured to try it.'

'Do you call Alexandra Lexi now, Stéphie?' asked Félicité, accepting the cake she was offered, in spite of the dark looks it produced from her mother.

'Yes. She doesn't mind,' said Stéphie.

'Can we all do it?' asked Henri. 'Alexandra is rather a long name.'

'Phff!' said Alexandra shrugging her shoulders. '*Comme vous voulez, mes enfants,*' she said in French.

'You get more Gallic every day,' said David, very amused. 'What have you children been up to today? Be prepared to write an essay about it tomorrow.'

'We went to see a friend of Papa's,' said Henri. 'He had a son. We all went truffle-hunting with their specially trained dog.'

'Was the son your age?' asked Alexandra. 'Did you play together?' She felt sorry for Henri, who never had other boys to spend time with.

Henri snorted and looked at his older sister. 'He was eighteen. He was more interested in playing with Félicité!'

Alexandra saw a blush creep up Félicité's neck until it reached her cheeks.

'There are girls too,' said Félicité quickly, 'but they were out. Which was annoying.'

'More to the point,' said David, apparently unaware of Félicité's reaction to the mention of the boy, 'did you find any truffles?'

'No,' said Antoine. 'They had a specially trained truffle hound, a perfect area of woodland and not a single one.'

'It was very disappointing,' said Stéphie. 'Can I have another slice of cake?'

'Is Jack back yet?' asked Henri. 'He said he might try and find a guitar for me.'

'You're not learning the guitar,' said Lucinda, without apparently needing to consider her answer. 'You are a brilliant cellist. You're not allowed to waste your time and talent on a guitar.' She drew breath. 'And I forgot to say, Jack is visiting my mother.'

'Really?' said Antoine, surprised.

'Yes. And my mother's old friend Gérard is also coming for dinner,' Lucinda went on. 'I came to invite myself to dinner here to leave them alone. The conversation will be very boring.'

'But Jack is there?' said David. 'Visiting your mother? How very curious.'

Lucinda shrugged. 'I would be jealous if I thought either man was romantically interested in my mother, but of course, they can't possibly be.'

'Why is that?' asked David, who, Alexandra could tell, found Lucinda highly entertaining.

'She's a grandmother!' Lucinda said, scandalised. 'She is far too old to have admirers.'

Chapter Fourteen

❧

Jack arrived back after supper, staying in the kitchen very briefly before going to bed. He was as polite and charming as ever, but Alexandra had no idea if he'd had a good day or not. He seemed distracted and unwilling or unable to tell them how his dinner with the children's grandmother had gone. It was very strange.

It was only later, when Alexandra was clearing up, that Antoine told her it had been arranged that Lucinda would take Félicité and Henri out the following day. Alexandra couldn't decide if she was annoyed that Stéphie had been left out or relieved. If Lucinda wasn't going to treat the three children equally, maybe it was better if Stéphie wasn't included.

'Do you know what they're going to do?' she asked Antoine.

'She wants to buy them clothes, and do something cultural, I expect,' said Antoine. 'She has asked me to look at the prospectuses she brought. Maybe they should go to boarding school. It may be the only sensible solution.'

'Stéphie will miss them terribly if they went away.'

David appeared in the hall. 'I'm going to take myself off now. It's been a lovely day but I'm tired.'

'Thank you so much for cooking us such a wonderful meal,' said Antoine.

'It's an absolute pleasure, old chap,' said David and went upstairs, making Alexandra wonder if he wasn't rather overdoing the English-gentleman act.

She was about to follow David when Antoine said, 'Don't go up just yet. Come back into the kitchen where it's warm and have a glass of brandy. I need advice about my children's education.' He sent her a glance. 'Even if you are only twenty.'

Inordinately flattered, Alexandra allowed herself to be seated in the comfy chair, which had become a bit more comfy since she had found better cushions. Antoine handed her the brandy.

'What do you think? Should I allow Lucinda to send them to boarding school?'

'It's hard to say. I did go to boarding school myself but I didn't like it. It was very old-fashioned and I'd been used to a certain amount of freedom, living in London with young women who never really knew what I was up to. I wasn't happy only being able to walk to the nearest town, which was very small, on Saturdays, with a friend, if we asked permission. I suppose I did enjoy being with girls my own age, but not enough to make me want to stay at the school.'

'And did you learn anything there?'

'It did fill a few gaps in my knowledge. I was considered bright and was advanced in some subjects but I was dreadful at arithmetic. David taught me sums.'

'Oh?' Antoine sat back in his wheelback chair with the rush seat.

'I met him when I was selling – or trying to sell – antiques at the Portobello Road market. Have you heard of that?'

He shrugged. 'It's a market; it sells antiques.'

That didn't quite sum up the bustling, colourful, cosmopolitan community she'd come to love but this wasn't the moment to comment. 'Well, I'd managed to wangle myself a bit of space on someone else's table. I had to look after the whole stall while the proper stallholder went shopping. David was next door and could see I was getting in a muddle with the money. And I didn't know the basic trading terms. He took me to the pub and made me learn my times tables and percentages. He taught me a lot of other things too.'

'You went to school without knowing your times tables? Surely you learn that when you are small?'

She nodded. 'I managed to miss learning them.'

He shuddered. 'I'll speak to Jack about it,' he said. 'My children must know that, at the very least.'

'Maybe you should talk to Félicité and Henri about going to boarding school,' said Alexandra. 'They're too old to be just sent to places, particularly Félicité. She should have the choice.'

'My ex-wife doesn't seem to believe in choice for children.'

'If she's unhappy, Félicité will run away. I think Henri may be all right about it. He needs other boys to play with. And he needs to continue to study the cello.'

'How do you know so much about children and what they need?'

174

Alexandra could tell Antoine was teasing her but he'd asked her advice and so she'd give it to him. 'I've been a child and I also had an unconventional upbringing. I had a lot of nannies, companions and governesses. You've met my cousins Clothilde and Aimée. They were the relations most concerned in my upbringing, but they didn't care enough to interview the applicants every time there was a change of staff.'

'Yet you seem so self-assured.'

'I learnt to look after myself to some extent. My life changed for the better when David let slip he needed somewhere to live and I realised there was more than enough room in the family property where I was living in Belgravia. First, I just shared with David, but later, two fellow students at the cookery school I went to moved in.' She sighed. 'We had a lot of fun.'

Antoine didn't speak for a long time. 'And then there's Stéphanie . . .'

The thought of Stéphanie being sent away to school tore at Alexandra's heart. But it wasn't her place to be emotional. 'Well, she'd be very lonely without the others. And, of course, you're away most of the time.'

'I know. It's far from ideal but we must eat, and I must keep the roof on this place.'

Alexandra hesitated. Should she tell Antoine that she and David had had a good look round and saw plenty of potential for renting out bits of the property to holidaymakers? She didn't think so. She stifled a yawn.

'I'll let you go to bed in a minute, but I should tell you I will be away all day tomorrow. Stéphie will need you to look after her.'

'You know Stéphie and I can always have a good time together.'

'Thank you, Alexandra.' He smiled and Alexandra's heart turned over and began to beat faster in response. 'I'm glad you lied on your form. If you hadn't, I might not have employed you.'

'I thought it was that terrifying woman who employed me.'

He shook his head. 'She took her orders from me. Now go! And goodnight.'

Chapter Fifteen

Alexandra and Stéphie cut short their reading the following morning in order to be first downstairs. Alexandra felt being the first one up would make Stéphie feel in control, as if she was the one making things happen. And they both enjoyed letting the hens out, seeing them emerge, clucking and pecking, waiting for the corn that she and Stéphie had with them.

Today they were going to cook *pain perdu* for breakfast which Alexandra knew as 'Poor Knights'. They had discussed why they had different names for it and put it down to living in different countries.

'I think Americans call it French toast,' said Alexandra, soaking the thin slice of baguette in eggs and milk. 'It has lots of names.'

'Why?' asked Stéphie, watching with interest as Alexandra put the first piece in the pan of sizzling butter.

'I think everyone in the world has to use up stale bread sometimes and no one says "Ooh, let's have stale bread for breakfast" as if it's a treat.'

'No,' agreed Stéphie.

'Now get the jam out. I found a jar of fig jam the other day. It's in the larder.'

They were soon joined by David and Jack. Jack didn't look terribly cheerful and David was being hearty to make up for it. Alexandra wondered if Jack's leg was bothering him. She didn't know how he'd got his limp and didn't like to ask but he looked strained, and not like the cheerful character David had first introduced.

'Morning, ladies!' David said. 'Another beautiful day!'

Alexandra gave David a look. 'It is. Do you want tea or coffee? Jack? What would you like?'

'Coffee please. Black, with sugar.'

Alexandra passed him a cup. She was familiar with the habit of serving coffee in bowls in France but as it meant a pot of coffee only provided enough for two people, she didn't endorse it.

'Alexandra,' said Jack. 'Can I have a word?'

'Come with me into the larder,' said Alexandra. 'I think we're going to need more jam.'

Once they were there, Jack spoke rapidly. 'I wasn't quite honest with you when I came to be a tutor. I've told David some of it, but I must tell you everything.'

'Jack! I realised you aren't yourself at the moment, but what is it?' Alexandra's heart was beating hard, hoping Jack wasn't going to confess to some dreadful crime so he'd have to leave immediately. He was a good tutor, a nice man and the family needed him.

Obviously seeing her anxiety, he gave her a reassuring smile. 'It's nothing too awful – at least not in the eyes of the world. I've been here before.'

'What? In the chateau?'

'In Saint-Jean-du-Roc. And in the grounds of the chateau, too, if I'm honest.'

That wasn't too bad so far. 'Go on.'

'I met Penelope – Grand-mère. It was before the war. She was a widow with a young daughter, Lucinda. We fell in love but . . . well, it was in 1939, and I had to go back to England to enlist. Inevitably, we lost touch.'

Alexandra turned her gulp of surprise into a cough. 'And you didn't try and find her after the war?'

He shook his head. 'My leg got mashed up in a parachute jump and I was invalided out of the army, and after that I didn't earn a lot as a teacher. When I first met Penelope, I was a promising musician, but after the war, and with my bad leg, I couldn't do the touring I'd have had to do if I joined an orchestra. I had nothing to offer her.' He paused. 'And then a friend of a friend told me they'd heard she'd remarried.'

'Ah. That must have been a blow.' It was heartbreaking, Alexandra thought. 'So, what changed your mind? What made you come back here now?'

'When David said he needed a tutor and was coming here, I couldn't resist, for old times' sake. But it never occurred to me I'd meet Penelope again, and that she'd be a widow once more.'

'But you *have* met, and she *is* a widow, so that's all right?' Alexandra very much wanted this to be true, but she didn't really believe in fairy-tale romances.

Jack sighed. 'She has other suitors, as you'd expect.'

Alexandra chided herself. It had never occurred to her that Grand-mère would have suitors. But why not? She was very well preserved and would have been beautiful in her youth, it was just that Jack and Grand-mère seemed a bit old for that sort of thing.

'Ah, well . . .' Jack still seemed upset, although he'd confessed his secret.

'Why don't you and David go out for the day?' she suggested. 'Explore the area a bit more? The older children are going out with their mother anyway. Stéphie and I will be very happy entertaining ourselves. You two take the day off! Antoine will be away working.'

'It would be good to talk it all over with David, step back from it for a little while. If you're sure you don't need us?'

'We'll have a lovely day playing with dolls or something. Don't worry about us. Now, can you reach that jar of jam on that shelf?'

Antoine was eating the last of the French toast when Jack and Alexandra came back with the jam. He smiled and Alexandra felt obliged to smile back. 'I have to leave for Marseille now,' he said. 'I'm not sure at what time I will be back.'

Alexandra noted that while his English was perfect there was sometimes something a little different about his word order.

'OK. Do you know when Lucinda is collecting Félicité and Henri?' she asked.

'Félicité will know.'

'If it's all right with you,' said Alexandra, feeling brave, 'I've told David and Jack they can have the day off.'

Antoine nodded. 'Will you and Stéphie be all right?' He turned to the little girl who nodded. 'I have to go to the city and work.'

'We'll have an adventure,' she said matter-of-factly.

'Of course,' said Alexandra. 'Ah, here are the others. Hang on a minute and I'll make more French toast.'

'We'll need to make more jam,' said David, who had taken the news that he had the day off without comment. 'Or there won't be any for next year.'

Alexandra smiled wistfully. 'Maybe that won't matter to us.'

'Oh, I think it will,' said David.

The kitchen felt very empty when everyone had left and it was just Alexandra, Stéphie, the dirty dishes and a thin layer of jam which seemed to cover everything.

'You don't fancy having a baking day?' said Alexandra. She never used to be such a fan of baking herself but she'd learnt it was a good activity for children.

'No, thank you. I want an adventure! Everyone else is having an adventure.'

'OK, we'll think of something . . .'

'I want to go truffle-hunting. Like we did yesterday.'

'But you went—'

'We have a bit of land just like the land that had truffles,' Stéphie went on. 'Papa said. We can take Milou. He'll be our truffle hound.'

'I think that sounds fun!' said Alexandra, thinking it sounded a recipe for failure. 'Why are you so keen on finding truffles? Didn't you do enough hunting yesterday?'

'I want to find truffles on *our* land. Then Papa won't have to go away to work. I want him to stay here.'

As she and David had spent time also looking for ways to stop Papa having to go away to work, Alexandra nodded. 'Well, it would be wonderful to find truffles on this land, but I have to warn you, it is unlikely. And there will be other ways we can make money from the chateau. Don't worry!'

'I'm not worried. We'll find truffles. They're very valuable.'

Stéphie seemed very certain so Alexandra put together a picnic. 'Do we need to take the car?' she asked.

'No, no. We just walk. Papa took us there once and said there might be truffles. We'll find them, I know.'

Eventually they set off. Alexandra had a knapsack with their picnic, a knife and a trowel in it. The trowel was found after Stéphie showed Alexandra to a shed she hadn't been in before. It was full of useful things, many of which would sell very well on the Portobello Road, Alexandra couldn't help thinking. Old agricultural implements were popular items to hang on pub walls back in England. Alexandra didn't say this out loud, but she made a note. She wasn't optimistic about the truffles; the chateau might have to rely on disused farm equipment to make its money.

Stéphie and Milou led the way, up through the field and then to where oaks and other large trees began, leading into the woodlands which climbed up the hills behind the chateau. Alexandra was beginning to find the picnic heavy to carry. The large bottle of orange squash had made it so, she knew; she hadn't been able to find anything that held less than a litre to put it in. If they had lunch – and it was nearly half past twelve – it would be lighter. She might also be able to persuade Stéphie it was time to go home afterwards. Alexandra's espadrilles weren't suitable for climbing in, and the ground was a bit muddy, too. But if her espadrilles were ruined, she could at least buy a new pair next market day.

'We need to find a branch of a pine tree and break off all the little branches and just leave some leaves on the top, like a little broom,' said Stéphie when she sensed Alexandra was flagging. 'And then we need to find trees that have no grass round their base,' she went on.

'How do you know all this?' said Alexandra, wishing Stéphie wasn't quite so keen.

'I listened carefully when the man told us. No one else seemed interested, but I was.'

'We couldn't have lunch first?'

Stéphie shook her head. 'Work first, lunch after.'

Alexandra sighed. Stéphie was on a mission and this was her special day out. Alexandra hitched up the knapsack so that it rubbed her shoulders some-where different and carried on.

'Look, here's a good tree,' said Stéphie. She was standing under an oak tree and there was a patch of bare ground beneath it. 'Now we need to see if there are flies. The flies like the smell of truffles to lay their eggs on. Help me find a branch so we can brush away the leaves and things, so we just have bare soil.'

Alexandra put down the knapsack with relief and obediently hunted for suitable branches. Luckily there were plenty to choose from.

Stéphie rejected all Alexandra's offerings and broke off the smaller twigs from her own chosen fly whisk.

Milou, who was usually the epitome of the patient companion, flung himself down in the shade with a groan, expressing Alexandra's feelings exactly.

'Get a branch, Lexi! It's not easy to find truffles, you know!'

'I do know, chicken, but you don't like any of my branches, and I think we should have lunch before we start.'

'No!' Stéphie was firm. 'I'll do it on my own if you don't want to join in.'

'I'll just watch you to begin with, to see what you do,' said Alexandra, perching on a convenient rock so she could see if she was getting a blister. It was quite stony underfoot here and her shoes slid about when she stepped on the rough ground.

Stéphie swept away for a bit and then suddenly lay on her stomach and started sniffing. 'The truffle hunter's most important piece of equipment is his nose,' she said, obviously quoting the expert they'd met the previous day. 'There are flies here.'

Milou got up and stretched before going over to find out why one of his people was lying on the ground. Then he started sniffing too. For a few seconds Alexandra thought he was just joining in out of politeness but then realised his nose was down and he was starting to paw the ground.

'Look at Milou!' said Stéphie, getting up. 'He's a truffle hound!'

'Has he done this before?' Alexandra joined the truffle hunters.

'I don't know,' said Stéphie, 'but look!'

Milou was really digging now, covering Alexandra and Stéphie with soil.

Stéphie went over, and then exclaimed in disappointment. 'Oh, it's only a rock.'

'Maybe the truffle is under the rock,' suggested Alexandra. 'Dogs have extremely sensitive noses. I read it somewhere. Let's help him get it out.' She found the trowel. She moved Milou to one side and started trying to prise the rock out of the ground. She had to dig quite a bit more and wondered if she should have left Milou to it for a bit longer. Then she paused. 'Stéphie? Can you smell something?'

They both lay full length on the ground, not caring about the mud, and sniffed. A strange, musky scent was discernible through the smell of earth. They looked at each other. 'I think that might be truffle,' said Alexandra.

Suddenly, getting the rock out of the way was their urgent goal and together they dug, heaved and waggled, as if at a stubborn tooth. At last the rock moved and eventually they managed to dislodge it completely. Milou was beside himself, digging furiously.

'Will he eat the truffle?' asked Stéphie.

'I don't know!' said Alexandra. 'It may not even be a truffle. It might be a dead body or something.'

Stéphie stopped and gasped. 'That would be terrible!'

185

'It would be of an animal or something. Not a person,' said Alexandra, backtracking slightly. 'Don't worry. Here, let me have the trowel. Milou, you have a rest for a while. Stéphie, you hold his collar.'

By now the ground was a lot looser and the digging was easier. Milou pulled harder and harder until he broke free of Stéphie's grasp, pushed Alexandra out of the way and dug furiously again until at last he stopped, something in his mouth. He dropped what he was holding at Stéphie's feet.

'A truffle!' she exclaimed. 'And it's huge!'

Chapter Sixteen

❦

'We can have lunch now,' said Stéphie after she and Alexandra had hugged each other and congratulated Milou. 'And I think we should give some of it to Milou for being such a good truffle hound when he hasn't been trained or anything.'

'I did bring something for him,' said Alexandra, rummaging in the knapsack. 'Here. Some ends of baguette that are rock-hard. We can put some pâté on it for him.'

When they'd all eaten a few mouthfuls, Alexandra said, 'Well, Stéphie, you're the heroine of the hour.'

'What's that?'

'It means you've been the one to save us by finding a truffle. A huge truffle.'

'Milou found it.'

'No! Milou didn't know where to look. He just smelt it. You did all the difficult bits.'

'Did I?'

'Yes. And you must have listened very carefully when you went truffle-hunting yesterday. Well done! Your papa is going to be very pleased with you. So will everyone else.'

'Will it mean Papa won't have to go away any more?'

Alexandra shrugged. 'I don't know, but it could certainly help.'

Stéphie drank some more squash. 'We will need to sell the truffle, not eat it,' she said.

Alexandra considered this. 'I don't think one truffle, even a big one like this, will be enough to keep your papa at home, but knowing that there are truffles here, on this land, that we could get more, might make a difference. Yesterday, while you were learning how to find truffles with Félicité and Henri, David and I explored the chateau. There are lots of little buildings that could be turned into accommodation for tourists. English people love staying in France. That could make money.'

Stéphie considered this. 'Papa might not want people staying here. But if Félicité and Henri go away to school, maybe there would be people I could play with?'

'Perhaps you could go to school locally? Then you'd have lots of people to play with.'

'They might not want to play with the girl from the chateau.'

Alexandra took the knapsack on to her knee, searching for something. 'They will when they find out that you're nice and not a snob.'

'What's a snob?'

'A person who doesn't like other people because they think they are better than they are. Here, I brought chocolate!'

'Can I give Milou some?'

'No,' said Alexandra. 'I heard that chocolate is bad for dogs. Let's give him the last bit of bread and pâté.'

'He deserved it,' said Stéphie, two seconds later, when the dog had gulped down his treat.

'He certainly did.'

No one spoke for a few moments, and then Alexandra wiped the crumbs from the corner of her mouth. 'Stéphie, you know that Lucinda is taking Félicité and Henri to buy clothes?' Stéphie nodded. 'Well, she may not buy you anything. So, if this happens, and you feel a bit sad to see your sister and brother with new things, I want you to know that I will take you shopping another time. If we can make him come, we'll bring Papa, so you can have a special day too.'

'But I've had a special day, Lexi. We found a truffle.'

Alexandra took Stéphie in her arms and hugged her.

Alexandra really hoped that Antoine would be back when they got home. Stéphie ran into the chateau through the courtyard into the kitchen. She was so full of joy and optimism Alexandra feared for her a little. She couldn't bear her to be disappointed.

David was in the kitchen, cooking, very happy in what he had turned into his own space. Jack was sitting at the kitchen table, peeling cloves of garlic, and seemed to be back to his old self.

'Hello, Stéphie. How nice to see you!' said David. 'Have you had a good day with Lexi?'

'Yes,' said Stéphie. 'We found a truffle!' She produced it proudly.

'Good God!' said David. 'It's enormous! Where did you find that?'

'Up in the woods behind the chateau,' said Alexandra. 'Stéphie remembered everything about hunting for them that she learnt yesterday and we did what she said, and *voilà*!'

'Is Papa here?' asked Stéphie, picking up the truffle. 'I want to show him.'

'Um – Antoine telephoned. He is coming back tonight but a bit later and he's bringing a business colleague who may need to stay the night.' David looked at Alexandra.

'He wants me to make up a bed?' she asked.

'He didn't say as much but he did say if there was a bed ready it would be very helpful.'

'Helpful is my middle name,' said Alexandra.

'Is it?' said David, sounding astonished. 'I thought it was something mad and aristocratic like Euphemia.'

Alexandra tutted and sighed at him. 'I see you chaps have been at the rosé. Are Félicité and Henri home?'

'Yes,' David said.

'And they really want to see you, Stéphie,' added Jack.

'I'd leave the truffle here—' David called, but it was too late. 'Oh well, I don't suppose it will come to much harm. We'll have to think how to cook it.'

'I think Stéphie wants to sell it. She wants to find a way so Papa doesn't have to go away to work.' Alexandra suppressed a sigh. 'Did you two buy lots of valuable antiques?'

'I won't know if they're valuable until I come to sell them,' said David, 'but we have got a lot of things. I may well have to hire a van when I go back to England.'

Alexandra wondered if he'd said 'I' instead of 'we' deliberately, and fervently hoped he wasn't planning to leave soon.

'We also bought lots of very good wine,' said Jack. 'We are drinking rosé by the pint and anything else nice that Antoine produces so we felt we should contribute.'

'Félicité has bought Stéphie a lovely dress,' said David. 'She told her mother that Antoine would pay her back for it, but what a nice child she is! So thoughtful, and of course she dotes on Stéphie.'

'Oh, good for her!' said Alexandra.

'But because we didn't know that Félicité would do that, we bought Stéphie something too. It's an old doll's house. It needs restoration but we can do that,' said David. 'At least, I thought that Jack might like to do that. But when we discovered that Félicité had bought her a dress we didn't give it to her – although of course we still can.'

'Maybe restore it, if you have time, and it'll be there if you need a present?' suggested Alexandra, aware her opinion was being sought. 'I don't know when her birthday is, for example.'

'That sounds like a good idea,' said Jack, 'as long as her birthday isn't next week.'

'Now I'd better make up a bed for Antoine's business colleague. I do hope he's nice!'

'Antoine wouldn't bring him here and invite him to dinner if he wasn't,' said David. 'Do you want me to help you?'

'Not at all! I'll do it now. Do you know when dinner will be?'

'We're having a nice bit of pork but it'll keep if Antoine is late. It'll be ready in about an hour.' He glanced up at the old grandfather clock that ticked away in the corner and always struck twice. 'So about seven?'

'I'll find out if the children are starving,' said Alexandra. 'Would it spoil it if they ate early? If we don't know when Antoine and his colleague will turn up.'

'We can do whatever suits.' He thought for a moment. 'We could always eat the pork early and I could make a nice omelette for the boss and shave the truffle over it.'

'No, you can't!' said Jack. 'If we're eating the truffle, I want to be there!'

'It's Stéphie's truffle,' said Alexandra firmly. 'She will decide. Now I must choose a bedroom for the colleague. I wonder if he needs to be near the bath-room?'

'I'm afraid I didn't ask how old he was,' said David. 'I don't know if he might need to get up during the night.'

'You're no help!' said Alexandra, laughing, and left the room.

Alexandra was looking for some sheets in the huge cupboard that was full of ancient linen when Félicité came up behind her.

'Have you got any more pads? I'd like to have some ready for next month.'

'Oh! Yes, I have. I'll go and get them.'

Félicité followed Alexandra to her room. 'We were in a pharmacy and I started to ask my mother about getting some but she misunderstood and said, "Oh, you're far too young to worry about things like that," and then I didn't feel I could say any more. Henri was there, of course.'

'Embarrassing,' said Alexandra, handing Félicité a paper-wrapped package. 'Although men do have to know about periods, you know. When I lived in London with David, he used to give me a hot-water bottle and a hot drink while I lay on the sofa in front of the gas fire and he cooked me comforting food.'

'I'm not going to tell my brother about this!' Félicité held up the packet. 'I haven't got used to the idea myself yet.'

'Fair enough.'

'And David is a bit different from other men, isn't he?' said Félicité.

Just for a second, Alexandra worried, then took a breath. 'Yes, he is. He explained to me that in the theatre people often share digs with each other – you know, accommodation – and so people weren't so private about things like that. I think it's a good thing! But you don't have to tell anyone if you don't want to. Although I'm glad you told me.'

'I had to tell someone, and you are my nanny!' Then Félicité gave a snort of laughter at how ridiculous this seemed and turned to go.

Before she did, Alexandra put a hand on her arm. 'Thank you so much for buying that dress for Stéphie. It was very thoughtful of you.'

Félicité shrugged. 'Well, it wouldn't have occurred to my mother to do such a thing.'

'Good for you for thinking about it.'

Before Alexandra could embarrass her any more, Félicité left to find her siblings.

When Alexandra had gathered an armful of linen she hoped wasn't too old in spite of being beautifully ironed, she decided to look in on her charges before worrying about bedrooms. They were all playing cards on the floor of Félicité's room and seemed very happy. Alexandra waved from the door and received waves of varying enthusiasm in response. Félicité may have wanted to appear to be a cynical teenager but she revealed herself as having a very kind heart.

There was a little room near Antoine's master suite that Alexandra thought would be all right for the colleague. She'd come across an old stone hot-water bottle and decided she'd put it in the bed, to make sure the mattress wasn't damp – looking at the ominous patch of damp on the wall, she feared it probably was.

After she'd put sheets on and found some extra blankets in case the colleague was chilly, she was about to go to the kitchen to fill the hot-water bottle when she caught sight of herself in the mirror. She was filthy!

Once she'd washed and changed her dress, she thought she might as well put a bit of make-up on. Her hair needed a trim so she twisted it up into a sort of chignon and secured it. Having gone this far she decided to add her pearl studs which were in a little velvet sack in her handbag. She was quite pleased with the end result and relieved she hadn't inadvertently spent the evening covered in soil from truffle-hunting and generally looking like a peasant after a hard day in the fields.

She was laughing when she went into the kitchen with her huge stone bed warmer.

'You look very glamorous, m'dear,' said David.

'Indeed you do!' Jack agreed.

'Thank you. I'm laughing because making up beds for people is really not what I would have predicted for myself a year ago. However, looking glamorous would definitely have been the plan. Now, this is going to take a lot of boiling water to fill but worth it, I think.' She put the stone hot-water bottle on the table.

'We can always boil more water,' said David. 'The children came down and Stéphie is wearing her new dress. It's a little big for her but looks very sweet.'

'And it will be clean!' said Alexandra. 'If I hadn't caught sight of myself I'd have come down covered in mud. Truffle-hunting is a grubby business. Any news from the travellers?'

'Antoine phoned just now. They'll be here in twenty minutes.'

Alexandra was aware of butterflies of excitement at the thought of seeing Antoine and she squashed them firmly. 'Is the table set?'

'Yup,' said Jack. 'And I've opened a couple of bottles of the wine we bought. I lit the fire in the salon, more for the welcome than for warmth, but it does look very charming. I put candles in the candelabra too.'

'Anyone would think we lived in a chateau,' said David.

Alexandra was back in her room redoing her chignon having put the bed warmer in the bed and found towels when she heard a couple of very loud, deep barks from Milou and realised Antoine was back.

To stop herself getting so nervous about seeing him that she'd stay in her room for ever, she left and ran down the stairs. She was nearly at the bottom when she stopped. Antoine was there being greeted by Milou as if he'd been away for years, not a matter of hours, and with him was a woman.

Alexandra's mouth went dry. Why hadn't it occurred to her that Antoine's colleague might be female? Even if it had, she wouldn't have imagined she'd be so very Parisienne, so extremely glamorous.

Antoine looked up and saw her, poised on the stairs. 'Alexandra!' he said in English. 'Come and meet Véronique. Véronique, this is . . .' He hesitated for the tiniest second and Alexandra rushed in.

'I'm Alexandra, the children's nanny.'

Véronique, who, Alexandra was convinced, must have stopped to titivate on the way here so she'd arrive looking soignée, seemed surprised. 'The nanny?' She addressed Antoine in French.

'Companion, rather,' he said smoothly. 'She has been running the house, engaging teachers, and of course you're right, Félicité and Henri are far too old to have a nanny—'

Alexandra didn't think this was the reason Véronique questioned the term. She straightened her back and lifted her chin.

At this moment Alexandra's charges clattered down the stairs and arrived in the hall. Stéphie flung herself into her father's arms. 'Papa! We found a truffle! Well, Milou did!'

'Milou?' Antoine hugged his other children in turn. 'I didn't know he was a truffle hound. Are we going to eat it?' He addressed the question to David, who had appeared in the hall.

'No, Papa!' said Stéphie. 'We're going to sell it, so you don't have to go away to work any more.'

Véronique smiled charmingly, and squatted down to be on a level with Stéphie. 'I'm sure you'd like that, sweetie, but it would take more than one truffle to make enough money for that. And your father's work is very important. But it's very good that your dog didn't eat it, so well done.'

'It's enormous,' said Félicité. 'Look!' She held out the truffle to her father.

Antoine was shocked. 'Good God! It *is* enormous! I've never seen such a big truffle,' he said.

'It was under a rock,' said Stéphie. 'Milou knew it was there and was digging and digging, then me and Lexi helped him and got the rock out.'

'We were covered in earth afterwards,' said Alexandra, 'but we were so excited we didn't care. Véronique? Would you like to wash your hands? And I think I may have given you the wrong bedroom.' She was glad she didn't know Véronique's surname so she couldn't be tempted to use it and thus lower herself in status.

'Why the wrong room?' asked Véronique.

'We were expecting Antoine's colleague to be a man.' Alexandra gave a little laugh. 'If you'd like to come and see we can make changes if necessary.'

As Alexandra led the way upstairs she realised she had no idea what changes she could make if Véronique did reject the little room with the patch of damp on the wall.

'It's small,' said Alexandra as she opened the door, 'but that lump in the bed is a stone hot-water bottle. You can see how large it is. The bed will be very cosy.'

Veronique froze in horror. 'I can't stay in here. It feels like a dressing room, not a proper bedroom.'

It occurred to Alexandra – belatedly – that it was indeed a dressing room, for Antoine's bedroom.

'Very well.' She made a quick decision. 'I will put you in my bedroom. If you'd like to use the bathroom' – she indicated where it was – 'I'll change the sheets.'

Making such a sacrifice was easier because she knew she was on the high moral ground. She also knew that Véronique was completely confused about whom she was dealing with.

Véronique went downstairs without waiting for Alexandra and eventually Stéphie came up. 'Dinner's ready. What are you doing?'

'I'm making sure my bedroom is spotless and tidy before Véronique sleeps in it,' she said. 'Does that look all right to you?'

'It looks utterly perfect,' said Stéphie. 'She couldn't possibly say that anything's wrong.' She paused. 'She's very pretty, but she's quite like Félicité's and Henri's mother.' She suddenly giggled. 'Supposing I forgot it wasn't you in here and got into her bed in the morning by mistake! Wouldn't that be awful!' For something that was awful it seemed to make Stéphie laugh a lot. 'You could sleep in my room with me if you like, Lexi. I don't mind.'

'That's so kind of you, Stéphie, but I've put a huge hot-water bottle in the bed I made for Véronique and I wouldn't like to waste it, so I'll sleep there. If we want to do reading, we can do it in your bed though.'

'Oh good.' She gave a sudden twirl and held out her skirt. 'Do you like my new dress? Félicité got it for me.'

'I love it! And isn't it a good thing you'd put it on? We got so dirty on our truffle hunt.'

'We did!' Stéphie paused. 'I think you should put on some perfume, Lexi. Véronique has a lot of perfume on.'

'OK . . .' said Alexandra. 'I've put it in the little room where I'll be sleeping.'

When a good splash of Bien-Être eau de cologne, bought in the local chemist, had been applied – although it was certainly not the sort of scent that Véronique would ever wear – she and Stéphie went to join the party.

They were standing round in the salon with glasses of wine. David was near the door, looking anxious. Alexandra moved within earshot.

'I want to serve up,' he said out of the corner of his mouth. 'Can I just announce that dinner is ready, do you think? Véronique is very grand!'

Alexandra tossed her head a little. 'Of course you can announce dinner. She's not as grand as all that!' Having had to give up her room for her, Alexandra wasn't going to give Véronique any ground on the grandness stakes.

David clapped his hands. 'Ladies and gentlemen, dinner is served!'

Alexandra hung back and gathered discarded glasses which she left on a tray and so was last to the dining room. Véronique was sitting next to Antoine, at the head, and Stéphie sat on his other side. The truffle, she noted, was placed on a saucer, doing duty as a table decoration. And a fine one too, she decided. She sat next to Jack at the other end of the table.

'How did your day go?' she asked him. 'What did you get up to?' She was longing to find out if they'd been to visit Penelope, and if the visit had gone well, but didn't feel she could ask.

'We had a good day, thank you. We found a market, the spoils of which you see before you. And then we had lunch with Penelope.'

'Was that – nice?' said Alexandra lamely.

Jack laughed. 'You want to know how Penelope and I got on, don't you?'

Alexandra nodded, laughing at herself.

'It was delicious!' Jack was teasing her now. 'Seriously, we were both much more relaxed now that we've had time to get used to the idea of seeing each other again after all these years.'

'Oh good,' said Alexandra, wishing she could press him for more details. But he seemed a lot happier. That must mean something.

When everyone was happily eating, Véronique said, 'So, Alexandra? You come from London?'

Alexandra smiled and nodded, acknowledging that she did.

'How do you find this sleepy little corner of Provence after the bright lights?' Veronique continued.

'Well, it's rural but very beautiful. I like it here very much.' Alexandra smiled again, in a way intended to end the conversation.

It didn't. Véronique seemed to find this amusing. 'Surely, a pretty girl like you needs to be with young people, and be out having fun.'

Alexandra shrugged. 'Félicité and Henri and Stéphie aren't all that old and we're always busy.'

'But you're so young—' Veronique began.

'Alexandra is an heir—' Stéphie began until she obviously spotted Alexandra's horrified expression.

Alexandra gave the tiniest shake of her head, which fortunately was enough to silence Stéphie on this particular topic. The last thing Alexandra wanted was a discussion about her fortune. That was something she wanted to keep private as far as she was able.

'What is Alexandra, Stéphie?' Véronique prompted gently.

'She's – very pretty!' said Stéphie.

'Véronique,' said David smoothly, rescuing Alexandra. 'Can I encourage you to have another egg? They're called Devilled Eggs in England. I'm not sure if you're familiar with them in France.'

'I'm not very interested in food,' said Véronique dismissively.

David was surprised. 'Oh. I thought all French people were interested in food.'

'That's just a stereotype,' said Véronique. 'In the same way everyone expects me to be male. I'm not and I'm just as powerful and effective as any man.'

David bowed. 'Madame, I would never have thought anything different.'

'Is that why Antoine described you as a colleague when he telephoned to say you would be with him?' said Alexandra.

'Of course,' said Véronique. 'He and I often work together. He knows better than to refer to my gender.'

'It would have been much easier for me had I known,' said Alexandra quietly. 'Then I wouldn't have had to change bedrooms.'

Véronique dismissed this protest with a shrug. 'It is important that women are given proper respect, and not just as wives and carers of children.'

'I think caring for children deserves respect,' said Jack. 'It's not easy but it is very important.'

'Yes,' said Véronique. 'But I have a brain! I don't want to waste it on what any woman can do!'

There was a very awkward silence. Then Antoine said, 'Have some wine, *chérie*.'

'I'll get the main course,' said David.

'I'll help,' said Alexandra.

When they reached the kitchen she said, 'Oh, David! You know I've always believed in equality for women but she's enough to make me change my mind.'

David laughed. He put his arm round her and gave her a hug. 'Don't worry about her. If she's not interested in food, she's not worth thinking about.'

Although Alexandra knew David was probably right and she shouldn't bother to think about Véronique, her mind wouldn't cooperate. When she went to bed that night she found herself analysing everything Véronique had said and when it dawned on her that her feelings of resentment were jealousy, she was mortified.

Chapter Seventeen

Alexandra was up and about early the following morning. She'd done the hens and now she wanted to grind coffee and make sure that breakfast would be properly organised; it was a meal that was often an informal free-for-all and not fit for the likes of Véronique.

It was possible that Antoine had had the same thought for he appeared shortly afterwards, damp from the bath and freshly shaved. He was wearing a very beautifully cut suit and looked so attractive, Alexandra couldn't breathe properly for a few seconds.

'Morning!' she said calmly, when she'd got her breathing back to normal. 'Have you thought what to do about Stéphie's truffle? She definitely wants to sell it, much to David's disappointment.'

'I'm going to telephone my friend the truffle expert before we leave for Marseille today and see if he can arrange to sell it. We could deliver it on our way if he can.'

'Do you have any idea how much money it might fetch?'

He shook his head. 'Not really. I don't suppose it'll be enough to make it possible for me to retire. Maybe I should put the money away for Stéphie's future.'

'Please don't do that! No amount of money in the future is as important to her as having her father at home – if not all the time, at least more often.'

As he regarded her down the length of his long, slightly crooked nose, Alexandra wondered if she'd spoken too frankly, but then she realised he was thinking. 'I'll put the money aside to do some repairs on the chateau. Stéphie will be so proud to know it was her efforts that made it possible. And yours, of course.'

'Stéphie would say it was all down to Milou.'

'He is a prince among dogs,' said Antoine, just the hint of a smile wrinkling the corner of his eyes.

Alexandra couldn't help smiling back. She jumped when Véronique said, 'Am I interrupting something?

'No! No, of course not,' said Alexandra. 'I've been waiting for you to come before I make coffee. What else would you like for breakfast? Toast and marmalade?' A fraction too late she remembered that toast and marmalade wasn't really an option as they hadn't any.

Véronique made a face at the suggestion. 'No, thank you. I'll just have coffee.'

After Antoine and Véronique had left for Marseille for the day, Alexandra took the time to telephone Donna in Paris. After quite a lot of enjoyable, gossipy chat, she established that Véronique was the gorgeous woman with Antoine the night he went to Donna and Bob's dinner party. The knowledge didn't make Alexandra feel any better about her.

Later, as she made her way to the kitchen to prepare lunch for everyone (leftovers were always so useful), she told herself she should really leave the chateau. She was never going to get over her ridiculous crush while she was living in Antoine's house. But she'd told her relations that she would stay until the spring, and she didn't feel she could leave before the children were settled with their father at home more regularly. Although Donna had said she'd be delighted to have her to stay in Paris. She could do Paris properly. It would be wonderful!

But Alexandra knew in her heart it was here, in rural Provence, in a slightly dilapidated chateau, that she really wanted to be. She would never be more than the nanny, or maybe the housekeeper, but it was still where she felt most at home.

It seemed to Alexandra that the chateau as well as its inhabitants gave a gentle sigh of relief when Véronique went back to Paris on the train a couple of days later. Antoine was due to follow her in a few days' time but not having Véronique – not interested in food but still surprisingly critical – at the dinner table lightened everyone's spirits.

Although it was November, it was a beautiful autumnal day, the colours of Provence as bright as a paintbox against a brilliant blue sky. Alexandra thought she'd take Milou for a walk – meaning she'd go for a walk and he might come too. She had time now she no longer had to worry about Véronique and her needs and wanted to think about her life and what to do. Walking would help. She was in the hall when the doorbell jangled.

It was Penelope, or Grand-mère, as Alexandra continued to think of her.

She seemed unusually diffident. 'Good morning, Alexandra.'

'Good morning!' she replied. 'Would you like to come in?'

'You've got your coat on. You were about to go out.'

She'd borrowed an old jacket of Antoine's she'd found hanging in a corridor, obviously long forgotten. It was embarrassing to be discovered wearing it by this daunting picture of elegance. 'No, no. I was only going to take Milou for a wander. It's such a beautiful day.'

'It is. I won't keep you. I just wanted to bring you this. It's the little Sèvres soup bowl I mentioned to you before. It has handles and one has come off.' She produced a tissue-wrapped package from her handbag.

Alexandra took it. It was beautiful, sky blue with a lot of gilt decoration. 'Oh goodness, it's fantastically valuable. I don't think I could—'

'*Chérie*, it isn't valuable without a handle. Just do your best.'

Penelope had never called her *chérie* before, she realised with a start. 'I will,' she said.

But even after Alexandra had taken the little bowl and put it in a safe place on the mantelpiece of the salon, Penelope showed no signs of moving. 'Can I get you some coffee, or a drink?'

'No,' said Penelope decisively. 'You have your coat on; I have mine. Let's go for a walk together. I've become a little homesick lately. Talking to a fellow Englishwoman will help.'

Alexandra was so surprised she couldn't speak for a few moments. Penelope was so entrenched in her part as a French *grande dame*, she would hardly admit she wasn't French. Now she was talking about being homesick, and wanting to go for a walk with the nanny. Somewhere, Alexandra imagined, hell had frozen over. Or, she thought, remembering what Jack had told her, perhaps she wanted to talk about her love life? This thought was even less likely than a sudden cold snap in hell!

Milou was on his best behaviour and followed the two Englishwomen meekly. Penelope didn't speak as they walked down the path through a neglected but still pretty walled garden that would have produced vegetables for the chateau at one time but now held only a few roses covering the walls and beds of salvias, rosemary and lavender.

'You must be delighted that Lucinda has come back from Argentina,' said Alexandra when she could stand the silence no longer. They had left the garden and taken one of the paths that led into the wood.

Penelope nodded. 'Yes and no. It is lovely for me to have her, but I don't think she understands the children, having been away from them for so long.'

'Oh?' Alexandra concentrated on sounding non-committal.

'She loves her own children, of course, but she doesn't pay attention to *la p'tite.*'

'Stéphie?'

Penelope nodded. 'Lucinda is an only child and doesn't understand jealousy. Not that Stéphie is ever jealous, but it's hard for her to see her siblings – even if technically they are not her siblings – being given attention and gifts when she is not.'

'I have tried to make sure she doesn't feel left out,' said Alexandra. Although I'm an only child too, she thought but didn't say.

'Yes! And I am truly grateful. You've worked very hard for the children and I do appreciate it.' They walked on in silence for a bit longer. 'You know, I had a sister who had a godmother who used to give her lavish presents. I understood that this godmother was special to my sister but it was hard. The pretty dresses from Harrods, the special Easter egg, wonderful crayons – I remember once I couldn't bear it and burst into tears. I was so ashamed.'

'That's dreadful!' Alexandra was stricken on her behalf.

'My mother couldn't do anything about it. It was a fact of my life. But I hate to think that little Stéphie might be feeling like I felt.'

'Well, I gave her an antique doll's stove that really works with little pots and pans that she loves. David and Jack are both aware of her possibly being left out too.' Alexandra took a breath, hoping Penelope would be reassured by this, and went on, 'But I feel the person who is suffering most is Félicité. She loves her sister, and she knows she must feel left out. The other day, when Lucinda took them shopping, Félicité bought Stéphie a dress. She must have been given the money by her mother, but I was so pleased with her thoughtfulness.'

'I'm glad to hear that, too,' said Penelope. 'Lucinda didn't tell me. We don't always communicate very well.'

There was another quite long silence as they walked through the woods. Alexandra was enchanted by the changing colours but she was waiting for Penelope to carry on. She could tell she had more to say.

'I have lived in France for a very long time. In many ways I am French,' Penelope said.

'Can I ask why you came to France?'

'I had come here before the war, with a friend's family. We had a wonderful holiday. I knew it would be quite different after the war, but my parents had gone to live near my brother and I wanted a complete change of scene. And I thought it would be good for Lucinda to become bilingual, and spread her wings a bit after spending the war at boarding school in England.' She laughed. 'She'd read so many stories about English boarding schools – too many possibly – that my parents had given her, she was convinced she wanted to go too.'

'It must have been hard, going to a country where you knew no one. I at least had the children for company when I came here.'

'It was hard, although having Lucinda helped. A neighbour – a friend of Hortense – took me under her wing. She had a daughter the same age as Lucinda and introduced me to her friends. It was through her that I met my second husband – you'll know that I lost him too . . .' She fell silent for a moment, and Alexandra heard the echo of grief. 'That's also how Lucinda met Antoine. Rosemarie was an Anglophile, which is partly why she was so kind, but she made sure I learnt French as quickly as possible. I felt her loss when she moved to Paris.'

The story sounded convincing, and yet Alexandra knew there was more. She was tense, wondering if Penelope would continue to be confiding or revert to being the starchy *grande dame* Alexandra had first met.

They had walked through the edge of the wood and come across a path that led back to the chateau.

'You may be wondering why I'm talking to you, instead of Hortense, whom I've known for nearly twenty years. I'm wondering why myself.' She smiled. 'But Hortense has always known me as an upright pillar of the community. I could never reveal to her that I wasn't always upright or a pillar.'

Alexandra laughed at Penelope's little joke but inside she braced herself. This was about Jack; she was sure of it. Could she tell Penelope that she knew something of her story? Then she realised that she couldn't.

'You're too young to know what love is but when you do fall in love you will feel that your love is the only thing that matters. Nothing else is important. You will be wrong – as I was wrong – but you will feel that just the same.'

Alexandra did feel she knew what love was but certainly wasn't going to confide in Penelope about her feelings for Antoine. She was going to suppress them completely. She was determined that no one should know about them – least of all Antoine.

'It is likely that, like most people, you will come to a place in your life when you have a choice. You can choose the safe, comfortable route that will give you security and possibly happiness. Or you can choose passion and risk losing everything you have built up for years.' Penelope seemed to hold her breath for ages until she slowly exhaled.

Alexandra waited as long as she could. 'Which is the right choice?'

'I wish I knew, *chérie*. I am middle-aged but I'm not sure I shall ever have the necessary wisdom to decide between head and heart.'

Alexandra cleared her throat. She was suffering a similar dilemma: her head said, leave the chateau, forget all about Antoine; and her heart said, stay as long as she possibly could. She was very surprised to find herself in the same situation as Penelope.

'Shall we go to the orangery?' said Penelope after a second or two. 'When Lucinda lived here, she and Antoine used to give parties in it.'

Alexandra was a quick thinker but she struggled with this change of tack for a second. 'Of course. But when David and I explored the other day we found it was locked.'

'I think I know where the key is.'

They walked to the building with its floor-to-ceiling windows that were now covered in creeper, one of which was like flames climbing over the roof. Penelope ran her hand over the top of the door and found the key. The lock was stiff but they got it open and went in.

'Ah,' she said with a long sigh. 'I remember this.'

Alexandra waited. She didn't think Penelope was remembering parties given by her daughter and her husband.

'I came here once, lifetimes ago. The chateau was closed up; it was before Antoine took it over. A friend and I were walking in the grounds. Trespassing, probably. Suddenly there was a summer shower and we came in here for shelter. It was like it is now, overgrown but very romantic; not like it became later, when it was clean and ready for Lucinda's parties.'

Alexandra's heart was in her mouth. Was Penelope talking about Jack?

'Nothing was the same after that,' said Penelope.

There was a long, agonising pause. 'I wonder how much it would take to clean this place up,' she went on. 'It would be a lovely venue for a celebration.'

Alexandra relaxed a little. It appeared there weren't going to be any more confidences, but as she considered herself a bit of an expert in turning large dirty spaces into somewhere suitable for guests and parties she just focused on the orangery for a few moments. 'A jolly good clean, plenty of flowers – it would be lovely.'

'Yes. It would,' said Penelope and then added, 'Shall we go back? I think I need tea now. However French I may appear, I still like to drink tea in the afternoon.'

Emboldened by Penelope's recent conversation, Alexandra said, 'Maybe you could give me some tips how to make tea properly here in France. I can never get it strong enough.'

'The secret is to persuade someone in England to send you proper tea, then it's simple.'

A few days later the postman delivered a large package to Alexandra.

'Oh, has someone sent you a present?' asked Stéphie, excited at the prospect.

'No, they've sent me a lot of papers which I have to read – a bit like someone sending me homework.' She smiled. 'And like the homework David and Jack set you, I have to do it. Why don't you go and see if David's made something nice for lunch?'

Antoine came into the hall. 'We're going to miss David when he has to go back to England.'

'And Jack,' said Alexandra.

'I think he may well stay a bit longer,' said Antoine, looking mysterious.

Alexandra undid the split pin that was holding the package together and peeped inside. Then she slid the papers out and saw that they were in closely handwritten French. She could barely read the words, let alone understand them.

'Let me know if you need help with your homework,' said Antoine.

She put the papers back into their envelope. 'I might need Maxime.'

'Maxime? Why?'

'It's legal stuff. From Switzerland. Very boring.' She smiled. It wasn't really a lie but it felt like it. She hated not being completely open but she didn't want Antoine knowing the details of her inheritance. It was bad enough that he knew she was due to inherit money without him learning that she could have her fortune now, if she just got married. She wanted him to see her as the nanny, not as an heiress.

*

213

It wasn't until the evening that Alexandra had the chance to look more closely at the papers. French legal language was as incomprehensible as she'd feared and she would definitely need help to understand it. She would ring Maxime when she could and ask his advice. He was a lawyer, after all.

Chapter Eighteen

It was early the following morning. Stéphie, who'd got into Alexandra's bed in the night, was fast asleep. Alexandra, unable to sleep longer herself, had come downstairs. When she'd seen to Milou and the hens, she had put a small, spotted mirror on the kitchen table and was cutting her fringe with the kitchen scissors when Antoine appeared through the back door. His arms were full of paper bags with baguettes emerging from the top.

'Haven't you got anywhere better to do that?' he asked. 'And don't you need a hairdresser?'

'I'm accustomed to doing it myself. Is it straight?'

Antoine put down his parcels and inspected Alexandra's handiwork. 'Close your eyes.'

She did and he blew on her, then he brushed away the remaining loose hairs on her face. 'There. That's perfect.'

She opened her eyes and wanted to shut them again. He was too near. He obviously felt the same because he stepped back quickly.

'It's funny, because I always cut my hair in the kitchen when I'm at home I do it here too. But you're right, the light is far better in my room.' Aware she was gabbling, she took a breath. 'But it's done now. The kettle's on the gas stove.'

Antoine seemed amused. 'I'll get the range going.'

Alexandra ground coffee in the hand grinder and found cups and plates for breakfast while he broke twigs and adjusted logs. He was humming and seemed happy.

'You seem full of the joys of spring,' said Alexandra. His English was so good she assumed he would understand her.

'I'm putting on a brave front. I can't put off leaving any longer. I'll have to go back to Paris again very soon.'

Alexandra's heart gave a lurch. 'Oh. The children will miss you.'

'Won't you miss me too?' he asked.

She turned away from him, unwilling to let him see how. 'Possibly a little bit. You're very good at dealing with the stove.' She was pleased with how matter-of-fact she sounded.

'Is that the only reason?'

Alexandra shrugged in a way that David would say was Gallic. 'What would you have me say? Milou will be very sad without you.'

He didn't reply immediately. He just looked at her in a way that made her wonder if she hadn't cut her fringe quite straight. 'You're very unusual for a nanny.'

'Nannies are supposed to be unusual. Haven't you read *Mary Poppins*? No, I don't suppose you have.'

'I'll miss you, Alexandra,' he said.

'Why?' She knew he wasn't going to tell her it was because he'd fallen in love with her, so she felt it was safe to ask.

216

'You're very good at putting me in my place. In my work I am accustomed to being treated like the boss.'

'Even Véronique treats you like that?'

'She does. As my second in command, she likes me to be top of the heap – does that make sense to you? – so that her position, as number two, has status also.'

'Antoine, would you mind if I asked you something?'

'Ask me anything!'

'What do you do that means you have to constantly keep coming and going away from home, away from your children?'

Antoine lost his flippancy. 'I am a management consultant.'

'Which is?'

'Companies get into trouble. Maybe they are threatened by their competitors and don't know how to respond, or they need new staff, or they have made financial mistakes. They need help. My company provides that help. When I go away, I spend time with these businesses that are in trouble.' He paused. 'We are not always welcomed by the staff and sometimes we cause people to be dismissed, but we help; we earn our money.'

Alexandra took time to think about what he'd said. 'Can I ask . . . No. I won't ask. It might be rude.'

'Why become tactful now, Alexandra? You are very good at speaking your mind even if you are only twenty.'

She was aware he was teasing her but felt she had nothing to lose. 'If you can tell people how to run their businesses so they're profitable and run well, why don't you look at the chateau as a business and see how it could be run to make enough money so you don't have to go away?'

He was silent for so long Alexandra refilled the kettle and put it on the range which was now going well.

'It hadn't occurred to me the chateau and the farm could be a proper business. It's always been a passion; I never thought it could be a way of making money.'

'You have several small outbuildings. You could turn them into accommodation for visitors. David had lots of thoughts about it.'

'I'll have to think about this.'

'You would need someone to run the bookings for you. And you'd need someone to organise everything, to arrange cleaners, to see about the bedding. A house-keeper.'

'And we need one here. I've just learnt that Mme Carrier isn't coming back.'

'If you did all this so that renting the buildings earned money, would you be able to stay at home more in future, do you think?'

He nodded. 'Possibly. I haven't thought about renting the buildings to holidaymakers before. My plan is for the children to go to boarding school, but not like the ones Lucinda has brought prospectuses for. One that could provide a cello teacher for Henri, for a start.'

'I do agree; the right school would be the best for them all, if you can find it.'

Stéphie was the first one down, rubbing her eyes and holding her book, which was *Snowball the Pony* by

Enid Blyton. 'You weren't there, Lexi. I wanted to finish the book.'

'I know, I'm sorry. I got up early. I had to cut my hair. Look!'

Stéphie frowned. 'It looks the same to me. Good morning, Papa.'

'Good morning, *ma petite*. Would you like a croissant? I've just brought them from the *boulangerie*.' Antoine held out the paper bag. Stéphie reached in and took one.

'Here,' said Alexandra to Stéphie. 'Have a plate for your croissant. Do you want butter or anything on it?'

'No, thank you,' said Stéphie.

'I'll make some hot chocolate,' said Alexandra. 'Ah, here's Henri.'

'Félicité is still asleep,' said Henri, taking a croissant from the bag.

'I'll need her to get up,' said Antoine. 'We're going out for the day.'

'Great,' said Henri. 'Or is it culture? I'm not keen on culture.'

'Dear boy, how can you say that?' asked David, coming in, Jack following him. 'Culture is all that matters in life.'

'You only think that if it includes food,' said Jack. 'Morning, everyone. What's the plan for the day?'

'I'm taking the family to visit an old friend of mine. He has young people around the same age and he's invited us to spend the day with them all.' He paused. 'I have to go back to Paris the day after tomorrow and I thought it would be nice to have a day out.'

Stéphie took a very deep breath. 'The day after tomorrow?' she said. 'The day after tomorrow? You are going away then?'

'Yes,' said Antoine gently, obviously trying to make it easier for Stéphie.

Stéphie threw down her croissant. 'It's my birthday the day after tomorrow!' she announced, and burst into furious tears.

Henri, who was nearest, gave her an awkward hug and patted her.

A few horrified moments ticked by.

'OK, I have an idea,' said Alexandra more calmly than she felt. 'In England the Queen has two birthdays. She has her own, ordinary birthday and an official birthday. Why don't we make your official birthday tomorrow? And then you can have another birthday on the actual day?'

'Ooh,' said Henri. 'Two cakes! How about that, Stéphie? There will be two cakes, won't there?'

'Of course,' said David.

'Does the Queen have two cakes?' asked Stéphie, whose tears had turned to outraged sniffing.

'Of course!' said David.

'How do you know?' demanded Stéphie.

'I know a thing or two about being a queen,' he said, giving Alexandra an almost imperceptible wink.

'I think two birthdays would be very special,' said Alexandra. 'And you can choose your cake. What kind of cake would you like?'

'I'd like one in the shape of Snowball the Pony,' said Stéphie, clinging to her indignation and still sniffing.

'Oh, darling,' said Alexandra. 'That will be quite difficult. I really meant what flavour cake.'

'I think it will be perfectly possible to have a cake shaped like a pony,' said David. 'Queens must have their wishes granted on their birthdays, real or official.'

'*Chérie*, I'm so sorry,' said Antoine, still at his most gentle. 'I didn't mean to forget your birthday. We can have it tomorrow instead. We'll have a lovely day.'

'It's horrible when a sad thing happens on your birthday,' said Jack, 'but maybe Antoine isn't going away for long?'

'I will be back before Christmas, I promise you,' said Antoine.

'And it's December tomorrow,' said Henri. 'We can have an Advent calendar.'

'I know it's December tomorrow,' said Stéphie. 'It's my birthday on the second!'

'I am so, so sorry, *chérie*,' Antoine said again, obviously stricken with guilt. 'How could I have forgotten?'

'What's going on?' said Félicité. 'Why did no one wake me?' Her hair was ruffled up at the back and she looked very young.

'Papa has forgotten my birthday!' said Stéphie.

'He can't have done,' said Félicité. 'It's the day after tomorrow.'

The grief and hurt went on until even Stéphie's siblings were starting to lose sympathy. Alexandra indicated that she wanted to speak to Antoine alone. They went into the courtyard to fill the log basket.

'Could you possibly put off leaving for a day?' she asked.

He shook his head. 'I need to be at the office first thing on Tuesday. I've put it off for longer than I should have done as it is.'

'Did you really forget her birthday?' Alexandra was still hurt on Stéphie's behalf.

'No! Yes! I got the day wrong in my head. I could kick myself. I have a present for her.'

'What she really wants is a pony,' said Alexandra.

'She can have a pony when I no longer have to go away to work.'

'When will that be?'

'Soon, I promise. I'll speak to David about his ideas and get a builder to come. Maybe David will tell him what is required—'

'In which case, promise her the pony,' said Alexandra firmly. 'But maybe you'll have to get three ponies.'

'If there's someone who can look after them, they can have as many ponies as they like,' said Antoine.

'Don't look at me! I'm a city girl.' She turned to go back into the house wondering if she was angry with him because she didn't want him to go to Paris either.

'What can I do to make it better?' he asked.

Alexandra shook her head. 'I don't really know. Maybe tell the people you're visiting today that you forgot her birthday. If Stéphie has a really lovely time she'll forgive you.'

'Can you come with us, Alexandra?'

For a moment Alexandra acknowledged how much she wanted to, but: 'I have to arrange a birthday. And make two cakes. One of them in the shape of a pony.' Now she'd said it, she began to feel daunted.

'I'm sure David will be able to do something creative. I need you with me.'

The words made her catch her breath. She came back sharply, desperate to mask her reaction. 'Then I really hope David will be able to make both cakes, M. le Comte!'

He put his hand on her arm. 'Alexandra, please don't be angry with me. It's bad enough with Stéphie and the others hating me for getting the day wrong for Stéphie's birthday.' His mouth was curling at the corners and she realised she couldn't stay angry with him for more than about a second.

She took a breath. 'Telephone your friends. Tell them about the birthday and warn them that I am coming. If they're cooking, they'll need to know that.'

'They've always thought you were coming, *chérie*.'

Alexandra felt she was on holiday as they set off in Antoine's car a couple of hours later. Still touched that he'd wanted her to go with them, she was determined to enjoy herself, although he confided (while they were waiting for Félicité to find the right jeans) it was because the friend, who lived quite far away, had mentioned his children went to a school that might be suitable. 'I need your opinion on these matters,' he said. It was still flattering even if he wasn't saying, 'I want to spend every last moment with you that I can.'

She turned round to look at the children. Félicité had been fairly maddening, trying to find exactly the right outfit. But Alexandra did understand. She'd always managed to feel fairly relaxed about it herself but there had been a couple of occasions when she'd been sent with a nanny to spend time with 'suitable' girls when she'd turned up in a smocked dress as approved by her relations and the girls in question had worn slacks.

Félicité was looking sharp, Alexandra decided. She was wearing well-fitting jeans and a white shirt with a sweater over the top. It was smart but casual. Stéphie's clothes were practically the same but she managed to look like a little girl in hers and not a sultry teenager. Alexandra smiled at them all. 'You're looking very nice, I must say.'

She was wearing a very similar outfit herself: jeans she had bought from the market and a Guernsey sweater of David's that had shrunk a little in the wash and he had passed on to her. Under it she had on a white shirt – the jumper was slightly itchy – and pearls in her ears. She had her Hermès scarf in her handbag in case Antoine's friends were smarter than she'd imagined. She'd recently acquired a pair of boots, designed for a young working man with a small foot, and felt they added a certain *je ne sais quoi* to her outfit. She didn't want to look like a run-of-the mill nanny.

'Mummy would want me to wear a dress,' said Félicité from the back of the car as they turned on to the main road, obviously not quite sure if she could trust Alexandra's assurance that jeans were fine.

'But you didn't want to wear a dress,' Alexandra reminded her.

'I know! But should I have worn the dress she bought the other day anyway?'

'I should just say that Henri and I are very proud to be escorting such stylish young women, aren't we,

Henri?' said Antoine, glancing in the mirror so he could see the back seat.

'What? Yeah. Of course.' Henri rolled his eyes but good-naturedly.

Stéphie giggled, quite over her disappointment about her birthday, for now at least. Alexandra wasn't the only one who felt it was like a holiday.

'We're going up into Haute Provence,' said Antoine. 'It's different up there, away from the tourist spots. It's beautiful, but rugged.'

'If this man is a friend of yours, why haven't we visited him before, Papa?' said Félicité.

'Because he lives a good hour away,' said Antoine. 'Also, I lost touch with him for a few years. He is married and has children. They are almost the same ages as you are.'

'Do they have young children?' asked Stéphie. 'I never have friends to play with.'

Alexandra saw Antoine looking guilty; he hadn't discovered the precise ages of the children and now felt caught out.

They'd driven up through hills and chalky mountains with scrubby bush and forests with oak and pine trees and eventually they arrived. The house was large and on a plateau, visible from the road a little way away.

There was a gate and Alexandra got out to open it. She felt a bit stiff and was immediately aware that the air was cooler here. Although it was nearly December, it had been warmer at the chateau.

A couple just a little older than Antoine were waiting as the car drew up in front of the house. And then several children appeared from different directions. They all seemed very pleased to see Antoine and his party.

There was a lot of kissing and then Philippe, who was Antoine's friend, looked at Alexandra, said, 'Antoine, you old devil, where did you find such a beautiful young woman and how did you persuade her to go out with you?'

Although Philippe had spoken in French, Alexandra responded in English. 'I'm the nanny, monsieur. Alexandra.'

'But you speak French, mam'selle?' asked Philippe. 'I do.'

Philippe shrugged and replied in English. 'If you tell me you are the nanny I have to believe you!' He gave the impression that he didn't believe this for a minute but in a way that was amusing rather than offensive.

'Forgive my husband,' said Nicolette, who was Philippe's wife. 'He is paying you a compliment but in a very clumsy way.'

The children, who were all teenagers, came up to Félicité, Henri and Stéphie, who were standing in a row not quite knowing what to do. A girl, about the same age as Félicité, said to Stéphie, 'Would you like to come and see some kittens? They are in the barn. We can also play ping pong?'

'What lovely children you have, Nicolette,' said Alexandra as they moved indoors.

'They like other children and Sandrine is very maternal. She will love having little Stéphanie to play with.' She handed Alexandra a glass of champagne from a tray and took one herself. Then Nicolette moved to the window, and Alexandra followed.

'What a beautiful view!' she said, and then realised it made her sound very English.

'But the chateau is also in a beautiful place?'

'Oh yes. I will be very sorry to leave it.' Alexandra hadn't intended to say anything remotely personal but possibly a few sips of champagne had loosened her inhibitions.

'I am sorry too, if you will be leaving. I think Antoine's children have been without a mother too long.'

'Oh, but Lucinda has come back! She's no longer in Argentina. She lives in town, with her mother.'

'Maybe I haven't remembered correctly but she is not the mother of the little one?'

'No,' said Alexandra. 'Sadly not.'

'And you can't stay? As their nanny?'

Alexandra shook her head, suddenly feeling emotional. 'No. I have relations in Switzerland. In the spring I must go and live with them, when the children are established in school, or have another nanny, or someone who can look after them when Antoine is away.'

'They will miss you!' said Nicolette.

'How do you know?' said Alexandra, smiling to cover the tears that threatened. 'They may hate me!'

Nicolette shook her head. 'They don't hate you. Antoine told Philippe all about you. Come, let us find the children. It is time for lunch.'

They were all in the barn. Félicité was playing table tennis with a boy who seemed a bit older than she was. Henri was looking at an old tractor with another of the boys and Stéphie was with Sandrine, on her knees, surrounded by kittens. They all looked extremely happy.

Lunch was hugely enjoyable for Alexandra, possibly because she wasn't responsible for any of it. A lovely young woman put dishes on the table, a man filled glasses, and she didn't have to get up once.

'This is delightful,' she said to Nicolette when the opportunity came up. 'Such good food and such well-behaved children. Yours are being so kind to ours.' Alexandra didn't notice her use of the possessive until it was too late. She did feel as if the children were hers, although it was a ridiculous thought.

'Their school – I can see Philippe is boring Antoine with the philosophy – focuses a lot on the children being kind to each other. And what are good manners if not kindness?'

Alexandra could think of people she knew who used what they considered to be good manners as weapons, to make others feel inferior. 'What indeed! So, are yours happy there?'

'Very. It's like a large family. Academic achievements are important but they are not the only thing. They do a lot of music and drama.'

'Henri will like that,' said Alexandra. 'He's very musical. But he will need someone to teach him the cello. He is really gifted.'

'The school has specialist teachers who come in for things like that. Henri would be encouraged and supported.'

Alexandra fell silent as she realised that Lucinda would have to agree to her children going to this school, and she probably wouldn't approve of it at all. And it might be very expensive, too. If it was small, it was bound to be.

'Can I pass you something?' asked Nicolette, indicating the *tartes* and gateaux that had been offered for dessert, possibly concerned by Alexandra's sudden silence. 'Or maybe more coffee?'

'No, thank you. I've had what one of my schools taught me to call "an ample sufficiency". English people don't really consider enthusiasm for food to be polite.'

Nicolette laughed. 'We must give you an opportunity to talk to my children about their school, when I'm not there. They will tell you the truth, possibly, because you are so much younger than their parents.' She smiled. 'Which is not to say that you are too young for Antoine. In many ways women are so much older than men, no?'

'Antoine and I aren't a couple,' Alexandra said urgently. 'Everyone makes a joke of it – I would do myself – but I am only the nanny.'

Nicolette seemed disappointed. 'Oh. I thought there was a spark between you.'

Alexandra was missing female companionship and she longed to share her feelings for Antoine. David was a close friend and she could tell him anything but she felt this needed another woman. Possibly if her feelings were brought out into the open, they'd melt, like snow in the sunlight.

'Shall we go for a walk in the garden?' suggested Nicolette a little later, as people got up from the table. 'We can meet the children in the barn.'

'I miss my women friends,' said Nicolette as they stood at the end of the garden and looked at the distant hills covered with scrubby pine and oak forest and the mountains beyond. 'Before I was married and had all these children, I had a job I loved and I worked with women. I don't regret giving it all up for this' – she made a gesture towards the view – 'or for my husband. But I miss other women.'

'I do too. I've lived most of my life in a fairly solitary way but recently I shared my house with girls my own age. I miss them now.'

'And you'd have told them if you were in love with your boss?'

Alexandra smiled. 'Yes. And I hope they would have told me how ridiculous I was being.'

'I don't suppose they would. Falling in love is very annoying. It's not always possible to choose the right person to do it with. Although Antoine is a good man, and of course very handsome. It's natural you should find him attractive.'

'I think I am too young for him.'

'Which is not to say that he is too old for you.'

Alexandra nodded. 'No. And in any case, when the children are settled, in one way or another, I will have to do my family's bidding and join them in Switzerland. I think they'd like me to marry my cousin Hubert.'

Nicolette was very amused. 'Does Hubert not take your fancy?'

'No, and more to the point, I don't take his. David, who is tutoring the children now, is of the opinion – and I believe him – that Hubert is . . . of the other persuasion.'

It took Nicolette a couple of seconds to interpret this and then she laughed. 'Don't give up on Antoine,' she said. 'Love has a way of getting what it wants in the end. Shall we find the children now?'

Getting the children to leave took some time. It was only when Antoine had been persuaded to let them take two kittens, pressed on them by Sandrine, that Félicité and Stéphie got into the car. Félicité also had a book, lent to her by Léo, the eldest boy. She'd blushed but taken the book willingly. Alexandra decided it wasn't her job to check the book was suitable. She'd recently discovered a stash of *Angélique* novels on a bookshelf in one of the bedrooms that she had recommended to Félicité, although Lucinda would no doubt be horrified. Alexandra felt no guilt; they were full of French history, which made them educational.

The first part of the journey was taken up with the kittens, who objected to being put in a box. It was only when they became tired, and accepted that sleeping on a warm lap being stroked by a gentle hand (the girls had a cat each) was an acceptable way to travel, that Antoine could really relax.

'It's a shame you were persuaded to promise everyone ponies when you could have got away with kittens,' said Alexandra quietly to Antoine.

He took his eyes off the road long enough to give her a look that made her stomach flip with desire. 'I hold you entirely responsible for the ponies.'

Alexandra suppressed a smile and looked out of the window. Perhaps Nicolette was right and there was a spark between them. Even the possibility made her very happy.

'I hope Milou will be kind to the kittens,' said Antoine as they approached the entrance to the chateau. 'You'll have to be very careful in the beginning. He's a big dog.'

'It's all right,' said Stéphie, full of confidence. 'Sandrine told me the kittens are used to dogs.'

'They have a dog that comes into milk when the cat has kittens,' said Henri. 'They'll be fine.'

Antoine and Alexandra exchanged an anxious glance. The kittens were tiny compared to Milou. They would have no chance if he decided he resented their presence.

The front door to the chateau was unlocked and a welcome warmth greeted them. Although it was warm enough when it was sunny, it was much cooler in the evenings now, and Antoine had begun to light the fire in the hall. David had lit it now and Milou was flat out asleep in front of it.

Before anyone could say or do anything, Stéphie put down the kitten she was holding. 'There you are, Snowball, that's Milou. He lives here too.'

Antoine put an arm round Alexandra's shoulder and clutched it, obviously terrified at the potential disaster.

The kitten, spotting the dog, jumped on all four legs towards him, every hair on end, looking like an angry feather duster made of swansdown. Milou, who had raised his head, hadn't taken in what was attacking him until the kitten gave him a biff on the nose. Then the ball of fluff ran up the dog's side and settled on his groin as if it were an established favourite spot. Milou looked at the little creature in utter amazement.

Félicité, seeing that Milou had yet to harm the little white kitten, set down the tortoiseshell kitten, as yet unnamed. This ran over to the dog in a much less aggressive manner, and the dog and the kitten sniffed each other's noses before this less assertive little animal snuggled in the dog's neck. Milou looked up at Antoine, obviously wondering what on earth had just happened.

'It's going to be fine,' said Stéphie as if this was never in doubt. 'Hello, David. I'm starving. Is there supper?'

'There's soup,' said David, looking at the kittens and the dog in amusement.

'What kind of soup?' asked Félicité.

'I can't be very specific. Let's just call it soup. I've had a very busy day getting ready for an official birthday.'

'Oh, I'd forgotten!' said Stéphie. 'Have you made me a cake?'

'Children!' said Antoine. 'You are being very demanding. David isn't here to cook for you.'

David smiled. 'Although, to be fair, I do cook a fair bit. I enjoy it. Now come along.'

'I'll just run up and wash my hands,' said Alexandra, not waiting to hear Stéphie ask why she needed to go upstairs to do it.

In fact, Alexandra wanted a moment to think about Antoine's arm round her shoulders. It didn't mean anything, she knew that, but she wanted to enjoy the feeling of connection it gave her. Just for a few moments she felt as if she was the mother in a family. Maybe it was because she'd grown up without close family of her own that she wanted to be part of this one. Looking at herself wonderingly for a few moments, she washed her hands, redid her plait and ran back downstairs.

Chapter Nineteen

Everyone was dipping bread in their soup and eating when Alexandra came back into the kitchen, except Stéphie, who was holding forth.

'Their school isn't all strict like the ones Félicité and Henri might have to go to. They don't have to wear a uniform and everyone is kind.'

She looked up as Alexandra came in. 'I do wish Papa would marry Alexandra, then when we go to school we can say we've got a mummy and a daddy just like the other children.'

'I'm not sure that's quite enough reason for them to get married, chicken,' said David.

But Stéphie had decided this was what should happen. 'Yes, but then if they have a little baby of their own, I can help look after it and I won't be the littlest in the family any more.'

'There are a lot of advantages to being the littlest,' David persisted, possibly aware that Alexandra, always so self-assured, was dying of embarrassment, particularly because Antoine was also there. 'Jack and I, and your grandmother, have spent all day arranging your party for your official birthday.'

'Ooh! Have you made me a cake?' asked Stéphie.

'Enough with the cake, already!' said David. 'But don't worry, there will be cake. Lots of cake. Penelope has invited us all to her house. It's going to be simply splendid.'

'Oh! I'd rather have it here . . .' said Stéphie, disappointed.

'You will have it where it has been arranged for you to have it, my little queen,' said Antoine, fond but firm.

'Penelope is looking forward to having it at her house,' David explained. 'She's gone to a lot of trouble to make it possible.'

'I think Stéphie is worried that Grand-mère is always so prim and proper,' explained Félicité, obviously not liking her sibling to be admonished.

'I do take your point,' said David. 'But Penelope is in a party mood! It'll be great fun. Jack is there now, helping.'

'How kind,' said Félicité, looking pointedly at Stéphie, obviously wanting her little sister to echo her words. Stéphie ignored her.

'The food's always great at Grand-mère's,' Henri piped up obligingly. 'Not that it isn't here, of course,' he added, looking doubtfully at David.

'We should check on the kittens,' said Antoine. 'And make a litter tray for them. Where are they going to sleep?'

'With me,' said Stéphie. 'With Milou. They can curl up together.'

'Well, go and see if they're still happy with each other,' said Antoine, 'and if the kittens have run up to the top of the curtains, we'll make another plan.'

*

Félicité came in to speak to Alexandra while she was finding a corner in Stéphie's room for a litter tray, which, she insisted, would have to be emptied every day or it would smell.

'Stéphie didn't really mean it when she said you wanted her to marry Papa. She's just little; she doesn't understand.'

Alexandra laughed. 'Oh, I know! And all that wanting to be the same as everyone else – she'll grow out of that. I wanted to be the same when I first went to boarding school and then I realised that the people I wanted to be the same as were really boring.'

As Félicité left the room Alexandra felt pleased that she'd been able to tell her something in exchange for being told Félicité wasn't remotely keen on her papa getting married again. Alexandra didn't blame her, and was heartily relieved that Stéphie had no notion about Alexandra's fortune being only a couple of marriage vows away.

Stéphie blew into Alexandra's bedroom early the following morning wearing jeans and a jumper, a kitten in each hand. 'I'm going downstairs now,' she said and vanished.

Alexandra lay in bed for a few minutes wondering if she should run after Stéphie and tell her to keep the kittens indoors, and wondering what on earth they were going to be fed on. Last night they'd had some leftover chicken. She knew she had to get up but couldn't face getting dressed. Her dressing gown would do.

'David!' she said as she arrived in the kitchen. 'No matter how early I get up, you're almost always here first!'

'It's a big day today, Lexi,' said David, ignoring her slight early-morning grumpiness. 'Let me tell you the plan.'

'I'd better check on those kittens before you do,' she said. 'I've no idea how to look after cats but I'm sure you don't just let them loose when they first arrive.'

'I'd agree with you, but if you look out into the courtyard, you'll see them running round after Milou like mad things. I think if you call him in, the kittens will follow. Stéphie too, if you're lucky.'

Stéphie came in first, red in the face and very happy. 'The kittens used the bathroom under the fig tree and Milou ate their leftover chicken which means it won't be wasted. I'm just going back out.'

'Well, there's a happy Official Birthday Girl!' said David. He turned to Alexandra. 'Perhaps you could have a cup of coffee and a croissant now. Yes, I have been to the *boulangerie* already.'

'Tell me everything then, David!' asked Alexandra a few moments later.

'Well, yesterday we went over to Penelope's and to her credit she understood right away that Antoine going away on Stéphie's birthday did constitute an emergency. She's organising the cake in the shape of a pony – although Stéphie will probably want a kitten now, or two kittens – and Penelope is going to make a proper Victoria sponge herself.'

'It's presents I'm worried about—'Alexandra began.

'No need! We heard of an antiques market, quite far away but so worth it! It was the last market of the season and it seemed everyone wanted to get rid of their stock before winter.'

'Oh! That sounds fun.' Just for a second Alexandra felt a stab of longing for the old days when she and David would have spent happy hours hunting out bargains together.

'It was. In fact, I did buy rather a lot of stock. It's being stored in someone's lock-up for now but sometime I'd like to get it back over the Channel and sell it.'

'I do appreciate how much time you've given up for me and the children, although it's for me really,' said Alexandra.

'Oh, darling! Don't apologise – I've loved it! And I've been thinking about getting a little place over here and specialising in all things French. I'd keep an eye on you, apart from everything else.'

'I'm going to be in Switzerland, David.'

'Not until next year. Anyway, let's get back to the matter in hand. Presents.'

'Oh, David I've been so worried! Although logically I'm sure Stéphie understands—'

'All sorted,' said David, not a little smug. 'Jack and I are giving her the nearly restored doll's house. We've done quite a bit of work to it since you first saw it.'

'Which is a very lavish present!' said Alexandra.

'And you are giving her the most divine toy bakery I think I've ever seen. It's at Penelope's. Jack is making sure it's in as perfect condition as it can be given it was made in the 1900s.'

'Jack stayed the night with Penelope?' Alexandra was a little surprised.

'He did; they are getting on rather well, I must say. Lucinda's there, after all, and she's being a brilliant chaperone.' He sounded a little acid, Alexandra thought.

'I suppose if it's your mother . . .' she began, trying to be fair.

'I understand that part,' he said, 'but Lucinda used the word "nanny" rather a lot yesterday – referring to you. And I know that technically you are the nanny, but you do have a name and she does know it.'

'Oh, David . . .'

'So while I was buying toy bakeries and a lovely little horse and cart – in case Stéphie's older sibs haven't got her anything – I bought you a jacket and some trousers which are new. The trousers are new, I mean, not the jacket, which is Chanel.'

'Chanel? David!'

'And – here's the best part – I managed to find some big pearls, just like the ones you used to wear in London.'

Alexandra got up and hugged him. 'My fake pearls! The ones that are in my trunk in Switzerland, that I love!'

'Very similar. I think it's important that you look glamorous for Stéphie's birthday party. She'd like that.' He was very firm.

'Would Stéphie care? She wants a party and presents. She won't care what I look like.'

'Well, I care. I didn't like the way Lucinda was referring to you.'

Alexandra smiled at David, thinking how much she appreciated having him in her life, to look out for her, to make her laugh, everything really. Then another worry occurred to her. 'Supposing Antoine hasn't got a present?' She jumped and blushed as Antoine came in.

'It's all right. I may have got the day wrong when I was making my travel plans, but I have got my daughter a present. I told you.' He sounded offended and haughty at the same time.

'Oh yes, so you did,' said Alexandra. 'Let me know if you'd like me to wrap it for you.'

'It's wrapped already,' he said. 'They did it in the shop in Paris when I bought it when I was last there. Véronique helped me choose it. She's very caring when it comes to my children.'

'Jolly good!' said Alexandra in English, glimpsing David rolling his eyes out of the corner of her own. 'I'll go and get dressed now.'

The party was to start at four o'clock, teatime in England. Everyone was dressed up in their best, apart from Félicité, who was going to wear her jeans if it killed her and everyone else around her. She came down the stairs last, when everyone else was waiting in the hall.

'Félicité!' said Antoine. 'Please! Put on a dress. You know your grandmother won't be pleased to see you in jeans.'

'She won't mind!' said Félicité with a toss of her head to indicate she didn't care. Although of course she did, Alexandra could see. She was fifteen and wanted to tell the world it was up to her what she wore, but she also wanted her father's approval.

'Why don't you put on that pretty pendant that Grand-mère gave you?' asked Alexandra. 'She'd be so pleased to see you wearing it.'

Félicité went back upstairs to put on the little gold symbol on a chain and Alexandra turned to Antoine. 'Just let her be. It doesn't really matter what she wears; this is Stéphie's day.' She spoke quickly, hoping he didn't think she was being presumptuous; she was a paid employee after all. Antoine was looking serious.

'Can I sit next to you in the front?' asked Stéphie. 'It is my birthday!'

'That's a brilliant idea,' said Alexandra. 'Here's Félicité! Let's all pile in. Just as well David went earlier. We'd never have managed to fit.'

'It's good that the kittens are having a nap,' said Stéphie, 'or they may have wanted to come with us.'

'Milou will look after them,' said Alexandra and slid across the bench seat so she was sitting in the middle.

'You're looking very smart, Lexi,' said Félicité, possibly grateful to her for having stuck up for her. 'I haven't seen those clothes before. And your hair looks very elegant in its chignon.'

Alexandra patted the back of her head, checking for escaping tendrils. 'Well, all my smart clothes are in Switzerland and David bought me this jacket from the *brocante*. It's Chanel! I put my hair up properly for once because it seemed only right that I should, for the jacket. But does it smell OK? Will your mother take one sniff and say, "Ugh! How unpleasant! It maybe couture, but it's still second-hand!"'

Félicité laughed. 'That's exactly what she'll say.' She sniffed. 'And then she'll say, "And soaking it with cheap eau de cologne doesn't help!"'

Alexandra was giggling now. 'I did slosh quite a lot on. And she'll probably tell me my pearls are obviously fake, too!'

Antoine turned round and looked at them, his expression one of complete bafflement. 'In France, women don't make jokes about clothes; they are too important,' he said. 'And it is considered bad form to be disrespectful about your mother.'

Alexandra and Félicité exchanged rueful glances, both trying not to laugh.

'So best behaviour, please,' he went on. 'OK?'

'Sorry,' said Alexandra, not at all ashamed. 'We'll be good, I promise.'

She could tell from the back of his head that he was laughing too.

Everyone was in a very good mood when they arrived at Grand-mère's elegant townhouse. Jack opened the door, holding it wide with a big smile. Inside it was *en fête* with flowers and candles, everything arranged to look festive and celebratory.

'Oh, I've never seen Grand-mère's house like this before!' whispered Stéphie, looking around her in awe.

'It's for your birthday,' explained Alexandra.

Félicité looked at her. 'We've had birthdays here before, you know, and Grand-mère has never put out candles and bowls of sweets.'

'It's probably my bad influence,' said Jack, looking pleased.

'We don't often have an official birthday to celebrate,' said Penelope, appearing from the salon, formal but obviously happy with the effect her efforts had produced. 'We also wanted to give Antoine a little party as he's going away tomorrow.'

Everyone was ushered through to the salon. Jack was opening a bottle of champagne seeming very at home when Alexandra caught a look Penelope gave him which he couldn't see. She was obviously very smitten. Alexandra felt a rush of joy at the prospect of Jack and Penelope finding love after being apart for so long.

She wondered if anyone else had noticed and was looking around to see when Lucinda came into the room. With her, arm in arm, was Véronique.

Just for a second, Alexandra was too shocked to move. She wasn't expecting to see Véronique and she had no idea that she and Lucinda knew each other. Seeing them together almost took her breath away. She was very grateful when David appeared at her side.

'I know they're looking as if they're bosom pals,' he said, reading her mind in a way that only he could. 'But they have only just met,' he breathed into her ear. 'I found out earlier. Véronique has an old friend in the area she's been staying with.'

Véronique having to stay at the chateau before with hardly any notice flashed into her mind. She could have stayed with her old friend and not made life so difficult for everyone in the chateau. And now she'd chummed up with Lucinda. Alexandra felt suddenly depressed.

'Antoine, darling,' said Véronique, leaving Lucinda's side. 'Surprise! I've been staying with my friend in the town and I met Lucinda and her mother in the *pâtisserie*, ordering her cake. I discovered that little Stéphanie was having a party and I thought, if I come, I can travel with you back to Paris. Won't that be fun?' She enveloped Stéphie in a hug which meant the little girl was crushed to Véronique's ear and smothered in silk jersey.

Alexandra longed to rescue Stéphie from suffocation, and was just about to cross the room to her side when Penelope put out a hand to the little girl and released her from Véronique's grip.

'Now, it is your party!' she said to Stéphie. 'Do you want to open presents? Or shall we have tea and eat cake first?'

'Cake! The obsession with cake!' said Lucinda, loud enough for everyone to hear.

Stéphanie looked at the mother of her siblings for a moment. 'Let's have cake first!' she said, sounding very English. 'I'm jolly hungry!'

Alexandra nudged David. 'That's my girl!'

Chapter Twenty

There was a long table set up in the dining room covered in party food and in the very middle was a horse made from choux pastry. It was sitting in a field of spun sugar and was very like the horse that Alexandra had repaired when she'd first arrived in France. Two large ovals held together by cream created the body and two smaller ovals made the neck and head. Cream exuded from the pony's sides, and all the details were in piped chocolate.

'Penelope had that made,' said Jack proudly to Alexandra while people were deciding where to sit. 'And while it does have a faint look of a very large swan, I think it's a really splendid effort at such short notice.'

'It's brilliant! I love it!' said Alexandra.

'Penelope made the Victoria jam sponge and I helped David make the chocolate cake. We wanted bridge rolls or little sandwiches but they're tricky in France so we have *tartines* instead. You see? Little slices of a *flûte* with butter and a bit of pâté on it. We all craved fish paste but actually the pâté is much nicer.'

'I'm sure!'

'And then we have a selection of gateaux from the bakery.' He smiled at Alexandra, his eyes crinkling at the corners. 'And now I'm on tea-making duty. You need an Englishman for that.'

'Can I help you?' asked Alexandra, falling on an excuse to leave the room.

'Of course,' Jack said.

But it was not to be. Véronique came bearing down on them. 'Alexandra!' She smiled. 'I'm going to be begging a room for the night. Antoine and I will be driving to Paris tomorrow but, naturally, we will need to leave early. It's more convenient for the main road from the chateau, rather than him having to drive into town and pick me up from here, so I will come home with you all later.' She wrinkled her nose. 'Too much perfume, darling. Far better to be more subtle about it. But you're very young, you'll learn.' Then she clicked her way across the parquet floor.

Alexandra didn't move.

'Penny for your thoughts,' said David, appearing from behind her.

'I'm just wondering if there's a more patronising person in the whole of France, or if she takes the prize.'

'Hm, well, she's certainly the most patronising person in this room. But I do see her point about the cologne.'

Alexandra regarded her old friend. 'I know, but eau de cologne is better than eau de brocante,' she said. 'Although I am so extremely grateful you bought me this wonderful jacket.'

His shout of laughter was loud enough to make everyone look at him. Alexandra went to stand by Félicité, who was keeping an eye on Stéphie. Not,

Alexandra was sure, because she might misbehave but because she might be enveloped by an adoring female who really wanted her father's attention.

'Can we all sit down?' said Penelope. 'Stéphie needs to blow out her candles and make a wish. And cut the cake,' she added, sending her daughter a look.

'That is a very beautiful jacket,' said Lucinda to Alexandra. Like Véronique earlier, she also wrinkled her nose but didn't comment on the smell.

The tea was over, and Penelope and Véronique were arranging Stéphie's presents in the salon. Véronique was taking a very personal interest in the process. Everyone else was standing around, chatting. Stéphie was beginning to get impatient so Alexandra was keeping her entertained.

'Yes!' replied Alexandra. 'It's Chanel. David bought it for me from a *brocante*.'

'A *brocante*? So it's second-hand? I could never wear second-hand clothes. But I suppose we have to cut our couture jackets according to our cloth.' She laughed to highlight her pun, which, annoyingly, Alexandra found quite funny although she didn't laugh.

Stéphie, who had overheard this conversation but only partially understood it, obviously felt her beloved nanny was being insulted. 'Lexi is going to inherit a fortune when she's twenty-five!'

'*Chérie!*' said Antoine, obviously hearing his daughter from a few yards away and heading to join them. 'We don't say things like that!'

'But it's true! Me and Lexi heard—'

Alexandra was too embarrassed to think of what to say immediately. She just put her hand on Stéphie's shoulder.

'One of you should teach that child that it's vulgar to talk about money,' said Lucinda.

'You started it!' said Stéphie.

Antoine and Alexandra inhaled sharply at the same time.

'Really,' went on Lucinda, still outraged. 'You're the nanny,' she said to Alexandra, 'and you consider yourself to be the child's father' – she turned to Antoine – 'you should teach this child better manners!'

Alexandra didn't hesitate. 'Come on, Stéphie, let's go and look at your presents.'

As she manoeuvred Stéphie out of the dining room, she saw Maxime in the hall.

'Do go and see Lucinda,' she begged, hardly giving him time to kiss her on both cheeks. 'I think you'll cheer her up. And I'd love a quick word later.'

'Alexandra!' said Maxime, throwing up his hands in a gesture of defeat. 'I was hoping for a very slow word later.'

Stéphie giggled and they went into the salon.

Véronique was tweaking her arrangements. She'd arranged the presents on boxes covered with a cloth on a table, so they looked as if they were in a shop window, although the presents were wrapped. There were little dishes with sweets and flowers in the spaces.

'Gosh!' said Henri, who had followed Alexandra's swift exit from the dining room. 'Look, Stéphie! Don't they all look special!'

Véronique inclined her head, looking past him to Lucinda, who had entered the salon hard on Henri's heels. 'It is so important to make things special for *la p'tite*. Poor little motherless child.' She said this last bit to Lucinda in a slightly gushing way that indicated not having Lucinda for a mother was a major setback.

Alexandra caught Félicité rolling her eyes and wondered how she felt about her father's colleague becoming matey with her mother. Not thrilled, she imagined.

'You've arranged the presents very prettily,' said Penelope in a way a teacher might congratulate a promising pupil. 'Jack? Antoine? Maxime? Come on in. Can you make sure that everyone has a drink and maybe Stéphie can open her presents?'

It occurred to Alexandra that perhaps Stéphie would like to do that without so much public interest and looked at Antoine to see what he thought, but the little girl seemed not to mind.

'Open this one first,' said Véronique, indicating the largest present. 'It's from your very generous papa. I helped him choose it when we were last in Paris together.'

'Yes, *chérie*,' said Antoine as Stéphie took off the paper. 'I do hope you like it.'

It was a toy *bureau de poste*. As Stéphie undid the box its beauty could be appreciated. It had everything and had obviously been expensive. There were toy scales, rubber stamps, envelopes, postage stamps, all sorts of forms to fill in, everything any self-respecting post office could possibly need.

Stéphie got up and ran to her father. 'Papa! It's wonderful! Thank you so much!'

'Ah,' said Véronique, fondly, 'I'm so glad you like it, little one. We tried very hard to find the very best one for you that we could.'

Stéphie gave Véronique a rather frightened smile. She picked up another box.

'That's from me and Jack, chicken,' said David. 'Actually, most of it is at your house. That's just something to put in it.'

Inside was a set of doll's house drawing-room furniture, elegant Louis Quinze style, with gold trim and velvet covers.

'What my friend is trying to say', said Jack, 'is that back at the chateau is a doll's house that we've been renovating for you. It's a bit of an antique, rather like its donors.'

Stéphie had some really lovely things and Alexandra was getting anxious about her present, as she hadn't seen it. It didn't need to be the best present the little girl received, but it had to be good enough.

It was a toy bakery. It opened out into a shop with shelves and for the shelves were a plethora of plaster cakes, baguettes, loaves, gateaux, croissants, everything a good *boulangerie* would sell.

'Lexi! Thank you!' Stéphie rushed in for a hug.

'I'm so glad you like it,' said Alexandra, returning the hug. 'David chose it. I didn't know about your birthday until too late, but it is lovely, isn't it? We can have a lot of fun playing with it together.'

'I am so sorry that I won't be able to play post offices with you,' said Véronique, apparently suddenly aware that playing with a child was something you were supposed to do. 'But I will be with your papa, on important business.'

Antoine came and crouched down, to inspect the bakery, which was already having its shelves filled with tiny meringues. 'When I come back, Stéphie, we will play together more. I promise.'

Stéphie looked around at the adults, who were all looking at her as if she were the main performer at a circus, and began to whisper in her father's ear. While she was telling her father what she needed him to know, she kept glancing at Alexandra. When finally she'd finished, Antoine said, 'It's simply not possible. I am so sorry, little one.'

Alexandra was convinced she had been the subject of the conversation and then was equally convinced she was being neurotic.

Lucinda had apparently become bored with not being the centre of attention. 'Maxime? Take me out to dinner, please. I find children's parties so exhausting.'

'It's too early for dinner,' said Penelope to her daughter. 'And I'm surprised you have found the occasion so tiring. You didn't involve yourself in the preparation.'

'Children are so overindulged these days. I'm sure I never had such extravagant gifts when I was that age.' She gave Stéphie, who was now selling croissants to Jack, a critical look. 'Of course I understand that you are all over-compensating for the fact that the child has no parents.'

Alexandra found herself confronting Lucinda, not quite sure why she was so outraged but before she could think of something cutting to say, Lucinda turned her disdain on to her. 'As for you, the nanny, I hope you don't think anyone believes those enormous pearls to be real. They are quite obviously not!'

Secretly delighted to have this insult to repel, Alexandra pulled out the end of the pearls. 'David? How much did you pay for these?'

He shrugged. 'They were part of a job lot of things I bought. A couple of francs, maybe?'

Alexandra took one of the pearls between her teeth and scraped, pretending to look for the gritty feel she knew would not be there. 'You were robbed! They're fake!'

Everyone laughed, enjoying the way Alexandra had turned the situation. Then Maxime took her arm and separated her from the group. 'Lucinda will scratch your eyes out if you're not careful. She is not a woman who likes other women, especially those who make jokes at her expense. Now what was it you wanted to talk to me about?'

It took Alexandra a second to remember. 'It's a legal matter. I have some papers from my family in Switzerland and I can't understand a word of them.'

'I'm sure I can help. Would you like to bring them to me? Or shall I collect them?'

'I'll bring them,' said Alexandra. 'I have some errands to run in town anyway. And Maxime?'

'Yes?'

'It will all be confidential, won't it?'

He was offended. 'But of course! Totally confidential.'

Alexandra gave him an extra warm smile to placate his wounded feelings. 'Thank you.'

*

Eventually, the party began to draw a close and Alexandra turned her mind to where she should put Véronique. She went into the hall so she could think and, to her surprise, Antoine followed her.

Partly because she was embarrassed to be on her own with him, Alexandra spoke quickly. 'Do you think, as it was short notice, Véronique would sleep in the little room beside yours?' she asked. 'It's got clean sheets on the bed, and—'

'No,' he said firmly. 'Véronique cannot stay with us. She can spend another night with her friend. I can pick her up from here perfectly easily.' He walked back into the group.

Alexandra watched his retreating figure as if he was a hero about to rescue a dog from a burning building.

'What did you say to Papa at the party that was so secret, Stéphie?' asked Félicité, when at last everyone was in the car (the children in the back this time) and they were finally on the way home.

Stéphie started to speak but Alexandra interrupted, worried about what she might say. 'She won't want to tell you in the car in front of everyone,' she said quickly before Stéphie, who was probably perfectly happy to do so, could confide. Alexandra couldn't be sure, but she was worried that Stéphie had said something to her father about her fortune, which was fast becoming a curse rather than a benefit. 'If it was a secret then, it's a secret now.'

There was a certain amount of huffing and tutting and almost audible eye-rolling from the back seat, and Alexandra exhaled.

'Véronique and my mother don't approve of you, Lexi,' said Félicité, possibly wanting to make trouble.

Alexandra saw Antoine frown and draw breath, possibly to tell off his eldest daughter.

'What makes you think that?' asked Alexandra, turning round so she could smile at Félicité.

'I heard them talking. You don't dress properly for a nanny and are far too sophisticated.'

'They're entitled to their opinion,' said Alexandra calmly.

'They don't think you should mix with people as if you were on the same level. At least, that was what Véronique said, and then my mother—'

'That's enough, *chérie*,' said Antoine firmly.

Alexandra mouthed 'tell me later', partly because she couldn't resist hearing what Véronique and Lucinda thought about her, and partly so Félicité wouldn't be mortified by being told off. Antoine couldn't really be described as strict, Alexandra thought, but he wasn't weak, either.

Chapter Twenty-one

Although it was very early, all three children and Alexandra got up to see Antoine off. Antoine had remembered it was Stéphie's real birthday and gave her a very grown-up box of chocolates – the kind of box you would want to keep long after the chocolates were eaten – and Stéphie was pleased.

It was heartbreaking but all the children were brave and no one cried, although Alexandra, who almost felt she shouldn't be there, felt tearful. The kittens and Milou did their best to help. Milou was serious, obviously understanding his beloved master was going away, and the kittens thought everyone had got up early to entertain them.

'Happy Birthday, Stéphie!' said Alexandra, the moment they had all come back into the chateau after seeing Antoine shoot off down the drive. 'Let's go and have a birthday breakfast. What about pancakes and chocolate spread?'

Although six o'clock in the morning was early for so much chocolate, it did help. But as she turned pancake after pancake on to a plate on the table whence they disappeared with terrifying speed, Alexandra decided the partings had to stop. It was just so sad saying goodbye.

When David appeared later it was to find them all smeared with chocolate, feeling faintly sick.

'Happy birthday, Stéphie!' he said. 'And good morning, everyone else. Pancakes for breakfast? Excellent choice. Later, if you're feeling up to it – maybe after a bit of a nap' – he nodded to Stéphie who was yawning – 'Jack and I thought you might like to see your proper present from us? But I warn you, it's a bit like this chateau . . .'

'How can it be?' asked Henri.

'It's beautiful, but needs a bit of restoration in places,' David went on. 'Look, the kittens have gone back to bed.' He gestured to where Milou was lying on his rug and the kittens were lying on him. One was in his groin, presumably because it was warm where he had less fur, and the other was on his neck. They all looked perfectly happy with the situation.

As he and Alexandra cleared up, the children having gone off, either to sleep or to read, he said, 'It's quite worrying to think that all the dog needs to do is turn his head and snap, and both those kittens would be gone. He reminds me of Antoine, rather.'

Alexandra wiped her sticky hands. 'Milou does?'

David nodded. 'He has a lot of power but chooses not to use it.'

A week later, Alexandra set off on her own into town. At home, the children were helping David and Jack renovate the doll's house. Henri was learning maths doing the measurements, Stéphie's nimble fingers were proving very adept at woodwork, making very tidy dovetail joints to create an *orangerie*, like the one in the chateau grounds. Félicité was painting a tiny piece of wallpaper with birds and exotic flowers which was destined for the salon in the doll's house.

'Who'd have thought a doll's house could be so educational,' said Alexandra as she said goodbye.

'The University of Life,' said Jack. 'It will teach us everything if we only open our minds.' He bowed, to indicate he knew he was sounding pompous and didn't expect to be taken seriously. 'Talking of which, I've heard of a group of young musicians that Henri could join. It would be good for his music and his social life. Do you think Antoine would approve?'

'I'm sure he would. You could take him? Bring him back?'

'Of course,' said Jack with a smile.

When Alexandra went upstairs a few minutes later she felt that it wasn't only Henri who would benefit from the sessions with other young musicians; Jack could use the hour or so while Henri was with the group to visit Penelope.

Alexandra had with her a very large parcel that was mostly layers of newspaper, wrapped round a box, in which the now mended soup cup nestled. David had packed it for her with all an antique dealer's care. The papers that had been sent from Switzerland and were going to be discussed with Maxime were in an envelope, thrust into the old post bag that was Alexandra's handbag.

Alexandra was looking forward to having some time on her own. Growing up, she had been very used to her own company and although subsequently she'd become accustomed to sharing her house, she found her present situation took up almost all her time and she missed solitude. And while she loved her charges and found looking after them very satisfying, sometimes it was nice only to have to think about what she wanted to do, rather than worry about the needs and wants of three children and a dog. (The kittens looked after themselves.)

Visiting Maxime was first on her list.

He had welcomed her with the friendly charm that always managed to make Alexandra feel better, and now she was sitting on the comfortable sofa and chairs he had in one area of his office. He had offered coffee and wine, and she accepted a glass of water.

'So how can I help?' he asked with his usual attractive smile.

Alexandra smiled back, wondering why she didn't fancy Maxime. He was so much more suitable as a love object than the man who occupied almost all her thoughts.

She handed Maxime the envelope that was showing signs of having been stuffed in a bag a little bit too small. 'Can you interpret this for me? I asked Hubert to send me something in writing about my possible inheritance. I've always known I wouldn't inherit anything until I was twenty-five so I've never thought about it much – it so far away from being mine. But the other day, when my relations visited—'

'The formidable cousins, the less formidable Hubert, and the very beautiful car . . .'

'You were there! Well, I overheard my female cousins talking about my fortune.' She smiled at his slightly shocked expression. 'Being brought up from a distance, as I was, I learnt to survive by stealth. I'm afraid listening at doors was sometimes necessary. Anyway! I overheard them saying that I'd come into my fortune before I was twenty-five if I got married. Which was a bit of a shock, I must admit. I felt I really should understand my inheritance properly and asked Hubert to send me details. He has, very kindly, but I'm not much better off as I can't understand what he's sent me. Could you look over it for me and check there's nothing else there I should know about? I speak French better than I can read or write it and these documents are full of words I don't understand.'

'Ah!' Maxime said, raising his hands in a way that told her there was no shame in not understanding. 'It is another language, even for a Frenchman. We learn it when we are studying to become lawyers. Would you mind if I looked now? Or would you prefer to go away and I'll tell you what I think another time? Perhaps look at the magazines we have provided for clients? Not that you need magazines to look chic. You are always so elegant.'

Alexandra found this genuinely amusing, thinking about the dresses and boiler suits she'd bought from the market. 'I'll happily sit here and read. It will be good for my French.'

A little while later Maxime put down the papers. 'There is nothing concerning in here. It says that if you were to marry, your fortune – quite a lot of money, Alexandra – now I understand the beautiful car! – will come to you. Otherwise, you have to wait until you are twenty-five. So nothing that you don't know already.'

'I suppose my cousins felt that if I knew I'd come into my fortune when I married, I might be tempted to accept the first boy who asked for my hand, just to get my hands on the loot, as we might say in England.'

'Have many boys asked you?'

'A few, but none of them were serious.'

'So what if Antoine were to ask you . . .?'

'He won't!' said Alexandra – too sharply, she realised afterwards. She laughed to soften her reaction. 'Why should he? I am the nanny for the children!'

'I hate to be the one to tell you this, Alexandra, but in France it is not unusual for the master of the house to—'

She broke in quickly. 'Antoine is different. I am different! He would never . . .' She swallowed as she realised just how true her words were. 'He would never take advantage of me.' While that was true, she also knew he wouldn't be tempted. She was too young. He thought of her almost as one of the children, she was convinced. 'Anyway,' she said, smiling, 'I won't get my inheritance if I just have an *affaire*, will I?'

'You are right when you say that Antoine is not like that. He wouldn't do anything dishonourable, but he might well want to marry you. You are beautiful, his children adore you as you adore them, you would make the perfect chatelaine for the chateau.'

'Maxime! Only in romantic novels does the hero marry the governess, or the nanny, or the serving wench. Not in real life!'

Maxime was not convinced. 'You are not the same as other nannies. Your presence at the chateau alarms Lucinda and Véronique.'

Alexandra shrugged. 'I am only temporary, until someone better can be found.'

'Has Antoine been looking? I feel he would have asked me for help if so. He hasn't asked me to help him with advertising for the post either, or with looking at candidates sent to him by an agency. I think he is very happy with you.'

Alexandra felt herself blush. It wasn't something she was prone to, but she was suddenly certain that Maxime had guessed about her crush on Antoine. She straightened her back. Even if he did suspect, he couldn't know for certain. 'I certainly love the children and I think Antoine appreciates that.' She paused. 'Should I leave those documents with you, do you think? For you to study? Or do we know all we need to know?'

'I think we know all we need to know for the present, Alexandra. If you consider getting married to anyone other than me, come back and we can discuss things some more.'

She smiled and got up. 'I most certainly will.' She put the papers he handed to her back into the post bag. 'Now I am going to have lunch with Penelope. I do hope Lucinda isn't there!'

Penelope was on her own and was very welcoming. Alexandra was ushered into the salon and given a glass of wine. When they'd made toasts and tasted the wine, she produced her wrapped parcel.

'Here it is. I hope it's all right. David wrapped it for me. He didn't trust me to do it.'

'This is very exciting. That little cup has been missing a handle for so long.'

They admired the shell-like bowl of deep blue with gold decoration. It was extremely pretty and when it was put back in the cabinet with its fellows, no one would have known it had been repaired.

Later, when Penelope had both thanked and congratulated Alexandra on the skill of her repair, they sat at a little table in the window of the dining room for lunch. Penelope had prepared an elegant lunch for them. She brought in plates with salad, hard-boiled eggs, ham and olives while Alexandra looked about her. Most of the room was used for playing and listening to music.

After a moment, Penelope said, 'I expect you feel a bit lonely, sometimes.'

Alexandra appreciated this disregard for conventional conversation although it was rather unexpected. Penelope had a reputation in the family for formality, but she seemed to have softened lately. She looked younger, as if a light had gone on inside her.

'David and I are very old friends and he's great company but I do miss my female friends sometimes. We were all on a cookery course together and they shared my house in London.'

'Why don't you ring them? Would that be possible? A long chat on the telephone can be very restorative.' She handed Alexandra an antique sauce boat with mayonnaise in it. 'For the eggs,' she said and then looked at Alexandra, waiting for an answer.

'I hadn't thought of it, to be honest. And of course I wouldn't want to run up Antoine's phone bill.'

'I would consider the occasional call home to England one of the perks of the job.' Penelope smiled. 'Sometimes English slang comes back to me. I am sure Antoine wouldn't begrudge you a phone call.'

'And I could always make a note and pay him for it.'

Penelope laughed. 'If you insist, but I doubt he'd want recompensing. How are the children's lessons going?'

'Well! I really admire the way David and Jack manage to turn everything into a lesson. They're helping with the renovation of Stéphie's doll's house and it's amazing how much maths is required.'

'This is how the school Antoine wants to send them to works, I gather. Lucinda is very opposed to it. She wants them to go to school in England, make influential friends and possibly be very unhappy. They've had such an unconventional beginning; I don't really think that's the answer.'

'I went to boarding school having had a very different upbringing from my classmates. Once I stopped trying to fit in and was just myself it was fine, but it took a certain amount of nerve.' Alexandra felt a bit awkward talking about schools with Penelope as she didn't really think it was her place. She changed the subject. 'This is delicious mayonnaise. Mme Wilson, who taught me and my friends cooking in London, would be very impressed.'

Penelope was not to be diverted. 'I don't like to think of my grandchildren being so far away, in England, in places where they may not understand them. And Stéphie is far too young to be sent away.'

'Would you never go back to England to live your-self?'

Penelope's shrug made her look very French. 'Well, possibly. I would prefer not, really. I have my friends here, my house. I am accustomed to the way of life now.' She paused and Alexandra thought she looked a bit embarrassed. 'What about your friends? Would they consider staying in France?'

'I can't answer for Jack, I don't know him very well, but David might easily. He could travel to and from England to do his antiques stall and I know he'd like to specialise in French antiques. I'll miss him when I go back to England myself.'

'You'd go back to England? Why would you do that?' Penelope obviously felt this was a very eccentric idea.

'I'm English! I live in London! I'm only here tempo-rarily.'

Penelope leant forward and put her hand on Alexandra's. 'It's up to you. When you find the one you love, do not run away because you fear they may not love you. Don't make the mistakes I made.'

But it wasn't the same for her, Alexandra thought. She might be in love with Antoine but he wasn't in love with her, and although she could hang around for months and months if she really wanted to, it wouldn't necessarily change anything.

Penelope seemed lost in her own thoughts and Alexandra didn't like to interrupt them. Eventually Penelope said, 'It's a funny thing but it seems to me that one gives advice to others that really you should be taking for yourself.' She sighed and smiled and then changed the subject. 'We have a couple of meringues for dessert. Having Lucinda here, who disapproves of anything she considers fattening, has made me want to eat sweet things even more.'

'She does have a lovely figure,' said Alexandra.

'So have you, but you don't wear a girdle or refuse to eat anything sweet. I'll make some tea. No one here appreciates tea. It's pleasant to share it with someone who does.'

As she was crossing the town square on the way to the chemist, Alexandra considered Penelope's words to her, repeated as she was leaving the house. Summed up, they were: don't turn your back on love; talking things over with an old friend is helpful; and, finally, don't be afraid to use the telephone, even for a call to England.

The doll's house seemed to be the focus of everyone's attention when she got back, and because of this, Alexandra was able to find some time to telephone her friend Lizzie. She really hoped that her friend would be able to have a chat.

Apparently she'd picked the perfect moment. Lizzie, being seven months pregnant, was perfectly willing to abandon her housework to talk to her friend. Alexandra made herself comfortable at the desk in Antoine's study and opened her heart.

When she finally went to the kitchen to make dinner she found Stéphie already there. Alexandra had left the study door open but she hadn't heard her pass. Still, she seemed happy enough, although she gave Alexandra a slightly strange look.

'I'm missing Papa,' said Stéphie a bit later as they ate the chicken casserole Alexandra and David had created. 'I want him to come home!'

'He's coming home for Christmas,' said Félicité.

'I want him home now!' said Stéphie.

'Oh, Stéphie!' said Henri. 'We can't make him come home now. He's working! You know how it is.'

'Christmas is nearly here,' said Alexandra. 'We should start getting ready. We've only got two weeks.'

'We don't really get ready,' said Félicité. 'We go to Grand-mère's on Christmas Eve. Her friends come too. It's quite boring. Then on Christmas Day we write thank-you letters for our presents. Twelfth Night is better.'

'Do we have to go to your grandmother's?' said David. 'Why don't we have Christmas here in the chateau instead?'

'We've never done that,' said Henri.

'But it doesn't mean it's not possible,' said Jack.

'We could have an English Christmas!' said Alexandra. 'Tell us what you usually do. Then we'll say what we do, and then we can do the bits that we like from both! How about that?'

'Planning it is the best part, I think,' said David. 'All the food, making the puddings, the mince pies, the Christmas cake.'

'I don't think we have any of those things usually,' said Henri.

'Will you be here for Christmas, David?' asked Alexandra, suddenly aware that David and Jack would be perfectly entitled to time off for the festive period.

'Darling,' said David, rolling his eyes in horror. 'I told you last year how utterly ghastly my Christmases often were.'

'What's "utterly ghastly"?' asked Stéphie, diverted, as David had intended she should be.

'Christmas for me if I can't spend it with you lot, that's what!'

'Do tell us,' said Alexandra, who knew he'd make the children laugh and so cheer everyone up.

'I have to go and stay with my two maiden – that means they're not married – aunts who live in a very dreary suburb in the outskirts of London. It's not proper London, with bright lights and festivity, and it's not the country, either, with pubs and carol singers. It's in between.'

'And what are your aunts like?'

'Well, they don't hold with alcohol as a rule,' said David, 'but as it's Christmas we're allowed a very small glass of sweet sherry each. They've been using the same bottle for years. When we've drunk our sherry, we have lunch. Everything has been cooking for a very long time which means we don't have to actually chew. We have boiled potatoes instead of roast ones because they're more digestible and we have lumpy Bird's custard with the pudding. Bird's custard is made with a packet, Stéphie, and should never be confused with proper custard. Then after lunch we listen to the Queen's Speech on the wireless. And then we open our presents, which doesn't take long. They give me socks, I give them handkerchiefs and a box of New Berry Fruits, which is what they like best. Then I go home and find an old friend to get drunk with.'

'Our Christmas won't be a bit like that!' said Alexandra. 'Jack? Will you stay for Christmas?'

'Certainly will!' said Jack, enthusiastically. 'I usually go to my brother and his wife – they're a lot younger than me and have children which makes it much more fun than David's Christmas. But this year, I want to spend it with you.'

And your lady-love, added Alexandra silently.

'We'll have a brilliant time,' Alexandra said. 'We'll do everything we like best and miss out the New Berry Fruits which are, I have to tell you, absolutely disgusting. We'll have chocolate truffles. We can make them ourselves. And, Stéphie, by the time we've organised everything, your Papa will be home!'

Chapter Twenty-two

❧

Antoine was due home in a week's time when Maxime, who had become a frequent visitor, called at the chateau with a message from him.

'He's bringing Véronique home for Christmas,' he announced.

The joy and excitement which Alexandra was feeling vanished like snow in the rain. 'Oh,' she said, handing Maxime a glass of wine. He'd already been invited to stay for dinner.

'Yes. He didn't want to surprise you with an unexpected guest.'

'Considerate of him,' said David, looking at Alexandra, who found herself blushing.

'Why didn't he tell us himself?' she asked. 'And wouldn't she be happier staying with her friend in town?'

'Maybe the friend didn't invite her,' said Stéphie.

Maxime, who was possibly feeling awkward at having to deliver bad news, sipped his wine. 'Apparently he tried to telephone several times but no one has ever answered.'

There was a pause. 'We've been busy!' said Alexandra, still feeling affronted. 'It's Christmas.'

There had been a lot of shopping, and Henri's music group was now meeting twice a week practising carols. Jack and Stéphie had started making characters to supplement the *santons*, the traditional clay crib figures that had been found in the attic. There weren't nearly enough animals, in Stéphie's opinion. They'd made a workshop in one of the old stables, out of earshot of the telephone, and so had missed Antoine's calls. Félicité was painting a background scene with palm trees, shepherds and sheep on the hills and a heavenly host with real gold paint.

'Does Véronique have to come?' said Stéphie. 'I hate the way she hugs me all the time.'

Alexandra and David exchanged glances. 'I know!' said David, who had completely taken over Christmas catering plans. 'Why don't we invite lots of people to come for Christmas? Could you come, Maxime?'

'For Christmas Day? Yes! Christmas Eve is the important day in France,' he said presumably for Alexandra's benefit, who already knew this.

'Excellent!' said David. 'We are having an English Christmas.'

'Penelope is really looking forward to it,' said Jack. 'We all are,' he added awkwardly. 'But can we just invite everyone here instead of going to Penelope's house? We just work here. We don't own the place,' he went on.

'I think it's perfectly permissible for you to invite people for Christmas,' said Maxime, after a quick glance at David. 'You will be doing the work and I'm certain Antoine won't grudge extra money spent on food and wine at this time of year. As his lawyer, I give permission on his behalf!'

'Oh, thank you, Maxime!' said Alexandra, putting an arm round his waist and giving him a little hug. 'If we choose who we invite we won't feel as if we're being invaded by Véronique. I don't think having her in charge would be much fun.'

'She'd want us to wear ghastly frilly dresses,' said Félicité. 'Like Grand-mère, although worse.'

'Have you got dresses like that in your wardrobe?' asked Alexandra, suddenly thinking she should know the answer. It hadn't occurred to her to go through her charges' wardrobes. She washed the clothes they wore and put them on their beds when they were dry.

Félicité nodded. 'I like the colour of mine, but it's very babyish.'

'If you can still fit into it, we could adapt it. Otherwise, we'll get rid of it,' said Alexandra. She pulled her hair over her shoulder and began to plait it. 'We're going to make Christmas really special!'

'Bravo!' said Maxime, raising his glass in a toast.

'Come on, let's eat,' said David. 'Félicité? Find a knife and fork for Maxime, there's a dear.'

Alexandra was doing the washing up and Félicité, who had become far more amenable lately, was drying, when Alexandra said, 'Where shall I put her?'

David, who was at the table shelling walnuts for a cake he planned to make, said, 'Well, you don't want to end up giving her your bedroom again.'

'You mean Véronique?' said Félicité. 'Isn't there a room near where you and Jack are sleeping?'

'There is, but it's a bit . . . well, put it like this: it needs work,' said David.

'A lot of work?' asked Alexandra.

'Not sure,' which indicated to Alexandra that he was sure, and it was in a bit of a state.

'Let's look at it tomorrow,' said Alexandra and reached for the last dirty saucepan. 'We can see what needs to be done then.'

Félicité came with Alexandra to inspect the walls of Véronique's potential bedroom the following morning.

'It's a pretty room with lovely views,' said Alexandra. 'And it's near a bathroom. We could ask David to share the bathroom with Jack at the end of the passage.'

'But it has a large damp stain on the wall,' said Félicité.

'Yes.'

Alexandra was just considering which was less work: repainting the wall, or giving up her room to Véronique, when Félicité said, 'I could paint a mural.' In spite of her casual tone, Alexandra could tell she wanted to do it and was nervous in case her idea was rejected. 'I've been wondering about doing one in my bedroom. I've enjoyed doing little ones for the doll's house and the crib, and have been thinking about doing a much bigger one.'

'What about paint? Where would you get it?'

'I'd use house paint, I think,' said Félicité. 'I'd need some small brushes for the detail. Do you think it's a good idea, then?'

'Excellent!' said Alexandra. 'Apart from looking really good, the smell of paint would disguise the smell of damp!'

Félicité laughed. 'You really don't like Véronique, do you?'

'Well, do you?'

'No. It's such a shame that Papa seems to.'

Alexandra deliberately didn't look at Félicité. She didn't want to see pity or anything like that in her eyes. 'Make a list of what paint you need. Have you an idea what you'd like to do?'

Félicité shrugged. 'I'd need to think about it for a bit. Then I'll get David or Jack to take me to buy what I need.'

'Good idea. We'll count you having to work out how much to get as a maths lesson.'

Félicité laughed, obviously delighted that her idea had been taken up so positively.

As Alexandra and Félicité walked back through to the main part of the chateau together, Alexandra reflected she was mad to let Félicité undertake a project like this when she herself was so busy and couldn't help. But she was delighted by Félicité's enthusiasm and her newly discovered love for art and design.

Four days before Antoine and Véronique were due to arrive back, David, Alexandra, Henri and Stéphie set about decorating the hall.

According to the children, usually no one did much about decorating the house at Christmas beyond setting up the crib. Antoine was always away until the last moment and whoever was looking after the children had their own houses to think about. Thus, when Alexandra, aided and abetted by David, announced they were going to be 'decking the halls' in a major way and explained what this entailed, everyone was excited. And while Milou just got in the way, the kittens obviously thought the whole venture was for them. They ran up every ladder, chased every spray of ivy and turned the curtains into a climbing frame and raced each other up and down them at great speed.

Henri and David went into the chateau grounds with saws and axes and buckets to gather greenery while Alexandra and Stéphie arranged the crib. It was set on a beautiful table in the hall, and the old clay figures and the newly carved wooden ones jostled for space in the stable. The baby Jesus was hidden behind the crib, to be put there at midnight on Christmas Eve. The Three Kings (on camels, with several donkeys, some the size of elephants) were on another table. They wouldn't join the stable scene until Twelfth Night.

After they'd found every vase, pot and jar – anything that held water and might be useful for greenery – Alexandra lit the fire. The weather had turned really cold in the past week and Alexandra had had to borrow a couple of old sweaters from David to wear on top of her boiler suits to keep warm.

When the greenery arrived, everyone went a little crazy and only recovered when all the receptacles had been filled and the banisters, the picture rails, every picture and mirror in the hall had been draped. The pots were distributed so every room (including the loo) had at least one vase of greenery including bay, rosemary or winter-flowering viburnum filling the air with fragrance.

The salon was perfect, with candles in every candlestick and candelabrum that could be found. Cushions were plumped, furniture was arranged just so and

Stéphie had declared that, from now on, no one was allowed to go in and sit down. All the best vases were there, looking stately and festive and smelling wonderful.

The hall was much less formal. There was greenery in buckets, branches of pine trees in chimney pots. It had a medieval feel to it, and was just a bit crazy.

The four of them, David, Alexandra, Henri and Stéphie, were just admiring their handiwork when Jack came in through the front door.

'Good Lord!' he said, having taken in his surroundings for a few seconds. 'Is it Christmas or is David putting on the Scottish Play, and this is Birnam Wood?'

'It's Christmas,' said Stéphie indignantly. 'Anyone can see that!'

'Sorry!' said Jack. 'I got confused for a minute.'

Then Félicité appeared; she had been painting her mural. 'It's very . . . lavish,' she said, looking doubtful. 'Not like we usually have it at all.'

David and Alexandra looked at each other. 'We should probably get hold of some tinsel,' said David.

'Or baubles, at the very least,' Alexandra said.

'No, no! It's perfect!' said Jack hurriedly. 'Don't add another thing. And the smell is wonderful! Oh, and Henri? I met Jules from your music group in town.' He produced an envelope. 'He gave me this for you.'

'What is it?' said Stéphie.

Henri had opened the envelope. 'It's an invitation to a party. The day after tomorrow. It says, "Please bring your pretty older sister."'

Alexandra's sprits slumped a little and she hoped Félicité and Henri would both declare they didn't want to go. She would have to ask Antoine and imagined speaking to the chain of command on the telephone until she got to Véronique. She would either say no on Antoine's behalf or refuse to let her speak to him. And of course they couldn't go without his permission.

'A party?' Félicité's eyes lit up.

'Yes,' said Henri, looking at the invitation. 'It's from a boy who's at the school we might go to.'

Alexandra became more anxious, especially as Félicité looked as though she definitely wanted to go. Could she forbid it? But maybe it would be fine. It might be a formal party, overseen by strict parents. That would be fine, she could surely say yes to that. But then again, if the boy was at the school Antoine had been thinking of sending his children to, the party wasn't likely to be formal.

'Can we go, Lexi?' asked Félicité, who, Alexandra noticed, had bright pink paint in her hair.

'When is it?'

'I said, the day after tomorrow,' said Henri.

'I'll have to think about it,' said Alexandra. 'I wonder if I can get in touch with your papa? Then we could ask him.'

Félicité rolled her eyes at the ridiculousness of this suggestion. 'Papa had to telephone Maxime to tell us he was bringing his "colleague".' The inverted commas she put round this word were audible. 'We'll never be able to track him down!'

'It's not the same . . .' Alexandra began and then stopped. Félicité's body language was telling her she didn't think her papa would approve. Which made her decision a lot easier. Except – Félicité and Henri were teenagers! They had very little social life. Was it fair to forbid them to go to the one party they'd been invited to?

She went into the salon, disobeying Stéphie's instructions, and lit the fire that had been laid ready. She wanted some time to herself to think about things. Jack came in with a glass of Muscat for her.

'Guaranteed to aid thought,' he said. 'I'm sorry. I shouldn't have just given Henri the invitation. I'm assuming you're in here wondering if you can let them go to the party?'

Alexandra nodded and took the glass. After a sip of the sweet but musky wine she said, 'Would it look crazy if I went to the party with them? I just feel they should be going to parties, having a nice time. Mostly they're here in the chateau, happy enough, but Félicité – she needs to meet boys! She's growing up! And Henri should meet a few girls who aren't his sisters.'

Jack sat down opposite her and added a log to the fire. 'I think that's the perfect solution.'

'The nanny going to the children's party with them? To make sure they eat bread and butter before cake and say thank you properly afterwards?'

Jack laughed. 'You don't look like a nanny and you're hardly older than they are!'

'I'm twenty!'

'That's not very old. Keep your hair in that plait over your shoulder you've been wearing lately, put on your blue jeans, you'll fit right in.'

'Thank you, Jack. It's a compromise. I'll ask them about it. They can choose to have me along or not go. But I feel I have to give them the opportunity.'

*

It was the day of the party – two days before Antoine and Véronique were due to arrive for Christmas – and the house was almost ready. Every downstairs room was decorated. Presents had been bought and wrapped and put in a huge barrel brought in from one of the stables to keep them away from the kittens, who had discovered a passion for unwrapping anything with paper on it. Another huge barrel contained the Christmas tree, cut from the grounds and lavishly decorated thanks to a bargain struck in the market by David, whose ability to get a bargain was not hampered by his eccentric use of the French language.

That evening, Stéphie (who had had to be heavily bribed) was already at her grandmother's making animals out of salt dough, a process Penelope had learnt from a German friend. So it was Alexandra, Henri and Félicité whose outfits were being given the once-over by David and Jack (who also wanted the address of the party).

Alexandra wasn't accustomed to dressing so she wouldn't stand out. Her style had always been a bit out of the ordinary, but tonight she wanted to look like a standard teenager. Under her leather jacket (another *brocante* purchase) she was wearing jeans, a black polo-neck jumper (without the outsize pearls she longed to add) with her hair in a plait. Henri and Félicité also wore jeans. Henri had a navy sweater with his and Félicité a stripey top. Alexandra and Félicité had added black eyeliner and mascara.

'I don't look like the nanny chaperoning her charges at a children's party, do I?' Alexandra asked. She had memories of uniformed nannies hovering over small children in frilly dresses in smart London houses. The nannies certainly hadn't made the parties any more fun.

Everyone inspected her. 'No,' said David and Jack, horrified and amused.

'You look fine!' said Henri. 'Now can we go?'

'You just look a bit older than us,' said Félicité. 'I could tell people you didn't want to be left alone in the chateau except I never tell anyone I live in a chateau unless I really can't help it.'

Alexandra nodded. 'I used to be careful who I told I lived in Belgravia – which is a rather grand part of London. So, I've got the car keys, we all know the address. I've got money for emergencies, in my bag and in my bra – we're set!'

Alexandra wasn't quite as gung ho about setting out in the dark to an unknown destination as she pretended, but logically she felt it should be fine so she was refusing to let herself worry. Getting Félicité and Henri to accept her going with them had been a bit tricky but when they realised it was either take her or not go, they'd accepted it. Alexandra was grateful they were in rural France and not somewhere where there was public transport. Otherwise she couldn't have stopped them going without her.

Eventually they found the house, on the outskirts of Saint-Jean-du-Roc, and Alexandra found a space to put the car. Most people had not so much parked as just stopped their cars, so finding somewhere near the house was tricky.

But the sight of the cars encouraged Alexandra. She wouldn't be the only slightly older person there. She was clutching a bag with a bottle of wine in it. According to Henri, it was expected. She wasn't sure how French parents would regard this sort of thing so just resolved to not drink at all herself and try and limit what her charges drank. She wasn't looking forward to the evening at all.

'We'll leave our coats in the car,' she said. 'Then we don't have to spend hours finding them.' The shenanigans that sometimes went on in bedrooms containing piles of coats was not something Alexandra wanted her charges to witness. 'Is everyone ready? Then *on y va!*'

Chapter Twenty-three

Johnny Hallyday singing 'Let's Twist Again' in French hit them as soon as the front door was opened by a black-clad boy with long hair and a pale face. He regarded them for a couple of seconds before nodding. They all went in.

It was a fairly wild party, far more grown up than the groups of girls and boys too shy to speak to each other that she'd half expected and definitely hoped for. Alexandra could tell that Félicité and Henri were half enchanted and half terrified. She felt a bit like that herself. It was so noisy, so hot, so full of young people dancing. The smell of aftershave and sweat was a heady combination. But it was too late to turn them round and take them home; they'd never speak to her again.

Henri spotted his friend and led the way to him. They exchanged some words in French that Alexandra couldn't hear or understand.

Henri shouted to Alexandra and Félicité that they should have a drink. Alexandra wondered if she could forbid them to drink alcohol. She decided not but she'd have to keep a close eye on how much they had. As Henri and Félicité followed Henri's friend the only thing she could do was to tag along behind.

There was a long table covered in bottles and paper cups. There was wine of various sorts, lemonade in big bottles, Orangina in little bottles as well as something called Pschitt! and bottles of beer.

Alexandra arrived just as Félicité was being handed something by the young man who'd let them in.

'It's just wine and lemonade,' Félicité said. 'Don't worry! I won't get drunk.'

Alexandra accepted a cup of the same thing and realised you could only taste the lemonade, which meant you could very easily get drunk quite quickly.

'Only have two,' Alexandra said to Félicité. Henri was having a beer, which she thought was preferable.

'Don't fuss!' said Félicité, gulping down her drink and holding out her paper cup for a refill.

Never had Alexandra felt so unqualified to do her job. How was she expected to keep her charges safe? She should never have said they could go to this party.

Just then a boy tapped Félicité on the shoulder. Félicité put down her cup and followed the boy on to the dance floor. Alexandra breathed more easily. She was delighted that Félicité had been asked to dance and was being accepted into the party. If she was dancing she wasn't drinking or doing anything else she shouldn't be doing.

Henri was talking to a group of boys and seemed to be on his first beer. As neither of her charges had had too much to drink, she could relax a little. She'd said they'd leave the party at eleven. She only had to keep them safe for another three hours.

Before she could think further, someone pulled her on to the dance floor.

As she could see Félicité dancing, she didn't object to this boy expecting her to go along with his wishes. She copied him and did the twist. While the dancing was fast, it felt safe. It was good to dance, she realised, and when another boy wanted her to jive, she remembered the steps from another party, back in England.

Alexandra soon found she was quite popular. No one spotted her as being older. In fact, the age range of the guests was quite wide. She was by no means the oldest, and nor were Henri and Félicité the youngest. Alexandra found this reassuring. It felt like a family party. There could be no objection to that.

However, a bit later, while Alexandra was drinking a bottle of Orangina to quench her thirst, the lights went down. It was apparently time for 'le slow'. Quite a few young men wanted to get Alexandra on to the floor for this one and she had to be quite sharp in her refusals. But then she thought that maybe she should have danced because she'd have been able to spot Félicité better. When the music changed and it was still slow, and some other young man tried his luck with Alexandra, she accepted. She allowed him to put his hand on the back of her neck but wouldn't let him dance cheek to cheek. She was here to look for her charges.

She saw Henri quite quickly. He was still chatting with other boys his age and, when the music ended, Alexandra got rid of her rather affronted dance partner and went to speak to him.

'Where's Félicité?' she asked in English.

He shrugged and shook his head. 'Dunno.'

'I really need to know where she is!'

'Are you looking for Henri's sister?' asked a friend, obviously proficient in English. 'She went outside.'

'Outside? Really?' Alexandra went to look for her.

The outside area was full of couples taking advantage of the darkness, which was relieved only by one light fixed quite low to the side of the building. It took Alexandra several minutes to find Félicité.

She was being thoroughly kissed. Alexandra's first instinct to grab hold of the boy doing it had to be suppressed because Félicité was kissing him back with enthusiasm. She wasn't being forced to do anything she didn't want to do. Alexandra turned away. What should she do? Watch from afar like some weird chaperone?

She moved to where the light was better so she could check the time. It was only ten o'clock. She couldn't drag her charges home yet. She'd promised that they could stay until eleven.

Alexandra went back to the dancing. 'Le slow' was being enthusiastically indulged in. She felt a bit surprised there were no parents visible. She'd always got the impression that French children were more closely chaperoned than English teenagers, but she remembered that Henri's friend went to the progressive school that Antoine's children might well go to and realised that his parents might have given their children more liberty. Although she'd never thought this before, now she felt a couple of stern parents turning on the lights and turning off the music would be a jolly good thing.

The air was blue with cigarette smoke – something else she now disapproved of. Alexandra had never

285

smoked after she'd nearly passed out when she'd tried it when she was at boarding school. All the party-goers' clothes would have to be washed before they could even be put in the wardrobes, they would be so impregnated with the smell.

She had just spotted Henri, who was in the control of a very attractive blonde girl who knew exactly what to do with a boy who had probably never been kissed, when a man came up to her.

He was wearing jeans and a leather jacket similar to the one Alexandra had left in the car. He had slicked-back hair and a medallion round his neck. His almost tangible air of entitlement was possibly caused by the admiring looks that the other young people gave him as he passed.

"Ello,' he said, in English. 'Why are you all alone? Has your boyfriend abandoned you? Let me take his place.'

He pulled her on to the dance floor and Alexandra wondered if anyone ever asked anyone to dance in the old-fashioned way, or if women were always pushed and shoved about as if they were cattle. But as she had to pass the time somehow, she went along with it. She kept her head turned, so most of what this man had access to was her ear. She was aware the other girls were looking at her with envy.

The man got fed up with not getting what he wanted from a slow dance. 'Come with me,' he said, and led her outside. Alexandra went because she wanted to check on Félicité, having decided she would try to make her leave the party early. The combination of boredom and anxiety she was currently enduring was deathly. Also the attentions of the probably self-appointed 'leader of the pack' might yet become seriously annoying.

She allowed him one kiss, and she put her arms round his neck so she could look at her watch. Carefully, she transferred it to the other wrist, so it caught the light and she could see it better. Time was going so slowly.

Kissing wasn't enough for this man who could, he seemed to think, have any woman he wanted; he pushed his hand up her jumper, trying to undo her bra. She was not having this! When grinding her foot on to his instep only made him more determined, she brought her knee up sharply between his legs.

'*Putain!*' he said, staggering back. Alexandra was braced for a further attack but the man just spat on the ground near her. 'English whore!' he said loudly and pushed his way through the small crowd who had gathered.

'I think we'd better go,' said Alexandra to Félicité who, hearing the commotion, had left her boy and joined her.

'We certainly should,' Félicité agreed.

'That's Tito,' said Félicité's boy, who had followed her over. 'No one crosses him.'

Alexandra suddenly felt a bit shocked. She'd probably been in greater danger than she'd realised. 'We need to find Henri.'

'I'll get him,' said the boy. 'You shouldn't go back in there. Go to your car and wait there.'

Félicité came with her. Once they were a little way from the house and the possibly hostile crowd, they stopped, waiting for Henri. Nerves got to Alexandra and she started to laugh. Félicité joined in. 'That was very impressive, what you did back there!'

Alexandra shook her head. 'It's a technique. I'll show you how to do it. Where's Henri?'

'He's coming now,' said Félicité. 'Jules will fetch him.'

Thinking that Jules was turning out to be kind and responsible, Alexandra began to feel guilty. She was the one who had nearly got herself into trouble, not her fifteen-year-old companion.

'Did you have a nice time, Félicité? Did I drag you away from a really nice boy?'

'It's OK,' said Félicité. 'We exchanged numbers. On a cigarette packet. And,' she went on, too excited to remember she shouldn't be confiding in the woman who was effectively her nanny, 'he goes to the school Papa wants us to go to but he comes home every weekend.'

'That's great!' said Alexandra. 'Ah, here's Henri. I hope he's all right. He seems to have make-up smeared on his face.'

'I'm glad we left our coats in the car,' said Henri. 'I saw the room where they were kept. The pile of them was a mile high. It would have taken ages to find them.'

At least he'd only seen a pile of coats, thought Alexandra as they all got into the car.

Alexandra enjoyed the drive home. Now they were away from the party and she could stop worrying, it seemed much more fun in retrospect. She must make sure Félicité learnt how to get rid of men she didn't want groping her – as far as it was possible; she was sure no one else would teach her.

'Did you enjoy the party?' she asked, accidentally slipping into being a nanny. 'I mean – was that fun?'

'It was a bit of a shock,' said Henri. 'I mean – girls! – but yeah, it was good. And it means I'll know a few people when we go to that school.'

'Mm,' said Félicité. 'It was a bit frightening, but yes, it was fun.'

'It was a bit frightening for me, that's for sure,' said Alexandra. 'But I've been through worse.' She was thinking of a time in England when she and her friends had had to leave a party in the country rather suddenly.

'What? Because of Tito?' asked Félicité. 'You were so brave!'

'No. He was a creep who felt he could do what he liked with women. I've met types like him before. No, I was worried because I was in charge of you two. I didn't want to spoil your fun, but I didn't want you to do anything dangerous either. But never mind. We'll soon be home, drinking hot chocolate, discussing boys.' She paused. 'Not you, Henri. You don't have to discuss boys.'

'I don't mind,' said Henri.

As Alexandra turned the car into the drive and saw a car parked in front of the chateau that hadn't been there before she had another strong attack of déjà vu, when her house in London had been full of lights when it should have been dark.

Please let this be friends of David or Jack, she prayed in the two seconds before it was clear whose car it was.

'It's Papa!' said Félicité excitedly.

'Tell me quickly,' said Alexandra. 'Are you two allowed to go to parties?'

289

'I don't know,' said Henri. 'We've never been invited to one before.'

Alexandra was going to drive the car round to the stable yard where it was kept when the door of the chateau opened and Véronique came out. It seemed rude to ignore her so she parked the car behind Antoine's.

'Where have you been!' demanded Véronique. 'And what have you done with Stéphie?'

Alexandra decided not to engage in conversation until everyone was out of the car and in the house.

Antoine was in the doorway with Véronique by the time this had happened.

'Papa!' said Félicité, running to his arms. 'You're home early!'

'And you're home late, *chérie*,' said Antoine, returning the hug. 'Where have you been? And where is your little sister?'

'We've been to a party,' said Henri, going in for a hug. 'Stéphie's with Grand-mère.'

'Thank God she's safe!' said Véronique, clasping her hands to her chest.

Alexandra didn't say anything. It was far better if the explanations came from the children, she felt.

Antoine looked down the length of his long nose at Alexandra, his expression entirely inscrutable. She couldn't think of a single thing to say. His children were safe, had suffered no injury, although now she heard them talking to their father she realised they may have had a little bit too much to drink. Yet she felt guilty, remiss and a bad carer.

'I can't believe you allowed the children to go to a party without their father's permission!' said Véronique.

'Excuse me,' said Alexandra. 'If I could just squeeze by you and get into the house?'

She had forgotten how beautiful the hall looked, dressed for Christmas and smelling strongly of pine, rosemary and sweet box. Alexandra found the fragrance very calming. Milou came up and gave her a gentle woof of welcome, his two satellites dancing along behind him. She rubbed his neck and under his chin. The kittens ran up her leg and landed on her shoulder. 'Hello, you lot. Have you been good?'

She was tired suddenly, and would very much have liked to slip upstairs and go to bed without any more conversation, but she knew that wasn't possible.

'Véronique, as Félicité said, you're earlier than expected and your room isn't ready,' said Alexandra.

'I've put my things in the room where I was before,' said Véronique. 'I threw all the clothes that were on the bed on to the chaise longue. You don't need to tidy it until tomorrow because I'm very tired and need to sleep now, but can you please put clean sheets on the bed?'

No, Alexandra decided, she could not put clean sheets on her bed so that Véronique could sleep in it. But nor did she have the energy to spend much time arguing. 'I'll certainly find you some clean sheets,' she said, smiling warmly as if this was a generous gesture. 'We are halfway through preparing you a very lovely room at the other end of the chateau, near where David and Jack have their rooms.'

Before Alexandra could go up to the linen cupboard, David appeared in the hall, wearing a very flamboyant dressing gown which he may well have acquired from a Noël Coward play.

'What on earth is going on?' he said. 'Oh! The master of the house has arrived! Welcome! Shall I make everyone a snack?'

Even Véronique found it difficult to continue to be so frosty now. David's presence was so benign and welcoming it affected everyone.

'I'm starving!' said Félicité and Henri, as one.

'So am I,' said Antoine. 'Let's stop standing round in the hall – which does look beautiful – and go through to the kitchen.'

Alexandra slipped upstairs and found sheets for her bed. She laid them on top so Véronique could find them and rescued a few bits of her own and took them to Stéphie's bedroom. She also scooped up anything she really didn't want Véronique to find and then went back downstairs.

David was the master of the creation of meals and hot drinks at a moment's notice and Antoine had got the range going in a way only he could, as well as producing a bottle of brandy and glasses.

Véronique obviously realised the wisdom of going with the general mood. She accepted a glass of brandy and a little piece of toast with pâté. David had obviously rustled up a plate of these to keep people going while he made a rich cheese sauce for Welsh rarebit.

Félicité and Henri got through nearly a whole *flûte* toasted with pâté.

'So,' said Antoine when there was a pause after everyone's initial hunger was satisfied. 'Tell me about this party.'

'You should never have let them go to a party!' Véronique said again, addressing Alexandra. 'What were you thinking?'

'I was thinking – or rather I thought – that it was nice for Félicité and Henri to be invited to a party at Christmas,' she said. 'But as I didn't know the hosts, I decided the best thing to do was to go with them and disguise myself as a fellow guest.' This last bit was meant as a joke but only David gave a humph of amusement.

'And we all came back safely,' said Félicité. She glanced at Alexandra. 'Alexandra didn't take her eyes off us, all party.'

Antoine laughed. 'How very – annoying of her.'

Alexandra looked at him properly now she wasn't overcome with unnecessary guilt. 'It must have been very annoying but I didn't know what else I could do to keep them safe.'

'You could have forbidden them to go!' said Véronique. Then she looked at the plate David had put in front of her: golden cheese sauce on toasted baguette, browned under the grill and sizzling. Her outrage subsided.

'I think we have established that the children were safe,' said Antoine calmly. 'We'll talk about it tomorrow, Alexandra.'

Chapter Twenty-four

Alexandra got up as soon as she was awake the following morning. She wanted to be first up, to take control, and also to see Antoine before Véronique was around to make things difficult.

She had seen to the animals, ground coffee, got the range going, washed up any remaining glasses from the previous night, set the table and put all suitable breakfast food on it and yet still jumped when Antoine appeared in the kitchen. She took a quick breath. Usually, she was a confident person, not afraid of anyone, but in the presence of Antoine she felt like a small child who'd done something naughty.

'Good morning! Would you like some coffee? Then I could make you scrambled eggs?' Too late she remembered they were in France and he probably wanted a croissant or bread and butter. 'I haven't been to the *boulangerie.*'

He regarded her in that slightly amused, slightly bemused way that he had, the way that set off the butterflies that had been perched in her stomach, ready for flight, ever since she'd first met him. She took another breath, wondering if she should open the conversation about the party or if she should leave it to him.

And then Véronique came in. 'Good morning! How are you, *chéri?*' she asked Antoine. 'Alexandra.' She gave her a formal nod and then sat down at the table. 'Oh, no croissants?' She looked questioningly at Alexandra and then gave a little laugh. '*Ah non!* I dare say you are suffering from *la gueule de bois.*'

Alexandra laughed politely at this pleasantry, which wasn't intended to be pleasant at all. '*Pas du tout!* I drank very little alcohol last night, and none at the party. I have no hangover.'

'Would you like me to fetch fresh bread and croissants?' asked Antoine.

Véronique shook her head. 'No, no. I wouldn't put you to the trouble. Milou!' She pulled away from the dog who'd decided to get up from his place in front of the range to check if there was anything likely to fall from a breakfast plate. 'You seem to get bigger and bigger! I'm sure you'd be far happier living in a kennel outside. And as for the cats—'

'They are Stéphie's,' said Antoine. 'They have grown a lot since we went away but are still very – kitten-like.'

'Of course I adore animals!' said Véronique. 'But they should be kept outside the house.'

'I could go to the bakery and maybe collect Stéphie at the same time,' suggested Alexandra, who suddenly wanted an excuse to leave. 'Although you'd have to wait a little while for breakfast.'

'I'm sure you have quite enough to do,' said Antoine with an easy smile. 'I'm more than happy to pick up Stéphie.'

'I'd love to come with you! Little Stéphie is so sweet!' said Véronique. 'And, Alexandra' – she said her name as if it were an honour that she'd remembered it – 'I slept very well in that bedroom so maybe if you take your things out of it, I can stay there.'

'I'm afraid that's not possible,' said Alexandra, her smile just as polite and cold as Véronique's had been. 'I have all my Christmas presents in there as well as my clothes. It would be quite impossible for me to move out permanently. Or even until the end of the Christmas holiday.'

'Surely it's only good manners to suffer a little inconvenience for your guests?'

'Of course, but we have been planning a very charming room for you at the other end of the chateau, where we normally put guests.' Alexandra realised she was making a rather grand statement here but ploughed on with it. 'Félicité has been decorating the room. Ah, here she is! And Henri.'

Never had Alexandra been more pleased to see Félicité and Henri, who now felt like dear friends. 'You've put a lot of work into Véronique's room, haven't you, Félicité?'

Félicité, whose hair needed brushing, nodded and sat down. Henri sat down next to her. No one spoke. Alexandra hoped that they weren't suffering from a *gueule de bois*. They may well have had more alcohol at the party than she knew about.

Antoine surveyed the table. 'I think maybe I will have scrambled eggs, Alexandra. If they are still available?'

'Of course.' Alexandra found the pan she liked best for eggs and put a large lump of butter in it.

'Of course they are available if you want them!' said Véronique, clearly thinking Antoine was being far too diffident about making his wants known. 'If English people can indeed cook eggs,' she added with a smile implying that they definitely couldn't.

'Can I have some?' asked Félicité, reaching out for bread. 'Oh, it's yesterday's.' She withdrew her hand.

'We don't eat yesterday's bread in France, you know,' Véronique explained kindly, as if it were possible that Alexandra didn't know this.

'Yes,' said Alexandra, her teeth beginning to clench. 'But I can't go shopping and scramble eggs. Not at the same time.'

She sent mental messages to David to come and take over the eggs so she could escape to the *boulangerie* to buy baguettes and *pain de campagne* and possibly a *pain au chocolat*, which she would eat in the car. They'd have to think about other meals too. Without Véronique and Antoine to be considered they'd planned very simple things so that attention could be paid to the Christmas feast. Now everything was going to be harder work and a lot less fun. Not that she'd think this if only Antoine had arrived unexpectedly early, of course.

David and Jack came into the kitchen when everyone except Véronique, who preferred to nibble on stale bread rather than anything Alexandra had produced, were eating eggs.

'So sorry I overslept,' said David. He looked across at Alexandra. 'But Alexandra's scrambled eggs are better than mine, so you've done well.'

'I might run out for bread,' said Alexandra, getting to her feet.

'I'll go,' said Jack. 'I expect you're needed here.' Too late he caught her silent message that she needed to escape. 'Although of course if you'd like to go—'

'We will need to think about food,' said David, who seemed to think of little else just at the moment.

'I'm sure Antoine will tell you what he wants, David,' said Véronique. 'Could I have some more coffee?' she went on, addressing Alexandra.

'Although I'm more than happy to help,' said David, suddenly very dignified, 'I am here as the children's tutor. Alexandra is their nanny. There seems to be some misunderstanding about our roles here.' He gave Véronique his most charming smile. For someone who was usually so affable and easy-going, he could be devastating if he wanted to cut someone down to size.

'I realise that our early appearance has upset your plans,' said Antoine. 'If you could give us a list, we can shop for you?'

'Can I go with you to get Stéphie?' asked Félicité. 'There's something I want to do in town.'

'We'll be busy when we go to town,' said Véronique. 'We won't have time for you to catch up with friends.'

'Oh, are you going with Antoine?' asked Alexandra, who knew perfectly well that was Véronique's plan. 'I was hoping to settle you into your bedroom.'

'Enough!' said Antoine, getting up from the table. 'I will go into town to collect my daughter. I will bring her siblings with me. Before I go I will see what needs to be bought for the household. Children? Can you please get ready to leave the house in five minutes.'

He stalked out of the kitchen, Milou and the kittens following, which made Alexandra want to giggle.

Véronique did not want to giggle. She was obviously furious but couldn't express it.

In the end Véronique got into the car while David was finishing the shopping list and Henri was finding his shoes.

Although Alexandra was annoyed that Véronique had gone against Antoine's express wishes and appeared to get away with it, having her out of the house was a definite relief.

'I can say this to you now she's not here. I find Véronique sucks the joy out of everything,' said Alexandra, gathering breakfast dishes.

'She does,' David agreed, filling an enamel bowl with boiling water. 'But we won't let her spoil our Christmas. There's always a difficult guest you have to invite. It's traditional.'

Alexandra laughed. 'You always make me feel better about things.'

'I'm so glad.' He carried on washing dishes in silence for a few moments while Alexandra wiped the table and put away the detritus of breakfast. 'Lexi?' he asked.

'Mm?'

'Have you had a chance to look at the mural Félicité is painting in Véronique's proposed bedroom?'

Alexandra's heart sank a little. 'No. Why?'

'Well, I haven't been in,' said David. 'But when I was passing and she'd left the door open I couldn't help seeing . . .'

'What?'

'It's a little bit – wild.'

'Let's go and look when we've finished here. I'm not giving Véronique my bedroom, I'm just not!' she said. 'Or is that silly?'

'Let's look at the room and then you can decide,' said David.

'Well,' said Alexandra a few eye-opening minutes later, 'it's certainly vibrant.'

'There wasn't a huge range of colours when we went to buy the paint. But there were lots of different shades of green,' David said.

'So a jungle theme makes perfect sense. And that parrot is brilliant!'

'Félicité copied it from an old book I got from the *brocante*. It's a shame the mural isn't finished.'

'Well, she thought she had another two days!' Alexandra was suddenly worried. 'Will Véronique be OK in here?'

'Yes, she will,' said David firmly. 'You need to be near the children and the animals. Our bathroom is bigger and tidier. Go and get her sheets. We'll find a nice big jar and fill it with scented foliage and everything will be lovely.'

Alexandra squeezed his arm. 'I don't know what I'd do without you, David.'

'You'd manage just fine,' he said comfortingly.

Alexandra and David spent an hour making Véronique's room as lovely as possible. Alexandra found some lace-edged pillowcases, and a cloth (which they suspected was really designed for altars) for the chest of drawers they'd turned into a dressing table. There was a china dressing-table set: little bowls, a tray for hair pins; they found candlesticks in a cupboard, washed and set them out too. They stayed there, 'set dressing' as David called it, until they started to get hungry.

'Lunchtime,' declared Alexandra and they set off back to the main part of the house.

Jack was in the hall. He was holding an envelope. 'The postman has just been.' He looked shocked, although he seemed to be holding an ordinary-looking Christmas card.

'Bad news, old chap?' asked David.

'I'm not sure,' said Jack. 'Very unexpected news, that's for sure.'

'Let's have lunch and you can tell us about it,' said Alexandra, who didn't want to be insensitive but didn't want to stay in the hall forever. Antoine and the children might be back at any moment, not to mention Véronique.

She passed the two men and had soup heating up and bread and cheese on the table by the time they joined her. David loved making soup and there was always some on the go.

'So what's your news?' Alexandra said gently after everyone had eaten a few mouthfuls, and had had a couple of sips of wine. 'Unless you don't want to tell me.'

'No, it's fine,' said Jack. 'The card is from my brother. He and his family are going to emigrate to Australia. They think I should go with them. We've always been very close – they're the only family I've got really.'

Alexandra couldn't help thinking of Penelope. How would she feel if Jack emigrated? Devastated, she was sure.

'Will you go?' she asked gently. 'Although you probably need to think about it,' she added, aware Jack hadn't had time to make up his mind.

'I don't know,' said Jack. He took a breath. 'I don't think I can. You both know how I feel about Penelope. Now I've found her again after losing her for all those years, I'm not going to risk losing her again.'

Alexandra put her hand on his arm. 'Then talk to Penelope about it. I think you should ask—' She stopped. 'This is nothing to do with me.'

'Ask Penelope what?' said Jack.

'To marry you!' said Alexandra.

There was a shocked silence. It wasn't what she'd intended to say. She was just going to say something vague like "see how she'd feel" but suddenly she felt it was time that Jack and Penelope stopped pussyfooting around. 'Unless you don't want to marry her, of course.'

Jack looked at her earnestly. 'I do! I do want to marry her. But what can I offer her? I have a flat in London, but not in the best part. I could support us, but . . .' He made a gesture that brushed against a vase of greenery and threatened to knock it over.

'Just ask her!' said Alexandra. One thing she was fairly sure of was that Penelope had her own money and wouldn't refuse Jack because he didn't have much of it. 'If she loves you, she'll say yes. And if she doesn't, she'll say no.'

'Can I borrow your car, David?' said Jack.

'Won't you finish lunch before you go?' asked Alexandra as Jack took the keys David offered.

Jack shook his head. 'I've wasted enough of my life being without her. Not a second more!'

'So where are you going?' asked David.

'To propose, of course!' Then Jack opened the front door and swung himself through it with great alacrity.

A few minutes after he'd gone, when Alexandra and David had gone back to their lunch, Alexandra said, 'I meant when the time was right, not that he had to rush off immediately.'

David laughed. 'You gave him the push he needed. He and Penelope could have a good life here, I think. It's a nice town, lots going on.'

After they'd finished their soup and gone on to the cheese, Alexandra asked, 'Could you have a good life here, David?'

He nodded. 'Yes, I think I could. I could buy a van, buy stock here and take it over to the UK to sell and make a very nice profit.'

'I know you were thinking of doing that,' said Alexandra, 'you told me.' She paused. She really wanted the answer to a different question. 'You said – I was wondering—' She stopped. She had never asked David about his love life and he had never volunteered anything. It was an unspoken agreement that this was a forbidden topic. Now she felt she wanted to know.

'You were wondering if, like Jack, I could find the love of my life?' He took another slice of cheese and neither of them spoke while he ate it. 'I think I could. In fact—'

'Don't tell me if you don't want to!' said Alexandra, thinking she may well have overstepped a line that had lain between them for years.

'You're being unusually tactful, Lexi. Usually you say what you think and ask any question you need the answer to.'

'I know but – this is different.' It *was* different. David's romantic life would be illegal in England and he wouldn't want to involve her in it.

'I do appreciate your discretion, chicken, and there is someone here who I . . . like. Is that enough to be going on with?'

Alexandra smiled. 'It's plenty. Thank you so much for telling me.'

'And while we're telling each other things – is there anything you'd like to confide in me? The house is always full of people and even more so now it's Christmas, so now might be our only chance.'

Alexandra sighed. 'Well, I don't suppose it's any secret, to you anyway, that I've got a huge crush on Antoine. I know exactly how silly it is, how much of a cliché it is – honestly, it's practically a direct copy of what happens in *Jane Eyre*, but I can't help it. I know my crush will go away in time and I'll end up marrying someone suitable, who isn't older, who hasn't got children and a rundown chateau—'

David laughed. 'I don't know when you last read *Jane Eyre* but I'm fairly sure Mr Rochester fell in love with the governess.'

Alexandra gave a little chuckle. 'Antoine is not at all like Mr Rochester!'

'And you're not remotely like Jane Eyre, but I think we should check the attics for mad wives anyway, just in case.'

Now Alexandra was laughing too. 'I don't think we need to; we know who Antoine's ex-wife is. And she's not in the attic!'

'How do we know he's only got one? There may be a room full of bodies up there. "Anne, sister Anne!"' he declaimed. '"Do you see anyone coming?"'

'Like in *Bluebeard*?' Alexandra was mildly hysterical now.

They'd taken things several stages further in which Alexandra was now Snow White, in love with all seven dwarves, when suddenly Véronique, the children hard on her heels, appeared in the kitchen.

'You seem to be having a party all on your own,' said Véronique, obviously wanting to object but unable to find a reason.

'Not really,' said Alexandra. 'David just made a joke that appealed to me.'

'Perhaps we could share it?' asked Véronique.

'Oh no,' said David firmly. 'Jokes never bear repeating. Have you had lunch?'

'We went out for lunch,' said Stéphie. 'Maxime was there and he sent you his love.' She rolled her eyes at this. 'Where are the kittens? Oh, here you are.'

Véronique smiled. 'Tell me, Stéphie. What is the name of the striped kitten? I know the white one is called Snowball.'

'Margaret,' said Stéphie instantly, although Alexandra had never heard her call the kitten that and was fairly sure no one else had either. Stéphie didn't like to appear lost for an answer.

'How charming,' said Véronique.

'Come up to my bedroom, Snowball, Margaret,' Stéphie ordered, and raced out of the room, the kittens skittering after her.

Antoine appeared. 'We must find out what sex those creatures are, before we find ourselves overrun with them.'

'Would you like to see your room, Véronique?' asked Alexandra.

Véronique winced slightly as if she wasn't happy with Alexandra using her Christian name, although Alexandra had used the formal *vous* form as always.

'I'm really very happy—'

Alexandra interrupted this oft-repeated assertion that Véronique was very happy in Alexandra's room. 'I've made your room very comfortable. Félicité? Come with me to show Véronique. Your mural is what is making the room so special.'

'Really?' Félicité obviously doubted this statement.

'I think so,' said Alexandra.

'And so do I,' David agreed. 'Honestly, Véronique, you're going to love what we've done with the room.'

'Come along, everyone!' said Alexandra briskly and set off, assuming people would follow. What she wasn't expecting was that Antoine would come too. And as the party passed Stéphie's door, she and the animals joined the procession.

'Well!' said Véronique after Alexandra had shown her into the room with a conjurer's flourish.

'Isn't it amazing?' said David. 'Antoine, did you know your daughter had such artistic talent?'

'No,' said Antoine, impossible to read. 'I didn't.'

The jungle mural depicting vast trees in a mixture of several shades of green with vivid parrots and tropical flowers was very well done, but it did dominate the room, there was no denying. For a few moments Alexandra wondered if she would have to give in and let Véronique have her room, just to save arguments. But the room was larger than hers, with a beautiful view, and the bathroom was next door.

'I don't think I can sleep here,' said Véronique. 'That mural will give me nightmares.'

'It wouldn't give me nightmares!' said Stéphie. 'Look how pretty the dressing table is.'

'The bathroom is next door,' said David. 'And you will have exclusive use of it. There's another bathroom, further down the corridor, that Jack and I will use.' He didn't mention that this bathroom was small, draughty and quite a long way away, obviously designed for use by servants only.

Alexandra took a breath, wondering why she and David were bending over backwards to make Véronique comfortable when she was not remotely appreciative. But it was for Antoine: she wanted to make his life as easy as she possibly could.

'I think you will be very comfortable here, Véronique,' said Antoine. 'And if your mother should change her mind and join us for Christmas, the room is easily big enough to share. We could find an extra bed.'

Alexandra caught the quick smile of apology he sent her and instantly forgave him everything.

'There's always room for one more in a chateau,' said David after what seemed a rather long silence.

Everyone had set off back to the main part of the house when the front door opened. In came Jack and Penelope. They were laughing and Penelope's chignon was beginning to come loose. They both looked young and silly and very, very happy.

'What's going on?' said Antoine. 'What have you two been getting up to?'

'We're engaged to be married!' said Penelope.

'She said yes,' said Jack at the same time.

Just at that moment, they realised they were standing under a bunch of mistletoe and Jack gave Penelope a hearty kiss.

'Grand-mère!' said Stéphie. 'I didn't know you knew about kissing!'

'Go into the salon, everyone, and I'll call Henri,' said Antoine firmly. 'This situation requires champagne!'

Chapter Twenty-five

Alexandra had decided to refuse the glass of champagne that Jack was offering her until she spotted
Véronique looking disapproving so she took it,
although she knew it would make her feel tired. They
were gathered in the salon and she was perched on a
little settee a little way away from the others. She was
plotting her escape.

'The thing is', said Jack, walking about in front of
the fire, still bubbling with enthusiasm, 'we need to
have the wedding quite quickly, before my brother
emigrates, so he and his family can come.'

'We want to come too!' said Stéphie. 'So do the
kittens. Milou doesn't care. He's a boy. They don't
care about weddings.'

'You and Félicité will be my bridesmaids,' said
Penelope. 'You will wear very pretty dresses and have
flowers in your hair.'

'I thought weddings, after your first, were usually
simpler, more austere affairs,' said Véronique, determined to suppress everyone's joy.

'Not in this case,' said Penelope.

'No, indeed,' agreed Jack. 'This is going to be a very
grand celebration!'

Stéphie was jumping up and down. 'I didn't know old people got married. It's very exciting.'

'It's very rude to refer to people as old,' said Véronique.

'Why?' asked Stéphie. 'Is it bad to be old?'

'It's better than the alternative,' said Jack.

Penelope's laugh in response was very like a giggle. She seemed to have turned from the strict grand-mother to a woman in love in an instant.

'The sooner these children go to school, the better,' muttered Véronique.

'What do you mean?' asked Henri

'I think you need to be at school, *chéri*,' said Véronique. 'I know your mother thinks you – I actually mean Félicité and Henri – should go in January.'

'We're not going to that school,' said Félicité firmly.

'No,' Henri agreed, 'we want to go to the school our friends go to.'

'Children!' said Antoine, quiet but firm. 'This is not the time to talk about schools. We are talking about Penelope and Jack's wedding.'

'She started it,' said Stéphie quietly, looking accus-ingly at Véronique.

Her father gave her a look which spoke volumes.

'Maybe Stéphie and I should—' Alexandra was on her feet, frantically thinking of some urgent activity that she and Stéphie could instantly embark on.

'Don't go,' said Jack. 'We want to talk to you about our wedding.'

'Yes,' said Penelope, looking at Antoine. 'We want to have it in the old orangery.'

'Of course,' said Antoine, looking extremely surprised. 'But it is not in a state for celebrations. Is there any particular reason?'

Penelope and Jack looked at each other and Penelope definitely blushed.

'Erm – well . . .' said Jack. 'We met in Saint-Jean-du-Roc before the war. We were both on holiday here. The chateau was empty at the time and we got into the grounds where a wall had broken down.'

'It started to pour with rain,' said Penelope. 'And we decided to take shelter in the orangery.'

'I see,' said Antoine. 'But still, it's not fit for anything like a wedding.'

'Far better to have a nice lunch in the local *auberge*,' said Véronique.

'It will be fit for a wedding by the time Lexi and I have finished with it,' said David, having shot a glance at Véronique, which, had she been looking, would have put her in her place. 'We might ask Félicité to do a mural.'

Félicité looked pleased. She had been somewhat abashed by the mixed reception her mural in Véronique's room had received.

'That will be up to Antoine,' said Véronique icily. 'Everyone seems to have forgotten that the chateau is his. He may not wish to have the wedding here.'

Jack looked embarrassed. 'I'm so sorry. It's just—'

Antoine raised a hand. 'I have already said, the chateau and its occupants would be delighted to host your wedding, Penelope and Jack,' he said, having sent Véronique a look that Alexandra wished she could read. 'Now, more champagne. Let us toast the *orangerie*, in the hope that it will be beautified in time. And, Félicité, I think a mural would be a very good place to start!'

Like a conjurer, David produced another bottle of champagne and filled the glasses.

'To the *orangerie*,' said Antoine raising his, 'and to my dear mother-in-law Penelope and her lucky fiancé, Jack!'

As soon as she decently could, Alexandra escaped to her bedroom, ostensibly to wrap presents, actually to lie on her bed and wonder what she should do. She knew that Véronique was here with Antoine, and knew she should leave, and was wondering when and how she should go about this, when Stéphie came in, one kitten sitting on her shoulder, the other in her arms.

'Oh, here you are! I've just been downstairs, outside Papa's study.'

'Why were you there, Stéphie?' Alexandra asked, thinking there couldn't possibly be a sensible reason.

'I heard Papa and Véronique talking.'

For a second, Alexandra fought with herself. She knew she should reprove Stéphie for listening to other people's conversations, but she was struggling. 'You know you shouldn't listen outside closed doors—'

'So don't you want to hear what Véronique said?'

Alexandra exhaled. 'All right, tell me. I can see you really want to.'

'She said that Papa should dismiss you.'

Alexandra gasped. Surely she hadn't done anything bad enough to get her the sack. 'Did she say why?'

'She said that you'd let "the children", although you didn't let me,' – Stéphie appeared to be a bit resentful about this – 'attend a party that was quite unsuitable. And you let Félicité paint on the walls.'

'And what did your papa say?' This was the important bit. Alexandra knew perfectly well that Véronique would do anything to get rid of her.

Stéphie seemed disappointed. 'He didn't answer. I looked through the keyhole and could only see his mouth, which was in a line. He opened it as if he was going to say something but I didn't hear. Milou woofed because one of the kittens bit his leg and so I had to run away up here.'

Alexandra didn't know what to say. She didn't want to tell Stéphie off for doing something she would certainly have done herself and they had already done together, but she didn't think she could just leave it either.

Stéphie seemed to understand her dilemma. 'Lexi, I know you think I shouldn't have listened, but you are pleased to know what Véronique said, aren't you? And sometimes you have to listen at doorways to find out important things no one is going to tell you because you're just a child.'

'That's very true,' said Alexandra, who'd done a fair bit of eavesdropping herself growing up. 'But we shouldn't do it unless it's really important. Now let's go and help David with dinner.'

As she followed Stéphie and her kittens downstairs, she felt she hadn't really handled the situation; she'd just let it ride. Maybe Véronique was right: she *was* a bad nanny.

Chapter Twenty-six

It was Christmas Eve and Alexandra and her three charges were squashed in the back of the car. They were off to have dinner – *le réveillon de Noël* – with Penelope.

Alexandra had suggested she should take the other car, with the children, and Véronique was keen on this idea. Antoine, however, decided they should travel as a family. Alexandra decided he still thought of his children as small. It wasn't a very long journey, after all.

Jack was already at Penelope's, and David had an engagement of his own for the evening. Alexandra wasn't terribly looking forward to the gathering. Véronique was being dreadfully possessive of Antoine and Lucinda was bound to be very maternal about her children. While there was nothing wrong with this, of course, it seemed to Alexandra to be a rather artificial sort of love and it set her teeth on edge. Also, when Véronique and Lucinda got together they seemed determined to condemn Alexandra as the nanny and while there was nothing remotely to be ashamed of, she found being haughty in the face of their disapproval quite tiring.

However, everyone seemed to be on their best behaviour. Penelope's old friend Gérard was there as well as a couple of older gentlemen; Alexandra suspected that Penelope invited everyone who was likely to be on their own. Christmas Eve was the big day of celebration in France, which was why she and David could do an English Christmas on 25 December.

Eventually, Gérard and the more elderly members of the party went home and everyone was called into dinner. Penelope told Alexandra that the old people were very happy to have a drink but didn't want a long and heavy meal which would stop them sleeping. 'And although traditionally we should be eating this meal after Midnight Mass, I couldn't have managed that even as a young person.'

'Nor could I!' said Alexandra. 'Is there anything I can do to help?'

But Penelope had engaged some young women from Saint-Jean-du-Roc as waitresses and Alexandra's help wasn't required.

Everything was going well, if slightly boringly, when Stéphie suddenly remembered something.

'Papa? You never told me what happened to the truffle? The one that Milou found in the forest?'

'Oh, *chérie!*' said Antoine. 'I am so sorry. So much has happened since then. I sold it to my friend – the one who taught us all about truffle hunting that day. I got quite a lot of money for it, and next season, we will hunt for more!'

Stéphie clapped her hands delightedly. 'So you will never go away to work again?'

'Stéphie,' said Véronique in a voice like honey, 'your father is an important man. He cannot stay at home and look after you.'

'And although I did get quite a lot of money for the truffle, all thanks to you and Milou,' Antoine added, 'it wasn't quite enough for us to live on. Although in the years to come we will find more truffles and earn more. There just isn't quite enough right now.'

Stéphie exhaled, obviously feeling thoroughly cheated. 'Well then, Papa must marry Lexi. Then she'll get her fortune and there'll be plenty of money!'

Alexandra wanted to disappear into her chair and it was obvious that no one else at the table was happy either. Several people started to speak at once but it was Véronique's voice that cut through the hubbub.

'Stéphanie! You must not tell lies! Alexandra is not a fairy princess with a fortune to solve everyone's problems.'

'Yes,' said Lucinda. 'I think rather too much has been made of this fortune. It's probably not very much at all.'

'She definitely gets it when she marries,' went on Stéphie, her clear voice audible to everyone. 'I heard her talking about it on the telephone to her friend.'

Alexandra got up and left the room. She wasn't easily embarrassed but now she was ready to die of it. 'Indigestion!' she said when she got to the door, hoping this explanation would satisfy the party.

Penelope found her five minutes later, leaning over the washbasin, her hands at her temples, hoping to soothe the headache that suddenly felt like knives. If only they'd come in two cars as she'd wanted, she could have gone home.

'Oh, Penelope!' she said in English. 'What can I do? This is a disaster!'

'Phff!' said Penelope, also in English. 'Why a disaster? A little girl has mentioned something everyone knew about anyway. And as for suggesting that Antoine marry you, no one will take that seriously. You have no reason to worry.' She paused. 'It probably was wise to let Antoine deal with the slight uproar Stéphie has created but really, child, it's a storm in a teacup. Take a few moments now and then come back in. No one will be surprised if you've had *une petite crise de foie* – it's traditional. I'll find you a Vichy tablet. Eat it and then join us in a few minutes for the pudding.'

'I do hope you're right,' said Alexandra.

'My dear girl, I would be disappointed in you if you were *bouleversée* by such a small social upset. I'll see you shortly.'

When Alexandra went back into the dining room everyone was eating and chatting merrily. Stéphie got up and ran over, flinging her arms round Alexandra's waist. 'I'm so sorry, Lexi! I didn't mean to embarrass you. Papa said I did?'

Alexandra hugged her back. 'Don't worry, darling, I just needed a moment because I had a pain in my stomach. Do you know . . .' Alexandra crouched down so only Stéphie would hear what she wanted to say next. 'Grand-mère gave me a tablet and I ate it, and then I burped!' She gave this word so much emphasis that Stéphie giggled. 'I feel much better!' she added. 'Now, are the desserts delicious?'

They went back to the table together and Alexandra accepted a macaron, offered to her by Jack with a small bow and a big wink. She didn't say no to another glass of champagne either.

Alexandra was up early on Christmas morning. She hadn't slept well and now wanted a soothing cup of hot chocolate. She had spent a lot of the night wondering how soon she could leave the chateau; Stéphie's question had made her feel very exposed. And when she wasn't worrying about that, she worried about how to make Christmas Day special for the family. There were no favourite routines for this day as they usually completed all their celebrations the night before. She wanted to produce an English Christmas for them.

There was still the crib to look at and complete. Stéphie had been asleep when they got back the previous night and everyone had felt it was a shame to put the baby Jesus in place without Stéphie there.

There were presents to be opened. Although Penelope and Lucinda's presents had been given and opened after supper, Alexandra, Jack and David had insisted on holding theirs back to make Christmas Day more like it was in England. Antoine withheld his, too, and so did Véronique.

Alexandra was whisking hot chocolate in a saucepan when David appeared. He was wearing his Noël Coward dressing gown and was sleepy but determined to wake up.

'Happy Christmas, honey,' he said. 'How was your evening?'

Alexandra told him, including every detail, every blush and slightly exaggerating her rush from the room. She found that telling David made it all less awful somehow.

'My poor little chicken!' said David. 'How crushingly embarrassing for you. And I don't think that even I knew that about you getting your inheritance on your marriage. I thought you had to wait until you were twenty-five.'

'I only found out about it myself when my cousins came, and I wouldn't have then if I hadn't overheard them talking about it. Stéphie was with me, and she now seems to have got into the very bad habit of listening at doors. But, as she frequently reminds me, I started it.'

'But Penelope rescued you? She grows on you, doesn't she? When I first met her I thought she was all prunes and prisms, to quote my favourite writer – starchy as all get out. But since she and Jack have been reunited she's really softened.'

'She was very kind. When I was lying in bed during the night, thinking about it, I thought it was so embarrassing I would have to leave, but now, well, maybe Penelope is right. It was only Stéphie saying something she shouldn't.'

'That's my girl!' said David.

'And how was your evening?' asked Alexandra, taking a sip from her foaming cup.

'Delightful,' said David in a way that did not invite further questioning but set Alexandra's heart at rest; at least that had gone well!

'So, Christmas!' she said.

319

'Yes! I didn't get up at this ungodly hour for my health. I need to make a proper plan.'

'David! You've been making plans for days!'

'Never finalised them. Too many variables. Do you know traditionally they have thirteen desserts in Provence?'

'Yes, I have been told several times, but we're doing an English Christmas, so we don't have to do that. It would be far too filling, anyway. So? What are we having?'

'I found a lovely recipe for a tart with walnuts and caramel, and I've done a *bûche de Noël* – or a chocolate log as my gran would have called it. I thought the kids could decorate that if things get boring.'

'On Christmas Day? That shouldn't happen, should it?'

'You know as well as I do about the longueurs of Christmas Day. I know we've always had fun since we got together but really? Having to wait until teatime to open your presents? The mad aunts and uncles who have to be invited because they've nowhere else to go? The Queen's Speech?'

'Well, I have experienced Christmases like that, but mostly, I've been in the mad aunt class. I had to be invited to other people's Christmases because I had nowhere else to go. The Swiss cousins always arranged it. Sometimes I had fun and sometimes I didn't.'

'Well, this Christmas is going to be fun, for the children, anyway!' said David. 'So . . .' He produced a hardbacked notebook. 'I have a potential plan. It's breakfast. A walk. Must have a walk on Christmas Day. Light lunch before our visitors come: they're invited for about three; we're planning to eat dinner at six. So when should we open presents?'

'Oh goodness, I don't know. The children have had some presents. They've got their stockings. Penelope gave them to me, filled and wrapped, and Antoine put them on their beds after they'd gone to sleep. Maybe we could wait until everyone is here?'

David wrote this down. 'So, light lunch after the walk, then charades, then everyone else—'

'Charades?'

'Of course! It's traditional! Proper charades when you act out half a word and then act out the second half. Lexi, darling, you have played charades, haven't you?'

'Yes, but I think it might be hard in two languages—'

'Nonsense! Ah! Here's Stéphie! Happy Christmas, darling!' he said.

'Happy Christmas,' said Stéphie sleepily. 'I brought my stocking down. Are the others up? We always open our stockings together.'

'Tell you what, I'll make some more hot chocolate and then we'll wake them,' suggested Alexandra.

'We don't need waking,' said Félicité. 'The kittens got into my bedroom and jumped on my face.' She was holding her stocking, a beautifully embroidered velvet example which she put on the table. 'Where's Henri?'

'Here. Wretched cats!' he said. He had his stocking too.

'Hot chocolate all round, then,' said David. 'Is the baker open on Christmas Day, do we think?'

Henri nodded. 'For a short time.'

'I'll go!' said Alexandra, glad of an excuse to get into the fresh air. It was surprisingly cold but she wanted to feel the air on her face and help her head to clear.

She got back to see everyone singing round the crib, in the hall. The last notes of 'Away in the Manger' to a different tune to the one she knew were dying away. Henri had accompanied it on his penny whistle.

'That was delightful!' she said, wondering if it was a family tradition and how lovely it was. 'Do you do that every year?'

'We needed to keep ourselves busy while we waited for our croissants,' said Véronique with a smile that didn't fool Alexandra for a tiny second. 'Now that our breakfast has finally arrived, let us go through to the dining room. It is a special day, we should celebrate!'

'Happy Christmas,' Antoine said to her, in English, kissing her cheek.

'Happy Christmas,' she said back, wishing that Véronique wasn't standing beside him.

Having found a basket for the croissants, *viennoiserie* and bread, Alexandra went through to the dining room. The table was set but Stéphie hadn't had a chance to bring out all the little accessories to make it festive. So instead of a cosy breakfast in the kitchen, with the fire in the range crackling, and the coffee maker bubbling on the stove, the children's opened stockings covering the table with toys, they had it sitting formally round the table of a chilly room.

'Well,' said David, after refilling cups of coffee and hot chocolate. 'As you all know, Lexi and I have claimed today as English Christmas Day, and so we will follow the timetable.'

Although he was usually the most easy-going soul, Alexandra noted that his training as an actor allowed him to speak with great authority when he wanted to. It meant that Véronique said nothing and everyone else paid attention.

'So, we're going for a walk. We don't have to go far, but we need to get out into the fresh air. Then we'll have a light lunch, perhaps a glass of champagne, and after that we'll play a parlour game or two. Our guests are invited for three o'clock.'

His enthusiasm was such that Alexandra wondered if he'd ever had a part as a games teacher; it made her smile.

'But it's so cold!' said Véronique. 'I was led to believe the climate was better in the south.'

'Wrap up warm,' said David bracingly. 'You won't feel it once you get going. Everyone meet by the front door in twenty minutes!'

Chapter Twenty-seven

It was a beautiful Christmas morning. There was mist and although there was also sunshine, it was bitingly cold. Alexandra walked with David and Félicité while Stéphie and Henri ran with Milou and the kittens (who had no intention of being left out). Antoine and Véronique were a little way away from the others and seemed to be talking earnestly.

Everyone's breath was visible and soon Félicité joined her younger siblings, forgetting her dignity so she could run around and keep warm. They went to a favourite tree on the edge of the forest and climbed it. The kittens chased them and Milou stood at the bottom looking up at them, irritated and disdainful.

'He seems to be saying, "I could climb up with you, if I wanted to,"' said Alexandra to David.

'And so could I!' said David. 'In fact, I definitely would, only I need to get back to put the turkey in the oven.'

'I thought it was traditional to put the turkey in at dawn,' said Alexandra.

'It's also traditional for the turkey to be overcooked and the vegetables like mush. The joy of this Christmas is that we can make our own traditions, ones that are a lot easier to endure.'

'Come on then, I'll race you back!'

The children, seeing Alexandra and David running back to the chateau, soon followed. When Antoine and Véronique finally arrived, the Christmas presents were arranged in the salon, Alexandra had put on a dress with her Chanel jacket and her big pearls and everyone had enjoyed at least two chocolates from the box David had hidden in the kitchen. Alexandra and David had enjoyed a quick glass of champagne too, and everyone was rather giggly.

By contrast, Antoine and Véronique were sombre. Véronique went upstairs after lunch, presumably to her jungle-painted bedroom, and didn't return for a little while. She joined the party in the salon (warmer now the fire had been lit for a little while) wearing a very elegant outfit and a fur jacket. She perched on the edge of the sofa and watched the charade that was being acted out in front of her. The team was led by Antoine and consisted of his three children and Milou, who didn't understand the concept of acting at all.

'The English,' she said after a little while. 'I think they are mad.'

Alexandra and David shared a look and then, as one, they got up and retreated to the kitchen. Here they peeled and prepared, chopped and sliced, making stuffing, sauces, sipping red wine and nibbling as they worked.

So engrossed were they that when the doorbell jangled, and Milou woofed, they were surprised. But their guests had arrived, seemingly all at the same time.

First came Penelope and Jack, Penelope looking radiant and Jack very proud of the woman on his arm, whose eyes sparkled and whose cheeks were gently flushed. With them was Lucinda, elegant but chilly, pleased to see her children but in a restrained way that didn't allow her hair or her dress and jacket to be disturbed, followed by Maxime who was also on top form, and looked handsomer than ever. Everyone was welcomed and ushered through to the salon where it was now quite warm, thanks to the tree trunk burning in the hearth.

The plan was for those who had presents to open to do that before the meal. This was partly so David could have extra time if he needed it to make sure the potatoes were brown and that there was enough gravy. The turkey was reposing under a pile of towels, already perfectly cooked, waiting to be carried through to the dining room.

Alexandra and David were summoned from the kitchen, Alexandra still in her apron. The demand to open presents was too urgent to be ignored.

Antoine and Véronique had presents for the children, although they'd had their presents from Penelope and Lucinda the day before. Alexandra, David and Jack had decided to stick to the twenty-fifth for present-giving, even though this caused a bit of eye-rolling from certain quarters.

Alexandra had bought Antoine a bottle of cognac and a box of chocolates and gave Véronique a handkerchief case she had bought from a woman in the market. It was edged with handmade lace and very beautiful. It was a bit of a wrench to give it away. In exchange

Véronique and Antoine gave Alexandra a rather grand bath set involving soap, bath salts and talcum powder.

Alexandra's charges were delighted with their presents. These were a very nice set of watercolours for Félicité, the music for a current pop song and a harmonica for Henri, and an antique model stable, including several charming horses, for Stéphie. As Lucinda, as usual, had ignored Stéphie's existence, Alexandra felt it was important that she had something a bit more special than her siblings.

At last all the present-opening was over, and David marshalled everyone into the dining room. Jack and Maxime were very helpful getting people organised, while Alexandra and Lucinda brought in the vegetables. The turkey, as golden and full-breasted as it was possible to be, was brought in by David and Antoine together, and placed at the head of the table so Antoine could carve.

The meal was very successful. Even Véronique and Lucinda were impressed, who both had reason to wish the food to be disappointing. But the turkey was moist, the stuffings different from what were commonly eaten in France, and even the bread sauce, new to many, was reluctantly declared delicious.

The desserts were a mixture of traditional French and English, including a very rich *bûche de Noël*, as chocolatey as anyone could wish and decorated with robins, and a Christmas pudding served with brandy butter. Maxime declared he was happy to eat only the brandy butter, it was so delicious.

It was a very merry occasion, but Alexandra felt relieved when it was over and people started to take their leave. Jack went to pack: he was going to England to see his brother and family, partly to tell them about Penelope and his wedding plans. David was also going back to England for a week or so, and Véronique, it transpired, although Alexandra suspected it wasn't what she'd originally planned, was taking the train to Paris in the morning.

While the clearing up was going on David took the opportunity to check on Alexandra's feelings. 'Now, you know I'll be away for about ten days but if it all gets too difficult, I could come back.'

'It won't be difficult! It'll be fine!' She said this so convincingly she was proud of herself.

'You'll be alone with Antoine, with only the children as chaperones.'

'Well, don't tell anyone, will you?'

'Hmm,' said David.

'Really! Antoine asked me if I wanted time off. In fact he tried to insist I had it, but I didn't want to go anywhere.' She paused. 'Although I'll have to go when the children go to school, obviously.'

'Has it been decided when that should be?'

'I'm not sure. I think money is involved. Lucinda is prepared to pay for the older two to go to boarding school in England, but Antoine wants the three of them to stay together here in France. And if that happens, then he'll have to pay.'

'It really would make life easier if you and Antoine got married!' David was teasing and Alexandra didn't take offence.

'I know!' said Alexandra. 'But Antoine is never going to ask me, is he?'

David nodded. 'Unlikely. Pity, really. Now, you must promise me you'll fry the leftover Christmas pudding in butter tomorrow?'

'All right.'

'And you'll be OK doing all the meals without me?'

Alexandra smiled. 'I managed when I first arrived; now I've got all these leftovers: turkey, ham, pâté, cheese, all sorts of delicious things. We won't starve even if I don't cook a thing!'

'I'm still annoyed I couldn't get us any Stilton. The French are very narrow-minded when it comes to cheese.'

Alexandra giggled. 'I know! They resolutely stick to their own hundreds of kinds and never open their minds to anything different.'

'It's the same with the bread,' said David. 'They insist on their long pointy loaves, or round crusty ones, and seem to ignore proper square white slices!'

'Which are what you want for real turkey sandwiches,' said Alexandra.

'It certainly saves all that slicing!' Then David stopped laughing, obviously still concerned. 'You really will be all right?'

'Of course! I'm not a bad cook even if I'm not nearly as good as you are and my speciality is meals made from leftovers.'

'You talk a good game, Lexi,' said David. 'But I'm still worried.'

At that moment, Antoine came in with a tray full of glasses. 'What are you worried about, David?'

'He's worried about me doing the cooking again. Quite unnecessarily. I cook perfectly well.'

'I will be cooking while you are away, David,' said Antoine, suddenly every inch the Comte. 'Alexandra can't have the time off she is entitled to, but at least I can take over her duties.'

Alexandra looked at him, open-mouthed. He put down his tray and then closed her mouth by lifting her chin with his finger. 'Don't be so astonished. I'm a very good cook.'

'I'm sure—' Alexandra began.

'In France, we doubt that the English can cook,' Antoine went on. 'It seems you doubt that Frenchmen can.'

Alexandra had had time to recover her aplomb. 'I've just had no evidence of it so far,' she said.

Antoine's eyes narrowed. 'You have a way of being insolent without being rude. Is it an English thing? Or one of your special skills, Alexandra?'

'Oh, it's special to her, believe me,' said David.

Aware suddenly of how intently Antoine was looking at her, Alexandra took the opportunity to fetch another trayful of dirty dishes.

Chapter Twenty-eight

David left the chateau very early on Boxing Day. Alexandra was awake so got up to say goodbye. He hugged her hard and told her to take care of herself. Surprisingly, she felt a little tearful as she returned his hug. They'd been in a happy bubble, cooking together, looking after Félicité, Henri and Stéphie, enjoying living in France. He promised to be back for Twelfth Night, but him going home for a break reminded Alexandra that her time here might be nearly at an end. If her charges went away to school in the New Year, she would have to go and live in Switzerland.

By the time Véronique came downstairs the kitchen was spotless. She refused breakfast beyond a bowl of coffee, which she drank standing up. Antoine was already in the hall, waiting to drive her to the station. Alexandra said her goodbyes in the kitchen. She and Véronique were very polite and formal with each other.

An hour or so later, the household was sitting round the kitchen range, feeling a little flat. Even the kittens had settled on Milou, who was stretched out in front of the fire. No one had eaten much breakfast and Alexandra was trying to think of something to do to restore a bit of Christmas spirit when Antoine strode in having returned from the station.

'This morning we will go into the woods and collect sticks and logs for the fires, and then we will go out to lunch!' He clapped his hands. 'Hurry, children!' He looked at Alexandra, definitely including her in the 'children'.

As everyone ran upstairs to change into more suitable clothes, Henri said, 'Papa used to take us into the woods often, before he had to go away so much for work.'

Even Félicité forgot to be detached and adolescent at the prospect of the trip. Alexandra was excited too, telling herself it was just because she needed fresh air and exercise.

There was a big, battered basket attached to a trolley on large wheels that they dragged behind them. When they got to the edge of the woods everyone separated, competing with each other to find the biggest logs. The basket was soon full and Henri volunteered to take it to the house and then bring it back for refilling. Antoine had a small saw with him and soon there was another pile of logs and bits of wood for burning, waiting for the trolley.

Alexandra pulled it back the next time and saw the untidy pile that Henri had left, and added her load to it. When she returned to the others she found them all inspecting boar tracks.

'You see here? The marks are quite clear in the mud,' Antoine was saying. 'Several animals and quite big.'

'I don't like boars,' said Stéphie. 'Can we go up behind the chateau? Away from them?'

'Most people shoot them,' said Henri. 'Why can't we?'

'I prefer to let them live until they do serious damage,' said Antoine. 'Besides, I haven't had time to do any shooting for pleasure although next time I do, I will take you, Henri, and show you how to be safe with guns.'

'Can we go and see the lake?' asked Félicité. 'It's so cold. I wonder if it's freezing yet?'

They walked through the forest that curved round the chateau to the lake. Alexandra was surprised. 'I didn't know this was here!'

'We've kept you far too busy indoors,' said Antoine. 'You haven't had time to explore the grounds properly. Do you like being in the woods? Or do you prefer cities?'

'I like both,' Alexandra said firmly. 'I've lived in London most of my life but I've always enjoyed the countryside when I've been in it.' She was certainly enjoying herself now, but that might not have been because of the fresh air and the beautiful forest.

Antoine was very knowledgeable about nature, showing them more than just boar tracks. 'I don't get out enough these days. I love the forest and the trees and yet I only seem to see them when I'm driving away.'

'Don't worry, Papa,' said Stéphie, putting her hand in his. 'You won't always have to go away to work. David said you could rent our outbuildings for people to have holidays in. The English will pay a lot to stay in a real French chateau.'

'Is this true, Alexandra?' Henri asked.

'If the buildings were converted into places where people can stay comfortably, of course,' she said.

'They'd pay extra for the aristocratic surroundings, I'm sure.'

'Let's explore the buildings,' said Henri. 'You'd like that, wouldn't you, Stéphie?'

As her brother made it sound like a huge treat, Stéphie instantly agreed. Alexandra was keen on the plan, too.

They found their way into a disused coach house, a wash house and a *pigeonnier*. They fought past veils of dusty cobwebs, climbed rickety wooden ladders and opened long-closed stable doors.

'Look at the view from here!' said Alexandra, having peered through a crack in the stonework.

'You're looking at a wall, Alexandra. You can't see anything,' said Antoine.

'You could put in a big window! Maybe double doors. These places could be charming,' said Alexandra, who didn't understand why Antoine didn't see the potential of it all. 'It's not very long since these buildings were full of farm vehicles and pigeons. Perhaps that's why you can't picture them being used for anything else.'

Antoine shrugged. 'All the animals have been over at the farm for some years now, which is probably why I haven't given these buildings any thought. Having a holiday in a place still full of pigeon droppings and cobwebs doesn't seem very attractive to me.' In spite of his snooty words, Antoine smiled at Stéphie to show that he was joking.

'Well, please give them some thought now, Papa,' said Stéphie sternly. 'Then you can stay at home more.'

Antoine looked at his watch. 'It is time to go back and make ourselves presentable. We're going out for lunch.'

'I thought you said you could cook!' said Alexandra without thinking. 'Did you really mean you know how to get us to a restaurant so we can eat?' Then she saw his expression and her mouth went dry. He was a man whose honour had been questioned and he wasn't taking it well.

'Come on, children! Race you back!' she said and set off for the chateau as fast as she could. She felt as if she had been playing with a kitten and it had suddenly turned into a tiger; she needed to get away quickly.

Back in her room, while she twisted her hair into a knot and found her oversized pearls, she instructed herself to remember she was the nanny, and shouldn't tease her boss. It wasn't (as Véronique would say) suitable.

The restaurant wasn't smart on the outside. It seemed to be behind a butcher's shop which was currently closed. But there were cars parked haphazardly around the building and far up the road which indicated it was popular. Antoine wriggled the car into a spot between two others and then led the way round the building.

The restaurant seemed full but the man in charge was there the moment Antoine opened the door. He obviously knew Antoine of old and the two men exchanged a few pleasantries before they were led to a table. Antoine nodded to many of the families and couples who were there. The restaurant was very crowded.

They were given menus immediately. 'And for madame,' said the owner, as he handed Alexandra hers.

Stéphie giggled. 'That's not madame, that's Lexi.'

'*Bien sûr*,' said the owner and Antoine felt obliged to provide more detail.

'Alexandra is the brave woman who has been taking care of my children while I've been away.'

Alexandra offered her hand and looked the man firmly in the eye in the hope that would stop any thoughts about her relationship with Antoine being anything other than professional. He shook her hand and bowed and left.

'He thinks you are Papa's girlfriend,' said Félicité with a sigh.

'It doesn't matter what he thinks, does it?' asked Alexandra.

Félicité shrugged. 'Everyone here knows Papa. They'll all be thinking the same thing. We come here quite often, but Papa has never brought a woman with him before.'

'Let us just enjoy our lunch,' said Antoine after a quick glance round the room. 'Everything is fine. We don't want to embarrass Alexandra.'

It was too late for that. Alexandra was indeed embarrassed. A bottle of champagne arrived at the table and now Alexandra became aware that the women were looking at her with speculation. She could only imagine what they were thinking: was this woman the right one for M. le Comte? Wasn't she far too young? Had he finally found a replacement for the lovely Lucinda? She didn't want to imagine what the men were thinking but consoled herself with the realisation that it was unlikely very many of them had met Lucinda.

Antoine clinked his glass against hers. 'Here's to you, Alexandra. Now drink up. Everything always looks better after a glass of champagne.'

She laughed and took a large sip. Too late she realised that although the tables were all crowded with bottles, theirs was the only table that had champagne on it. He must have ordered it specially. Everyone would have noticed.

Then the food started to arrive. Alexandra immediately understood why this unassuming restaurant was so popular – the food was superb.

There were hardboiled eggs served with tapenade, salty and full of olive flavour, a soup made with mushrooms and served with grated truffle (much to Stéphie's delight), a green salad, and then a chicken casserole which made all the festive food they'd had the day before seem mundane and tasteless.

'I love the fact you enjoy your food, Alexandra,' said Antoine. 'So many women think only of their figures.'

Alexandra was at that moment helping Stéphie extract a piece of bone from her bit of chicken. She turned back. 'I'm glad I do something that pleases you. Quite often I think I just annoy you.'

'You do many things that please me,' he said and then directed his attention to his older children. 'A little more wine and water for you both? Stéphie, do you want more lemonade?'

Alexandra picked up her wine glass, closer to blushing now than she had been before. His words had been simple enough and she knew she shouldn't imagine they were particularly significant, but somehow they were. At least to her.

After the chicken, when Alexandra thought she couldn't eat another mouthful, even to please Antoine, pears poached in red wine appeared, served with thick cream. After that came macarons and chocolate truffles.

'I just want to go home and go to sleep!' said Stéphie. 'Is it all right if I pick my teeth in public?' She had a paper-wrapped toothpick in her hand.

'I'm not sure,' said Alexandra. 'Personally, I'd prefer it if you didn't. Take the toothpick for later.'

Antoine laughed. 'Your English nanny is very strict, *chérie*. I'll go and settle up.'

Before he did that, however, he visited every table, exchanging news, making jokes, and looking back at Alexandra often. He's explaining who I am, she thought.

'Can I eat your second truffle?' asked Henri.

'As long as you're not sick in the car on the way home,' said Alexandra.

'Ergh!' said Stéphie. 'Don't be sick!'

'I won't be,' said Henri. 'Oh, look, there's Jules. The boy you met at the party.' He indicated someone who was sitting behind Alexandra.

'Oh God,' said Félicité. 'I can't have him seeing me like this! I'm probably bright red in the face, and I'm not wearing any make-up.'

'It's fine,' said Alexandra calmly. 'Look at me. Now laugh at something funny I've said. There! Now you look lovely. If you catch his eye he'll be impressed.'

338

'You used to be much more fun when you weren't interested in boys,' said Stéphie to her sister.

'She's still fun,' said Alexandra. 'And you'll be interested in boys too, soon.'

'Are you interested in them, Lexi?' asked Stéphie.

'Lexi's just interested in Papa,' said Félicité, making Alexandra wish she hadn't stuck up for her.

Alexandra sighed and rolled her eyes. 'Your papa is my boss,' she said calmly. 'It would never be appropriate for me to think about him like that.'

'Now you sound like Véronique,' said Félicité. 'And even if you're not interested in him, like every other woman who ever comes near him always is, everyone here will assume you're sleeping together.'

'Please don't talk like that in front of your sister. And why don't you think about your own love life and stop concerning yourself with mine?' said Alexandra.

Jules did indeed steal a few glances at Félicité, with her pretending not to care. Then his family got up to go and he paused at the table to say hello and goodbye. Alexandra made sure not to look at him and trusted he wouldn't recognise her. She didn't want him referring to the party. While she still felt she'd done what was best, she wasn't sure if Antoine would see it that way and she was having such a nice time, she didn't want it spoilt. But when Jules finally left, Félicité turned her attention back to Alexandra.

'Don't you care what people think about you, then?' she asked.

Alexandra considered for a moment. She had to make sure she was teaching the right lesson here.

'Well, I know I'm doing nothing wrong, which is the most important thing. Although I would care a lot more if these people were part of my community. But when you children go to school, I'll go to Switzerland and never see any of them again.

'Oh,' said Stéphie. 'That's sad.'

'Not really,' said Alexandra, not believing what she was saying. 'You won't miss me when you're at school, having fun. And I'll send you postcards with pictures of the snowy Alps on them.'

'But will you miss us?' asked Henri.

'Yes,' said Alexandra. 'Of course I will. I've very much enjoyed looking after you.'

'Then you should stay!' said Stéphie. 'You could look after Papa!'

'Your papa doesn't need me or anyone else to look after him,' said Alexandra. 'Is that not true, Antoine?' she added as he joined them to say it was time to go.

'That's quite true,' said Antoine. 'Now let's go home.'

Chapter Twenty-nine

❧

The following morning, Alexandra was wakened early by Stéphie, quickly followed by Antoine, who was carrying a tray. On it were coffee, rolls, butter and fig jam.

'Breakfast in bed,' he stated, settling the tray on her knees. 'And then you must get up. The lake is frozen and we're going skating.'

'I haven't got skates . . .'

'There are dozens of pairs here,' he said. 'It's been a pastime at the chateau for years.'

'So don't take too long eating,' said Stéphie, in case Alexandra hadn't got the message. 'I'll teach you to skate. Don't worry.'

Alexandra didn't dawdle. She put on as many of her clothes as she could get on at the same time, ending with one of the boiler suits she had bought at the market, and then presented herself downstairs.

Antoine regarded her critically, made her put on a battered leather flying jacket, a scarf and an extra pair of gloves. 'You will soon get warm but at first it is cold. What size are your feet?'

There was a bit of confusion because she was uncertain what her continental shoe size was but eventually she was found a pair of skates which nearly fitted when a pair of socks had been added to the two pairs she was already wearing.

'Apart from looking like Bibendum – or a Michelin Man,' she said, 'I can hardly walk, I'm wearing so many layers.'

'You can take things off when you're warm,' said Stéphie. 'No, kittens, you can't come with us. You'll get cold.'

Although Stéphie had strong maternal instincts, the kittens didn't recognise her authority and insisted on dancing out of the door behind Milou.

'Are you sure the ice won't break so we'll fall into the freezing water and drown?' Alexandra said to Antoine.

'If the ice breaks we might get wet but we won't drown. It's more of a swamp than a lake. Come along. I'll hold you.'

The children had all put on their skates and glided off with elegance and style. Antoine's arm was strong about her waist and somehow Alexandra got to the ice.

'Now, step on,' he said firmly.

She stepped, slipped and fell over. He laughed.

'Excuse me,' he said. 'I'm sorry to laugh but you are always so poised, so elegant, I can't help being amused.'

'In England it is not considered good form to mock the afflicted,' said Alexandra, as haughty as it was possible to be while sitting on the ice with her limbs sliding underneath her.

He picked her up and set her on the ice again. 'Hold on tight.' He was certainly holding her tightly. She was clamped to his side. 'Now move when I move.'

Henri, seeing her difficulties, swooped to her side and took her hand. 'Come on! Papa and I have got you. One, two, one, two.'

Suddenly Alexandra found she was moving over the ice, if not with grace, at least without falling over. Henri, convinced she'd got it now, abandoned her, and for a moment, she thought she was going to fall again.

'Just relax into it. I won't let you go. You're safe with me.'

Although Alexandra was concentrating very hard on relaxing, not something that was easy, she allowed herself a moment to imagine Antoine was using those words in a different context. Still, it was not to be. She must enjoy what she had and not pine for something she couldn't have.

'I think I've got it,' she said. 'Let me go but don't move away.'

'Very well. Bravo! You have got it!'

Alexandra stayed on her feet for a few minutes until Stéphie came racing towards her and couldn't stop, making Alexandra fall over again.

Now she'd tasted the joy of skating, Alexandra became determined. No matter how many times she landed on the ice, she insisted on getting up again and striking off across the ice, only to fall over again.

Antoine helped her up again. '*Chérie*, you don't have to do this. We can go inside and drink hot chocolate.'

'No, no. I hate to give up on things. I'm going to get to that tree' – she pointed to the edge of the lake – 'and back, without falling over, and then hot chocolate would be lovely.'

It took her three more attempts before she finally made it. Antoine helped her up every time, getting her back on her feet and watching her tentative, staggering steps until, at last, she realised she was doing it properly. She was skating. She turned round when she got to the tree and headed back towards Antoine.

'Come on, Lexi!' he called. His arms were open and he was smiling, willing her to make it.

Nothing would have stopped her. She flew across the ice and into his arms. For a few wonderful moments he hugged her to him. 'Well done, *chérie*, well done!' He kissed the top of her head and mumbled something into her hair. Her heart knew it was something fond and loving but her mind told her it couldn't be.

He released her. 'Come on, let's get you into the warm. I'll make my special drink which will cure all your aches and pains. Sit down – let's get your skates off.'

Alexandra hadn't been aware of suffering any aches and pains until he mentioned them. Now, she sat on the frozen ground and let him deal with the laces and ease off her skates. Then he picked her up and carried her into the house, leaving skates, shoes and various discarded scarves and mittens lying on the ground.

'I'll get them later,' he said.

She closed her eyes as he carried her, drinking in his smell, relishing his closeness. But her moment of bliss was short. He put her down when they reached the chateau.

'Go and make yourself comfortable,' said Antoine. 'I'll be with you in a minute.'

The children rushed past, Félicité to the office so she could telephone Jules (Alexandra was willing to

344

bet), and Stéphie up to her room, taking Milou and the kittens with her. Henri, more relaxed than his sisters, ambled upstairs too, muttering something about playing some music.

Alexandra collapsed on to the most well-sprung sofa, the one that had been drawn up close to the fire. She pulled a rug over herself and tucked her feet under her. She should go to her room and put on her slippers, but she didn't want to move. Just for a few moments she wanted to think about Antoine and how lovely it had been in his arms, having him close.

He brought her a steaming mug of chocolate. 'Here you are. This will warm you up.'

She sipped. 'Oh! It's got something in it!'

'Brandy. You drink it up and relax. I'm making lunch.'

'I should—'

'No, you shouldn't,' he said. 'This is your time off. I'll ask one of the children if I need help.'

A little later she was aware of having drifted off to sleep, affected by her early start, a lot of fresh air and exercise, and a large measure of cognac. She was also aware of someone putting a cushion under her head and rearranging the blanket. She could easily have stirred and done these things for herself but while she had her eyes shut she could pretend that Antoine was doing it because he loved her and not just because he was a kind man who cared about his employees.

The next two days would always be special, Alexandra felt. She wasn't allowed to cook or wash up (although she did sneak down and tidy up early one morning).

The washing was piled up in front of the new washing machine, waiting for the young woman who usually came in daily but was currently on holiday. During the day, they skated, rambled in the woods, read, painted or played instruments. In the evenings, Antoine taught them card games on which they gambled with matchsticks. Stéphie couldn't have been happier.

'It's as if you and . . .' Stéphie paused, obviously having been told she mustn't say anything to embarrass Alexandra. 'It's like having two very kind parents.'

'Maybe,' said Alexandra. 'Now, who would you like to read you a story? Me or Papa?'

'I'd like you to, Lexi. You won't be here forever.'

Alexandra followed the little girl up the stairs with a lump in her throat.

Next day, the weather was suddenly warmer and the ice on the lake had melted. Luckily, later in the morning, when Stéphie announced this sad fact, Penelope and Jack arrived. They were a little bit breathless and excited, holding hands and giggling. It was very endearing, Alexandra thought. Penelope was naturally a rather serious person.

'We've come to talk about our wedding,' said Penelope.

'I found out from my brother when they're planning to emigrate – they'll be Ten Pound Poms!' said Jack. 'Which means the Australian government will let you emigrate for only ten pounds, subject to certain conditions. Emigrate means leaving your own country to go and live somewhere else,' Jack explained to Stéphie, who had her mouth open to ask the question.

'Has Lexi emigrated, then?' Stéphie said.

'Not really,' said Alexandra quickly. 'I've just come to live in France for a bit. It's not quite the same thing.'

'But my brother and his wife are leaving for Australia quite soon,' said Jack. 'We have to have the wedding by the first of April at the latest.'

'And you have very kindly said we can have it here, in the chateau,' said Penelope, smiling firmly at Antoine, who was looking taken aback.

'We were also wondering if it might be possible for you to put up some family and friends in your outbuildings,' said Jack.

'Really?' said Antoine. 'Don't you like your English guests? Have you seen the outbuildings?'

'The thing is, Antoine,' said Penelope, now more like her usual brisk self than she had been at first. 'If you got a move on, you could have some of those buildings ready, and we would pay for people to stay in them. After that, you can hire them out to *les Anglais* for the rest of the year. They would pay lots!'

'It would be a great deal of work,' said Antoine, considering the matter.

'Although of course the building I am most interested in is the orangery, for the reception,' said Penelope.

'Penelope,' said Antoine. 'I would love to help and had we more time I would be delighted, as I said before . . .' He paused. 'But we have just a couple of months—'

'Three months. And Alexandra will help you,' said Penelope. 'The children will go to school in the New Year—'

347

'Actually,' said Antoine. 'The school – I mean the progressive one that Philippe's children go to – can't take them until the following term. I haven't had an opportunity to discuss it with Jack and David yet. Let alone Alexandra.'

'Oh,' said Penelope.

'I heard just before Christmas and I didn't want to talk about school during the holiday.' He seemed embarrassed not to have told the family sooner. 'I know Henri and Félicité were looking forward to going.'

'It's OK, Papa,' said Félicité after a moment. 'We understand.'

'Well,' Penelope went on, 'if Alexandra is here, but isn't really needed to look after the children all the time—'

Alexandra opened her mouth to say that if the children didn't need her, she would have to leave. But she didn't want to. Nor, it seemed, did Penelope want her to speak.

'No, Alexandra, just a moment. If the children aren't going away to school until after the wedding, they will be taught by David and Jack,' said Penelope. 'So although Alexandra will need to be here, in case Antoine has to go away, she will have time on her hands.'

Alexandra felt she should object strongly to having her time allocated without her being consulted but as the thought of overseeing the building work thrilled her, she merely gave a little grunt of agreement.

Antoine was more vocal. 'Perhaps Alexandra doesn't want to oversee the renovation of old buildings, or clear out the orangery. We mustn't take advantage of her.'

Alexandra found her voice. 'A project like this would be wonderful. I'd love to do it,' she said. 'If you didn't mind?' This she addressed to Antoine.

He shrugged and smiled. 'If it makes you happy, I am happy.'

Although delighted with his reaction, Alexandra felt obliged to protest a little. 'Except that it will be expensive to renovate the buildings.'

'We've got my truffle money,' said Stéphie.

'And we will pay in advance for everything,' said Penelope firmly.

'Would you mind if I talked to Alexandra about this in private?' said Antoine. Without waiting for an answer, he ushered her out of the room.

When they reached the study Alexandra remembered he was someone who told other people what to do with their businesses and wasn't just a father who loved spending time with his children.

'Before you take this on, Alexandra,' he said seriously, 'you must give yourself time to consider what it entails. You will have to deal with French builders, planning approvals, buying supplies at the best prices, all sorts of things which will be new to you and you may well not wish to undertake.'

'Won't you be here?'

'Not all the time. There are some loose ends that need tying up with my last project. If we went for this, you would be in charge. Although of course I hope we'll have David, too. And Maxime for the legal part.'

'I've never done anything like this before,' she said, suddenly filled with doubt.

'If you want to do it, you will do it. I have perfect faith in you. We'll do what we can and not worry about the rest.'

Alexandra felt a sudden flip of excitement. It was a massive project but so exciting. 'I'd love to do it! And I know David and Jack will help when they're not teaching.'

Antoine smiled and Alexandra felt she'd been breathed on by the sun itself. 'Thank you, Alexandra.'

Chapter Thirty

The following day, Antoine and Alexandra surveyed the buildings with much more concentration than they had before. Alexandra had a notebook and pencil and Antoine had a builder's tape measure. Alexandra found it easy to visualise how things would look if a wall was knocked down or moved. She had done a fair bit of knocking down walls in London, in her home there, although mostly she had crossed her fingers when it came to knowing whether or not the ceiling might come down too. Luckily for her it had been a successful strategy.

Here, there would be builders, people who knew what they were doing. But they might also say: No you can't do that. She would have to accept that – at least until she knew a bit more about what they were hoping to achieve and the building process.

'There is a father and son who do a lot of work in the area,' said Antoine. 'They will know other tradesmen. We'll ask them to come and look at what's required. It'll be a big job; they may prefer not to take it on. If they don't, we'll have to find someone else.' Antoine frowned. 'I want you to know what you're taking on, *chérie.*'

He was looking at her so intensely she had to look away.

'Let's go and see the orangery,' she said. 'That's where Penelope wants the party.'

They turned away from the outbuildings and walked across to the orangery, which was on the other side of the chateau.

As they approached the building, Antoine said, 'It is rather inconvenient that Penelope is so set on having her wedding breakfast in the orangery, but the reason for it is romantic. I suppose, as a Frenchman, I should encourage romance.' Alexandra turned away so he wouldn't see her blush. 'Now,' he said, finding the key on the ledge, 'let's see if we can make it suitable for a celebration.'

As Alexandra and Penelope had discovered before, the orangery was mostly in need of sweeping and painting.

'It's because it's part of the chateau and it has been used more recently,' Antoine explained, examining what appeared to be a patch of damp in the corner. 'The other buildings have been ignored for so long.'

'Félicité's mural will improve it, but it will need to be quite big. Maybe she could get Jules, the boy she likes, to help her.'

'Hmm,' said Antoine. 'Maybe not, considering the history this building has.'

Alexandra laughed. 'We'll get Stéphie to be their assistant. Henri too. They can be chaperones.'

But as Antoine locked up the *orangerie* she couldn't help feeling wistful about her feelings for her boss. Unrequited love could be rather draining.

*

Once the world had gone back to work after the Christmas break, Antoine and Alexandra visited the builders in town. It was an old-established business, handed down from father to son for three generations. The father was not hopeful they could take on the work. He explained why at length, sucked his teeth and shook his head. But once his son came into the office and saw Alexandra and discovered she was going to be in charge of the operation, everything became a lot more positive.

'Well,' said Antoine afterwards, 'you had an effect on Luc. Suddenly, they can take on the job right away. He obviously has a penchant for English roses.'

Alexandra couldn't stop herself blushing at this, but she brushed off the compliment. 'I expect he thinks he can do what he likes and I won't notice. He's wrong, of course.'

'But how will you know?'

'David will help me. And I'm good at knowing when people are trying to cheat me. In the antiques world, although most people are kindness itself, there are sharks – as in all businesses. I learnt how to spot them. And I don't think Luc is a shark.'

'I don't either. Let's go and tell everyone the good news. We have builders! *On y va!*'

The days started early. Each morning, Antoine went to the farm after a cup of coffee and a piece of bread and Alexandra went to where the building work was going on. She wrapped her hair in a scarf and donned her boiler suit supplemented with extra layers of clothing. She liked to arrive shortly before the builders did, so she was there, smiling, and alert.

She did struggle with the language to begin with. But the men were all very willing to help this English girl who was so interested, knew what she wanted and cared how work was done. She praised good work and just a look was enough to make people redo anything that was sloppy. She trained Stéphie to bring English cake in the afternoon, and the work went on apace. The old stable would soon be a comfortable place to stay, with two bedrooms, a reasonably sized kitchen, and a sitting room with double doors that opened on to a terrace.

'I'd stay here!' said David, who came to inspect progress. 'It's going to be splendid. Good idea to put a big window in that wall. It lets the light in and makes it all look bigger.'

'They had to put in a stone lintel, which was quite difficult,' said Alexandra. 'But Luc is so willing and helpful.'

'I wonder why that is?' said David wryly.

Alexandra didn't protest. Even she had been forced to admit the men did work well for her and, so far, no one had tried to get away with anything underhand.

As word of what was going on went round, people came to inspect progress. Most of them were interested and admiring but one morning, when Alexandra was particularly covered in dust and cobwebs, having just inspected the upper floor of a barn, Lucinda appeared.

Alexandra brushed herself down, waiting for Lucinda to say something, hoping there wasn't anything actually alive on her head, crawling over her scarf and about to drop on to her face. Eventually she said, 'Can I help you?'

'Oh, I've just come for a look round. Everyone says how *wonderful* it is here, so I thought I'd find out for myself.' She surveyed the barn they were in, where currently nothing had happened. Alexandra had been looking to see if it might be a project for later. 'I'm not impressed so far. I was hoping some of my friends could stay here, but that's obviously not going to be possible.'

'We won't do any work on this barn until after the wedding. Why don't I show you the rooms we're planning to have ready in time for that?'

This was a different matter. There were two buildings currently being converted. One was part of the old stables and the other was a *pigeonnier*, where pigeons used to provide food for the chateau.

'This one is coming along well,' said Alexandra, showing Lucinda into the old stable. 'You can see the sitting room with its terrace, and the kitchen, but we haven't done the stairs to upstairs yet, so you'd have to climb a ladder to look at the bedrooms.'

Lucinda laughed prettily, gesturing to the narrow skirt she was wearing under her tweed coat with long boots. 'And obviously I can't do that in this skirt. Can I look at the other building?'

'That's not nearly ready.'

'Still, I'd like to see it. You can call me nosy if you like.'

Alexandra had been silently calling her nosy since she first appeared. 'You're welcome as long as it doesn't take too long. I am very busy.'

'Everyone knows how busy you are,' said Lucinda as the two women walked to the next building. 'They are *astounded* at what a good job you're doing!'

'Oh . . .'

'But what nobody talks about is how much this is all costing.'

Alexandra opened her mouth to explain that the rental money was going towards the cost of renovation, but she had no real idea if it would be enough. She decided it was none of Lucinda's business. She shrugged. 'I don't know about that.'

'Obviously not. I heard that Antoine had sold a piece of land to raise money and he's refusing to pay for the children to go to boarding school in England.'

'I'm so sorry. That's not my business.'

Lucinda seemed pleased to hear this. 'Well, just bear it in mind before you plan on turning all the dozens of outbuildings there are here at the chateau into holiday accommodation that no one will ever want to rent. Unless you're going to finance it with your own fortune, of course.'

'I beg your pardon?'

'Oh, sorry, I forgot. You have to get married to get it, don't you? And that would only be worth it for you if you and Antoine were very much in love. And it's highly unlikely that Antoine will so much as glance at you if you go on looking like a char lady on a bad day.'

Alexandra stood even taller than usual and lifted her chin. 'If you've seen everything you want to see, can I show you out? As I said, I have a lot to do.'

Watching Lucinda walk away a few minutes later Alexandra realised she wasn't quite sure who'd won that argument. But on balance she felt that she had been the more dignified, which definitely scored points.

One of the many things that had been worrying Alexandra in a low-level way was the mural in the orangery. Félicité was painting it, and sometimes Jules, her boyfriend, helped her. Alexandra had promised not to go and look at it on her own and Félicité seemed very secretive about it. But Alexandra really wanted to see it while there was still time to paint over it and do another one. She knew Penelope had said she wanted to inspect the orangery too and she certainly didn't want her walking in to see something outrageous.

When she went into the kitchen for a snack a few days after Lucinda's visit and saw Félicité spreading butter on a bit of bread, Alexandra decided that now was the time.

'Félicité,' she said, sitting down opposite her. 'The mural. I need to see it. Your grandmother wants to come and show the orangery to her caterers. I don't want her to see it before I have.'

Félicité chewed agonisingly slowly. ''K,' she said. 'It's not finished but it's near enough.'

'You'll let me look?' Alexandra hadn't realised until now quite how much she'd been worrying about it. In the scheme of things it was a tiny issue, but the orangery was the heart of the wedding for Penelope and it had to be right.

'Yup. But not on your own. I'll come with you. When I've finished my breakfast.'

'No hurry,' said Alexandra. 'I want something to eat myself. Is Antoine still at the farm?'

'Yup. I don't want him seeing it until it's done.'

'Fine.' Alexandra took the end of baguette that Félicité had left and buttered it. 'When it's finished we should have a grand unveiling.'

'Could we invite Jules's parents?'

Alexandra nodded. 'I'm sure you could.' She paused, waiting for Félicité to explain why she wanted this.

'They don't believe he's been helping me. They think he's been getting into trouble with the other boys, on their mobylettes, down by the river. They're talking about making him stay at school at the weekends.'

'I see.'

Félicité chewed for a while. 'They're probably just being nosy.'

'Honey, many of us are nosy a lot of the time, and that includes me.'

Half an hour later, Félicité unlocked the door to the orangery and Alexandra went in.

She felt her throat catch with unexpected emotion. One wall was entirely taken up with a picture of the chateau with the woods and mountains behind.

The chateau had roses climbing up it which weren't there in real life and, in front of it, stood the open carriage they'd found in the old stables, a dapple-grey horse between the shafts. Milou and the kittens played by the carriage. Although in real life they were young cats, here they were still small. One of them was swinging on Milou's tail.

Next to the animals was Antoine, his two older children alongside him. In front was Stéphie. She was holding a bunch of flowers and offering it to Alexandra,

358

who was instantly recognisable in her boiler suit and scarf. Félicité had added her big pearls.

'Oh, you put me in!' said Alexandra. 'You shouldn't have! I won't be here for much longer.'

'But you were here,' said Félicité. 'And I can always paint you out and put in another woman if Papa gets married again.'

Alexandra had to laugh. She really liked Félicité but she had her mother's sometimes acerbic tongue. Still, as her use of it was always funny as well as cutting, Alexandra couldn't hold it against her. Now she put an arm round the girl. 'That's very true. But I must say, you could have put me in wearing something a bit nicer than my work clothes.'

Félicité shrugged. 'It's all you ever wear these days.'

'You sound like your mother,' said Alexandra before she could stop herself. These days, she never criticised Lucinda in front of her children. 'I mean, she said something like that to me.'

'Well, she's right.'

'I'm too busy to pay attention to what I look like. Now, let's go back to the mural. How near finished are you?'

'You can see that a lot of the greenery is just sketched out and needs to be painted. I want to put a bit of the lake in if I can.' Félicité paused. 'I wonder if Papa would let me carry it on to another wall. Then I could paint us all skating.'

'Maybe after the wedding? It would be a shame to have to rush it. I love your style. It's very clear and a bit naïve like Rousseau – remember? The tiger in the forest?'

'David said something like that to me after he saw the mural in Véronique's room. He made me realise that being a bit childlike isn't necessarily a bad thing.'

'Not when it's like this, no. Will there be art teaching at your school, do you think?'

'It depends which one I go to. I don't expect the one my mother would prefer will be very keen on it. Or they won't like my painting anyway.'

'You never know,' said Alexandra, feeling that she probably did know and that Lucinda's preferred school would be more interested in teaching Félicité to be a lady than in encouraging her artistic side. 'Can I let your grandmother see it now? She's desperate to come and I've been putting her off.'

'You really think it's all right?' Félicité looked anxious suddenly.

'I do. I think it's really, really good. David will tell you the same.'

Félicité sighed happily.

In the end Félicité and Alexandra decided to ask Jules's parents (and Jules, of course) to come on the same day that Penelope arranged to come with her caterers.

'We can open some fizz and I'll ask David to do some little nibbles for them,' said Alexandra. 'He and Jack can come and it'll be like a party.'

'David's seen it lots of times,' said Félicité. 'But I'll ask Papa.' She paused. 'He hasn't seen it yet.'

Alexandra nodded, sensing Félicité's nerves about her father seeing the mural. She shared them; the way the figures were arranged made it look a little bridal, although she realised she was probably reading a whole lot of things into it that weren't there.

Alexandra had intended to put on a dress and make herself look less like a workman and more like someone who arranged weddings, but time got away from her so she was restricted to putting her hair up in a loose chignon and putting the scarf she usually put round her head round her waist instead. For the sake of the mural, she put on her pearls. David was there when Alexandra and Félicité arrived and he winked, which meant he thought she looked OK.

Penelope and her two caterers were the first of the visitors to come through the door of the *orangerie*.

'Goodness!' said Penelope. 'Félicité did that? It's amazing! But where are my manners. Let me introduce you. These ladies are the best caterers in the area. Madame Pam Hopkins and her colleague, Madame Elizabeth Pollard. This is Alexandra, who works for my son-in-law. Very hard to say what her job is now but she came here as a nanny.'

After the how-do-you-do's Pam said, 'How nice to meet you. I've heard such a lot about you.'

Then Elizabeth said, 'I expect you're wondering how two Englishwomen came to become caterers in France; everyone does.'

'We met at the market,' Pam continued. 'Elizabeth was with her husband and I heard her speaking English. I said hello; we became friends and discovered we both have a passion for food.'

'And I would like an English element to the food,' said Penelope, 'for Jack's sake.'

'We'll be serving things like devilled eggs, angels on horseback – things the English love and the French will enjoy too, I think,' said Pam. 'We're still discussing the main courses. Cold only, obviously. So . . .' Pam addressed Alexandra. 'Where can we serve from?'

While Alexandra was talking to the caterers, she saw Antoine arrive with Jules and his parents. They went straight to the mural and Alexandra could tell how impressed they were.

'Is this a private party? Or can anyone come,' said Lucinda in a loud voice. 'Oh, darling!' she said to Félicité. 'Did you do that? It's really quite good, isn't it?'

Feeling protective, Alexandra made an excuse and joined the group in front of the mural.

'It's really *very* good,' said David. 'Your daughter has great artistic talent.'

'Oh,' said Lucinda, apparently not sure if she should be pleased or annoyed.

Antoine put his arm round his daughter and kissed her head. 'I am so proud of you.' He smiled at Jules. 'And you – I gather you helped.'

Jules nodded. 'I only did the background; Félicité wouldn't let me do the important bits. Oh! Here are Henri and his sister.'

Lucinda opened her mouth and shut it again. Alexandra suspected she was about to deny being Stéphie's mother, and was glad she changed her mind.

Soon everyone was milling about, drinking *crémant* and eating the snacks that David provided.

'It's a lovely space for a party, isn't it?' said Penelope, who had been joined by Jack.

'It is,' Alexandra agreed. 'And isn't the mural lovely?'

'So charming!' said Penelope. 'We might have wished she hadn't painted you wearing a boiler suit, but it is all we ever see you in these days.'

'That's what Félicité said when I questioned it. Can I get you another glass of wine?'

'I think I've had enough, thank you. Can I take Jack and inspect the accommodation?'

'I'll come with you,' said Alexandra, happy for an excuse to leave what was developing into a party. She felt embarrassed being part of the mural; it made her look as if she was one of the family and she really wasn't.

Chapter Thirty-one

Suddenly, it was mid March and the wedding was only a couple of weeks away. Time had rushed on without anyone noticing how that had happened. And in spite of everyone's hard work there were still things that needed to be done before the converted farm buildings became comfortable, glamorous places to stay.

Alexandra had been busier than ever, doing the things that seemed to be nobody's job – a bit of grouting here, painting a skirting board there, putting candles in the candle holders and of course buying things for the kitchens. In spite of the days ticking by remorselessly, she loved it. She was worried things wouldn't be finished in time to receive guests, who, annoyingly, were arriving a few days before the wedding, but she had faith. David was a great ally and good at placing large mirrors, urns and in one case a bird bath in strategic places.

A couple of days before Jack's family arrived, everyone was going to the dressmaker in Antibes that Lucinda had recommended, to have final fittings for their wedding clothes. Afterwards they were spending the night with friends of Antoine's who had a chateau near Nice.

In spite of careful planning, when Jack, Penelope and Lucinda arrived in their car, so they could travel in convoy, no one at the chateau was ready.

'Milou went missing last night,' explained David to Jack through the car window. 'Stéphie won't leave until he's found.'

Lucinda sighed deeply and Penelope declared she might as well get out of the car and use the bathroom. So everyone got out and Alexandra made coffee.

'Milou is a big dog,' said Antoine patiently to Stéphie, not for the first time. 'He will come back. There is no need to be worried about him, *p'tite*.'

'I expect he's gone off hunting,' said Jack.

'He's never done it before!' said Stéphie.

'Actually, he went off for a couple of hours a few days ago, and came back,' said David.

But nothing that anyone could say would persuade Stéphie that her beloved dog wasn't gone forever.

Eventually, Alexandra, who'd only been going to Antibes as an adviser anyway, said, 'Stéphie, you go now, have a lovely time and don't worry about Milou. I'll stay and wait for him and if he's not back by – say – six o'clock I'll go and look for him. But he *will* be back by then because he'll be hungry. You know how much Milou likes his dinner.'

'You won't! You'll forget!' said Stéphie.

'How can I forget Milou?' said Alexandra. 'He's going to keep me company this evening when David is out and you're all away having the finishing touches added to your outfits and having a lovely time!'

365

Eventually, after this scenario was repeated in different forms many, many times, the two cars set off to Antibes, Stéphie finally having been convinced.

'Are you sure you'll be all right this evening?' David was standing on the step next to Alexandra. 'I'm going to an art exhibition but I could skip dinner afterwards and come back early.'

Although he never ever said anything about his love life to her, Alexandra knew that David was planning to see his friend in town.

'I'll be absolutely fine,' she insisted. 'I've got quite a lot I want to do today and am secretly very grateful to Milou for getting me out of the dressmaking trip. Now I can finish grouting the tiles in the bathroom in the stable. It's my new favourite thing!'

'Honestly, Lexi, I fear for your sanity sometimes . . .'

'And then I'm going to come back, eat the most unhealthy, delicious food I can find and sink into a deep bath. Then I'll wash the grit out of my hair and probably fall asleep.' She paused and then remembered. 'Provided Milou comes back.'

The two kittens ran up to her at that moment and rubbed themselves against her legs. 'Why don't you find your big brother, or uncle, or whatever Milou is to you! Being cute isn't all that useful, you know!'

'I'm sure he will come back,' said David. 'He's gone hunting, or maybe courting. He'll make a nuisance of himself and some farmer or other will throw him out, or telephone.'

'I know. The farmer will telephone just when I've submerged my head in the water. But I'll go and collect him if that happens. Now, I've got work to do! Don't hurry back tonight. I'll be in bed really early.'

'Well, don't forget to fully load up the range with logs if you want hot water. The immersion heater is on the blink.'

Alexandra tutted. 'I knew I had to ask the electrician to do something else when he was here yesterday. Never mind, he's coming again tomorrow. As long as it's done before the guests arrive.'

Once he was satisfied, David went off and Alexandra went back to work. Her unexpected extra day felt like a gift. There was still so much to do before everything was ready.

When Alexandra returned to the chateau at lunch-time she spent some minutes calling for Milou, but only the cats came running. She went into the kitchen and ate some leftover croissants heated in the range, adding a few logs to the fire. Although she'd believed every word she'd said to Stéphie about Milou coming home when he was hungry, she missed him. She went out and called from all parts of the garden, willing his large black and white form to come bounding up.

But it wasn't dinnertime yet, she told herself, and returned to her grouting.

Milou's whereabouts was at the back of her mind all afternoon, and when the workmen all went home and she felt she could too, she hurried to the chateau quickly. There was no sign of him and no response to her cries.

She called from all parts of the garden again and then went inside, still not too concerned. The days were lengthening and it wouldn't get dark for some time.

She was whisking eggs for an omelette when the telephone rang. She hurried to answer it, hoping it was a farmer with Milou, and also hoping his accent wouldn't be too hard for her to understand.

It wasn't a farmer; it was Stéphie. They'd had a very nice day making sure their dresses were perfect (they were) and shopping for little handbags to put handkerchiefs and confetti in; then they'd driven to Antoine's friends, who had a very beautiful chateau. But she really only wanted to know about Milou.

Just for a second Alexandra considered lying to her, so that she would enjoy her evening and go to bed happy. But she couldn't. Lying to children was hardly ever a good thing and if – please God, this wouldn't happen – Stéphie came back tomorrow to discover that Milou wasn't there, she would never trust Alexandra again.

'No, darling, he's not back yet. But it's not his dinnertime just yet, is it?'

'His dinnertime was half an hour ago,' Stéphie said with a wobble in her voice.

'But we all have dinner late sometimes. What are you having for yours?'

'Lexi, don't try and make me talk about food when all I care about is Milou.'

'All right. I'll eat my omelette really quickly and then I'll go and look for him. And I'll ring when I find him.'

'However late it is?' asked Stéphie.

'Yes. Give me the number, and ask your papa to warn the people you're staying with there might be a late call. Can you do that?'

'Yes.'

They disconnected. Alexandra ate her omelette and tried not to think about the bath she couldn't have. There was hardly any point in building up the range now.

Once she'd resolved to look for Milou, she was determined to make proper preparations. She wasn't going into the woods as it was getting dark without a plan.

First, she found a good torch. Then some rope so she could make a lead for Milou if she located him. Somehow, she couldn't bring herself to take his actual lead: it seemed like tempting fate. She packed half a baguette filled with butter and ham into her rucksack. And, although it would be heavy, she added a bottle of water. Matches, a candle, a ball of string. She put in a spare scarf (she didn't know why she might need this but since she had to take a rucksack she thought she might as well pack it out with light things) and a tin cup. She took a newspaper and a packet of biscuits and some cheese.

She made sure she was wearing the right clothes. Sturdy shoes (although they didn't have very thick soles), spare socks and an old anorak that had probably been Antoine's, which she put over her jumper. She felt ready to climb Everest, let alone take a stroll up some gentle hills through the woods to find a dog.

Then she left a detailed note for David, should anything bad happen to her. She was determined no one would have any excuse to reproach her for being stupid. She even drew a sketchy map of where she intended to go, which was up a rough footpath to where they'd found the truffle.

Eventually she felt there was nothing else she could do, and heaved the rucksack on to her shoulders. It was heavy, but she knew the glass bottle with water in it was the heaviest thing, and that she shouldn't go without that. She decided she'd get used to the weight of it quickly and went on her way.

She had just got going when she remembered she had forgotten to shut the hens in. She didn't want Stéphie to come back to find they'd all been eaten by the fox, so she went and did it. Then she set off again.

She was tired after her day with the builders but she enjoyed the exercise to begin with. Then she looked up to see a big black cloud hovering over the forest where she was headed. For a second she debated going back for another coat, sturdier than Antoine's anorak, but she couldn't bear to after a long day doing physical work. She persuaded herself she'd be fine. She was going into a wood – the trees would protect her.

Alexandra walked up the hill, calling every few minutes, and although it was nowhere near being dark when she set off, once she got in among the trees, things changed. She considered using her torch, but although she had checked it worked when she took it from the small room where such things were kept, she didn't know how long the batteries would last. She should keep it for emergencies. She didn't allow herself to consider what that might consist of.

By now the forest was almost entirely silent apart from her calling, the occasional sound of her feet on the ground and the odd sudden rustle in the distance. It wouldn't be wild boar, or anything dangerous, she told herself. It would be birds. Large birds. Boar wouldn't be in the forest so close to civilisation. But she couldn't forget the wild-boar tracks they had seen and examined when they'd been skating. Those tracks were very much closer to civilisation than she was now – although they were in the woods on the other side of the chateau, she told herself quickly. Anyway, her calling the dog was bound to scare them away. Wild animals almost always keep away from humans, given the chance.

At the same time as she had this more encouraging thought, she realised that walking and calling had made her thirsty so she decided to have a break. She found a rock to sit on and got her rucksack down from her back. She drank quite a lot of water and nibbled a bit of baguette. She considered finishing the water so she could get rid of the bottle but wisdom prevailed.

A distant memory of a *Swallows and Amazons* book made her leave a sign – 'patterans' they had called them, with a few twigs that were lying around. Anyone looking for her – it would be David – would know she'd been here.

She set off again.

It was only after she'd finished her water and shouted herself hoarse that she saw she'd climbed much higher than she'd realised. She was concentrating on setting one foot in front of another and it was only then that she appreciated it was almost completely dark. And then she heard a sound and realised it was rain, pattering on the leaves. This was not good.

She swung down her rucksack and got out her torch. If she had doubted the wisdom of her mission before, she doubted it even more now. If Milou hadn't heard her by now he wasn't going to. And climbing the hills in the dark and rain would only put her at risk. She already felt stupid for coming so far without thinking about this before.

She would switch on the torch and go back.

But going down was harder than travelling up had been. She slipped on stones and branches, and now the rain was finding its way past the leaves and adding mud to the hazards. She nearly fell several times. And then she did fall, dropping her torch, bumping down the hill, bouncing off rocks and tree roots. The thought was flashing through her mind that this was a much faster way to get down than walking was when she banged into a large rock and stopped. She was breathless and frightened, not daring to move in case she'd broken something.

She seemed to be sitting in a stream and realised that rain was running off the mountains and through the woods. But being wet and cold was the least of her problems. Did anything hurt? Eventually she decided she was all right – bruised, shaken, covered in mud, feeling like an idiot, but not hurt. But she didn't move for a little while, as she let herself get over the effects of shock. It was going to be a lot harder without the torch.

She felt suddenly tearful at the prospect of making her way back through the forest in the dark when it was so slippery underfoot. But crying wouldn't help. She had to get on.

'Right!' she said. 'Let's get going!' Then she wished she hadn't spoken her thoughts out loud. Her voice among the dripping trees sounded so lonely and vulnerable she almost wanted to cry again. The forest seemed darker than ever and the rain to be coming down harder.

She got to her feet and instantly they slid from under her, making her sit down hard on a rock. A few more tears came but she was determined to fight this useless self-pity. She had to move – she couldn't stay where she was all night, sitting in a stream getting wetter and colder with every second.

She should have brought a walking stick, she realised. There was a good collection of them in the umbrella-stand by the front door but it hadn't occurred to her that she might need one. She'd have to improvise.

There was just about enough light to see a fallen branch to her right. It was so slippery underfoot she'd be safer if she crawled to reach it but once there, she might be able to break off a bit to use as a stick.

She took off her rucksack, which kept banging into her and making things more difficult; then she got on her stomach and began crawling. It was horrible lying in the freezing cold mud and she could only move very slowly, pulling herself along on her elbows, and the branch seemed further away than she'd first thought.

She was just reaching out for it when she heard what sounded like stampeding cattle. Instinctively she curled into a ball, making herself as small as possible, pulling her hands under her body. A creature thundered past, inches from her. When she opened her eyes, she saw it was a boar, and racing after it was Milou.

'Milou!' Alexandra shouted as loudly as she could, but her voice was small and croaky. 'Milou! Stop!'

She clambered to her feet so she could go after him, managed a few steps and then tripped on a log and fell again, but this time much further. She bumped and slithered down the hill and when she stopped everything hurt and one ankle was folded under and hurt a lot more.

This time she couldn't muster any positive thoughts. She was in a pitch-dark wood, freezing cold and soaking wet, and it seemed to be raining harder by the minute. Her ankle was incredibly painful and moving in these conditions could be dangerous. Getting home no longer seemed possible. It would be better to just stay put and hope David would find her in the morning. It was either that or crawl home on her own. She swallowed a lump in her throat; crying would make her feel even worse. She pulled her knees up to her chin and rested her head on them and closed her eyes.

The time passed so slowly. Every minute seemed like an hour. Her ankle hurt more than any other part of her and the rest of her was badly bruised. She was stiffening and her muscles ached as well as her bruises. She was shivering convulsively.

Even if David did come looking for her, he wouldn't be able to find her in the dark. He wouldn't see her *Swallows and Amazons* patterans; he had no idea where she was. She was stuck in a French forest that was full of wild boar. A sob escaped her and sounded so feeble and pathetic more sobs followed. She huddled down closer to the ground.

Suddenly there was a loud snuffling and whimpering and then her ear was being licked. It was Milou!

'Oh, Milou! I've been so worried!' she said as she wrapped her arms round him, holding as much of him as she could, burying her face in his wet fur.

He seemed very pleased to see her too. He licked her ears and whimpered with joy, and she hung on to him. 'You must stay with me now, Milou. I had a rope for you but I've lost it now. You'll just have to stay by me and not go off after boar.'

She wished she hadn't mentioned them. The memory of those galloping hooves missing her by inches added to her fear. But she had Milou now. He would keep her warm. They'd go back tomorrow and everyone would be so glad to see them. Well, they'd be glad to see Milou, she thought. They'd just think that she had been incredibly stupid.

They huddled together in the wood, Alexandra with her eyes tight shut, clinging on to the dog. He was her friend and source of precious warmth. Her ankle was throbbing and all her aches and pains surrounded her in a blanket of discomfort. But she had Milou.

Then suddenly she didn't have him! He'd escaped from her arms and bounded up the hill. He must have heard another boar. Having him and losing him again tipped her over into despair. The one good thing about this desperate situation was Milou, and now he'd left her.

She looked up the hill, although she knew it was far too dark to see him, and saw lights dotted around like fireflies. There were voices, men shouting to each other in the darkness. There was someone there! Someone who could help!

'I'm here!' she shouted, her voice hoarse and pathetic, and then she realised she'd said it in English. *'Je suis ici! Aidez-moi!'*

She took a breath to shout again and then Milou was suddenly on top of her again, licking her face. And shortly behind him was Antoine.

Alexandra didn't believe what she was seeing. Antoine was supposedly miles away in Nice, yet somehow here he was.

He didn't speak at first; he just pulled her up from the ground and took her into his arms, holding her so tightly she could hardly breathe.

'Oh, thank God, thank God! You're safe!' he whispered, adding endearments in French, pulling her head in under his chin. Then he seemed to come to. 'I am so relieved to find you safe. When we found your rucksack I thought anything could have happened to you!'

'But why are you here? You went to Nice!' Alexandra whispered.

'I couldn't stay there when I realised you were going after that wretched dog. But he found me and led me to you, so at least we have to thank him for that.'

Alexandra started to shake uncontrollably. 'I was so frightened,' she said, 'I thought I'd be here all night.'

'We must get you home. Are you hurt in anyway?'

'My ankle . . .'

'Can you put weight on it?'

She tried and winced. 'A little. It's not broken.'

'It may be sprained.'

'We could use my scarf to tie it up.' She put her hand up to her head and realised that she'd lost her scarf somewhere along the way. Now she was safe she felt even more aware of the danger she'd been in. She felt obliged to explain herself. 'I tried to be sensible. I left a note. I left signs—'

'And I found them. Can you walk?'

'Of course!' said Alexandra, her courage returning just a little. She tested her ankle again, and whimpered. 'You may need to hold on to me. But can *you* walk? It's so slippery.'

'I brought a ski stick. I won't let you fall. Now, can you hold Milou's lead with your other hand?'

Antoine obviously hadn't thought it was tempting fate to bring a lead as she had done. 'I'll put it round my wrist. He seems to want to stay close anyway. But if he hears another boar—'

'There were boar? Oh, Alexandra! Were you frightened?'

'No,' she said, and then corrected herself. 'I was absolutely terrified.'

Chapter Thirty-two

Antoine held on to her, tightly, as she walked step by limping step. Alexandra realised he was taking almost all her weight but it couldn't be helped. Being close to him kept her going. She felt almost as if they were the same person.

At last they reached the bottom of the wood where a man was waiting with a battered Citroën Deux Chevaux with its headlights on.

Antoine and the man had a conversation in a dialect too broad for Alexandra to understand. Then Antoine lifted her into the front seat and got in the back with Milou. As they bumped along it occurred to Alexandra that Antoine spoke two sorts of French, one for the drawing room and one for the people on his farm. She had picked up some dialect words when she was working with the builders but she didn't understand much of what Antoine and his friend had just said, although she recognised the word *sanglier*, which meant boar.

When they reached the front door of the chateau, Antoine jumped out of the car, ran round to the front and picked her up off the front seat. Then he carried her into the house and sat her in the big hall chair.

Milou followed. The two young cats ran out to meet him, delighted to have their leader back home.

David was there. 'Oh, Lexi! What on earth has happened to you? You're all mud. And here's Milou! You horrible dog! You had us all so worried.'

'Look after her for me, David,' said Antoine. 'I must just talk to Hervé and thank Bruno and the men who came with me to search for Alexandra. And then I must telephone Nice, so Stéphie knows that Milou is safe.' He looked at Alexandra, who was starting to shiver. 'No need to mention anything else.'

David didn't hesitate. 'Let's get you into the warm,' he said to Alexandra. 'Although you may want to have some sort of a wash first. Can you walk?'

'Give me your arm as far as the loo door. I'll be fine then.'

She deliberately didn't look at the mirror over the sink. She didn't want to know how awful and bedraggled she looked. She just got the worst off with cold water and the towel which would probably bear signs of mud on it forever.

David was waiting for her and helped her through to the kitchen where there was a blazing fire in the range.

'I put as much wood on it as I could in the hope of getting some hot water,' said David, helping her over to the chair that was pulled up close to the fire. 'I don't suppose I've done much for the water, but it'll warm you if you sit by it.'

She sat down gingerly as her aches and pains began to make themselves felt. David helped her get her shoes and socks off and wrapped her bare feet in a towel.

'I'll get your slippers in a minute but I'll leave the brandy with you while I feed Milou. He must be starving.'

Alexandra drank the brandy that David had poured, relishing the warmth of it as it went down.

'Right,' said David, 'now you need something hot.' He added more brandy to her glass. 'What do you fancy? Hot milk? Hot chocolate? Soup would take longer. Toast? Scrambled egg?'

She interrupted him. 'David? I've just remembered. Aren't you supposed to be looking at art?'

'I popped back to see if you'd gone out to look for Milou and found your note.'

'So you abandoned your date?'

'What's a date compared to looking after my surrogate child?'

Alexandra suddenly wanted to cry. She knew it was partly the brandy. 'You can leave me. Your surrogate child will be fine. I'm warm; I have alcohol. And Antoine will look after me.' She could tell David was tempted. 'Seriously. I've caused so much trouble tonight, people out searching for me and everything. Please don't make me feel guilty about you, too.'

David considered for what seemed a long time. 'Are you sure?'

'Absolutely!' Although she wouldn't have admitted it, even to herself, she had her own reasons for wanting him out of the way.

He stood looking at her, as if thinking up more reasons why he shouldn't leave her. 'I'll be here early tomorrow. But if you really and truly don't mind, I will go back.'

'Good! You're always getting me out of scrapes, David. I don't want your social life to suffer because I've been a bit of an idiot.'

'A brave and well-meaning idiot . . .'

'Go!'

He kissed her cheek and left.

Antoine came in. 'Well, I spoke to Stéphie and she is delighted. And very, very grateful.'

'I was a fool really. I shouldn't have gone into the wood when it was raining and getting dark.'

Antoine didn't speak but Alexandra was in no doubt that he agreed with her. 'We must get you into a hot bath,' he said instead.

She nodded. 'I am so very cold!'

'And so very dirty!' He smiled through his concern. 'But food first. I'll make an omelette.' He refilled her glass.

Alexandra looked at the brandy, knowing she'd already had quite a lot to drink. But it was making her feel better so she took another sip.

Antoine made her an omelette which she ate but she felt too tired to finish the bread he put with it.

'Sorry,' she said as he looked disapproving. 'All that chewing. I just haven't the energy.'

'Let's get you into the bath and then into bed.' He made as if to pick her up, but she baulked.

'I can walk! Just give me your arm.' She had no desire to be carried up the stairs like a film star when she felt so very unstarlike.

He almost did carry her up he had to support her so much, but Alexandra felt better moving at least partly under her own steam. She did feel quite wobbly but he was there to support her.

'How is your ankle?' he asked when they reached the top of the staircase.

'I think it feels a little better,' she said and smiled.

'OK, I'm going to start running your bath. You have to keep a check on the hot water and as soon as it starts running cold you must turn off the hot tap.'

Alexandra wondered why he felt obliged to explain this when she'd been running baths most of her life, but she did as she was told. She watched him run the water until it came hot, and only then did he put the plug in.

'Now I'm going to boil a kettle to top up the hot water,' he said. 'But don't you let any cold water in. This bath is not going to be very hot. You won't be able to wash your hair.'

She smiled again. He seemed to have got her muddled up with Stéphie but he was being so kind, she didn't like to complain.

She turned off the hot tap the moment it went cold and shortly afterwards Antoine appeared with a kettle. Alexandra had experience of heating baths with kettles; it was never really very satisfactory. But she had to get the mud off somehow and it would do.

'Don't be too long,' said Antoine, 'you need to get into bed.'

She nodded. 'I know.'

'Call if you need help getting out of the bath.'

'I will,' she said, knowing that the bath would turn to a block of ice before she'd ask for help.

Unfortunately, her injured foot slipped as she got into the bath. She wasn't hurt but it meant that she went under the water and so got her hair wet. Antoine had definitely told her not to try and wash her hair but now her hair was wet, she might as well.

She got as much mud off her body and hair as she could, and rinsed herself. The water was very murky. As she hauled herself up, using the taps for support, she decided she would clean the bath out tomorrow, when she was a bit more mobile and not so freezing cold.

She leant on the wall as she dried herself and dragged her nightdress and dressing gown on over her still damp body. Then she did what she could do to dry her hair and opened the door.

Antoine was there. His disapproval was evident when he saw her hair was wet.

'I fell,' she said before he could say anything. 'Just help me get into bed.'

Although Antoine had replaced the hot-water bottle, Alexandra was still cold and shivering.

'It's because your hair's wet,' he said. 'I'll get another towel.'

He rubbed her hair, which was still a bit gritty. 'A hot drink,' he said. 'I'll get it.'

Alexandra curled into a ball, thinking she'd never be warm again but at least she was safe and not lying in a stream waiting for a boar to trample her.

'Here,' said Antoine. 'Hot milk. I hope you like it.'

Alexandra drank it and it did help but she was still cold. 'I can't decide if I want the hot-water bottle on my feet or on my body,' she said through chattering teeth.

He stood watching her for a few seconds before kicking off his shoes and getting into bed with her.

'We must get you warmed up' he said.

He put his arm under her head, pulling her to him. She put her arm over him, and then she put her head on his chest and closed her eyes.

All the brandy she had drunk must have sent her to sleep for a few seconds, she realised, because suddenly she was awake and knew what she had to do. It would be hard but it would give her a memory she could hold in her heart forever, along with the moment in the forest when she really felt he loved her. If she let the moment pass she might never forgive herself. David had told her that, for the most part, it was the things you didn't do that caused regret, not the things you did.

'Antoine,' she whispered.

'Yes?'

'Will you make love to me?'

She felt shock jolt through his body and hurried on, before he could stop her. Not being able to see his face made it easier.

'Because I know that soon I'll have to go away, get on with real life, and put all the time I've spent at the chateau, where I've been so happy, behind me. I know one day I'll meet a suitable man and will probably get engaged to him and sleep with him.' She took a breath. 'And it'll be fine. I won't marry someone I don't love but I want you to be the first. I want the first man I fell in love with to be the man I first . . .' She swallowed. She wasn't quite brave enough to go into too much detail. 'I just want you to be the first,' she repeated.

The few seconds' silence before he replied went on for hours.

'*Mignonne,*' said Antoine. 'I don't know what to say. I am so . . . flattered—'

'You don't need to speak,' she said quickly, before he could say anything even more devastating. 'Just – do what I've asked. Please.'

He shifted so his head was resting on his hand, so they weren't so entwined and he could talk to her. 'I love you too much to do that.'

'If you love me, why won't you make love to me?'

'There are so many reasons . . .'

'Like what?'

'The most practical reason is you could become pregnant. I know people say it cannot happen the first time—'

'But it can. I know that,' said Alexandra. 'What are your other reasons?'

'We can't get past the first reason. If you were pregnant we'd have to get married and I can't marry you!'

'Why not?' There was a catch in her voice. 'What's wrong with me?'

'There is nothing wrong with you. Every hair on your head, every cell in your body is beautiful. You are the most wonderful woman I have ever met. You are intelligent, brave, kind, funny, you seem to love my children almost as much as I do, and you risked your life for a dog! Or maybe it was for Stéphie – it's not important. You are a true heroine.'

'But?'

'I am too old for you and you are an heiress. If I marry you, what will everyone think? And say?'

'Do we have to care what people think and say?'

'Perhaps not, but nothing is going to change the age gap, or the fact that you work for me. You've been in a vulnerable position. Your reputation—'

'Surely people get married to save their reputation?'

'Not in this case!'

She held on to his jumper. 'I want a beautiful memory—'

'You'll have a life full of beautiful memories. Go to sleep now. Think how happy Stéphie is going to be when she sees Milou. Rest. You've had a huge adventure. You need to sleep.'

He wriggled out from under the covers but stayed on top of them, stroking her forehead until she went to sleep.

She woke up with a headache. Too much brandy, she thought. And then the memory of what had happened with Antoine swept over her like a tidal wave. Sweat prickled her hairline. She felt sick. How much was hangover and how much was crushing embarrassment she couldn't tell. She only knew that she wanted to die – or, better, be hundreds of miles away from Antoine.

She got out of bed slowly. Her muscles were very stiff but her ankle seemed better. She could almost walk on it properly. She still limped as she went to the bathroom but she was moving much more easily than she had been the night before.

A quick glance was enough to tell her how ghastly she looked: pale, with hair that stuck up at funny angles and was still damp.

She went back to her room and got dressed. It took ages. She put on a skirt that she could wear with her Chanel jacket. She found tights and her one pair of court shoes. She was leaving.

At the top of the stairs she listened for sounds of Antoine. There were noises from the kitchen and then she heard David's voice saying something to Milou. This gave her courage to think that maybe Antoine wasn't around. She tiptoed to his door and listened to see if he was still asleep. Nothing. The door wasn't properly shut so she pressed it with her finger so it opened enough for her to see that he wasn't there.

Relief and disappointment battled for a few seconds before relief won. She couldn't face seeing him ever again. Leaning heavily on the bannister, she got down the stairs.

'Lexi! You should have called! I'd have helped you down,' said David. His gaze flicked over her, obviously taking in her clothes, her state of mind. 'Are you all right?'

She nodded. 'I have to leave. As soon as possible. Do you know where Antoine is?'

David nodded. 'We met on the drive. He's gone back to Nice to pick up the family.'

Alexandra sank on to a chair. 'He obviously can't face seeing me. I can see his point – I can't face seeing him.'

'OK, tea first and then tell me why. If you want to.'

It was cathartic telling David everything. He didn't comment, he just refilled her mug of tea, put food in front of her and listened.

'I don't suppose there's any point in trying to persuade you to change your mind about leaving?' he said at last.

'No. I can't face seeing Antoine again. I have to go. Please explain to Stéphie and the others that I was called away suddenly. They won't mind if they've got Milou.' She got up. 'I must find train times to Paris and ring Donna.' She paused. 'And if she can't have me I'll go back to the little *pension* I stayed in before. I'll be fine. I'll get a train to Switzerland as soon as I can.'

'Really?' said David. 'Why not enjoy Paris for a little bit first? You had planned that originally, remember.'

She nodded. 'Well, if Donna can have me, maybe I will.'

'I'll find out train times while you pack,' he said. 'You don't need to take everything, just things you need for Paris. You won't be needing a boiler suit when you're living with your relations.'

Although she had felt she would never laugh again, this did make her chuckle. 'Especially not one that's covered in brick dust.'

'Just leave everything you won't need. I'll sort it out later. Get your things together and then ring Donna. I'm sure she'll be delighted to hear from you.'

Chapter Thirty-three

David was right: Donna was thrilled to hear from her, and insisted she came to stay. David had also given her quite a lot of cash in exchange for a cheque so Alexandra didn't hesitate to get a taxi from the station to Donna's apartment when the train finally pulled into Paris. Her ankle, although improving, wasn't up to all the walking that somehow the Métro always required. It was a little bit of a struggle getting up the stairs but once she'd rung the bell, Donna flung it open.

'Oh, honey!' said Donna. 'What has happened to you? Come in! Let's have champagne!'

To her huge embarrassment, Alexandra burst into tears.

'Alexandra! What's wrong? Have a brandy.'

'I'm never drinking brandy again,' said Alexandra through her sobs.

'Do you want to tell me?'

Alexandra found that she did. She had been very happy living in the chateau and was disappointed at the thought of missing Jack and Penelope's wedding, but she had missed female company she could confide in.

The two of them sat at the small kitchen table nibbling potato crisps. After her first glass of champagne

Alexandra sipped Perrier water; alcohol could get you into serious trouble.

When Alexandra got to the bit where she asked Antoine to make love to her, Donna gasped in shock. 'That was brave,' she said.

Her look of absolute horror made Alexandra feel even worse. 'It was the brandy. I must have drunk far more than I thought.'

'I don't blame you for wanting to sleep with him,' said Donna. 'Antoine is so gorgeous. But to ask him! If I want to have sex with Bob I just undress in a way that makes him want it. I would never, ever come straight out with it. Not that I think it's wrong for women to do that; I just never would myself.'

'So you don't think I was mad to run away, then?'

'I do not! But now, why don't you have a hot bath, to make up for the cold one you had last night, and get dressed in your best clothes and we'll go out to eat? There's a darling little *bistrot* around the corner, where the waiters are friendly and we can comfort ourselves by eating *steak frites*. I do hope you can stay at least for a few days. I want a girlfriend to go shopping with!'

'If you have a constant supply of hot water, I think I probably can stay! Oh, Donna, one more big, big favour? Could you ring my friend David at the chateau and tell him I got here safely? I should have done it sooner really.'

It was good to be going out, Alexandra told herself firmly, dressed up, with make-up on. She'd spent a lot of time recently wearing a boiler suit doing manual work. Now she was back to being a girl again.

Donna approved her appearance. 'You look great!' she said. 'You've obviously decided to get back on the horse.'

Alexandra smiled. Inside she thought she'd be heartbroken forever but felt she had to put a brave face on it. Donna was obviously so pleased to have her to stay. 'Well, maybe I'm not ready to get back in the saddle, but I am willing to put a foot in a stirrup.'

Donna had been a country girl back in the States and appreciated this analogy.

The following morning, after breakfast with Bob, who was very kind and welcoming, Donna decided that Alexandra needed to go shopping. 'There's nothing that cheers a girl up more than a new hat – as my mother used to say. I'd prefer a new dress myself,' she said, wiping breadcrumbs on to her napkin.

'Well, I could certainly do with some new clothes. I only seem to have bought things from a stall for farmers or a *brocante* since I've been in France. Maybe it's time to try the fashionable shops of Paris!'

Alexandra had a bit of money saved up, having hardly spent anything while at the chateau. And something pretty to wear would cheer her. It would also disguise her inner feelings quite well. No one would believe a girl in a new dress could be heartbroken. She put her hair up into a chignon, to give her new look a start.

Yet in spite of Donna's helpful suggestions, Alexandra found it difficult to find anything she really liked. Paris had such lovely shops, even if many of them were quite outside her budget. But her ankle was hurting and she wasn't in the right frame of mind for shopping.

They had just decided to give up finding things to wear and take up finding somewhere for lunch when Donna suddenly disappeared into a tiny shop Alexandra had missed. She shot out again almost immediately.

'Come in here! They've got lovely things. And so reasonable!'

Alexandra was aware that Donna's idea of what was reasonable was different to hers, even though she had set out intending to spend money, but she followed her into the boutique anyway. They might have a chair she could sit on for a while and rest her ankle, she told herself.

The *vendeuse* came forward and spoke in English. 'Can I help you, madame?'

'My friend needs something lovely but not too expensive,' said Donna. 'She needs to look gorgeous.'

The sales assistant nodded and addressed herself to Alexandra. 'You have a very elegant figure, lovely hair – although it does seem to need some attention – and perfect skin. You will look enchanting in anything. But for now, something very simple, I think.' She put her arm into a rack of clothes without apparently looking and produced a sleeveless dress in the most heavenly shade.

'I love the colour!' said Alexandra,

'I would describe this as Schiaparelli pink,' said the assistant. 'It is a strong colour, not one for a little girl but for a woman. Although I'm sure many would argue with me exactly what that colour is. It has a matching coat.'

392

Before she quite knew what had happened, Alexandra found herself in a changing room.

'Please put the scarf over your head,' she was told, 'so as not to get lipstick on the dress.'

Before she could even attempt to zip the dress the assistant was with her, doing it up. 'Now come out and show your friend.'

'You need heels!' said the assistant next, producing a pair. 'And here is the coat.'

It was a simple, sleeveless dress that ended an inch above her knee. The coat was fractionally longer and had a stand-up collar and large gold trimmed buttons.

'There is a hat, also,' said the assistant, putting a straw hat with a rim that went downwards on her head.

Donna gasped. 'You look wonderful!' she said.

The assistant tweaked the collar of the coat, adjusted the angle of the hat. '*Voilà!* You look like a model.'

'Buy it!' said Donna.

Alexandra laughed. It was good to see herself looking glamorous and sophisticated, to remind herself who she had been before she went to Provence. She loved the hat.

The *vendeuse* mentioned a figure that was more than double everything Alexandra had spent on clothes since she'd last been in Paris.

She shrugged. 'Why not? But I won't take the hat. I'll never get it to Switzerland in one piece.'

Donna flapped a dismissive hand. 'Oh, you'll manage somehow. It sets off the outfit perfectly. Now, settle up and then let's have lunch. I'm starving!'

Both girls got the impression that the *vendeuse* didn't approve of such open admission of hunger.

The following morning Alexandra was in the salon, writing postcards, having been sent there by Donna. Donna, Alexandra and Bob had enjoyed a very pleasant evening but it couldn't last forever. Alexandra felt it was time to tell her relations in Switzerland that her return was imminent. She had chosen a postcard to tell them so as to avoid having to go into too much detail.

She was wearing her new dress because Donna wanted to do more shopping shortly (Alexandra wasn't sure her ankle could cope), and then Donna wanted to take her to a new restaurant which had become the favourite of the ex-pat community.

She heard the front door click open but kept writing as she was fitting in her cousin's address on a space too small for it. Then she looked up. Antoine stood there. He seemed unusually diffident, not sure of his welcome. For an unending moment, he said nothing.

Then he held open his arms. 'My darling, the family have thrown me out of the house and won't let me back unless I have you with me. I've come to take you home.'

Chapter Thirty-four

Alexandra didn't know if she wanted to laugh or cry. She was shocked, delighted, dismayed and confused, all at the same time.

'Will you forgive me for my stupidity?' Antoine went on. 'I thought I was doing the right thing for you, letting you go, but now I know I was very wrong.' He set off across the room to where she was sitting. 'You are my guiding star, my world, my very precious love.' He drew her to her feet and suddenly she was in his arms, and his mouth was on hers. She felt faint from the force of his passion and her own.

She was breathless when she said, 'Am I not too young for you?'

'You're perfect for me. And I'm going to spend the rest of my life making sure I'm perfect for you.'

'You're quite perfect enough already,' she murmured, hanging on to his lapel and pulling him down so she could reach up to kiss him again.

When Donna tapped on the door and came in a little while later, she found them both on the sofa. Alexandra's hair was no longer in an elegant chignon but was now down over her shoulders.

'Antoine?' she said quietly. 'Your driver is downstairs. What shall I tell him?'

'Your driver?' said Alexandra. 'Last time I was with you, you were in a Deux Chevaux, bumping over the fields.'

'But I had a driver!' he said indignantly.

Alexandra laughed, remembering the farmer who'd been so kind and, to her, incomprehensible.

'The office sent this one. I had to sign some papers and so they collected me from where I was staying this morning.'

'You were in Paris last night?' she said, thinking of the pleasant but, for her, desolate evening she had spent with Donna and Bob, who had gone to such lengths to make her happy. To think that Antoine, who had filled her thoughts so completely, had been in the same city and she hadn't known!

'I couldn't come to you last night, however much I wanted to,' said Antoine. 'I couldn't rush off immediately after arriving at my godmother's house, which was already late in the evening. She would have been deeply offended and shocked at such rackety behaviour. And everyone – all the family – said I had to propose to you properly.'

'Oh!' said Donna, excited, looking at Alexandra. 'And did he?'

Alexandra considered. 'No, I don't think he did.'

Antoine instantly went down on one knee. 'My darling Alexandra, will you do me the great honour of becoming my wife?'

She laughed and took hold of his hands. 'I think I will,' she said, pretending to think about it. 'I might like being a countess.'

Antoine got up and hugged Alexandra, and then Donna hugged them both. 'So, is it time for more champagne?' she said.

Bob, who hadn't yet set off for the office, came in. 'My wife has become addicted to champagne since we've lived in Paris but there was never a better reason for it.'

'Do you have to carry her back to the country immediately?' said Donna wistfully. 'Could we keep her in Paris for a little longer?'

'We probably should get back,' said Alexandra. 'I was organising a wedding, after all.' She was suddenly filled with longing for the chateau and everyone who lived there; it was her home and the people in it were her family.

'I think the wedding will manage quite well without us,' said Antoine. 'I want to show you Paris. We must buy an engagement ring and there is a fairly elderly lady I must introduce you to. No marriage without her consent will be quite legal, I'm afraid. We'll go home when we've done all those things and the wedding is safely over.'

'But Stéphie—' Alexandra protested.

'Stéphie will understand completely. It was she who gave me very strict instructions that I wasn't to come home without you.'

'Are you only marrying me to please your daughter?' asked Alexandra.

'*Pas du tout*. But if I don't marry you, my daughter – in fact none of my children – will ever forgive me.'

Donna sighed. 'I am very, very happy for you.' She paused for a second. 'Bob, will you take me to that

397

restaurant that all our American friends rave about? I was going with Alexandra, but she won't want to come now.'

'Why wouldn't we want to come?' said Alexandra. 'It sounds delightful.' In spite of everything, of her and his feelings at last being acknowledged publicly, she suddenly felt a little shy of being on her own with Antoine.

'We can celebrate in company,' said Antoine, 'and perhaps postpone the champagne?'

'Oh,' said Donna, clapping her hands. 'Think how cool it will be if we arrive with a real French *comte* and his beautiful fiancée! I just hope all my ex-pat friends are there!'

'We'd love to join you, if you don't mind?' said Antoine. 'But before that, I must make some arrangements.'

'So must I!' said Alexandra. 'I must tell my relations I'm going to be married!' She suddenly felt wildly happy; the man she'd fallen in love with the moment she saw him loved her back. 'Do I have to write a whole new postcard, do you think? Or can I just say "Forget all that, I'm getting married"?'

Donna tutted and shook her head, apparently disapproving of Alexandra's flippancy. 'I think you should add that he's a *comte*. They need to know that.'

Alexandra gave her a delighted hug.

When they were alone again, Antoine said, 'Will it take you long to write your postcard? I want to take you to buy an engagement ring. If I don't, when I take you to meet my godmother, who is formidable, she'll make you have a family piece which will be very old-fashioned.'

'I like old things. It's probably why I fell in love with you . . .' She bit her lip, not sure if he'd find this amusing.

He raised an eyebrow but the corner of his mouth twitched. 'I must get used to the fact that I'm not marrying a woman who worships her husband.'

'I do worship you,' she said, 'but I don't think I should tell you too often in case you become bossy.'

He laughed. 'You are the bossy one, I think. Luckily, I like that. Now, about an engagement ring—'

'I would like an antique. There's something extra romantic about jewellery that comes with a story of its own, one we'll never know. That's partly why I love antiques markets.'

'Then we will go to an antiques market and find you the ring of your dreams.'

'I've got the man of my dreams; I don't need a ring as well. I mean, it doesn't have to be expensive.'

He kissed her for a long time. 'Stéphie would never speak to me again if you didn't have a very large diamond on your finger when we come home. That said, if you want it from a market, we must wait until tomorrow. What shall we do this morning?'

'When shall I meet your godmother?'

'She will need notice.' He took a breath. 'Because of the way we met I haven't had a chance to woo you properly, or even take you out to dinner. Now is my opportunity to put all that right. And this morning, we can be tourists. Do you want to go up the Eiffel Tower?'

399

She shook her head. 'I want to do what I planned to when I met Donna and my life changed.'

'Which is?'

'I want to climb up the steps of Montmartre and see the Sacré-Cœur.'

'But, darling, your ankle!'

'I'd forgotten about my ankle.' Alexandra considered. 'Well, it was at the bottom of the steps where my life changed. There was Donna, with her shopping bag broken, surrounded by onions and potatoes.'

He hugged her to him. 'Your kind heart made you help her and so we met.'

Alexandra gave a little sigh of happiness. 'On the other hand, I really want to see the view from the top. Fancy helping me get up there?'

'I will carry you up as a proof of my love!'

Alexandra giggled. 'Just give me your arm; you can prove you love me in other ways.'

When they'd climbed to the top and got their breath back for a few moments, they turned and looked at Paris all laid out before them.

'I've dreamt of looking at this view for ages. I didn't realise you could see the Eiffel Tower from here.' What Alexandra didn't say was how she'd dreamt of seeing Paris with a man she loved. Tears caught in her throat; all her dreams had come true.

'Darling, I hate to say this, but I don't think we've got time to actually look round the basilica today if we're having lunch with Donna and Bob.'

'Do you mind doing that?' asked Alexandra. 'They've been so kind . . .'

'I feel I owe them my happiness,' said Antoine simply. 'There is nothing I would not do for them.'

Alexandra wondered if there was a limit to how much you could love someone and decided there wasn't. She kept on loving Antoine more and more.

After a very jolly and champagne-filled lunch Antoine got Alexandra on her own for a few moments. 'There is nothing I would like to do more than to take you to a lovely hotel and make love to you. But I am very old-fashioned, very traditional and I think we should wait until we are married.' He paused to let her absorb this. 'More to the point, I am staying with my godmother who will be noting exactly how long I am out of the house with you and if she even suspects we've done more than kiss our lives will not be worth living.'

Alexandra laughed.

'I do hope you're not going to insist on a long engagement,' he added.

'Not at all!'

'I am relieved. Now I will let you go home with Donna and Bob. Sadly I can't join you for dinner but can I collect you early in the morning so I can buy you an engagement ring?'

'What time is early?'

'Seven o'clock?'

'Seven o'clock! That's late by David's standards.'

Paris could not have looked more beautiful in the early-morning mist that promised a beautiful day. There was no official car; they walked to the Métro which took them to the flea market.

401

'How is your ankle?' he said as he took her arm.

'It'll be fine. Isn't this fun? And Paris is so lovely at this time of day.'

He kissed her cheek and they set off.

Although there were several stalls selling jewellery it took a while before Alexandra's eye was caught by a ring that looked different from the others. It was a single diamond, quite large, surrounded by gold and dark blue enamel. She reached out for it and then noticed the price and turned her attention to a smoky topaz set in silver. 'What about this one?'

'Try it on. Do you like it?' said Antoine.

'Yes I do.' She did like it. It was quite a large stone and looked nice on her hand. 'And it fits!'

'We'll have it then!' said Antoine. 'Darling? I can see a crêpe stall over there? I knew something was making me hungry. Could you get me one with cheese? Breakfast? I didn't have any.'

'Nor did I,' said Alexandra. 'You won't forget to haggle for the ring, will you?' she said quietly. 'You should never pay the asking price.' She felt guilty leaving him. Buying antiques at a stall was not for a novice.

Antoine took his wooing seriously. He took her every-where: to the tourist spots, to the spots only Parisians knew about and everywhere else they could think of. They went up the Seine on a *bateau-mouche*, they stood on bridges and they drank coffee in little cafés and they ate *baguettes jambon-beurre* in the street.

They also took Bob and Donna out to dinner the next evening but still Antoine wouldn't give her

her engagement ring. He said it was being cleaned and wasn't ready.

Alexandra was enjoying life very much but her conscience was pricked by the knowledge that the wedding that she had been organising, had been asked to organise, was happening far away in Provence and she wasn't there to make sure every detail was perfect.

She had said as much to David on the telephone, after she had given him her news. David was very clear in his advice. 'Penelope and Jack can get married without you. You've got everything ready. There are lots of local people who can help if necessary and I'll be there. You enjoy the time of your life.'

Eventually, David convinced her, up to a point. Then she found herself telling Donna how guilty she felt about it, too.

She was equally certain. 'Honey! Just leave it all to them. They'll be fine. You'll never have time like this again. You'll get married, you'll have babies and you'll work hard! This is like your honeymoon, without the sex.'

Alexandra laughed, slightly doubtfully. 'I'm a bit worried about that part now.'

'No need,' said Donna. 'It'll be fine. Trust me. You fancy each other like mad and he'll make it work for you.'

'I'll take your word for it. I know from the outside I seem very sophisticated, as if I know what I'm doing in life, but sometimes I'm just a girl who hasn't got a mother.'

Donna rubbed her arm. 'You're great. Brave, kind and funny as well as beautiful. And Antoine is a good man. I got Bob to check him out a bit and he is truly honourable.'

'I know that. Adopting his friend's daughter and bringing her up as his own was a great thing to do. Although having Stéphie is no hardship.' She paused. 'And what about you? Is it rude to ask? Are you thinking of having a family?'

'Thinking of it, certainly,' said Donna, suddenly looking secretive. 'In fact . . . it's too early to say really but . . .'

'Oh, Donna! That's lovely! So exciting!'

'We're cautiously thrilled,' she said.

Alexandra hugged her, unexpectedly tearful.

'So, why are you so nervous about this lunch?' asked Donna. 'You know which knife and fork to use.' Donna was doing Alexandra's hair into the neatest chignon it had ever experienced.

'It's the table manners thing! In England we put our hands in our laps every time we put down our knife and fork, which is while we're chewing. I know it's the opposite way in France, and you have to keep your hands visible at all times. I'm convinced nerves will make me forget and that'll make the godmother stop Antoine from marrying me and I'll have to go and live in Switzerland after all.'

Donna laughed. 'That is not going to happen! Even if it does, and the godmother does forbid it, Antoine won't accept her decision. He loves you! He wants to marry you! And you' – she paused to examine her handiwork in detail – 'are the most elegant young woman in Paris!' Then she sprayed Alexandra's hair so thoroughly it couldn't move.

She was in the salon, looking out of the long windows at Paris and the Eiffel Tower when she heard a noise.

It was Antoine.

'Oh, you startled me! Have you been there long?'

'No. I was trying to decide if you are more beautiful when you look like a woman on the cover of *Vogue* or when your hair is all over the place and you are covered in mud.'

'And what conclusion did you come to?' asked Alexandra, going to him.

Antoine shrugged. 'I could only think that I love you more every time I look at you. Are you ready for your ordeal by elderly Frenchwoman? You look *le dernier cri du chic*.'

She was wearing her new dress and matching coat, new patent leather court shoes with kitten heels and a discreet bow on the toe. Donna had not only made sure her hair was perfect but had manicured and painted her nails. (There had still been traces of mud under them which Donna had picked out with an orange stick and a lot of tutting.)

'*Merci du compliment, M. le Comte.*' She wished she could mention her engagement ring but somehow she couldn't. He was looking at her in such a way, she didn't want to risk spoiling the moment.

'Shall we go?' he said. 'I have the office car downstairs.'

Alexandra had the impression that he was a little bit nervous too.

Chapter Thirty-five

❧

Apart from her lack of an engagement ring, there was one other thing that was worrying Alexandra.

'Are you ever going to be able to give up work and devote yourself to the farm and the chateau?' she asked as she folded her legs neatly into the back of the car.

'I have left Véronique in charge, and told her she can consult me as often as she needs to but that I'll only go away once a year, and never for more than a month.'

'And is she happy with that?'

He shrugged. 'She has to be – she's certainly pleased about being in charge. I just hope Stéphanie will be happy too!'

'I am sorry to have missed Jack and Penelope's wedding and seeing the girls in their bridesmaids' dresses.'

'There will be photographs,' said Antoine, sounding a bit distracted.

Alexandra wondered if he was worrying about earning enough money for the family, the chateau and the farm. She thought of her own fortune, which he would have access to when they were married. Would she ever be able to mention it? He was proud; he wanted to provide for his wife and his family. Her money would have to be introduced by stealth, she realised. But she'd manage. She looked out of the window and tried to enjoy the drive.

'You don't need to worry,' he whispered as they stood waiting for the door to be opened. 'I've told her all about you.'

'That doesn't help!' It mattered to her hugely that as Antoine's prospective bride, who already had so many marks against her (English, too young, his children's nanny), didn't do or say anything out of place. 'In fact, it probably makes it worse!'

The door was opened by the manservant to reveal an apartment very like Donna and Bob's, only this one was full of antiques. It looked to Alexandra as if a museum had had to move to smaller premises but had left nothing behind.

Although Antoine was currently staying there, they were ushered through to the salon with all due ceremony to meet his godmother.

La Comtesse de Saint-Hubert was tiny, wearing a skirt and jacket that she'd probably had since before the war, and would definitely have come from one of the top Paris fashion houses. Her hair was perfectly coiffed and her diamonds were enormous. Alexandra held on to Antoine's arm a bit tighter. She'd never been particularly impressed by class or wealth and felt perfectly relaxed about spending time in stately homes. But this time it mattered if she was approved of or not.

La Comtesse de Saint-Hubert insisted on speaking in highly accented English and reminded Alexandra of Mme Wilson, who had taught her cooking in England and where she had met her two best friends.

Introductions were made, champagne was offered and accepted (gratefully) and everyone was seated.

'Well, my dear Alexandra – I may call you that? I have taken the liberty of looking up your family – you are to be marrying my godson who is very dear to me – and I am pleased to discover that yours is a family I know of.' She inclined her head graciously.

Had Alexandra been standing up she'd have curtseyed.

'Thank goodness for that,' said Antoine. 'It would never have done for me to marry someone who wasn't of noble birth.'

'You tease, Antoine, but these matters are very serious.'

'I apologise, Godmother.'

'I am so sorry about your parents,' the Countess went on, addressing Alexandra. 'A tragedy.'

'I don't remember—'

'These things happen. Think about little Stéphanie's parents.'

Alexandra nodded. She was not expected to wring her hands over her misfortune. The stiff upper lip was not just an English concept, she realised.

'And now I have seen you for myself I can see it was not just your fortune that attracted Antoine to you.'

'Godmother, please!'

'He didn't know about my fortune when we met,' Alexandra pointed out.

A perfect eyebrow ascended a little. 'He may say that, but he could have found out, had he done a little research.'

Antoine was obviously becoming increasingly embarrassed by his elderly relation. 'Godmother! You know perfectly well that I didn't do any research.'

The eyebrow was raised again and she turned back to Alexandra. 'Can you tell me why you aren't wearing an engagement ring? I have several family pieces that would be suitable—'

'I have Alexandra's ring here,' said Antoine, patting his pocket. 'It has been cleaned and made to fit.'

But it fitted perfectly when he bought it, Alexandra thought, hoping it still would.

'I hope it is appropriate,' said the Countess.

Alexandra could only hope that she had failing eyesight and wouldn't instantly see it was a cheap if very pretty ring.

Antoine took a ring box out of his pocket and took Alexandra's hand. Deftly he opened the box. Inside was not the one Alexandra had chosen, it was the first ring, the one she had pulled back from.

He took it out of the box and slid it on to her finger. 'There,' he said. 'A perfect fit.'

She gasped. On her finger was the large, cushion cut diamond surrounded by gold with blue enamel. It was absolutely beautiful.

'Show me, please.'

Alexandra crossed the room so that her ring could be inspected. 'Not bad. Not quite what a future countess should have on her hand, but not bad.'

Alexandra took her hand back and returned to her seat. She kissed Antoine's cheek. 'It's wonderful! Thank you so much! How did you know—'

'That this was the ring you really wanted? I saw you look at it, check the price and go for a cheaper option. I bought both rings so I could get the size right for your proper ring.'

'I don't understand,' said the Countess, 'why did you have to buy two rings? Surely the jeweller would measure your finger?'

Alexandra looked to Antoine to answer this one.

'We bought it from a market stall, Godmother.'

'It's always been a romantic dream for me,' Alexandra explained, to support him. 'To buy an engagement ring from an antiques market.'

The Countess obviously thought she was mad. 'English girls! They are very different.' Another thought struck her. 'Antoine, I understand your fiancée is – unusual – in many ways, but I trust you and she won't be living under the same roof when you return to Provence? It would be very wrong.'

Alexandra took a breath. If it had been all right for them to share a home when she was just the nanny, what was different now? But a second later she realised it was different in every way.

'We don't plan a long engagement,' said Antoine.

'And I have an older English friend who lives in the town. I am sure I can stay with her until we are married,' said Alexandra. She couldn't remember if Jack and Penelope were going on a honeymoon or not, but she was sure she could arrange something.

'Good! I am reassured,' said the Countess. 'Shall we go through for lunch?'

Chapter Thirty-six

A couple of days later Alexandra and Antoine were on their way back to the South on a train that was unlike any train Alexandra had ever been on.

'Golly,' she said to Antoine, in English. 'I've travelled first class from time to time but I've never been on a train where it's *all* first class. And pale pink carpets and upholstery! So de luxe!'

Antoine smiled at her. 'It doesn't go to Saint-Jean-du-Roc but Maxime is meeting us so we don't have to change trains. He agreed with me, everyone deserves to travel this way sometimes.'

'It's lovely. Thank you.'

As she settled into her pink seat with her feet on the pink carpet she reflected how different this journey was from last autumn, when she first travelled to the chateau. Then she had been travelling to a strange place, to do a job she had no qualifications for, all for a man she had barely glimpsed. Now she was travelling at speed through France on a luxurious train with the man of her dreams, who just happened to be the man of her dreams when she had met him all those months ago.

*

Although it hadn't been very long since she'd left Provence for Paris, when Alexandra saw Maxime waiting for them next to a very smart car she hadn't seen before, she felt as if she'd been away for a lifetime.

'Maxime!' she said and went into his arms. He felt like a long-lost brother.

'Alexandra! Antoine! How could you tear yourselves away from Paris?'

'Me?' Antoine said. 'I'd have stayed far longer, but this girl was determined we had to get back.'

'I wanted to come home,' she said simply.

Maxime nodded.

Alexandra grew more and more excited as they neared the chateau, but when they arrived and she was out of the car, she put her fingers to her lips. 'I want to surprise them,' she whispered.

They tiptoed into the hall and Alexandra realised that the door to the kitchen must be shut or Milou would certainly have come out. Antoine opened the kitchen door so quietly no one heard. And then, suddenly, Stéphie looked up, Milou barked and one of the kittens ran up Alexandra's coat to her shoulder.

'You're here!' said Stéphie, getting out of her chair and rushing towards them all.

'Lexi!' said David, who was nearer, and pulled her into an enormous hug.

'Papa!' said Félicité and hugged him.

Henri came over and gave Alexandra an awkward embrace that touched her heart. Then Félicité joined in. 'Are you engaged?' she asked. 'Can I see your ring?'

The ring was inspected and admired by everyone while David tried to get everyone to sit down.

'When did you last eat? Are you hungry? There's soup, or bread and cheese. We've got plenty of eggs if you want an omelette?'

'Shall we open champagne, Antoine?' Maxime asked.

'I'd just prefer a glass of rosé, from the demijohn,' said Alexandra. 'Then I'll know I'm home.'

'So,' said Stéphie when everyone was seated and eating, drinking or both. 'When are you going to get married?'

'We haven't discussed it yet,' said Alexandra. 'Quite soon, I hope.'

'Can I be a bridesmaid?' asked Stéphie.

'Of course, but it won't be a large wedding, I don't think,' said Alexandra diffidently. 'Just close family.'

'Why?' demanded Antoine. 'I think we should invite everyone we know. I want the world to see how proud I am of my beautiful bride, and how much I love her!'

'You will have to invite your cousins from Switzerland,' said Maxime. 'We could use Hubert's beautiful car to drive you about.'

'And you can't get married without Lizzie and Meg from England. It wouldn't be legal,' said David. 'Perhaps they could stay and help you get ready?'

Alexandra began to laugh. 'I did telephone Lizzie from Donna's when we first got engaged and although she didn't say anything I know she'd be disappointed not to come and stay for a bit. I asked her to tell Meg, too. Is that all right, Antoine?'

'Of course. As long as you can put up with my starchy relations, you can invite as many of your friends as you like. In fact, it's a good idea, it will dilute the formality of my family.' He paused. 'We must keep room for your family too, *chérie*.'

'I suppose we must,' said Alexandra reluctantly. 'But maybe they'll prefer the hotel in town. I'll tell them there is no room in the chateau and that everything is very rustic in the stables. Just the word "stable" might be enough to put them off.'

'Will you have the wedding here, like Grand-mère and Jack?' asked Stéphie.

'Of course,' said Antoine. 'Where better? Unless Alexandra prefers somewhere different?'

'Oh no,' she said. 'It has to be here.' Her voice constricted with emotion. 'It's our home.' She cleared her throat. 'So, was Grand-mère and Jack's wedding wonderful?' she asked.

'A bit,' said Stéphie. 'But it would have been better if you had been there.'

'My mother took charge,' said Félicité. 'She didn't let me invite Jules.'

'Or Milou,' said Stéphie. 'He and the kittens had to stay locked in a stable all day!'

Antoine looked at Alexandra. 'I officially invite Milou and the kittens to our wedding. They are a very important part of our lives.'

'Penelope and Jack looked very happy,' said David. 'And they were so thrilled to be celebrating in the orangery. All Jack's relations were very impressed.'

Later, when Maxime was saying his goodbyes, Antoine took Alexandra aside. 'I'm going to stay with Maxime,' he said. 'For form's sake.'

Alexandra huffed and sighed but she knew he was doing the right thing. 'I'm going to see how soon my English friends can come and stay,' she said. 'Then they can chaperone me. Lizzie wants to make my dress and Meg will want to do the cake, even if she doesn't do all the catering.'

Antoine kissed her cheek. 'We will let her make the cake with pleasure, but not do all the cooking. She will be a bridesmaid, *non*? She will need to look after you.'

Alexandra laughed. 'I suppose so.'

She was woken very early the following day by Stéphie, who got into Alexandra's bed but couldn't settle. Now Alexandra was awake she found she couldn't either.

'I know,' she whispered to Stéphie although no one was in earshot. 'Let's get up and make your papa a cake. He is coming early because he said he'd bring bread and croissants, but wouldn't it be fun to have a cake for him?'

Stéphie got out of bed and jumped up and down. 'We haven't made a cake together for simply ages! Let's go!'

'What sort of cake shall we make?' asked Alexandra as she and Stéphie walked through the yard having collected the eggs.

'His favourite is lemon,' said Stéphie, 'but I like chocolate.'

'He likes chocolate too, I'm sure,' said Alexandra. The cake-making project was for Stéphie; her papa would be delighted with anything his youngest daughter produced.

It was still only half past eight when they heard a car. Alexandra and Stéphie exchanged excited looks. 'But the cake isn't ready!' said Stéphie.

'It very nearly is,' said Alexandra. 'When it's cool, we can put on the ganache, but if we do it too soon it will all just fall off.'

They heard the front door open and footsteps travelling across the hall. The kitchen door was opened. But instead of Antoine it was Lucinda.

Alexandra's beaming smile froze and Stéphie said, 'Oh!' her disappointment evident.

'Good morning, Lucinda,' said Alexandra. 'We were expecting you to be Antoine, with breakfast.'

'Sorry to disappoint you. I am early because I have a car booked to take me to the airport. I have to leave very soon. I have come to say goodbye to my children!' She said this with a dramatic toss of her head.

'Oh,' said Alexandra. 'I don't think they're up yet . . .'

'I'll go and wake them,' said Stéphie, aware this was what was wanted.

When they were alone, Lucinda said, 'So you got what you wanted: a ring on your finger, a count and a chateau. Pretty good going for a nanny.'

Alexandra heard the bitterness and decided to ignore it. She was the winner here; she could be magnanimous. 'Indeed. So where are you off to?'

'Back to my husband in Argentina. I only left to teach him a lesson, really.'

'And to see your children?' suggested Alexandra.

'Oh yes, that too, of course. I wanted to make sure they were being educated correctly.' She paused, giving Alexandra a look that would have turned a lesser woman to stone. 'Which they are not!'

'I'm sure Antoine is sending them to the school which is best for them.'

'He could afford to send them to a decent school now he's marrying money!'

Alexandra wished Félicité and Henri would hurry up. Their mother was being particularly poisonous this morning. 'Do sit down. Let me make you some coffee.'

'You want to offer me cake as well, I suppose. You should know by now I don't share your obsession with confectionery.' In spite of this, Lucinda pulled out a chair and sat down. 'You do know he married you for your money? You have very little else to offer him.'

Alexandra decided to bite back. 'I think he does quite well out of the deal. He has a mother for his children, current and future. He has a chatelaine for his home. He has a bargain even without my fortune.'

'I do indeed!' said Antoine, who had appeared in the kitchen from the back door without anyone hearing his approach. His arms were full of baguettes and paper bags, presumably containing croissants and pastries. 'And Alexandra's fortune is exactly that, *her* fortune.' He put down his packages. 'Are you planning to stay for breakfast, Lucinda?'

'No,' she said, her bitterness apparently fading. 'I've come to say goodbye to the children. I'm going back to Argentina. My husband is desperate to have me back and I have no life here.'

'Sit down, Antoine,' said Alexandra. 'Thank you so much for bringing us breakfast. I'll have coffee ready very shortly.'

Much to her relief, Félicité and Henri appeared with Stéphie. They were dressed, but looked as if they'd only very recently got out of bed.

417

'Maybe you'd like some time alone with Félicité and Henri?' suggested Alexandra, eager to escape from this painful scene. 'Stéphie, let's see what your papa has brought us, and go and eat it on the terrace. It's a lovely morning.' She picked up a couple of packets, hoping for Stéphie's sake that one of them contained a *pain au chocolat*, and went out through the back door, trusting that Stéphie would follow. Milou and the cats obviously felt it was a good idea.

They stood on the terrace, looking out at the parkland towards the woods. It was going to be a beautiful day.

'I'm pleased she's going,' said Stéphie, blowing crumbs. 'Is that bad of me?'

'No. It's your opinion, and Lucinda has never been very nice to you.'

'I don't mind her not being nice, and never buying me any presents, but I don't like her thinking I'm sweet.'

'Oh, Stéphie!' said Alexandra, laughing. 'I completely understand. It's really annoying to be thought sweet by someone you don't like!'

A little while later, Antoine's family, including Alexandra, stood on the steps of the chateau, waving as Lucinda's car disappeared down the drive. When she was out of sight, Stéphie ran off and everyone else went inside. Alexandra found herself next to Félicité.

'I'm sorry. I hope you don't mind too much about your mother going away again when you were just starting to get to know her.'

Félicité shrugged. 'It's OK. She wasn't like a mother to me, really. She was just a grown-up who thought she had the right to tell me what to do.'

'We'll go and visit her in Argentina when we're older,' said Henri, marginally more enthusiastic. 'That might be good.'

'That will be wonderful!' said Alexandra. 'You can gallop over the pampas on beautiful horses and have a lovely time!'

Félicité and Henri looked at her wonderingly. 'Can you really see our mother doing that?' Henri said.

Alexandra smiled. 'Maybe not now, but people change . . .'

'If you don't mind,' said Henri. 'I'm going to see if there are any more *pains au chocolat* left.'

His sister followed him and Alexandra was reassured that Lucinda's departure was not something that had upset either of them.

Chapter Thirty-seven

Alexandra had thought she was busy when she was getting ready for Penelope and Jack's wedding. Her own was even busier. But one of the first things she did was to invite her friend Lizzie and her family to stay. They consisted of her husband, Hugo, and her small baby, Letty. The plan was that having delivered his wife and child and stayed for a couple of days, Hugo would go home and come back for the wedding. Lizzie would make Alexandra's wedding dress.

Meg, another friend, was arriving as soon as she could get away from her job cooking directors' lunches. She was set to make the cake. A third friend, Vanessa, would travel with her. Vanessa was going to do anything that was required of her, but really, she admitted to Alexandra on the telephone, she was just going to join in the fun.

The arrival of Lizzie, Hugo and their baby caused a lot of excitement and rejoicing. Stéphie instantly wanted to hold Letty and she handled the baby so well, her parents felt she was in safe hands.

'This was Antoine's room,' said Alexandra, when all the greeting food and drink was over. 'He's moving into the barn until after the wedding, but I thought it would be nice to have you close by.'

'Handy for dress fittings,' said Lizzie, looking around with delight.

'I thought if you wanted Letty to have her own room, she could have this little room, which is very close.' Alexandra remembered Véronique's horror when she'd been asked to stay there.

'Doesn't Antoine mind moving out of his bedroom?' asked Lizzie.

'His godmother is very correct. She said we had to be chaperoned and while she wouldn't really know, I think Antoine would find it difficult to look her in the eye if he hadn't obeyed her instructions.'

'I do like Antoine,' said Hugo. 'I'm glad. If I didn't, I might have to forbid the banns or something.'

'Although I appreciate your concern, Hugo,' Alexandra said teasingly, 'I don't think that will be necessary.'

David was delighted to be reunited with the girls and the first evening everyone sat up reminiscing and regaling Antoine with stories from their life together in London. It was only when Letty, asleep in a cradle behind the sofa, woke for a feed, that everyone realised how late it was and all went to bed.

Stéphie was in her element with a baby to look after and even Félicité blossomed being surrounded by women not so much older than herself, who treated her like an equal and genuinely admired her artwork.

Vanessa, who had arrived with Meg, came in an organisational mood and made lots of lists.

One of the first things that had to be done was for Alexandra and Antoine to visit the *mairie* to sort out the legal aspect of the ceremony. Alexandra produced her birth certificate and it was all very straightforward. That Antoine was an old friend of the mayor didn't hurt either.

They arranged the date for the legal part of the wedding; the blessing in church would take place the day after.

'I know your friends are organising a brilliant wedding for us,' said Antoine on the way home. 'But what do you want to do afterwards? Go away on honeymoon? We could go to London, or Switzerland – anywhere your heart desires.'

'Can we pull over and have a proper talk? It's all so busy at the chateau we hardly ever get a chance to see each other.'

Antoine found a farm gate to put the car into. 'I know. My godmother could not have arranged it better.'

'It's a bit frustrating, isn't it?' said Alexandra.

'Luckily we don't have to wait long to be properly married and be able to live together in the chateau,' said Antoine.

'Which brings us to the matter of our honeymoon. Would you think I was very strange if I said I didn't want to go away just yet? The children are just starting at their new school. I'd really like to know they're properly settled before we disappear.'

'Sometimes I think you love my children more than you love me!' he said indignantly.

'Oh, Antoine! I'm sure in time I'll come to love you just as much—' She collapsed into giggles as he tickled her and inevitably they ended up kissing.

They arrived back to lunch in the garden. The spring sunshine made it perfectly warm enough and it felt festive. But it was, it transpired, to be a working lunch.

'We just need to pin you down on a few things,' said Vanessa, who had her ever-present clipboard on the table beside her.

'For example, what sort of cake do you want?' asked Meg. 'To be honest it's a bit late for a traditional rich fruit one but I'd manage if your heart is set on that.'

'I've never had to think about cake before,' said Alexandra.

Antoine shrugged. 'A traditional cake in France would be a *croquembouche* but I know they are tricky.'

Alexandra saw her friend's eyes flash with excitement as she looked at David, who had been her partner in crime when they all lived in London.

'David?' said Meg. 'Could we do it, do you think? Or should we ask a local *pâtisserie*?'

Alexandra knew that Meg longed to take on the challenge. 'I'd love it if you felt you could do it, Meggy. I'd rather have it a bit wonky made by you and David than have it perfect from a shop.' She glanced at Antoine, hoping he'd understand.

'We would be so honoured if you would make our wedding cake,' said Antoine, who obviously understood perfectly.

'That's decided then,' said Vanessa, writing on the clipboard. 'Could someone pass the quiche? I'm suddenly quite hungry.'

'Would you want a sit-down do, or people standing around eating canapés?' asked Meg, who had her own list.

'People will have travelled, lots of them are staying, I think they should have a proper meal,' said David, who liked nothing better than to feed people.

'I agree,' said Antoine. 'We will be in the *orangerie*, after all.'

'I'm doing a new mural, or at least a new bit,' said Félicité. 'One for you and Papa.'

'Nothing too outrageous, please, *chérie*,' said Antoine.

'Oh, I don't know,' said Alexandra. 'I think you should have a free hand.'

After Antoine, David and Henri had gone off to do other things, the women remained, sharing another *pichet* of rosé and a plate of macarons – Meg's first attempt at making them. There was still important planning to be done.

'I've done some sketches for the dress,' said Lizzie. 'Obviously we won't get fabric until Alexandra is completely happy with the design.'

'I just want something very simple,' Alexandra began.

'And chic,' went on Lizzie.

'Long or short?' asked Vanessa. 'You'd look lovely in either.'

'I think you should wear a long dress,' said Stéphie, 'with a crown.'

'So do I!' said Alexandra, glad to fit in with Stéphie's ideas.

'And me,' agreed Lizzie. 'I'll make a toile. I've got time.'

'What's a toile?' asked Stéphie.

When it had been explained that a toile was a version of the dress in cheaper fabric so it could be fitted perfectly, Stéphie said, 'Can I have it afterwards?'

'Of course you can,' said Alexandra. 'We can take it up a bit.'

'What about bridesmaids' dresses?' asked Félicité.

Alexandra overheard a small gasp from Lizzie and realised it would be far too much work for her to make them as well.

'Can't I wear the one I wore for Grand-mère's wedding?' said Stéphie. 'I love that dress! Do I have to have something different?'

'Did you like the dress, Félicité?' asked Lizzie nobly, probably hoping the answer would be yes.

'It was all right,' said Félicité. 'I don't mind wearing it again.'

'I was really sorry to miss seeing you in the ones you had for Penelope and Jack's wedding,' said Alexandra. 'But only if you're sure . . .'

Félicité hadn't been as excited to have another wedding to plan as Stéphie had, although she had enjoyed the way Alexandra's friends had drawn her into the group. 'I'm sure,' she said.

'So you and Félicité will have dresses,' said Alexandra. 'What about my English bridesmaids?'

'I'm sure we can buy dresses,' said Meg. 'How do they put it? *Prêt-à-porter?*'

'Ready to wear?' said Lizzie. 'Would they be nice enough?'

'The shop where we had our dresses made in Nice had some nice things,' said Félicité. 'My mother recommended the shop so of course it was terribly expensive.'

'No need to worry about that, I'm about to come into a fortune!' Alexandra couldn't help laughing. It was all so crazy. 'We can go and look and if they're not nice enough, we'll try another shop. Now, can you pass the macarons? They are awfully good, Meggy.'

'It was difficult to get them off the paper but I am quite pleased with them,' said Meg, inspecting the pale green circle she was holding.

Later, when Lizzie and Alexandra were alone in the room that had been Jack's bedroom and was now the dressmaking room, Alexandra sighed.

'I know you got a bit frustrated with your mother and her plans for your wedding,' Alexandra said to Lizzie while her friend measured her from armpit to floor. 'But a few plans would come in handy. There's so much to do, so many decisions to make.'

Lizzie noted down the measurement and then hugged her friend. 'I'm so sorry. It must be hard for you, not having a mother at a time like this.'

Alexandra cleared her throat. 'I always assume that I manage perfectly well without parents, but maybe they do have their uses! But while I haven't got a mother and father, I do have lots of people who love me and look after me.'

'David adores you. He's the best kind of father, I think,' said Lizzie. 'He doesn't boss you about but he'll always help you out of a scrape and doesn't shout.'

'I don't know what would have happened to me without David,' said Alexandra, thinking of the time when she lived with him in London. 'He's agreed to walk me down the aisle.'

'And I think Stéphie will make an excellent mother substitute,' said Lizzie. 'She's bossy, knows what's best for you and loves you very much.'

'And Penelope and Jack! Penelope only had a really short honeymoon because of my wedding.'

'She's a little scary but determined that everything will be perfect. She still needs convincing that Meg's food will be good enough and that's just for the dinner the night before!'

Alexandra smiled. 'I know! That's partly because the caterers are friends of hers. Pam and Elizabeth. Both English and both very good cooks. Although I don't know what Penelope will say when she finds out that Meggy and David are making a *croquembouche*!'

'Although I know Meg and David would have done a wonderful job with the food, I'm glad you've got caterers. Then David and Meg can join in the party properly.'

'That's what I thought,' said Alexandra. 'And if the *croquembouche* collapses, so be it!'

Lizzie laughed. 'Can I measure you across the shoulders? You can be relaxed about your *croquembouche* if you like, but we want your dress to look as if it really has been made by Givenchy.'

'And as if I really am Audrey Hepburn!'

*

427

Several days later, everyone agreed that Lizzie had, in David's words, 'played a blinder'. Alexandra, in her simple column wedding dress, sleeveless with a stand-up collar, looked more beautiful than Audrey Hepburn. Her hair was arranged (by Donna, who'd come down from Paris with Bob and who was by far the best at it) into a chignon. A long veil held in place by a tiara (lent by Antoine's godmother) floated down her back.

But the buckle had fallen off Alexandra's shoe and Lizzie was sewing it on again. Inside the church Pachebel's canon in D could be heard playing (Henri and a friend had practised and practised and were now playing beautifully).

David was striding about, as anxious as any father about to walk his daughter down the aisle. Maxime was there too, impossibly handsome in his wedding clothes.

'It doesn't seem very long ago when we were arranging your wedding,' said Meg to Lizzie, making conversation, possibly seeing that Alexandra was getting nervous. 'And now we're organising a wedding in Provence.'

'Your turn next, Meg,' said Vanessa.

'I'm not planning on getting married,' said Meg. 'At least not for years. I'm going to have a career.'

'Good for you, Meggy,' said David. 'I feel as if I'm about to go on as Hamlet at Stratford.'

'*Courage, mon brave!*' said Maxime, and clapped him on the shoulder. Alexandra happened to be looking and saw the look that was exchanged between the two men. Ah! she thought. Of course! Maxime is

David's special friend. How lovely! She smiled broadly at them and David made a face, unable to hide his happiness.

'There, that's done,' said Lizzie, who had missed all this.

'Thank goodness,' said David. 'Now put your shoe on, Cinderella, and I'll escort you to your Prince Charming.'

'But Papa is only a *comte*, not a prince,' objected Stéphie.

'I know, darling,' said Alexandra, kissing her cheek. 'But sometimes you have to lower your standards a little. And I do love him!'

Epilogue

Antoine and Alexandra stood on the steps of the chateau, holding hands. They were looking at the party still going on in the orangery, which had spilt out on to the lawn. They had left it a couple of hours ago to much cheering and bouquet-throwing (Meg had caught it and had swiftly thrown it back).

'It was a wonderful wedding,' said Alexandra. 'Everyone I love was there. And a few people I didn't know I was really quite fond of. My Swiss relations, for example.'

'Yes! They really took their hair off – what?'

'Let their hair down,' said Alexandra, 'but I like what you said.'

He shrugged. 'Anyway, they are now close friends with my godmother, who is planning to visit them in Switzerland.'

'And David . . .'–

'Ah yes. David and Maxime. I didn't see it, but it's perfect. I think David will make a very good business selling antiques between the two countries.'

'I'm so happy to think they'll live here and so go on being part of our family,' she said.

'My children are having a very good time, I think.'

'They behaved so well, didn't they? I don't think Lizzie had to hold Letty once, Stéphie enjoyed carrying her around so much. And the older two, they were a credit to you.'

'They were a credit to their English nanny, I think,' he said and kissed her again.

'It's not the family you start out with that's important,' said Alexandra, still feeling philosophical. 'It's the family you create, I think.'

'Quite right. Which reminds me, there's a little matter regarding *that* which we need to attend to . . .'

Have you read them all?

Living Dangerously
For Polly, life is complicated enough without a relationship.
Surely, love is only a distraction . . .

The Rose Revived
May, Sally and Harriet decide to kick-start their own business.
Is it too much to hope for the same in their romantic lives?

Wild Designs
When Althea loses her job, she decides to transform her life and
pursue her passion for gardening.

Stately Pursuits
Hetty is drawn into a fight to save a crumbling stately home.

Life Skills
When Julia goes to work on a pair of hotel boats, her past follows her . . .

Thyme Out
Perdita runs into her ex-husband unexpectedly. Can love blossom
between them for a second time?

Artistic Licence
Thea runs off to Ireland with a charming artist and finds herself
having to choose between two men.

Highland Fling
Jenny Porter dashes off to Scotland and gets caught in a complicated love triangle . . .

Paradise Fields
Which man can Nel trust to help preserve the meadow and
farmers' market she loves?

Restoring Grace
Ellie and Grace embark on restoring a stately home, but have to reckon
with the help of the disconcertingly attractive Flynn Cormack.

Flora's Lot
Flora joins the family antique business and finds herself fending off dinner
invitations from the devastatingly handsome Henry.

Practically Perfect
Anna decides to renovate a beautiful cottage that is perfect on the outside
and anything but on the inside.

Going Dutch
Jo and Dora live on a barge boat and have both sworn off men until
they meet Marcus and Tom . . .

Wedding Season
Complications ensue when wedding planner Sarah agrees to plan two
weddings on the same day.

Love Letters
When the bookshop where she works has to close, Laura agrees to help
organise a literary festival, with complicated results . . .

A Perfect Proposal
Fed up with living her life for others, Sophie jets off to
New York for the trip of a lifetime.

Summer of Love
Sian moves to the country with her young son to start a new life.

Recipe for Love
Zoe is invited to compete in a televised cookery competition.
There is only one problem; one of the judges is too tasty to resist . . .

A French Affair
When Gina inherits a stall in the French House and meets the owner,
the last thing she is thinking about is love . . .

The Perfect Match
Bella is dismayed when the man who broke her heart,
many years ago, turns up in her life again.

A Vintage Wedding
Beth, Lindy and Rachel set up a business organising beautiful vintage weddings.
Could their own happy endings be right around the corner?

A Summer at Sea
Emily decides to spend the summer cooking on a 'puffer' boat in Scotland.

A Secret Garden
Lorna and Philly work at a beautiful manor house in the Cotswolds. Could everything change when they discover a secret garden?

A Country Escape
Fran has a year to turn a very run-down dairy farm into profit.
What could possibly go wrong?

A Rose Petal Summer
Will this be the summer Caro and the young man she met in
Greece many years previously finally fall in love?

A Springtime Affair
Gilly falls for the charming Leo, while her daughter Helena accepts a helping
hand from Jago. Can both these men be too good to be true?

A Wedding in the Country
It is London in the 60s, and Lizzie is so thrilled by her new, exciting life that
she forgets all about her mother's marriage plans for her . . .

Keep in touch with

Katie Fforde

Step into the world of Katie Fforde at

www.katiefforde.com

**Be the first to hear Katie's news by
signing up to her email newsletter,
find out all about her new book releases
and see Katie's photos and videos.**

You can also follow Katie on Twitter
and Instagram or visit her dedicated
Facebook page

 @KatieFforde

 /KatieFforde

@ffordekatie